The Rise

Book One of the Prophesied Trials and Triumph Trilogy

Kenneth E. Nowell

The Rise

by Kenneth E. Nowell

For information, contact:

Vero House Publishing, Corp.
5460 Corsica Place
Vero Beach, FL 32967
www.VeroHousePublishing.com
Telephone or fax: **888-292-7160**
Email: admin@VeroHousePublishing.com.

A previous version of this novel was offered by Vero House Publishing, in very limited release, in November of 2010, with the title, "Until I Return: Dawn of the Shining Darkness."

Printed in the United States of America.

Library of Congress Cataloging -in-Publication Data:
Nowell, Kenneth E.
The Rise / by Kenneth E. Nowell.
p. cm.
1. Suspense fiction 2. Christian fiction
3. Historical fiction 4. Prophecy
I. Title
813.6-dc22 LCCN: 2011937212
ISBN-10: 0-9828279-4-6 ISBN-13: 978-0-9828279-4-9

The author and publisher recognize and accept that the final authority regarding apparitions, miracles and prophecies rests with the Holy See of Rome, to whose judgment we willingly submit.

I dedicate this book ...

... to those who encourage my faith,
particularly Ruth and Fabian Werkowski
and Fathers Michael Massaro and John Merricantante.
Your humble service is inspiring.

... to those who revive my hope,
especially my children and extended family.
I trust that people like you
will make the world a better place.

... to those who teach me love,
including my mother and uniquely
my high school sweetheart,
life-long partner and beautiful bride,
Betsy.

Finally, to John,
patron saint of writers, theologians and book producers.
Thank you for your example.

Foreword

Occasionally, authors of fiction are asked whether they start with a detailed plot outline or, instead, proceed with only a general concept and wing it, so to speak. Each approach has its merits. However, the outline approach, while producing a highly structured tale, may result in one that is highly predictable. On the other hand, winging it may inspire surprising developments yet finally produce a story that is unfocused and unsatisfying.

This story, however, is not a typical work of fiction. I did not adopt either of the traditional approaches to plotting. Instead, I felt compelled to follow a third way. I let hundreds of prophecies, from over thousands of years, plot the story for me.

In doing so, I did not depend on Scripture exclusively, but neither did I accept any prophecy that contradicts the Bible. Instead, I relied heavily on supplementing the Biblical accounts with the numerous, but little-known, prophecies of many of the holiest men and women in history. These saints sacrificed their lives for their Savior. Many of their predictions were accompanied by miraculous signs and wonders. Some lived for many years consuming nothing more than the consecrated Eucharist. Others demonstrated amazing powers of bi-location, levitation and healing. Some even bore the *stigmata,* the wounds of the crucified Christ. These numerous miracles were not just witnessed and documented – as some might imagine – by gullible Christians. Oftentimes, doubters, agnostics and even atheists confirmed the accounts. Today, those who insist that science can explain these mysterious phenomena simply have not studied the evidence.

Nevertheless, it is important to emphasize that this is a work of fiction and not intended to be predictive of specific details. The current-day people, places and events in this book are completely fictionalized. If the reader, however, wishes to pursue a more detailed study of prophecy, the works cited at the end of this book – including, first of all, the Bible – are recommended sources.

For an author, however, there is no greater aspiration than for his fiction to illuminate truth. As Pablo Picasso observed, "Art is a lie that makes us realize truth." Accordingly, the prophecies cited in this work are described accurately and references for their supporting documentation are included in endnotes. Whether they shall be fulfilled remains to be seen. But the amazing clarity of numerous past prophecies – that, in many cases, revealed unlikely events that already have proven true – should lead even a Doubting Thomas to wonder, at least, about the cataclysmic predictions that may yet occur.

Finally, I wish to emphasize that this novel is a work of love. It is not written to judge others or to pretend superiority over anyone. Of course, I also fall short of God's standards. So, I draw comfort from the advice to, "Love the sinner, but hate the sin." That said, however, I also feel a loving responsibility to proclaim St. Peter's admonition:

> First of all, you must understand that in the last days scoffers will come, scoffing and following their own evil desires. They will say, "Where is this 'coming' he promised? Ever since our fathers died, everything goes on as it has since the beginning of creation." But they deliberately forget that long ago by God's word the heavens existed and the earth was formed out of water and by water. By these waters also the world of that time was deluged and destroyed. By the same word the present heavens and earth are reserved for

fire, being kept for the Day of Judgment and destruction of ungodly men.

But do not forget this one thing, dear friends: With the Lord a day is like a thousand years, and a thousand years are like a day. The Lord is not slow in keeping his promise, as some understand slowness. He is patient with you, not wanting anyone to perish, but everyone to come to repentance.

But the day of the Lord will come like a thief. The heavens will disappear with a roar; the elements will be destroyed by fire, and the earth and everything in it will be laid bare. (2 Peter 3:2-10)

K.E.N.

If I want him to remain alive
until I return,
what is that to you?

John 21:22

For the secret power of lawlessness
is already at work;
but the one who now holds it back
will continue to do so
till he is taken out of the way.

2 Thessalonians 2:7

Corruptio optimi pessimum est
"The corruption of the best is the worst."
Ancient proverb

1

Capernaum, Israel
Late 20th Century

The boy admired flickering flames that danced on dozens of candles as their leaden smoke ascended into the bright oculus above. He was comforted by somber organ strains that rumbled out of an old tape player. Then, when candles were moved, he giggled at the golden glow that wavered across jagged cave walls and over bloodstains on a chiseled pentagram.

Was he too young to understand?

The redheaded prodigy still possessed the qualities of a five-year-old: always living in the moment, never fearing the future, nor embittered by the past. His pale, delicate features suggested a fragility that might destine him to a future in the arts or in studious solitude. His appearance, however, like almost every other thing about him, was deceiving.

Beneath the ruins of Capernaum, the boy grinned as he welcomed the rise of the Shining Darkness[1] into the hidden Cave of Secrets. But his smile quickly faded when his parents lifted and laid him on the cold, stone altar.

Three men chanted under the oculus, wearing black hoods, masks and consecrated vestments that had been stolen from a Catholic church. The one in the middle — the kneeling high priest — prayed in Latin, but with a distinctly American accent. Only their eyes revealed that, after many months studying countless prophecies, the three emissaries of darkness had found the object of their obsession.

Surrounded by a familiar collection of pagan and satanic antiquities, the child had witnessed blood sacrifices here before. Tonight, however, no animal or aborted fetus would be offered. This strange, ancient rite was not another memorial to death but, rather, a celebration of life — the life that would prepare the way for the perfect holocaust.

While kneeling on pages torn from a Bible, the high priest proclaimed, "It was prophesied: In the twentieth century,[2] by the power of Satan,[3] from a Hebrew nun[4] of the bloodline of Dan,[5] a child of fornication[6] shall arise out of Syria[7] and be nurtured in secret."[8]

"It is fulfilled," the two junior priests chanted.

"From the land of seven hills,[9] with signs, wonders,[10] and the pretense of sanctity, the Cunning Blasphemer shall entice the adoration of Jews and Gentiles alike.[11] Kings and leaders shall submit to Antichrist, without whose approval no man shall hold power."[12]

The priests chanted, "It shall be fulfilled."

"Small and great, rich and poor, free and slave, shall receive the mark so that no one may buy or sell without it.[13] The Master of Deceit shall befriend Israel and then divide it;[14] shall drive the great apostasy into the very heart of the Church of God;[15] shall unify the Ishmaelites[16] and enflame the fury of the Red Dragon;[17] and shall promise peace, yet deliver desolation."[18]

"It shall be fulfilled."

Becoming uncomfortable, the boy turned his head to seek reassurance from his mother's exotic but cold, cat-like eyes.

The high priest continued, "With power and knowledge superior to all others..."

Suddenly, a hailing signal jarred the child and interrupted the litany. His mother rushed across the cave to the two-way radio that sat next to three large candles. The Syrian woman held the receiver to her ear as the luminous flames flickered across her flawless bronze face.

"*Assalamoualeikoum...*" She listened carefully and whispered, "*Naam... Naam... Shookran.*"

When she disconnected the call and turned back to the altar, her eyes were tense with fury. She growled to herself a stream of Syrian curses and then barked at the priests, "They're coming! Quickly, take the boy now!"

So be on your guard;
I have told you everything ahead of time.
Mark 13:23

2

Holy Sacrifice Monastery
Yashar, NY
May 16
23 Years Later

The old convent bells softly chimed six times as Pedro Lopez rolled his mop bucket across the rough tile floor. Just clearing the treetops, an extraordinarily golden dawn beamed through leaded glass windows and onto dark paneled walls. In the streaming light Pedro admired dust particles floating in the air around him. He thought of them as his little angels; always there, but rarely seen.

In his flannel shirt and rolled up jeans, the short, heavy Honduran was the image of a simple man in a complex world. The lonely widower was hardly ever noticed by the beautiful-but-lost, the brilliant-but-lost, or the powerful-but-lost. Even so, God noticed him. His simplicity was his salvation.

Pedro knew that the nuns had made their way to the chapel by now but, out of respect for their silent lifestyles, he still mopped the hall as quietly as possible. He paused to appreciate the spiritual peace that seemed to envelope this convent. This was his sea of solitude. However, he never paused for long. He quickly returned to mopping and softly whispering his rosary prayers.

Pedro admired these cloistered nuns. Perhaps, now, less than twenty were left – far fewer than when he first arrived almost forty years ago. Many of them had lived very difficult lives as missionaries before coming here. He never spoke directly to them and rarely even saw one up close. However, he sensed their profound dedication to God and he felt sure that they prayed for him.

His job was to take care of the mowing and landscape work that the nuns couldn't handle. Every month he made a special sacrifice, mopping all the floors without charge.

He knew that, like him, they were all getting old and their lives were becoming increasingly difficult. However, he never heard them complain, even when, now and again, one fainted from the heat.

Why do they have to dress so hot? he asked himself.

Pedro was jarred back to reality when he rolled his bucket into a travertine pedestal that supported Our Lady of Guadalupe. Hearing the "CLANG," he blurted out, *"Mierda!"* jerked around and lunged forward just in time to stabilize the teetering statue. The red-faced little man looked around to make sure that none of the nuns had heard his outburst. He sighed deeply and, amused at his good luck, grinned broadly at the Virgin's face. Pedro thought she may have smiled back at him. But he quickly disregarded his over-active imagination.

With crisis averted, he moved on. Pedro hoped to get his work done early. He was already craving the ice cream that he always picked up after work. Today, if he could finish mopping each nun's cell before they returned from Mass and morning prayers, he would finish work before lunch. So Pedro proceeded quickly and quietly to the sleeping quarters.

As he rolled down the darkened hallway, he could tell he was drawing closer to the chapel where he could hear Mass being said. The first cell was where Mother Liguori slept. Even though he knew the nuns were now away, Pedro always knocked before entering. After a brief pause, he opened the door and moved in with his bucket and mop. The room was colorless and small, only 6' by 8'. It contained an undersized bed and a bed-side chest with three drawers. It looked neat, just as he had expected. Mother Liguori tolerated nothing less than perfect order and simplicity. Her cell was spotless. The walls were windowless and bare, except for a crucifix that was hung over the tightly made bed. One small lamp sat on the chest next to a Bible.

Pedro dipped his mop into the bucket and squeezed off the excess water. As always, he mopped in broad circular strokes, saving the two oval depressions in the tile floor for last. Those indentations were where, next to their bed, a succession of nuns had knelt in prayer for almost two hundred years. Their persevering knees had overcome and eroded the rock-hard tiles.

Whispering another *Our Father*, Pedro rinsed his mop and finally swabbed the tile depressions. Then, sloshing his bucket here and there, Pedro rolled out the door and toward the next cell.

Here, Sister Mary Clarita slept. Numerous rumors swirled around town about her. Many people claimed that she was a *stigmatist,* a person who miraculously displayed the five major wounds of the crucified Christ. Pedro could not say if this was true. Many times, he had watched her from a distance, but she always wore gloves and her feet and side, of course, were always covered.

Some believed the *stigmata* was the greatest blessing that God could bestow upon a living saint. Others, who knew Sister Clarita well, claimed that the wounds were so painful for her that it could be nothing but a curse from hell.

For fifteen years, Pedro had secretly observed and admired this thin, quiet saint. He was one of the few who had learned her secret: that she loved to laugh. In fact, he sometimes saw her giggle to herself and then, like a child, hold her hand over her mouth as if she had been caught doing something naughty.

As the distant Mass continued, the priest's words reverberated through the hall, "This is the Lamb of God who takes away the sin of the world. Happy are those..." Pedro knocked on Sister Clarita's door and, as he opened it, the door stopped with a thump. Apparently, it was obstructed from inside the room.

"Sister?" he inquired.

How could she leave and still block the door inside?

"Sister?"

Pedro exerted a sustained push on the thick oaken door and it gave way enough for him to squeeze through the opening. The room looked like it had been ransacked. The bed had been knocked over, on its side.

He pushed the chest back to its usual place and reached to pull the bed back onto its feet. He pulled but then realized something was blocking it. Pedro looked over the bed, to see what was between the mattress and the wall, and screamed, "Sister!" He almost didn't recognize her. It was Sister Clarita, but with her head uncovered.

Pedro pushed the bed away from the wall to clear enough room to get to her. He kneeled beside her and placed his hand behind her head. He lifted it a few inches and whispered, "Sister?" He felt something on the back of her nearly bald head. It was warm and wet.

Mama Mia ... blood! His heart was pounding. His breath was rapid with panic. *The stigmata?*

He glanced at her feet and hands but they were covered and did not appear to be bleeding profusely. He lifted her head again, tilted it back, and saw her mangled neck. Pedro cried, "No! No! No!" He looked closer and thought he saw a thin rope deeply embedded under the skin. Fighting revulsion, Pedro fingered to remove it. But, as he pulled it out of her neck, he found it wasn't a rope. It was a rosary ... a rosary he recognized.

He screamed, "Juanito, why? No, dear God, no! How could you do this Juanito?"

Soon, he heard people pounding on the door. "Pedro, what are you doing?"

They tried to push the door open but the bed blocked it.

Father Alonzo shouted, "Pedro, open the door! Please, what's happened?"

Kneeling in blood, with a saint's head in his hand, Pedro could not answer. He could only cry.

Fortune favors the bold.
Terence

3
Four Seasons Hotel
Washington, DC
May 16

The Secretary of State was pleased with the rousing welcome that her introduction initiated from the assembled celebrities, politicians and political junkies. Even the wait staff watched at the perimeter of the auditorium and stopped to applaud. This was the annual Endangered Species Advocacy Council (ESAC) dinner that her supporters and staff had long anticipated. New York's Secretary of State, Angela Concepcion, was now announcing her run for President of the United States.

Just three years ago, Angela had hosted a popular, nationally syndicated, daytime radio show. Mingled with interviews of politicians and celebrities, Angela offered her devoted audience surprising new ways to understand and improve their lives. She was the queen of self-improvement advice. However, she did not limit herself to physical fitness and diet programs. A full range of parapsychology and psychic gifts were popular topics. She had reinvigorated the imagination of many Americans with stories on the power of crystals, trance channeling and the god that each of us can become.

Politically, her shows featured guests who espoused unconventional and, sometimes, even shocking perspectives on America and its history. Many of her most debated topics focused on a national and, even, global redistribution of justice. She argued that so-called equal rights in America are a sham, until there is a mandated equality of results. On these issues, the ESAC members appreciated her line of thinking, particularly when she demanded a new focus on eco-justice.

Her large American audience encouraged her untraditional and, sometimes even, confrontational ideas. Whatever she read, they read; whatever movies she liked, they liked; whatever philosophy she believed, they believed. ESAC members saw her as compassionate, articulate and still stunningly attractive at fifty.

In politics – the acting profession for ugly people – she was a rising superstar.

However, Angela Concepcion not only inspired admiration but also ridicule. To her supporters, this dark beauty was an "Angel," to her detractors, "A. Con." Whenever she bragged on the size of her radio audience, her opponents argued that she had never really run anything but her mouth.

Though her political experience was light, she had an interesting biography. Three years ago, she had achieved a dramatic, last-minute campaign surge that had confounded all the analysts and brought her victory in the New York Secretary of State's race. During that campaign, Angela had been fond of introducing herself to the voters with an endearing family tale.

In April of 1961, her father, Fernando, was an accomplished surgeon in Cuba. Her mother, Elizabeta, was a well-known university professor and pregnant with Angela. Then the American-supported Bay of Pigs invasion took place. It turned out to be a foreign policy fiasco for America and a deadly debacle for the Cuban resistance. When the dust settled, Fidel Castro was not satisfied with simply defending his regime. He sought to consolidate power and identify scapegoats. He accused capitalists and the intelligentsia of attempting to steal the people's paradise for their own selfish ends. The Concepcions could see what was coming.

With barely more than the clothes on their backs, Angela's parents fled in a ten foot skiff even though Elizabeta was eight months pregnant. Without a motor, rowing was their sole means of propulsion. However, fortune was with them. They caught the Gulfstream current and soon were safely delivered to shore, a little south of Miami. A newspaper later reported that there, on the beach, "the Miracle Baby of Miami" was born.

It was that kind of tale that had Angela's supporters insisting that her storytelling talents surpassed the best of politicians'. Her detractors, on the other hand, felt that her stories surpassed the best of reality. If Angela were to be believed, even as a child her family had realized she possessed the iron will of a leader. In reality, however, she remembered little about the early years with her family. In fact, she had felt, in some sense, almost unrelated to them. They did not understand her determination to become "somebody."

Angela did not have to share with the voters the details of her controversial past. Those stories were already well known.

After arriving in America, her parents struggled but, with Church assistance, managed to survive. Twelve years later, her mother and father were working as a maid and a mechanic. In some ways it was quite a come down. However, in America they never complained.

Angela attended a Catholic elementary school near Miami and was already pushing her boundaries. Perhaps, reminders of her "Miracle Baby" reputation had led her to believe that she was destined for greatness. But, whatever the reason, she yearned for fame and, with youthful impatience, was starting to exhibit signs of teenage rebellion. Her father tried to crack down – too hard, she believed – so she stepped up her resistance and mocked him with defiance.

Then, something happened that set off a series of important events. This twelve-year-old child became pregnant. The newspaper accounts were short on details, but Fernando reportedly had discovered that Angela was pregnant while driving her to school one morning. Upon hearing this, he flew into a rage and lost control of the car. Crashing into a telephone pole, he was killed immediately. Angela suffered only minor injuries.

Though personally tragic, the story wasn't front page news until a police report leaked that the girl was so fearful of naming the father of her child that the investigator planned to interrogate her own father. *That would explain why Fernando was outraged to the point of losing control of his car.* The local newspaper ran with the allegation and the public reveled in the hypocrisy. It became the perfect story for the national media: Was the conservative, church-going Catholic actually the sexual molester of his only child? *Of course he was!*

Initially, Elizabeta wept for her husband. However, the cruel news rumors drove her into a suicidal depression. She wandered the house, moaning, "It can't be possible!"

After she checked Angela out of the hospital and the small, private funeral was over, Elizabeta questioned her daughter. "Angela, I know you must be confused and afraid but I am here to help you. Tell me baby, who is the boy you slept with?"

"I didn't Mama!" she cried.

"Then, how is this possible," she moaned to herself. "How is this possible?"

Over time, the thought of the whole world knowing about this scandalous baby horrified Elizabeta as much as young Angela. So, in an attempt to escape the media and prying neighbors, they quietly packed up and moved to a small town in southern Alabama. There, with Angela's consent, her mother arranged to terminate the pregnancy.

* * *

ANGELA STIFFENED when Elizabeta escorted the man into the bathroom. “Call me doctor,” he said as he dragged in what looked like a trash can filled with plastic sheets and tools. He had a pale, pitted complexion. Obviously, he hadn’t shaven nor brushed his teeth for a few days. He seemed unnaturally calm, almost numb, which spooked Angela a bit. But, if he was a doctor, he must be okay. The procedure was conducted in the bathtub and was quicker than Angela had expected. None of the horror stories she had imagined materialized and, soon, her spirits lifted as her mother tucked her into bed.

“Cash, no checks,” the man called out while superficially rinsing the tub. Later, as the “doctor” dragged his trash can through the living room, Elizabeta paid him two hundred dollars.

“Is that it?” he asked, hoping for a tip.

From her bedroom, Angela watched her mother nod, close the door behind the man, and nervously look out the window to make sure he drove away. Angela was finally relieved that this emotional burden had been removed forever … at least, that was what she thought.

Within days, the “doctor” had an argument with his drug-addicted girlfriend and, undiplomatically, asked her to leave. Booted off the gravy train, she looked for money any way she could get it. She quickly called a national tabloid magazine and embellished the story she had heard about a famous little girl.

Soon, Elizabeta and Angela were national news once again. They, and the doctor, were charged under the strict anti-abortion laws of the state of Alabama and the abortion issue ignited into a national firestorm. With the help of an abortion advocacy group, the case quickly went all the way to the Supreme Court. In a surprising 7 to 2 ruling that would divide the country and eventually lead to more American deaths than in all wars combined, the Justices overruled every state law and found, for the first time, a Constitutional Right to abortion.[1]

Young Angela did not comprehend the gravity of her circumstances, but she soon came to enjoy the widespread publicity she received. It was the beginning of a craving she would never lose. This determined, twelve-year-old girl had become the international poster child for women's independence.

ANGELA'S SPEECH DAZZLED even herself. She now realized how much this admiring ESAC audience had suffered withdrawal pangs, over the past three years, missing her words of wisdom on the radio.

So, she focused on this group's specific concerns and proved that she had her biodiversity facts down cold. She pointed out how only 271 species were listed as endangered in 1979. However, within twenty years, that number had grown almost five-fold.[2] She promised that under her administration, the trend of protecting an ever-increasing list of endangered species would continue.

"After all," she liked to proclaim, "when ***men*** create the problems, fearless government leaders must find the solutions."

She had directed her campaign operatives to spread the word that, in this campaign, the world would see Angela unleashed. She had been married for twelve years to an establishment-style congressman. During that time she had played the good political wife and kept her political views private. However, many on the left loved to discern from her radio show various words and phrases that truly indicated her progressive leanings. "Angelistas," as her most radical supporters were often called, knew that she must have been inwardly seething to have married such a devout, free-market capitalist. That, the Angelistas argued, was why she never changed her last name.

She claimed to be confident about winning the upcoming primaries. Her dramatic last-minute victory in the Secretary of State's race had cemented her reputation as a strong finisher in a large state campaign. From her radio years, she had developed national name recognition and a high likeability rating. So, with "Washington experience" now viewed by most voters as a negative, her potential primary opponents bowed out when she hinted at a presidential run. However, the general election would be more difficult. Attempting to become the first female Commander in Chief would require her to show a tougher side than her critics thought possible.

For now, however, she knew that she was losing no one in this audience. They were not the kind of people she naturally would want to be around. They were a bit too zealous for her tastes. But Angela appreciated what they could do for her.

As Angela's speech wound down, she described her political philosophy. She called herself a "Perfective." Angela explained that this label best suits a candidate who seeks to perfect the Constitution, to perfect the American way of doing business and, indeed, to perfect life on earth.

Then she tossed the ESAC attendees the red meat they really wanted: "Our planet urgently needs a 'bailout plan' to protect its biodiversity." The attendees responded with applause and closer attention. "A fifth of mammals, 30% of amphibians, 12% of known birds, and more than a quarter of reef-building corals – the cornerstone for livelihood of 500 million people in coastal areas – face extinction. If we don't come up with a big plan now, the planet will not survive!"[3]

The Council loved it. So she got to the specifics: "And regarding our endangered friends, I will never forget the Hawaiian Hoary Bat."

The relieved Hawaiian delegation applauded loudly for the federal money that would soon come their way."

And down south, we'll protect the Alabama beach mouse and the Gulf Coast Jaguarundi."

The southern delegates upped the ante by cheering and whistling.

"And, my friends in Florida, how about our beloved Choctawhatchee Beach Mouse, Florida Salt Marsh Vole and the Everglade Snail Kite?"

The Floridians stood on their chairs and screamed their support.

"Oh my Gawd, this may get out of control!" she joked.

Everyone laughed, so, Angela switched into rapid-fire mode to entice a crescendo of applause: "The Coastal California Gnatcatcher … the Fresno Kangaroo Rat … the Ozark Big-eared Bat … the Sonoran Pronghorn … the Spectacled Eider … Jeez, I better stop before I start a riot!"[4]

She had them in the palm of her hand. This group had no doubt that a President Concepcion would invest billions of dollars into this new national priority. With her sense of humor and exceptional ability to communicate, Angela felt unstoppable and, as she finished her remarks, her audience laughed with, and cheered for, her.

At the back of the room, however, a big, foreign waiter was not laughing with Angela. He was not even smiling. As John Eben Malek reached his coffee carafe between a redheaded young guest and another man in a motorized wheelchair, he could not take his eyes off Angela. He discerned a familiar Dark Presence in the dining hall. Its power was unmistakable; its impatience, alarming. John did not know exactly how or when, but only that, like so many times before, he would have to confront it.

We must go through many hardships
to enter the kingdom of God.
Acts 14:22

4

Police Station
Yashar, NY
May 16

Detective Tim Lassiter glared down on the little Honduran who was sitting at the interrogation table.

"I'm not hiding anything," Pedro insisted. "Nobody is more upset about this horrible … sick … thing than me. Just let me go home now."

"Just a few more questions, Mr. Lopez," Lassiter said as he returned to his seat. The young police detective slowly and deliberately leafed through his yellow note pad again, to make sure his inexperience would not cause a lapse that could compromise the investigation. He knew his chief was observing this interrogation from behind the glass window at the end of the room so he refreshed his memory on the various tactics that might be useful. He had hoped his tall, thin, athletic presence would compensate for his boyish looks but Pedro did not appear intimidated.

"I see that Father Alonzo and Mother Liguori heard you shouting 'Juanito' after you found the body. That's what you call the church handyman?"

"Yes."

"But I hear John Malek is a big man. Why would you call him 'little John' in Spanish?"

"It's kind of a nickname. He's like a big kid. He … he never made me feel small."

"So you like him?"

"Yes, very much."

"But you accused him of murder. Everyone heard it."

"No! I did not! He couldn't have killed Sister Clarita. It's impossible."

"Then why did you blame him when you saw the dead nun?"

Pedro fidgeted with his fingers. "I … I don't know … but he couldn't have done it."

Frustrated, the detective raised his voice, "We're gonna be here all night if you don't start cooperating! Why did you blame Malek?"

Pedro didn't answer. Lassiter's eyes nervously wandered the stark room and settled on the darkened window. Pedro's face tightened with tension.

The detective decided to change directions. "Where can we find him?"

"I don't know. He's out of town."

"How do you know?"

"He got a weekend job in Washington. He'll be back soon."

"Where in Washington?"

"I don't know."

"So … when did you first meet him?"

"About three years ago."

"And?"

"Father Alonzo told me some new guy needed a place to stay. So, I set up a bed for John in the room over the garage."

"What did you think off him then?"

"Right off, I felt something special about him."

"Special?"

"Yeah, calm and spiritual. Father Alonzo and Sister Clarita felt it too."

"So, you know him pretty well?"

"Yeah. He's my best friend."

"Your best friend … And where's your best friend from?"

"I … I'm not sure."

"Does your best friend have any family?"

Pedro paused as he realized how little he really knew about this man. "I don't know."

Flippantly, the detective asked, "Has your best friend murdered before?"

"No!" Pedro yelled.

Lassiter snapped, "How can you say that, when you know nothing about him?"

Pedro sighed. "I don't know the insignificant details of his life. But I know the kind of man he is."

"Then, what kind of man is he?" the detective asked, impatiently.

"Look, sometimes we'd meet in the garage under his apartment. After he would finish a hard shift at the soap factory, he liked to play this old record over and over again … *Ave Maria* … He'd just sit there molding clay while I led prayers on his rosary. Then, a lot of times, we'd have ice cream and tell stories. He knows more about history than anybody I ever met … really interesting stories about evil people trying to destroy holy ones."

There ya go! Lassiter thought. "So," he asked with feigned disinterest, "what did he say you should do to evil people?"

"Oh, come on!" Pedro complained. "Pray for them … love them. He's a holy man, not a killer ... I mean, look, he volunteers in our soup kitchen and … and whenever he can help people."

Pedro paused for a moment. "You know, now that I think about it, it's kinda strange how he took charge at the clothing drive last January."

"Yeah," Lassiter prodded with anticipation. "Why is that?"

"He didn't even have a good coat for himself."

The detective now realized this line of questioning was going nowhere. He leafed through his pad again. "You said something about molding. What d'ya mean by that?"

"He had this potters wheel … you know … you spin soft clay on a wheel until you make a pot or a jar."

The detective nodded.

"He liked to mold pottery in his spare time." Pedro sighed. "Look, Juanito could never kill anybody."

"Hey, it had to be an inside job. That convent is too secure. So, if it wasn't Malek, the only suspect left is you."

"For the fiftieth time, when I found Sister, she was dead," Pedro insisted. "You know what Sister Gertrude said: She saw me go in and I wasn't in there long enough to do anything."

The detective tried not to cringe when he heard Pedro knew information that should not have been available to him, yet.

"Anyway," Pedro continued, "if I had done it, why would I give myself away by screaming? Give me a break."

Lassiter stood and leaned over the table. "Look, little man, I don't give a flying flip about giving you a break! I don't care about you, your buddy, or any of your religious hocus pocus. All I know is that I got a dead nun on my hands and a murderer on the loose."

Pedro had no response for him.

"Okay, then tell me what you know about this." He opened his briefcase and tossed a sealed, clear evidence bag onto the table. Inside it was the unusual rosary that belonged to John. Pedro stared at the blood-soaked beads and remembered how fascinated he had been the first time he had seen those little pebbles stranded on sturdy, knotted twine. The detective could tell this piece of evidence struck a nerve.

"It's … a rosary," the little man mumbled.

"Who does it belong to?"

Pedro remained silent and did not look at the officer.

"Look, Pedro, Father Alonzo already told me who owns it," the detective lied. "Pedro, just agree with Father and you're off the hook. It's your buddy's rosary, isn't it?"

Pedro shut his eyes. His lips moved, almost imperceptibly, as if in prayer.

Realizing that no more cards would be dealt, Lassiter bet on a complete bluff. "Oh … I think I understand," the detective said, pretending to have a revelation. "I see why you're protecting him." He walked around to Pedro's side of the table. "You're in on it, aren't you? You may not have been the one who strangled her, but you made sure it got done. Didn't you?"

"No," Pedro groaned. "I loved Sister Clarita."

"It was a sexual thing, wasn't it?"

"That's sick!" the Honduran snapped.

Trying the only remaining tactic that came to mind, the detective jerked Pedro up by his flannel collar and shoved him against the wall. "You murdering, little, son of a bitch," he growled. "You were in on it. That's why you're protecting that bastard, because if you turn on him, he'll turn on you."

With their noses almost touching, the detective snorted in Pedro's face and whispered, "It isn't gonna work little man. You got your kicks. But now you're gonna rot in prison … fry in the electric chair … and burn in hell."

Pedro closed his eyes and appeared to pray.

"Is that what you want? You wanna rot, fry and burn?"

Pedro whimpered.

"Answer me, dammit! Who owns that rosary?!"

Our lives begin to end
the day we become silent
about things that matter.
Martin Luther King, Jr.

5

Four Seasons Hotel
Washington, DC
May 17

The ESAC Conference breakfast was almost finished. As Angela ended her reflections on the importance of her highly-publicized appearance at the U.N. overpopulation summit in St. Moritz, John and the other waiters cleared the tables as quietly as possible. Secretary Concepcion had agreed to answer questions and, again, John could see that her audience was impressed. For the last question she announced that she would reach out beyond the privileged attendees and into the working class, "the heart and soul of America." So, she proposed that any server could volunteer a question. When none of the waiters raised his hand, John saw her point his way.

"You sir, what's on your mind?"

John was stunned, at first. Perhaps, she had picked him because he was the closest waiter to the dais. But, then again, he became even more uncomfortable as she looked his muscular frame up and down with a sly smile that signaled an eerie sexual flirtation.

John, however, knew that every surprise is a hidden opportunity. He set his plates down on a nearby table and gathered his thoughts as a staffer rushed over to hand him a microphone.

"What bothers you the most?" she urged empathetically.

"Well," John hesitated, "do you have a while?"

Angela laughed with the audience.

"Take all the time you need," she encouraged.

John realized that she expected a soft ball question about how she might get the government to do more for him. Angela never failed to find an ill that a new government program couldn't cure. Indeed, other people's money fuelled her political ambitions. However, John also suspected that, like himself, under her cool exterior lay volatile passions. He had learned to control his emotions but he doubted that she was that self-aware.

Moved by the Spirit, John observed, "Secretary Concepcion, I see in your literature that you list human rights as one of your highest priorities."

"Yes, that's correct ... absolutely. It is shocking how human rights are violated here and around the world. When I am president, my administration will hold everyone – and I do mean everyone – accountable for their human rights violations."

"Then," he asked softly into the microphone, "why don't you respect the humanity of the unborn? A right to life is the most fundamental human right of all."

Angela's sly smile faded as she scanned the room that had suddenly become silent. "Are you serious?"

John nodded.

"Well, in case you haven't heard, a woman has a right to choose. It's her health, her body and her decision. I am proud of my record of defending women's health."

John felt compelled to continue: "I'm sorry, you don't seem to understand my question. I'm not asking about human health. I'm asking about human death. Pregnancy is not a disease and abortion is not health care."

"Don't be ridiculous," she argued. "Plenty of scientists and doctors agree that the ba... I mean the fetus ... well, it's ... it's not a person yet."

"Then when is that magical moment?"

She snorted her disgust at the question.

"It's an important question. I mean, after all, we're talking about possible infanticide.... Murder?"

"I'm not a scientist..."

"Are they 'persons' when everything but the baby's head has been removed from the birth canal?"

Everyone knew Angela was a leader in defending the practice of partial-birth abortion.

She chided him, "Now look, we're trying to have a civilized breakfast here … If you're not willing to engage in a rational discussion without being hateful, then ..."

"I don't hate you ... I feel sorry for you."

She chuckled, along with a few others in the room. "You feel sorry for *me*?" She looked down on him as if preparing to verbally pounce on an audacious fool. "What, in heaven's name, do you pity about me?"

John goaded her with, "Your confusion."

She rolled her eyes. "Oh my Gawd, this I gotta hear!" The entire room burst into laughter. This was Angela's specialty. After years of taking live radio calls, she had perfected the art of verbal jousting.

John said, "You are confused by a spirit of invincible ignorance."

"Oh?" she mused, "This is the first time I've been called 'ignorant' by a busboy." Again, the audience loved her humorous jabs. "Tell me, oh wise one, of what am I ignorant?"

John seriously continued. "Human rights, for example."

This comment irritated her. However, she was distracted even more when she noticed a disturbingly familiar fat, greasy man sitting near the stage. He looked like a deliberately forgotten acquaintance from the past, but she quickly moved her attention back to John.

He continued, "What rights are left when politicians and judges refuse to protect life?"

"Wow!" she said, finally ready to get serious. "Truly, you must be the last of the knuckle-dragging Neanderthals ... What century are you living in? Where do you think human rights come from?"

"God," he answered without hesitation.

"Look, I believe in God as much as anybody," she said with a hollow chuckle. "But every time I'm burning the midnight oil crafting human rights legislation ... well ... He's on break."

She paused for a few snickers in the audience.

Then she quickly dropped the humorous facade. "Look, laws don't get written magically. He's up there, not down here. What legislation has God written for women's rights or minority rights? Enlightened progressives like myself have always had to fight Bible thumpers like you in order to create those rights!"

Some of the attendees applauded.

"Women's rights?" John countered. "Madame Secretary, it is baby girls who are overwhelmingly aborted around the globe. In fact, it has rightly become know as 'gendercide.'[1] Minority rights? Since 1973, abortion has taken thirty six times as many African-American lives as violent crime![2] In fact, African-Americans are being aborted at three times the rate of white Americans.[3] With all due respect..."

"I don't want your respect!" she interrupted. "I want what the people want. That's why I'm New York Secretary of State and you're a busboy!"

A few more chuckles sprinkled the room.

John remained composed and undeterred. He understood people like Angela and continued pushing her. "Why do you believe that the egg of an endangered bird should be legally protected but a child in the womb should not? Would you finally be outraged if I performed partial birth abortions on baby seals?"

Some in the audience gasped. "That is sadistic!" She knew she had to regain control of the situation. So, she ordered, "Take his mic. away. Take it."

As he watched her face blush, he continued calmly, "Human life exists, even when you choose to ignore it. Do you realize that the 20th century brought us almost *one billion* induced abortions worldwide?[4] Total world population never even reached a billion until 1804.[5]

"Cut him off … cut him off!" In the crowded dining hall, her aides unsuccessfully tried to get to John while she looked down on him, frustrated that this simpleton was ruining her big moment. Angela's anger was about to boil over.

"Madame Secretary, it is the unspoken holocaust. Human life is not to be feared. It is the most precious resource on earth. It is not for us to tamper with or destroy."

"Shut that lunatic up!" she shouted as aides fumbled with the sound system.

"Please, seek God's …"

"This is not a prayer meeting!"

When she reached for a carafe of water, he turned to address his comments to the entire audience. "When will you let life become *God's* choice? How many would-be inventors, healers, peacemakers and saints have been lost by …"

The carafe slammed against John's head and crashed on the floor, shattering into a dozen shards. Gasps and mumblings from the audience blended into the squealing of John's microphone as a staffer finally snatched it out of his hand. Addled, John could only rub his forehead to assess his injury while

Angela stared through him and panted with anger. As John scanned the audience members, each dumbfounded from the surreal attack they had just witnessed, he suspected that he might have achieved his purpose.

Her beautiful face was now contorted with anger and she could not contain the boiling vitriol within her. "I'll do whatever I want with my damn body! Keep your religious fanaticism to yourself!"

John stood there, not looking angry, but like the victim of a bully.

However, as the adrenaline receded, and the room grew quiet, her tightened eyes widened. Suddenly, no one was more shocked than Angela at the impulsive battery that she had just committed in public and on camera. So, she fumbled around for the words that might bring the audience back to her side.

She attempted humor. "Crazy zealot!" This time, however, no one laughed.

She fumbled through her notes for an embarrassing moment and then got serious. "I think everyone here realizes that it's not that simple. Ohhh Gawd," she nervously chuckled, "wouldn't it be great if it were as simple as that? You think I want more abortions? Of course not … I … I love kids. If I could just wave a magic wand to get rid of them … I mean … get rid of abortions … I would."

John knew what was coming next as Angela's tone became more confident. "But, until that time, you have my pledge that I will always defend a woman's right to choose…" and then she added, with tears welling in her eyes, "especially when she's been raped by her father!"

As usual, the victim card was the right one to play. The audience rose for a standing ovation and, for a brief moment, Angela seemed to relish her hetorical feat. She beamed as she soaked up the applause that invigorated her. But when her eyes finally turned back to John, she glowered at him.

Angela and her staff knew that the journalists and videographers around this stubbornly calm troublemaker would preserve her embarrassing outburst. Today's video could dog her for the rest of her political career ... unless she could find a way to neutralize it.

As the ovation continued, two big men from her security detail directed John to leave. He cooperated and they followed him out of the dining hall.

Outside, John commented, "See you later, guys," but they kept following. Then, when John reached the parking garage, he finally stopped, turned and addressed the leader of the two, "Okay. I'm leaving. God bless."

The man did not respond. But just before everything went black, John saw him pull a Taser® out of his pocket.

We love death
more than you love life.[1]
Major Nidal M. Hasan
American Soldier/Accused Muslim Terrorist

6

Metro Rail Subway
Washington, DC
May 17

Qurban smoothly slipped into the plastic seat and slid his backpack under it. Across the aisle, his eyes immediately gravitated to forbidden territory, which was exposed more than hidden, under layers of sheer fabric and a plunging neckline. The woman was standing, steadying herself with a raised hand on a silver rail. Her lips were red, and her blouse was too tight. He despised it all, but that did not stop him from looking.

Qurban suspected that the Metro railcar would get crowded at the Rosslyn stop since Washington rush hour was approaching. However, when the train departed the station, they were still less than half full.

I will wait.

He felt uncomfortable without his beard and did not like the polyester suit he had been given. He was too muscular for its slender styling and, in his twenty four years, he had never before dressed like this.

But Qurban smiled broadly when he saw a man with his daughter at the front of the car. She was, perhaps, only six and was playing with a plastic pony and singing to herself. The small, heavy man with her was wearing a *yarmulke.*

Qurban scanned the car for a look at the other passengers. At the back were four loud Europeans, young men about his own age. He suspected that they were arguing over a recent soccer game but could only minimally understand their French. Most of the other passengers just looked like middle class Americans, as they read their newspapers or listened to their iPods.

Then the scandalous woman moved toward Qurban and asked, "Do you mind?"

Silently, he shook his head, without making eye contact, and she sat in the open seat next to him.

He was thrilled with the power he had over her now. If he wanted, he could turn and kiss her on those full, red lips. *What could she do about it?* He could do even more ... much more.

But, instead, Qurban stared at the floor. He wanted to get it all over with as soon as possible.

At Arlington Cemetery Station a few people boarded and more departed. Again, the plan would be delayed. However, the next stop was the Pentagon.

Pentagon, yes! That will be perfect. Soon, I will be a hero... a very great man.

Trying to remain inconspicuous, he continued to studiously glance around the car. At the front, on his side, was an unusual trio. A man in a motorized wheelchair was flanked by two men, one was a younger redhead and the other had the mature but fit look of a bodyguard. The man in the middle was wearing a hat, pulled down over his face, almost as if to hide his identity.

The Metro car rumbled along loudly, but Qurban still could feel his heart beating.

When they arrived at the station, Qurban was angry to see the Jewish man and his daughter stand to depart, but he felt better when he saw hundreds of Pentagon workers waiting to board.

“Excuse me,” the woman asked Qurban, “is this where I get off for the Pentagon City stop?”

The doors opened and a mass of humanity elbowed its way into and out of the car. Still, over the shuffling tumult, Qurban could hear his heart pounding. He suddenly felt disoriented. He angrily turned to the woman but all he could look at were her red lips. They were smiling at him.

Qurban’s mind raced in confusion.

He saw the Jews leaving the car.

Why is that man in the wheelchair hiding his face?

The passengers pushed past Qurban.

Something’s not right.

He snatched his heavy backpack that was loaded with forty seven pounds of Semtex, nails and infected hypodermic needles. He threw it over his shoulder and slipped out just as the door closed behind him.

Qurban’s seventy-two virgins would have to wait.

Lord, make me pure...
but not yet.
St. Augustine of Hippo

7
Outside Washington, DC
May 17

Ricky Zipp quickly hit the brakes, pulled over and stopped the old blue Beetle on the shoulder of the road. After all, he knew how hard it was to catch a ride on this busy highway. He watched the hitchhiker in the rearview mirror as the tired, bruised man approached the car.

When John looked into the open passenger window, the anorexic old hippie yelled, "Where ya headed?" John could hardly hear him over the blaring sound of a radio rocker shouting, "I'm on the highway to hell."

"Yashar," John answered.

"Hop in. That's where I'm goin'."

John tossed his backpack into the back seat of the car, slid in and slammed the door. As he reached over to shake hands, Ricky could tell that John had noticed his T-shirt.

"Yeah," Ricky answered the unspoken question. "It says, 'Come over to the dark side… we've got cookies!'" He laughed, "Cracks me up!"

The passenger offered a sincere, "Thanks for the ride. I'm John," and the driver immediately took a liking to the stranger's dark eyes that were not quite smiling, but peaceful and calming. With just those few words spoken, Ricky detected a humble sophistication in his bedraggled passenger. He was a welcome change for Ricky because, these days, Ricky rarely had a positive connection with anyone.

"This bug wasn't built for a big guy like you."

John just smiled.

"You get mugged?"

"Hmmm?" John asked. Then he realized that the driver was asking about the bruised lump on his forehead. "Oh, no. Just an accident."

As the car's engine revved and they merged back into the traffic, Ricky offered, "I felt sorry for ya."

"Why's that?"

"Wel … uh …" the driver turned down the radio and continued with a chuckle. "I don't mean to be insultin', or anything, but ya kinda got that middle eastern look goin' on and … ya know … I figured 'that poor guy looks like he's been through hell. Ain't nobody gonna pick him up.'"

"God must have put you on my path."

"Yeah, sure," Ricky said. "But I got a selfish reason, too. I been drivin' since Nashville and I'm gonna fall asleep if I don't start doin' some talkin' … By the way, you mind if I smoke?"

"No problem." John ran his fingers through his wavy black hair, settled back into his seat and turned his nose toward the open window.

Over the next two hours, Ricky monopolized the conversation. He complained about the police officer who had injured him in a recent eco-riot and the bank that foreclosed on his house. At one point, the driver dangerously took his hands off the wheel so he could flash John a view of his fists that had one letter in the phrase "Eco Warrior" tattooed on each knuckle.

John soon learned Ricky hadn't been able to find steady employment for decades. He listened quietly to the balding, long-haired hippie as Ricky described each disappointment and resentment in a disjointed, rambling story that rarely required taking a breath. He only paused for sniffles, coughs or drags on his cigarette.

The only dream he had left was to "get the hell out of New York, buy a little boat and set sail for paradise."

When Ricky finally wound down, they drove in quiet for a while.

"I guess you've got a real mess on your hands," John later commented.

"What are you talkin' about?" Ricky asked warily with a couple of sniffs.

"You talk like everything is messed up."

Ricky turned off the radio. He realized he had opened up too much to the stranger.

"No. My life is not messed up. It's great … *real* great." His eyes focused hard on the road and his cheeks turned a little red as he pulled out a pill and swallowed it.

John responded softly, "I don't think so."

The driver barked, "What d'ya mean by that? You don't know nothin' about me. I'm happy … Okay, if you know so much, tell me all about me. Go ahead. What do you know about me? *Bupkis!* That's what you know. *Bupkis!*"

John started slowly, "My guess is that you've probably had three wives … The marriages all ended in divorce … bitter divorce. They don't speak to you anymore."

Ricky's facial muscles tightened and he listened closer.

"Your only child is a son, your pride and joy … but he doesn't speak to you anymore, either … because of the way you treated his mother."

"How do you know me?" Ricky demanded as he turned his eyes from the road to study John's face. *You don't look familiar.*

"I've never seen or heard of you before today." John continued, "You've got two steady girlfriends. Neither one knows that the other exists. Both think that you want to marry them. I'm not sure where they got that idea."

Ricky laughed until he choked out a cough. "You are one hell of a good guesser. You know women are impossible to live with these days. So, chances are, a sharp guy like me probably has all that stuff goin' on. I bet you got a few on the side too, don't ya?"

John pressed on, knowing – just like sand in the oyster – his talent for irritating sometimes produced precious pearls. "Your son's name is Jeremy."

Ricky suddenly realized that this was no trick. He snapped at John, "What d'ya know about my son?"

"He needs you, Ricky. You should go see him … Don't put it off … You mean well, but you have a habit of putting things off."

Ricky calmed and almost imperceptibly nodded as they quietly passed the New York state line.

"So," John ventured, "will you try to heal the family wounds?"

A few miles passed without a response, and then Ricky said, "I'm done tryin' to make them understand. It's too painful."

John responded almost optimistically, "Pain can be good."

Ricky shouted, "Man, what are you talkin' about?"

John backed off, in silence.

They drove mile after mile quietly. Then, perhaps ten minutes later, Ricky asked, "Okay, why is pain good?"

With deliberate slowness, John continued, "Pain, is a means to an end, not an end in itself. Pain illuminates ... Pain educates ... Pain motivates ... And as every athlete knows, pain is what we experience when weakness leaves the body. Pain is not a choice, it is unavoidable. However, each of us chooses how we respond to it. We can try to ignore or numb our pain and, consequently, never break free from its controlling power. Or, on the other hand, we can become illuminated, educated and motivated by pain, responding in a way that prevents its return."

Ricky nodded and said flatly, "Yeah, maybe."

"But there is also a third response we can have," John added. "We can embrace the pain we must endure."

"Look," Ricky warned, "I'm not takin' you to Yashar if this is gonna turn into some kinda church service."

Ricky despised these kinds of conversations. He was happy to talk about anything – politics, sports, sex, even bathroom habits – anything but this.

"Ricky, you will always be in hot water, as long as you are lukewarm ... And, by the way, you *aren't* taking me to Yashar."

"What's all that mean?" He asked with a baffled laugh.

John picked up where he left off. "Ricky, pain can be invested or it can be squandered. We all have to carry our crosses, but every cross is a victory if it is surrendered to God."

"Man, you're a real buzz kill."

"Like an athlete preparing for the Olympics, or a law student preparing for the bar exam, or a father supporting his family by the sweat of his brow, some things are worth the pain. Isn't there something in your life that is worth the sacrifice?"

Thinking of his son, Ricky sniffed, "I guess."

"Ricky, Jesus Christ is like the professor who will give you all the test answers, if you just come to his office and ask for them. You will still have to take the test but, with the answers, you will be sure to pass. He's like the football scout who will tell you all the plays the opposing team will run, if you just ask him for them.You still have to play the game but, knowing your opponent's plan of attack, you will surely win. He is like the rich grandfather who says he will leave his entire estate to you, if you just come visit him in the hospital before his dies. Yes, you will have to spend some time with him, but you will become rich beyond your wildest dreams for it. You see what I mean?"

"Will you stop talkin' if I say yes?"

John returned to his earlier theme. “Pain also warns. It warns the athlete when his body is reaching the breaking point. And it warns each of us when our relationships are self-destructing. But its greatest attribute? Pain is persistent. It keeps nagging us until we learn what it is trying to teach.”

“So, what’s it tryin’ to teach me?”

“Where there is no love, there is no sacrifice. Where there is no sacrifice, there is no trust. Where there is no trust, chaos prevails... Ricky, the path to misery is paved with pleasure.”

After a few moments, Ricky mumbled, “Yeah, well, I guess you gave me somethin’ to think about.”

“It may not be today. But one day – perhaps a month from now – you ***will*** think about it. And when pain forces you to start asking the right questions, you will realize they all have just one Answer.”

A few miles later, Ricky changed the subject to small talk, “You’re pretty smart for a young guy. What are you … maybe, early thirties?”

“Roughly,” John shrugged.

“Uh oh,” Ricky said as he noticed the gas gauge, “hey, we got 20 miles to Yashar but if I don’t stop for gas we’re gonna be walkin’.”

He immediately pulled into an approaching gas station and up to the pump. As he was getting out of the car, Ricky asked, “Ya gonna help with the gas?”

John dug into his pockets and said, “Sure. Here’s ten dollars.”

“Hey, it’s been a pretty long drive. Ya got any more?”

John removed everything but his change. “How about another ten?”

“Great. Why don’t ya go pay ‘em while I gas ‘er up.”

As they got out, John assured the driver, “Ricky, life’s a trial in which you get to prove your guilt or innocence.... But you’ll be okay.”

Ricky shrugged with a snort. He still didn’t have a clue.

* * *

JOHN FELL INTO LINE behind two men in the dingy old gas station. An Indian woman, in traditional dress, was behind the counter teaching her pre-teen daughter how to work the cash register. A news channel could be heard from the television in the corner.

The first man moved along quickly, but the second had a complicated transaction. To pass the time, John listened to the news.

XBC REPORTER: "… The quake, estimated at 6.8 magnitude, was part of what the U. S. Geological Survey is calling a "swarm" of recent earthquake activity along the coast of Baja California…"

Looking out, John saw Ricky in the car with the engine running.

XBC REPORTER: "… In other news, a congressional investigation began today into allegations that XCyst Industries, the parent company of XBC News, illegally sold Cyst-Blanc supercomputers to a Russian front company that diverted the computers to the Iranian nuclear weapons program. XCyst Industries denies all allegations. Finally, on a happier note, first there was the "morning after" pill and now the FDA has approved what is being celebrated as the first safe and effective "week after" pill…"[1]

After reaching the front of the line, John paid the cashier and headed out the door. Outside, he heard the Beetle revving and looked up to see the old car merging into traffic. John's backpack was left, next to the pump.

Still, John smiled at the departing car. He found satisfaction in the realization that he had returned a favor today.

I knew you weren't taking me to Yashar.

Dusk was approaching. He never had any luck hitching a ride in the dark so John abandoned his plan to get home tonight. He pickedup his pack and dragged himself over to a school bus stop. He sat on a bench with a thump and searched his pants pockets for his rosary.

Hmmm, I must have left it at the chapel.

Just like he had done many times before, the big man stretched out on the bench and rested his head on the backpack as a makeshift pillow. As he lay there, he stared at the nearby sign that read, "Yashar 20" and thought about Angela Concepcion's story of her parents at sea. After a while, he dropped into a deep sleep, unaffected by the sounds and lights of the unrelenting traffic.

Soon, the dreams returned … or were they memories?

Fear not, nor be dismayed,
for the Lord God, even my God, will be with thee.
He will not fail thee, nor forsake thee,
until thou hast finished all the work
for the service of the house of the Lord.
1 Chronicles 28:20

8

Adriatic Sea
67 A.D.

John's sleep was interrupted by a splash. His brown tunic was soaked. He struggled to sit up, uncovered his wet head and squinted under the bright sunlight. Slowly, John scanned every horizon and, just as he had witnessed for six days now, no land was in sight.

So much water. So much thirst.

Day after day, his tiny sailboat had wandered aimlessly on a windless sea. Though he was happy at first for the calm waters, he now continually prayed for a breeze. It appeared that John's prayers were about to be answered. The wind was picking up and the waves were getting rough … too rough for his small craft.

John adjusted his simple sail to catch the southwesterly winds and let them take him somewhere … anywhere. He reached for his only paddle and dipped it into the water so that this makeshift tiller would keep him on a consistent course.

His tongue was sticking to the roof of his mouth. He tried to summon saliva, but he had none left. His face was blistered and his lips cracked. He had never experienced thirst like this.

After the splash, the boat had taken on some water though not enough to be dangerous. But, anticipating rougher weather,

John bailed with one cupped hand. After all, he still had to sleep and sit on the inside, bony skeleton of this uncomfortable, wet hull.

John's life, it seemed, had become an endless race to stay one step ahead of evil and the pain that it wished to inflict upon him. He had become hunted prey with only his faith to save him. However, he lived without complaint or regret and knew that his important work was not yet finished. Indeed, he was humbled and honored to share in the Divine Sacrifice of his Savior.

Twenty five years ago he had fled Judea, along with the other apostles, to escape the persecutions of Herod Agrippa I. He had ventured to Jerusalem only once, since then, for the Apostolic Council. That was sixteen years ago. More recently, he had settled in Rome, where he thought it would be safer to save souls. However, Nero had renewed the Christian persecutions soon after the *Lupercalia* Festival that promised to challenge evil spirits and purify the city. Peter already had been executed and Paul would soon follow.

John did not seek persecution but, as his followers had warned, spoke too bluntly to avoid it. His famous temper was better controlled, these days, but even Jesus had called him and his brother, James, "the sons of thunder." It was not in his nature to hide his beliefs or control his emotions but, for now, preserving his life required it.

Once John discovered that he was marked for death, he developed a plan of escape from the roaming soldiers of the city. He had his friends hide him under a load of grain in a donkey cart. For three days, they wandered the *Via Salaria* northeast until they reached the seaside town of *Castrum Truentinum*. There, they found a friend with a small boat and, six days ago, John had sailed away from the peninsula, alone.

By now, he believed, his three accomplices would have been betrayed. They, most likely, had sacrificed their lives to save one of

Rome's most wanted men.

John carried with him only two clay jars: the first contained one *congius* of *Caecuban* wine for his long journey at sea. The second, perhaps eighteen inches tall and six inches in diameter, contained something far more precious.

The savagery John had witnessed and heard about, during the purges, was almost unimaginable.

How is such evil possible?

Just three years earlier, Rome had experienced a massive fire. The angry public quickly began to suspect that the Emperor had caused the conflagration in order to rebuild Rome as he wanted. To shift the blame onto Rome's harmless Christian minority, Nero became obsessed with elaborate persecutions. Many known Christians were seized, tortured and convicted, not for the burning, but for hatred of the human race. Soon, they were made to be sporting spectacles: covered with animal skins and thrown to vicious dogs; nailed to crosses and set aflame; or, in Nero's own gardens, wrapped in combustible materials, dipped in tar and set aflame, to light the evening's festivities.[1] Indeed, it was on Vatican Hill's Neronian Gardens that Peter was crucified, upside down, as John tearfully watched from a distance.[2]

John fully realized that the Christian persecutions were based on unreasoning hatred, that the trials were illogical, that the "crimes" were for nothing more than loving Christ, and that lies were readily accepted as proof of a variety of so-called Christian perversions. Because of the Eucharist, Christians were called cannibals and accused of infanticide, and their requirement to "love one another" brought charges of incest. John, however, knew it was actually the Romans who exposed their unwanted children to the elements, aborted their unborn and lived such lustful lifestyles that incest was inevitable. Christians were blamed for causing earthquakes, floods and famine. *But hadn't these all occurred even before Christianity?* Believers would not swear by the godhead of Caesar but they were loyal and even prayed for him. Romans, on the other hand, were more inclined to revolt and slaughter.[3] Yet, John would soon enough see that one million Christians would be martyred over the first three centuries of the Church.[4]

Why hate Christian love? Why murder the most innocent among us?

Clearly, John still had much to learn. However, his wandering thoughts returned to his present danger when a large wave slammed against the bow and soaked him to his loincloth. The sail was now full and the boat was heeling dangerously. His mind raced. *What can I do?* No answer came to mind. His life was now in God's hands but, then again, wasn't it always?

The empty wine jar accidentally had fallen overboard days ago. So, John held the more important jar tightly, protecting it from the salty spray.

Soon, wracked by the unmerciful wind and waves, he reached his limit.

John struggled to stand in the listing boat and shouted at the sky: "Lord, why are you doing this to me?"

He dropped the jar into the boat, leaned over, and picked up the oar. John screamed, "Let me die now!" He repeatedly pounded the hull of the boat, trying to puncture it.

"Sink me!"

"Drown me!"

"Kill me, now!"

Unable to pierce the thick hull, John smashed the paddle against the side of the boat until the oar finally broke. Exhausted, he hurled what was left of the paddle as far as he could throw it and collapsed in the boat.

If he could have cried, he would have, but no tears were left.

Then, with his rage exhausted, a sudden gust of wind burst forward and he heard a "pop!" A lashing had broken and his small sail collapsed onto the bow.

"Why have you done this to me, Lord? I am dying of thirst!" He then whispered, "I cannot go on."

The wind and waves continued their assault. Lacking sail and paddle, he bobbed aimlessly over a watery desert.

John covered his head from the sun and prayed, "Lord Jesus, please forgive my weakness. Please, have mercy. I am not as strong as You. Please let me die now." He was ashamed because he knew that more souls needed to be saved. He felt that his weaknesses would always prevent him from enduring to the end. Even before this ocean voyage, he had become exhausted from fleeing those who sought to torture and kill him. Perhaps, God was no longer listening. Perhaps, He had become offended.

Beaten, John collapsed onto the deck and stared at the blue sky. Finally, he whispered, "Thy will be done, Lord," and laid his head down, hoping his eyes would never reopen.

Moments later, a great downpour of rain burst out of the sky. At first John protected himself and the jar. Then, abruptly, he sat up. In front of him, he watched the disabled sail catch rainwater and funnel it his way. John quickly put his mouth under the end of one of the folds and gulped to his heart's content.

Later, when the wind and waves subsided, John smiled to heaven, thankful for the water he had so desperately needed. Cooled and refreshed by the rain, he laid down again with his precious clay jar. Even though he was soaked, he slept soundly, until he ran aground.

Don't be surprised
by the fiery troubles that are coming in order to test you...
but be happy as you share Christ's sufferings.
Then you will also be full of joy
when he appears again in his glory.
1 Peter 4:12-13

9

Outside Yashar, NY
May 18

John's eyes opened with a jolt. Coming into focus was the sign: "Yashar 20." He sat up on the bench, ran his fingers through his wavy black hair, and stretched with a grumbly exhale. The sun had not quite risen above the trees, yet, but the gas station had already opened.

When John shuffled into the store, he listened to the television behind the counter as he filled a cup with coffee.

CRITIC: "Would you pay $24.95 for the Book of Genesis? How about for a comic book of Genesis? Based on its French publisher's initial print run of 100,000 copies, apparently a lot of people will. That's because this Biblical account has a twist: plenty of bare breasts, relentless sex, violence and nastiness …"[1]

The young Indian girl was alone at the register watching the show but she jumped to attention when her customer approached. John pulled out his change and admired her innocence. He silently prayed for her triumph over the cultural pollution that she would soon test her. He handed her the exact amount and said, "You know, you're doing a very professional job. I'm impressed."

The little clerk looked up into his smiling brown eyes and giggled with a sweetness that is rarely found in the world today.

***

A RUSTY PICKUP TRUCK pulled over when the driver saw John's thumb out. The old man motioned John to get in and, when he opened the door, John asked, "Going through Yashar?"

"You betcha," the old farmer answered without enthusiasm.

John jumped in and put the backpack in his lap. The driver wore denim overalls and was listening intently to a radio program. At first, not much was said between the two men, except introductions. John could see the sadness that shaded the man's face.

XBC REPORTER: "… Last month, atheists marked Blasphemy Day at gatherings around the world, and celebrated the freedom to denigrate and insult religion ..."[2]

The driver muttered to himself, "Oh my."

XBC REPORTER: "…The more outrageous the message the better, says P.Z. Myers, who writes an influential blog that calls, among other things, for the end of religion. On Blasphemy Day, Myers drove a rusty nail through a consecrated Communion wafer and posted a photo of it on his Web site ..."[3]

John grimaced and the driver snapped off the radio. "That's sad, real sad."

"You a religious man?" John asked.

"You betcha," he barked. "You got a problem with that?"

"No," John smiled, deflecting the angry man's eruption. "No problem at all."

"Good, 'cause I'm in no mood to argue with another know-nothing know-it-all. We got too many of them from Hollywood, to Washington to Wall Street ... For the life of me, I cannot understand how they get so rich while they plunder everything they touch."

John nodded, "The simple truth is free. For elaborate sophistry, however, most people will pay."

"Ain't nobody willin' to live by the rules. Nobody cares anymore. You know what I mean?"

John said, "Well, not everybody ..."

"Yeah, yeah," the man interrupted, "but there's way too many. We might as well just get rid of the Constitution, the Bible, even the ol' rules of common decency … The hard work of raisin' kids right just ain't that important anymore. 'If it feels good, do it.' That's all anybody thinks about anymore … I tell ya, sooner or later, the Day of Judgment's comin'. You know what I mean?"

"Unfortunately, I ..."

"You believe that 'end of the world' stuff people are talking about?"

"I don't believe we can pick a particular ..."

"Yep, nobody knows the day or the hour," the driver finished the thought. Then, more forcefully, he said, "But when I hear the dinner bell ringin' I know supper's not far behind."

The man shook his head slowly and began to ramble. "Ya know, I've lived through the most murderous century in world history. From the 'People's Revolutions,' to the gas ovens, to the battle fields of world wars, to genocide and terrorism, we sure figured out how to kill … You know what I mean?"

John nodded.

The farmer continued with John's quiet encouragement. "How is it possible, in this supposedly enlightened age, that there's a global sex slave industry? How come we still got drug addiction here causing drug wars around the world? I tell ya why, 'cause Americans haven't learned that addiction is evil … Ya know, a kid today ain't got a chance. It's just shockin' the way people refuse to be responsible parents. Right here, in history's most prosperous country, five children a day die from the abuse or neglect of their parents."[4]

The man said, "I guess we're all to blame for toleratin' all that cultural sewage being pumped into our homes … Kids today got

Internet and video games that are ... disgusting. I mean, fifty years ago, you'd have to hang out with the perverts in big-city back-alley porn shops to see that trash. And a hundred years ago you wouldn't find it anywhere. No wonder murderers and rapists keep gettin' younger. And you can't even call them young girls prostitutes anymore 'cause they do it all for free! I know it's not all the kids, but it's way too many … Ya know, they can't pray God's name in school but they sure can curse it whenever and wherever they want. I mean, 'hallowed be Thy Name,' that's the very first sentence in the Lord's Prayer!"[5]

The farmer snorted with disgust. "I know I'm not very Christian right now … I'm mad … People today don't realize who they're playing with. You mess with the devil, you're gonna get burned. No wonder we got a society full of everything from Ponzi schemers to throat slitters … And, dear God, please save us from pedophile priests and get-rich-quick evangelists! Again, I know it ain't all of 'em, but it's way too many. It's like everything I hold dear is under attack: faith, family, country … Yep, we are lost … We just got too big for our britches. One of these days God's gonna lower the boom … And I won't blame Him for it when He does."

John thought about those words and added, "But He is merciful."

"You betcha," the farmer said flatly, "And He's also just."

John couldn't argue with that.

They drove a while longer before the farmer added, "I'm sorry I unloaded on you, like that.... I just buried my wife, yesterday."

"Ohhh ... I'm sorry to hear that."

"I tell ya, the way this world's goin', she's better off up there." Then the farmer's face reddened, his lips tightened and tears streamed from his eyes. "That bastard was out on parole." He repeated with seething anger, "On parole!"

They drove silently for a few miles until the farmer spoke up again. "Yeah, we been together … were together ... since we was twelve."

John attempted comforting words. "I'm sure it's hard to understand this now, but that was an extraordinary blessing to have shared your love for so long."

"I know. I just needed to get that off my chest." He took a deep breath. "I feel better now … I'll try to *be* better … not get so aggravated."

John smiled.

The farmer continued, "I gotta quit tryin' to change the world. Best I can do is get prepared for what's comin'." Then, he brightened a little. "I'm not ready yet, but I'm workin' on it."

John nodded.

"How 'bout you?" the farmer asked.

As they entered Yashar, John softly answered, "You betcha."

JOHN SAT AT HIS MOLDING WHEEL in the musty garage below his apartment. Around him, he had strewn newspapers on the floor to catch the clay drippings. The scratchy, old record played *Ave Maria* as John whispered prayers and delicately manipulated the soft spinning mud. When the record ended, it reset itself at the beginning.

His days were spent in continuous prayer but each evening at this time he had solitude. He was distracted when he thought he heard something outside. He stopped spinning the clay so that he could listen more carefully.

Suddenly, a battering ram crashed through the door causing it to burst open violently. Someone shouted, "Police!" as five SWAT members rushed in and threw John to the ground, causing the molding table to topple over on the floor. Two men held John's chest and face to the floor as another maneuvered his arms behind him and secured the handcuffs.

The SWAT leader asked, “John Eben Malek?”

“Yes, I am,” John grunted as he felt the blunt force of a knee in his back.

“You have the right to remain silent …”

LATE THAT EVENING, Mother Liguori raced across the darkened grounds almost tripping on her long black habit. When she reached the rectory, she banged on Father Alonzo’s kitchen door.

“Father, please open the door,” she shouted.

A moment later, the light came on and the priest opened the door. “What is it Sister?”

“I’m sorry it’s late, Father. Please come right now,” and, this time, slightly lifting her dress, she bolted back toward the convent. After all they had been through lately, he could only think: Dear God, what next? But, without hesitation, he jogged after her in his T-shirt and gym shorts.

She led him into the convent and then to the small alcove known as the Adoration Chapel. There, in a golden monstrance, a consecrated Host was always on display in front of a statue of Jesus Christ.

When she entered the chapel, she quickly dropped to her knees on the hard, tile floor.

He whispered, “What’s wrong, Sister? What are you doing?”

Her head remained bowed, as if in prayer. “Look, Father. Please tell me you see it too.”

The priest scanned the darkened room, studying the fresh flowers, the lit candles and the small altar. He carefully observed the sunburst monstrance and the consecrated Host it contained, under glass, at its core. At first, nothing seemed unusual, but then something dripped on the monstrance. Father Alonzo raised his gaze and witnessed what has become surprisingly common, around the world, in recent years: Tears oozed from the eyes of Jesus.

The priest dropped to his knees. "Yes, I see it!"

Mother Liguori was deeply moved. She had always taken pride in the fact that she prayed more than any other nun at the convent. *Why would He show His unhappiness to me?*

They meditated quietly until Mother Liguori began to sob. She whispered, "I was looking into His eyes, reciting the Fatima Prayer,[6] when He started crying." She choked out, "Why is He crying, Father? Why is He ...?"

Nothing more was said. They prayed quietly for two hours, until the statue's tears dried. Then they agreed that it must have been some kind of message for just the two of them, so, the matter should be kept private. If Jesus wanted the miracle made public, He would cause it to happen again.

That night, Mother Liguori could not sleep. She was tormented by the question: *Why is Jesus crying?*

Father Alonzo believed that he knew the answer.

Men never do evil so completely and cheerfully
as when they do it from religious conviction.
Blaise Pascal

10

Luxuriant Cleansing Company
Yashar, NY
May 19

Everything in his tiny office was old. Almost everything was the same as when his father had run the place ten years ago. The paneling was cheap pegboard. The floor was concrete. The only source of natural light was from the small, scratched acrylic window that he used to monitor the production floor employees. They stayed busy around the only new equipment Clarence owned: the towering, stainless steel churning vats that sparkled under the warehouse skylights. Yes, most of everything was old, but Clarence Porter felt a sense of pride as he sat behind his dad's old desk, in his dad's old chair. After all, the family business was experiencing a Renaissance.

By the time he had reached forty, Clarence had become one of the country's most successful African-American small businessmen. His mission had been to create the most luxurious hand soap in the world. By all reports, he had accomplished his goal but it had not always been easy. Only two years ago, he had expanded too fast and found himself teetering on the brink of bankruptcy. He maneuvered through the difficulties, however, when a wealthy silent partner invested time and money, helping him get the business back on its feet. Porter expanded production by purchasing larger churning vats. He also received guidance on opportunities regarding immigrant labor and on landing some "big-league" export accounts.

Now, operating at full production, three shifts a day, he had been unable to meet demand. However, that only added to the mystique of his product. For some people, this soap was not available at any price. That was because some customers, particularly the Saudi Royal Family, had contracted for volume purchases, ordering a forty foot container-load every quarter.

His son, Jamal, was just twenty-two but enjoyed his work knowing that someday he would be the third generation Porter to run the show. In fact, he had skipped college in order to expand his knowledge of the business. The father-son team worked well together but, like all ambitious young men, Jamal chafed whenever his Dad had to rein him in at the factory. Today, with Jamal working as floor manager, would be no different.

"Hey dad," he said as he plopped down in Clarence's office, "got a minute?"

Clarence looked up from his calculator, "Yeah, sure."

"Bad news: John's been arrested."

"Are you joking?" his father asked, as he turned in his chair.

"They think he had somethin' to do with that nun's murder."

"Man, that is crazy."

"Typical. They always grab the wrong guy."

"You got another floor manager in mind?"

Jamal thought for a moment. "Not really."

"Are any of the Saudis ready yet?"

The three Saudi Arabians were a bit odd but had come highly recommended and had turned out to be some of the company's better production workers. Clarence felt they had brought him luck because it was not long after they were hired that he landed his biggest account, exporting to the Saudi Royal Family.

"I don't know. John doesn't seem to trust 'em at all. He watches 'em like a hawk. Maybe that's why they don't get along. Or, then again, maybe they just resent takin' orders from a Jew."

"But they show up on time, work hard, don't take breaks," his father said.

"They've only been here a year, dad."

"Look, let's give 'em a chance. Who knows? Maybe the Royals will be impressed with our open-mindedness and then … maybe," he said with a smile, "they'll buy more soap."

Jamal frowned. "I don't think the Princes are gonna lose any sleep if these guys don't get promoted. Anyway, they're Shi'ite, dad. The Royal Family is Sunni. That's like oil and water."

Clarence overruled, "Naw, they'll be okay. Put 'em on the midnight shift. It'll be slow then. They can't botch that up too bad."

Jamal sat shaking his head. The father and boss tried to find a silver lining in the situation: "Maybe it is best John's not here. It'll give the Saudis a chance to show us what they've got."

That night, Jamal assigned the three Saudis to the graveyard shift after giving the men a key and a stern lecture about working diligently without supervision. They did not complain or argue about it but, at midnight, they did not show up for work. However, they were outside, watching the facility from a distance. When it was clear that the previous shift's workers had left, the men entered the building. They did not bother to punch in at the time clock.

The three Saudis walked through the entire plant, including the bathrooms and kitchen. They found no one else inside the building. Then, without talking, the men removed yellow haz-mat coveralls, latex gloves and facial breathing masks from their backpacks. Accompanied only by the churning sound of the three 10,000 gallon vats, the men quietly covered every inch of their bodies. Next they removed three thermos jars from their backpacks, climbed the stairs up to the catwalk, and went to the churning vats that were marked "Saudi batch." They unscrewed a small cap on each of the vats and poured in the contents of the Thermos® bottles.

Within minutes, the three men left the warehouse, making sure to lock the door behind them. Outside, they removed all of their haz-mat protection and placed the materials in a large garbage bag. They tied the bag and tossed it into the company's dumpster. Then, they drove off without saying a word.

Inside the plant, however, a mysterious note had been left: "Remember Abolhassan Hamdim."

To one there is given ... the message of wisdom, to another the message of knowledge ..., to another faith ..., to another gifts of healing ..., to another miraculous powers, to another prophecy, to another distinguishing between spirits, to another speaking in different kinds of tongues, and to still another the interpretation of tongues. All these are the work of one and the same Spirit, and he gives them to each one, just as he determines.

1 Corinthians 12:7-11

11

St. Francis of Assisi University
Yashar, NY
May 20

Father James Alonzo stood before thirteen students, far fewer than he had hoped to be teaching this semester. However, he realized that a night course called "Revelations of God" would not have the appeal of day classes that covered modern music, movies, politics or other enticing but inconsequential subjects. Youthful hormones, he knew, generally trump ancient wisdom.

"Okay, everybody, let's get started," he began. "Look, I may not be up to speed tonight. We had a horrible tragedy at the monastery recently. You probably heard about it on the news."

The students mumbled around the room as the uninformed were told what had happened. One girl meekly raised her hand and Father Alonzo recognized her with, "Yes?"

"I heard Mr. Malek was arrested. Is that true?"

Around the college, John was very popular. In recent years, Father Alonzo had let him attend and participate in many of the classes. John demonstrated such a detailed knowledge of every turning point in Christian history that his input always stimulated conversation among the students. His interest in, and excitement for, history was contagious.

The priest tried to minimize the importance of the question. "I'm sure they will talk to anyone who might have seen something of importance. You never know what clue might help the investigation."

Then, changing the subject, he continued, "Anyway, tonight's material is important. Can anyone tell me why?"

All eyes diverted from the priest. Still, Father Alonzo had always found a way to affirm and encourage the students and they liked that. They also liked that this class was an easy elective course with a surprisingly open-minded teacher for a Catholic college. Though, at sixty, grey was now weaving its way into his short blond ponytail, he still had a look that conveyed his youthful attitude to the students. They thought his clear blue eyes and dimpled chin belonged in Hollywood a generation ago, not on the face of a New York priest.

"Okay ... Well, as you know, we've covered God's Revelations from the prophets, the New Testament authors and, of course, Jesus Christ Himself. The Bible contains the 'General Revelation' upon which our faith is based. That Revelation ended with the last of the apostles. But, tonight, we will be diverting from Sacred Scripture and studying the Church-approved Revelations of the saints. These are called 'Private Revelations.' They are outside the scope of the Church's infallibility. So, even when they are deemed 'worthy of belief' it is up to the individual whether to believe them. Can anyone tell me about the process of Church approval and what an approval means?"

He scanned the students and pointed at the safest bet in the class, a shy girl in the back who always knew the answers but was too afraid to volunteer one. "How about it?"

"Well," she began, as always, slowly, "the Catholic Church doesn't seem to really want to approve any prophecies or miracles or visions. I mean, they take forever investigating. Usually, everybody is pretty much dead by the time they reach any conclusions."

"Okay," the priest approved tentatively. "But let me elaborate on that. You know, there is a sarcastic saying: The way the Church sees it, the only good mystic is a dead mystic. That's a crude way of recognizing the difficult position the Church is put in every time one of these mystical experiences is reported. First, every legitimate mystic is still human and, of course, subject to human error. What kind of human error might come into play?"

The first boy raised his hand to redeem himself.

"Go ahead," the priest said.

"Ya know, God doesn't seem to pick the best people sometimes." Some of the students giggled. "I mean, if He really wants to get His message out. I mean, like, He picks a lot of uneducated people and even kids, sometimes."

"I know what you mean," the priest responded. "Like Bernadette Soubirous in 1858. She was a thin, sickly, girl of eleven from a family that was not very respected in the French community of Lourdes. She had shown no outward signs of piety and had not yet been taught her catechism. So, when she reported seeing a "Beautiful Lady" in visions, the community, Church officials and even her own family thought that she was lying. It was not until Bernadette told her doubting pastor that the woman in the vision said, '*I come from Heaven. I am the Immaculate Conception*' that he started to take her seriously. The priest realized that she did not even know what the name meant."

Father Alonzo continued, "Today Lourdes is where thousands have claimed miraculous healings and it is one of the most sought after places on the planet for that purpose. Bernadette's body rests encased in glass, miraculously uncorrupted for over a hundred years. Now, what other human errors are possible?"

The Hispanic boy chimed in, "Ego?"

"Exactly. We are always our own worst enemy if we fail to find and keep humility. Human virtue is like a delicate flower ... Any more?" All student eyes returned to their books. "Think about this," Father Alonzo prodded. "Who is the most interested in messing up God's message?"

No one volunteered an answer.

"Let me tell you a story about Magdalena de la Cruz who lived in sixteenth century Spain.[1] She was a contemporary of, and more famous than, St. Teresa of Avila. She demonstrated amazing powers of prophecy, levitation, and decades-long fasting. She even displayed what some believed was the ultimate sign of holiness, the *stigmata.* However, on her deathbed, she received the rite of exorcism after confessing that she had bargained with Satan, in exchange for her soul. She explained that the fasting and *stigmata* were elaborate fakes, but that the prophecies and levitations were achieved by demonic power. You might say that Magdalena de la Cruz is the poster girl for the slow, steady approach that the Vatican takes in approving apparently miraculous activities. Whether tarnished by ignorance, youth, ego, or demonic influence, we just don't know the purity of a mystic's message until life's last chapter is written and the prophecies are fulfilled."

The tall boy in the back asked, "Do any of the prophecies indicate that the end times are near?"

"Let me read you a few and then you can tell me what you think."[2] Father picked up a book, thumbed through its pages, and then began to read, "In the fourteenth century, St. John of the Cleft Rock predicted, '... *twenty centuries after the Incarnation of the Word, the Beast in its turn shall become man. About the year 2000 AD, Antichrist will reveal himself to the world.'* Almost two centuries ago, the *stigmatic* Sister Bertina Bouquillon said, *'The beginning of the end shall not come in the nineteenth century, but in the twentieth for sure.'* Finally, two hundred years ago, Blessed Anne Catherine Emmerich described from her detailed vision of hell that, "*... Lucifer ... will be freed again for awhile fifty or sixty years before the year 2000 AD.*"[3]

The boy continued, "Doesn't the Bible say that the Antichrist will come from Rome?"

"Be very careful," the priest warned. "The Book of Revelation describes the woman who is drunk with the blood of the saints as symbolic of the city that sits on seven hills. However, the Book of Revelation also admonishes, *'I warn everyone who hears the words of the prophecy of this book: If anyone adds anything to them, God will add to him the plagues described in this book.'*[4] Yes, Rome was built on seven hills ... but so was Moscow, Melbourne, and Macau ... and those are just some of the cities that begin with the letter M. In fact, there are at least 45 major cities that claim to have been built on seven hills.[5] And, by the way, Vatican Hill is not one of the hills upon which Rome was built."

The boy persisted, "So, what city is Babylon the Great?"

"I cannot speak with certainty, but it may not be a city. Perhaps, it could be a centralized power that would have been impossible to describe during the age of St. John. For example, how would he have understood concepts like global non-governmental entities or global corporations? We must approach our faith with humility. Oftentimes, prophecy is not obvious until we have the benefit of hindsight. For example, Old Testament prophecies — particularly in the Greek Septuagint — unquestionably predicted the birth, life, passion, death and resurrection of Jesus Christ at least 200 years before his time.[6] Over 300 prophecies were fulfilled by Jesus Christ, confirming Him as the Messiah.[7] Yet, even many who were well-versed in Scripture, failed to recognize the Christ while he was still alive. Perhaps each of us would have been just as skeptical. We are all capable of sin and error." Father Alonzo continued turning pages to find more prophecies.[8] "In the eighteenth century, Blessed Rembordt said, '*God will punish the world when men have devised marvelous inventions that will lead them to forgetting God. They will have horseless carriages, and they will fly like the birds. But they will laugh at the idea of God, thinking that they are very clever. There will be signs from heaven, but men, in their pride, will laugh them off. Men will indulge in voluptuousness, and lewd fashions will be seen.*'"

The priest paused to gather his thoughts and then went on. "In the sixth century, St. Columba warned about 'the latter days of the world' saying, '... *people will read and write a great deal; but charity and humility will be laughed to scorn, and the common people will believe in false ideas.*' Bishop Christianos Ageda described, '*In the twentieth century there will be wars and fury which will last a long time; whole provinces shall be emptied of their inhabitants, and kingdoms shall be thrown into confusion. In many places the land shall be left untilled, and there shall be great slaughters of the upper class. The right hand of the world shall fear the left and the north shall prevail over the south.*' This description fits precisely what happened throughout the Soviet Union and, particularly in Ukaraine, before the terms 'right and left' had ever been used for the political spectrum. And just one more, out of many: In 1936, Teresa Neumann warned, '*The furies of hell are now set loose. Divine punishment is inevitable.*'"

Father Alonzo continued, "You know, it is fashionable today, even among Christians, to blind ourselves to the fact that evil is infiltrating our society. Walk though any major bookstore today and you can't help but conclude that never before in human history has there been such a supply of, and demand for, spiritually harmful material. Listen to what various Catholic prophets predicted. Sister Bertina Bouquillon said, *'All these things shall come to pass once the wicked have succeeded in circulating large numbers of bad books.'* The Trappistine Nun of Notre Dame des Gardes predicted, *'Chastisement will come when a very large number of bad books have been spread.'* And Abbe Voclin prophesied, *'Horrible books will be freely available. Intellectuals will argue fiercely among themselves. Then the war will break out ...'*

The priest asked, "Why do you think that books are important enough to include in prophecy?"

No one responded.

"Because a fascinating book can engage your mind almost as deeply as a sexual act can engage your body. The lingering residue of evil books can cling to your mind like a sexually transmitted disease clings to your body."

Now he had their attention.

"But please don't forget," the priest advised, "Blessed Mother has repeatedly told us, in her appearances to the saints, that the Chastisement can be lessened or delayed if we will just repent and turn to prayer."

The shy girl asked, "But, Father, how can we be sure prophecies are true?"

"It's okay, even advisable, to be skeptical while keeping an open mind. Just don't be cynical. There is one entity in the world that has compiled and exhaustively researched two thousand years of Christian history: the Catholic Church. In the Archives of the Vatican there are voluminous files on every mystic who has been studied. For example, by now there have been close to four hundred credible *stigmatists.*[9] What makes them credible? Well, when fakery is involved, the wounds will heal, over a natural length of time, or become infected; the miraculous ones may heal unnaturally fast or last for fifty years. The blood type oozing from the wounds is, sometimes, not the same blood type as that of the *stigmatist* and it often has a perfumed scent. The blood has even been known to defy gravity. It is well documented that some *stigmatists* survived many years without any nourishment, except that which came from the daily or weekly Eucharist. For example, the prophet St. Nicholas of Fluh lived on nothing but the Holy Eucharist for the last twenty years of his life. But, as the story of Magdalena instructs us, all of these are just signs and not what really matters. What really matters is the message. Jesus Christ warned us, '*Watch out for false prophets. They come to you in sheep's clothing, but inwardly they are ferocious wolves. By their fruit you will recognize them.*'[10] So, the Church must be very careful to evaluate the Spiritual Fruit in its investigations. For example, if the message does not foster greater love of God and man – as Jesus Christ directed – it does not pass the test. Also, here is what the Apostle John wrote, '*This is how you can recognize the Spirit of God: Every spirit that acknowledges that Jesus Christ has come in the flesh is from God ....*'"[11]

The polite boy in the back asked, "Father, did you hear about the piece of toast with the Virgin Mary on it?"[12]

Some students giggled.

"No, I'm serious," he continued. "A casino bought it on eBay for $28,000."

Another student mumbled, "Father, Son and the Holy Toast?" The laughter increased.

Father cautioned, "Look, I'm not going to believe anything that has not undergone a stringent evaluation, but it sounds ridiculous and that is why it will get widespread media attention. Our popular culture loves to mock matters of faith. However, there have been many thousands of miraculous phenomena that simply cannot be explained by science. Many of them are happening today, with no rational explanation except the Spiritual."

"Father," a girl asked, "why don't we just rely on the Bible?"[13]
He answered, "No apparent revelation is credible if it contradicts the inspired Word of God. The 'General Revelation' of the Bible is the foundation of our Faith. But don't forget that, during the persecutions of the early Church, the faith was conveyed by word of mouth. The early disciples thought Jesus would return soon, so they did not see the need to write everything down on paper. In fact, the Church existed before the Bible. Many Protestants accept the inerrancy of Sacred Scripture but they forget that it was the Catholic Church that compiled the books of the Bible. The Catholic Church, on the other hand, adheres not only to Sacred Scripture but also to the Traditions that were passed down by the apostles. Occassionally, those Apostolic Traditions are not explained in detail in the Bible just as the nature of the Trinity - three Persons in one God - is not explained. Still, these early Traditions were documented by Christians and non-Christians alike and St. Paul, himself, commanded, *'So then, brothers, stand firm and hold to the teachings we passed on to you, whether by word of mouth or by letter.'*[14] Actually, the doctrine of *'Sola Scriptura'* did not exist until Martin Luther preached it sixteen centuries after Christ."

He continued. "The Bible itself tells us that not everything is included in its pages. The Apostle John wrote, *'Jesus did many other things as well. If every one of them were written down, I suppose that even the whole world would not have room for the books that would be written.'*[15] On the subject of 'Private Revelations,' Holy Scripture does not assert that there will be no further Messages from God. On the contrary, in both the Old and New Testaments we find, '*In the last days, God says, I will pour out my Spirit on all people. Your sons and daughters will prophesy, your young men will see visions, your old men will dream dreams.*'[16] But careful, prayerful discernment is required. Remember St. Paul's warning that '*... no one can say, "Jesus is Lord," except by the Holy Spirit.*"'[17]

Another asked, "How often do mystical experiences happen?"

"Before becoming Pope Benedict XVI, Cardinal Ratzinger said, '*One of the signs of our times is that the announcements of 'Marian apparitions' are multiplying all over the world.*'[18] However, claimed apparitions are not simply accepted at face value. The Church never presumes supernatural causes for things that can have natural explanations. Many alleged miracles and revelations are dismissed, either for having natural causes or resulting from outright fakery. However, the Vatican has issued a press release observing the '*surprising increase*' in recent claims of '*... presumed apparitions, visions, and messages*' associated with the Virgin Mary. The Church knows of hundreds of credible visionaries reporting appearances of the Madonna just since 1950. That doesn't include apparitions of Jesus Christ or the saints. In Medjugorje alone, there have been thousands of claimed apparitions since 1981.

He scanned the room for more questions and then continued, "Look, I guess what I want to emphasize is that it is delusional to think that, someday, you will stand before God and successfully argue that you did not believe because He never made Himself known to you. Rise above your natural blindness and open your eyes. Open yourself up to the Revelations of God: the Inspired Scriptures, the life and teachings of Jesus Christ, and the prophecies and warnings of the saints. It is your choice. It is the most important choice you will make in life."

The American Republic will endure
until the day Congress discovers that it can
bribe the public with the public's money.
Alexis de Toqueville

12

State Capitol
Albany, NY
May 21

The receptionist announced, "Mr. Whitehead? The Secretary will see you both now." Fred Whitehead picked up his briefcase and proudly led his administrative assistant into the New York Secretary of State's office, strutting as if he owned it.

Whitehead entered tall and lean. His stark white head of hair uniquely proclaimed the upper limits of what modern chemistry can contribute to the process of hair coloring. It was his calling card, so to speak.

Secretary Concepcion rose from her desk and flashed a knowing smile. "Fred, it's about time you came to see me." He responded with the chiseled grin that always seemed to disarm her.

Fred glanced around the office, observing tasteful splashes of color from illuminated oil paintings that hung on dark cherry paneled walls. He admired the marble bust of FDR, the antique empire desk, the Tabriz oriental rugs, and the delicate silken draperies.

"Looks like you've done alright for yourself, Madame Secretary."

She could have corrected his overly formal salutation but just smiled, instead. After all, this was business. Yet, she was not pleased to see that, entering with him, was an attractive young aide … *too attractive … too young.*

Whitehead extended a hand knowing that his starched French cuff would slip beyond his pin-striped Armani suit sleeve and expose what every Washington lobbyist wanted: a presidential cufflink. Angela was more focused, however, on caressing his tan manicured hand again. How she had missed his soft touch and enticingly exotic accent.

So unusual for an American! Maybe there's more fuel for this bonfire, after all.

Fred quickly withdrew his hand and added, "Madame Secretary, this is my associate, Amy Laugherly. She's quite a smart young lady. You mind if she sits in with us?"

Angela did mind but responded enthusiastically, "Of course not."

Amused, the Secretary sized up the young woman. She found it hard to avoid staring at her bizarre outfit: a black rayon dress patterned with large ripe tomatoes, red stiletto heel shoes, and periwinkle blue, fishnet stockings.

Gaudy ... very gaudy ... She must be Senator Laugherly's daughter ... much too young to be that old fart's wife ... but, then again, for an Appropriations Committee Chairman, who knows?

Fred volunteered, "Amy is the Senator's daughter."

"Oh, Senator Laugherly. Of course." Angela flashed a toothy smile. "Wonderful statesman ... love the dress."

She directed her guests to a couple of upholstered chairs in front of the desk just as the intercom buzzed.

Angela punched the intercom button and barked, "Betsy, I told you to hold all calls."

"I'm sorry to interrupt but this sounded important. Your mother is on line one. She fell again. They took her to the emergency room but she's back home now."

Angela picked up the receiver and turned in her chair to speak more privately. “Okay ... tell her I’m out of the office and take a message. Send her a card.”

Angela hung up before hearing a response and proceeded with her conversation. “Fred, I think that the last time I read your name, you were playing polo with the Prince.”

“That’s right, last month at Coworth Park.”

“You must be the best of friends by now. So, what do you call him... Charley?

Fred played along, “Chuck, actually.”

“Is he any good?”

“Not as good as he thinks.”

“You rascal,” Angela chuckled. “Now, I know you’d rather talk about your Venezuelan polo ponies but you didn’t come all the way from Washington for that. So, what can I do for you.”

Yes, business it was, the business at which Fred excelled. He was the highest paid lobbyist on K Street, heading governmental relations for the most influential company in Washington: XCyst Industries.

“Madame Secretary, we’ve been admiring your leadership skills and, particularly with regard to the global warming crisis…”

As he spoke, Angela’s mind wandered to the last time she had seen Fred. Last August, he had arranged to host her and a half dozen state senators at his beloved retreat, *Palazzo di Mare,* on the Grand Canal in Venice. However, when the legislature entered extended session, the senators and their wives had to cancel. Angela welcomed the change of plans. For twelve days, Fred taught her Italian and the history of the fabled city. The two of them became regulars, dining casually at Fred’s favorite *trattoria* near the Rialto Bridge. They loved strolling the *Piazza San Marco* and she laughed hysterically when a *piazza pigeon* messed in Fred’s perfectly micromanaged hair. Then they attended Mass together under the glimmering ceilings of the *Basilica San Marco.*

During Mass, a rainstorm had hit and, after, Angela looked out onto Venice's infamous *acqua alta.* The always-prepared Venetians had quickly constructed *passerelle* walking platforms in the *piazza* over the floodwaters. Though Fred had left his Wellington boots at the *palazzo,* he pulled two pairs of yellow plastic bags out of his backpack. With all seriousness, he showed her how to slide them over her shoes and tie them just below her knees. They both smiled when he accidentally stroked her thigh in the knave of the *Basilica* while saints in golden mosaics looked down with disapproval. When they exited the church, the tourists shuffled along on crowded platforms, while the two of them proudly waded through the waters, just like the locals.

Later, the New York tabloids would frown upon "the love birds of Venice" but that was okay with her. After all, she was single. She had lost her congressman husband six years earlier. His untimely death resulted from a tragic accident while scuba diving the "Blue Hole" off the coast of Belize. He had just speared dinner and, as he reached for the dive platform of *I'd Rather Be Me!* – his luxury yacht – the powerful legislator was reduced to hammerhead shark bait. That fateful day, he probably would have preferred to be someone else.

Angela's husband had introduced her to the upper echelons of Washington's political circles. However, soon after the funeral, she promised herself that a man would never control her again. Now, with her $18 million inheritance, she could afford to be self-sufficient.

Fred, on the other hand, had discretely divorced his two previous wives. Though their splits were amicable, their settlements came with hefty price tags. So, since Angela and Fred were unattached now, the "Venice love birds" felt they had nothing to hide.

Angela's enemies back home, however, did not see it that way.

Soon, Angela's attention returned to Fred's tribute as he continued to lather up the praise. "... and, when history is written, you will be named foremost among the green pioneers who saved the planet."

The assistant, Amy, had listened attentively. Her head nodded slightly but her long, slender legs stayed motionless and a blinding-white smile remained frozen on her face. It was hard for Angela to tell whether the young lady's unchanging expression of delight was from self-discipline or, more likely, a young woman's first foray into the wonders of Botox.®

However, Angela pretended to take Fred's praise at face value. "Well, thank you, Fred... Appreciation accepted." The Secretary stood, "Now, how about a tour of the capitol and then we'll have lunch? I'd love to hear what you've been up to lately."

The two guests remained seated.

"By the way," Fred inserted, "how's Green E doing in the House?"

Angela sat again, irritated that her lead was not being followed.

Green E was the nickname for the Green Energy Bill. That legislation proposed putting all New York public facilities on an "eco-friendly" transformation timeline. Light fixtures would be changed to the new energy efficient mercury vapor bulbs (made by XCyst Industries); state cars and trucks would be scheduled for replacement by new "zero emissions" electric powered vehicles (made by XCyst); and the new exchange for calculating carbon footprints and trading carbon tax credits would be managed by a division of XCyst. Angela had taken it upon herself to spearhead the passage of the bill because of her national reputation as a climate control advocate and her good relations with both sides of the aisle in the New York Legislature.

Before Angela could answer, Fred added, "Did I mention that XBC News has another 'Green Week' of programming next month?" It was one of Fred's specialties: making sure that the inside players who benefit most receive fawning coverage of their selfless virtue.

Angela liked the sound of that but she knew that the once red-hot issue of global warming had cooled a bit, ever since the credibility of some of the scientists at the forefront of temperature data collection had been called into question. Then, when U.N. officials announced that diminishing biodiversity is a larger threat to mankind's survival than climate change, most progressives could read the writing on the wall.[1]

Once again, for those who wished to save the world, a shift in emphasis was necessary, just as it had been necessary after panics over the ozone layer crisis and the dying oceans crisis had diminished. Like so many other computer modeled cataclysms, disapearing ozone and dead oceans and planetaery warming could only keep the public's attention for so long. Eventually they lost their pizzazz, presenting little hope that more laws and regulations could be changed, and more money could pass hands.[2]

Fred continued, "We'd like to feature you again as one of our environmental heroes … that is, if you don't mind, of course."

"Oh, no. I would be honored." Angela then grew serious. "Fred, I can see you're concerned about delays on the bill. As you well know, Fred, I am your biggest advocate on Green E. I'm twisting arms every day. But I need some help with talking points to squelch the critics."

"Amy and I are happy to help any way that we can."

I don't need her help, Angela thought, perturbed that she was not getting the alpha-female treatment she deserved. Her resentments, however, remained veiled. "Well, Fred, some of your … I mean ... our opponents are using scare tactics. Let me lay their arguments out for you and I'm sure you'll be able to educate me as to why these concerns are unwarranted."

"First," the Secretary began, "in terms of buying and installing new compact florescent light bulbs and fixtures, the cost is substantial."

Fred nodded for Amy to take the lead. "Please remember, Madame Secretary, a CFL uses 75% less energy than an incandescent light bulb and lasts at least 6 times longer. So, fixture replacement costs can be amortized over about two years."

"Yes," Angela countered, "but then we're trying to make an argument for a cleaner, healthier environment and, yet, these bulbs contain mercury vapor ... a serious neurotoxin."

"The highest source of mercury in our air," Amy countered, like a third grade know-it-all, "comes from burning fossil fuels such as coal. A power plant will emit 10 mg of mercury to produce the electricity needed to run an incandescent bulb, compared to only 2.4 mg of mercury needed to run a CFL for the same amount of time."

"Yes, I realize that, but what about the disposal issues? A bulb that is broken in the home or office poses a health risk and I am told that it is best cleaned up by a haz-mat contractor."

"No, no, nonsense!" Amy barked. Angela stiffened and Amy wisely tuned back a notch. "I mean, uh, that is not exactly in line with the facts. A contractor is not required as long as the homeowner follows our detailed nine-step process during disposal."[3]

"Wow, all that fuss over a cracked bulb." Angela responded flatly. "Fred, what about ground water contamination? Surely millions ofthese bulbs will not be disposed of properly and the mercury will eventually seep its way into our groundwater."

Amy wouldn't back down. "No problem. By the end of the year, the XCyst advanced technology water filtration systems will be available and able to remove the vast majority of mercury contaminants."

"Okay." Angela mulled over what she was hearing. "Let me lay out what someone asked me at a town hall meeting: How can these bulbs be so important to our health and welfare when they are made in China – a country that manufactures with a much higher pollution rate and competes against American manufacturers while paying, essentially, slave labor wages – then the bulbs are shipped by diesel freighter half way around the globe, and then shipped by truck to the store?"

Amy didn't have a quick statistic to cite or product to offer, this time. She looked at Fred but he just sat there with a sage look of contemplation. Amy punted, "Madame Secretary, I'll get back to you on that one."

Angela remembered how disappointed she had been when Fred never followed up, after Venice, with a personal call. He simply mailed her a "Thank you, Madame Secretary" note a week later. *Not even hand written!*

"Fred, dear, I'm just passing on the questions that I've encountered."

Fred warily responded, "I certainly understand. We will get you answers to every question you have."

Angela felt underappreciated. The more Amy had talked, the more Angela resented Fred's insensitivity. Maybe she and Whitehead were too much alike, anyway. They both loved to live the good life while delegating the workload to subordinates. If they eventually married, who would take the subordinate role? Angela thought, *I sure as hell won't!*

Angela mulled her options, but then chose to demonstrate why she should not be taken for granted. "And one more thing, Fred. Your bulbs are manufactured in Fujian Province, right?"

"That's correct." Fred shifted uncomfortably in his chair.

"One of my top labor supporters told me that, three months ago, the plant's quality control supervisor was asked by a Chinese government official to assemble the thousand, or so, employees for a 'pep talk.' With the supervisor by his side, the government official explained to the workforce that they were failing to meet four specific quality control standards. He told the workers what needed to be done and said he would return in a month to inspect their progress."

"That's right," Fred interrupted proudly, "we take our QC standards very seriously."

"When he returned," Angela pressed on, "the government official had the quality control supervisor assemble the workforce again. He explained to them that they had met only three of the four quality improvement requirements. So, in front of them all, he shot the supervisor in the head."[4]

Uncomfortable silence prevailed for a moment.

Then Fred added, "Angela … surely I don't have to remind you of the devastating consequences of global warming. Green E is an important part of the solution. The future of mankind hangs in the balance. We must act quickly. Rest assured, XBC News will give you the credit that you deserve. So, Angela, I hope I'm not detecting hesitancy, now, in your commitment to save the planet."

Angela looked directly into his eyes, but did not smile. "Why would you think that, Fred?"

And they did not understand
until the flood came
and swept them all away.
Matthew 24:39

13

Holy Sacrifice Monastery
Yashar, NY
May 21

Detective Lassiter sat across from Mother Liguori with his pen and notebook in hand. Between them was a metal screen, with diamond-shaped holes, that they talked through. This was the usual practice whenever an outsider communicated with one of the cloistered nuns. The detective's tape recorder was running as he leafed through his notebook pages.

"So, Mother, I'm having a hard time piecing together your evaluation of Mr. Malek and Father Alonzo. On the one hand, you say you have seen nothing that causes you to suspect either of them was involved in the murder. But why do I feel that you are deeply suspicious of them, nonetheless?"

The nun remained stoically silent. Lassiter observed how the nun's frown lines seemed to be permanently chiseled into her face. Her only adornments were a crucifix around her neck and a silver ring on her finger. He knew that the ring symbolized her complete commitment to Christ.

"Sister, please. I want nothing but justice here. Please don't withhold your suspicions. Sister Clarita deserves the truth to be told. You know, 'The truth shall set you free'?"

The nun studied the detectives face and suspected that he had no clue about the origin of those words. She whispered, "But I do not know the truth. Rather than speak without certainty, I should speak of only what I know to be true."

"I understand, Sister. Just tell us what you know. Now, why are you suspicious of them?"

"Detective," she answered slowly and softly, "are you familiar with Blessed Elena Aiello?"

Lassiter shook his head.

"She was a *stigmatist* who said that Christ told her in 1954, '*The world is flooded by a deluge of corruption.*' He warned of '*Innumerable scandals*' coming and of '*...the pleasures of the world which have degenerated into perversions*'."[1]

"Mother," he interrupted, "that's very nice. But I need to know about Mr. Malek and Father Alonzo."

She continued, "Our Lord Jesus said, '*The world no longer merits pardon, but deserves fire, destruction and death. There must be much penance and prayers by the faithful to mitigate the deserved chastisement that is now detained by the intervention of My dear Mother, who is Mother of all men.*'"

The detective was about to give up on the interview when she added, "Our Lord then warned, '*The people do not subject themselves to the Church, and despise the priests, because there are so many among them who are the cause of scandals.*'"

"Scandals?" He delicately ventured, "So, you think Father Alonzo may have done something scandalous?"

"I did not say that. In the seventeenth century, however, the Blessed Virgin told Venerable Mary of Agreda, '*I will tell you a secret: there are demons, whom Lucifer has expressly ordered to watch for the religious, who come forth from their retirement, in order to beset them and engage them in a battle and cause their fall.*'"[2]

"Then, Sister," the detective pressed with mild irritation, "what are you saying?"

"The Fatima visionary, Sister Lucia of Jesus, warned us in 1961, '*The devil has begun a decisive battle against our Lady, because what most afflicts the Immaculate Heart of Mary and the Sacred Heart of Jesus is the fall of the souls of religious and priests. The devil knows that when religious and priests fail in their beautiful vocations, they carry along with them many souls into hell.*'"[3]

"Sister, please. Can't you just tell me what you mean, plainly?"

She continued, softly, as if she hadn't heard the question. "Venerable Sister Marianne de Jesus Torres, in the seventeenth century, said that Jesus Christ revealed to her what the twentieth century would be like: '*The demon will try to persecute the ministers of the Lord in every possible way, and he will labor with cruel and subtle astuteness to deviate them from the spirit of their vocation, corrupting many of them. These [corrupted priests] who will thus scandalize the Christian people, will incite the hatred of the bad Christians and the enemies of the Roman Catholic and Apostolic Church to fall upon all the priests.*'"[4]

The Detective interrupted again, "Are you saying all priests are bad?"

She did not seem to hear his question. "Our Lord continued, '*This apparent triumph of Satan will bring enormous sufferings ...*" she raised her voice, "*... to the **good pastors** of the Church, to the **great majority of good priests,** and to the Supreme Pastor and Vicar of Christ on earth*'."

"Okay," the baffled detective mumbled to himself, "I guess you're saying priests are not all bad." He squirmed in his seat as she continued her agonizingly slow, soft lecture.

"Moreover, our Lord said, '*In these unhappy times there will be unbridled luxury which, acting thus to snare the rest into sin, will conquer innumerable frivolous souls who will lose themselves. My justice will be tried to the limit by the evils and sacrileges of the twentieth century. Innocence will almost no longer be found in children, nor modesty in women, and, in this supreme moment of need of the Church, those whom it behooves to speak will fall silent.'"*

With those final words, she stood and started to walk away from the interview.

"Sister!" he pled.

She stopped but did not turn toward him.

"Just tell me one thing: What did you think of Sister Clarita?"

She released a long audible sigh. She turned and, for the first time, did not speak in a soft, respectful whisper but with coarseness in her voice.

"She was a phony."

Then Mother Liguori left for her afternoon prayers.

BEFORE HE COULD UNLOCK the car door, Detective Lassiter heard something around the corner. He walked to the side of the monastery and saw Father Alonzo cutting the hedge with hand clippers.

"Father Alonzo?"

"Hi Detective."

"I thought Pedro handled all that."

"Yes, he trimmed them yesterday. Don't tell him I fine-tuned his work. He'd feel bad about it."

"You mind if we talk for a minute?

"Sure. I need a water break, anyway."

He gathered the clippings and led Lassiter into the rectory's kitchen.

"Have a seat," the priest instructed as he filled a couple of glasses with ice and water. He sat the glasses on the table, dropped into a seat, and asked, "So, what would you like to know?"

"Father, I don't mean to be disrespectful, or anything, but that Mother Liguori is one strange bird."

The priest laughed. "You have discerning powers of observation."

The detective noted, "It's good to see you're laughing again."

"Yes," Father Alonzo reminisced, "it's been a while. But I'm comforted to know that Sister Clarita is where she belongs. She deserves what she now has."

"Father," Lassiter turned more serious, "why are there hard feelings between you and Mother Liguori? She hasn't admitted it but I think there's something eating at her. I believe she also has a problem with John Malek. Why?"

"Oh, what a wonderful world we would have," the priest said as he looked to Heaven, "without gossip and suspicion."

"That doesn't really answer my question, Father."

The priest answered directly, "She disagrees with my decision to assign John Malek as the Spiritual Director for Sister Clarita."

"I don't understand. Why wouldn't you be her Spiritual Director instead of some stranger off the street?"

"John is a very holy man and Sister Clarita recognized that."

"Did Mother Liguori?"

"No … But she means well. She just doesn't get it … yet."

"I don't get it either, Father. I mean, you told me that this stranger just showed up at your door one day and you took him in, no questions asked. Why?"

"Are you familiar with the Didache, detective?"

Lassiter shook his head, rubbed his eyes and tried to suppress his laughter. *Ohhhhhh, not another religion class!*

"The Didache is the earliest written Christian Catechism that we have. It dates back to the time of the apostles before the Bible was compiled. In it, we are instructed: '*Receive everyone who comes in the name of the Lord, and prove and know him afterward; for you shall have understanding right and left. If he who comes is a wayfarer, assist him as far as you are able; but he shall not remain with you more than two or three days, if need be. But if he wants to stay with you, and is an artisan, let him work and eat. But if he has no trade, according to your understanding, see to it that, as a Christian, he shall not live with you idle.*'"[5]

The priest continued, "John wanted to stay, so I got him a job at the soap factory."

The detective considered cutting the interview short for fear of yet another religious lecture. However, he could not stop himself from asking, "It just seems unusual to take in a stranger, like that. Why waste church funds on him?"

"It is strange for the natural man, but not strange for the Spiritual one. The Didache also says, '*Every true prophet who wants to live among you is worthy of his support.*'"

Lassiter was again squirming, anxious to leave this unproductive line of questioning.

"Detective," the priest warned, "with all due respect, you hear but you do not listen … I have been blessed, and you have been blessed, with the gift of a prophet."

Just then, they heard a knock at the door. The priest shouted, "Come on in."

As the guests entered, Lassiter grabbed the priest by the arm and whispered, "Father, what did you think of Sister Clarita?"

He answered firmly, "She was the holiest woman I ever met."

Six older parishioners filed into the kitchen. "Detective," Father Alonzo invited, "come join us for our rosary. I can answer more questions afterward."

As quickly as possible, Lassiter gathered up his notepad and recorder, and bounced to his feet. "Ohhh, I'd really love to but I have a lot of work to get done. Man, I didn't realize how late it is. I have to go. See ya."

The amused priest invited the departing detective to come back any time, but Lassiter was out the door before he could finish the sentence.

The Jews are a nervous people.
Nineteen centuries of Christian love have taken a toll.
Benjamin Disraeli

14
Burgers, Brew & BBQ
Yashar, NY
May 21

Under an ignored video of dazed, bleeding and dust-covered Haitians, an Elvis impersonator performed his version of *Love Me Tender* to a rowdy crowd. As the bar song continued, spectators cheered and jeered Gloria, a drunken middle-aged regular on the dance floor. The raunchier she danced, the more they hooted.

However, Ricky Zipp felt nothing, neither pain nor pleasure. He sat quietly at the bar staring into his double shot of bourbon on the rocks. Here, he could tune everything out: the stale aroma of beer and cigarettes, the flashing Blue Ribbon Beer sign, and the stench of the deep-fryer grease that should have been changed long ago. He even ignored the seven flat screen TVs around him and the bar patrons who periodically shouted at the ones that were tuned to various sporting events.

One screen, however, everyone seemed to ignore. It showed an XBC newscast of the devastating earthquake that had recently leveled much of Haiti. An estimated 200,000 were suddenly dead and millions were now homeless and suffering. The report's closed captioning described how life had never been easy in this impoverished country but that, in the blink of an eye, hardship had immeasurably increased.

Standing outside a church that had survived the earthquake, a reporter commented on the music he was hearing. He said he could not understand why children, inside, were still singing prayers of praise to God. Then the report switched to a relief aircraft that had been forced to return to Florida because it had been unable to land. Unfortunately, the airport runways had been overrun by the higher-priority planes that transported needy politicians who were desperate for photo opportunities.

Ricky noticed none of it. Once again, he was immersed in contemplating his own persecutions and problems. These days, it seemed, he couldn't even pick up a hitchhiker without getting lectured on how he screws everything up.

Then, when the music stopped and "Elvis" took a break, Ricky happened to look up and notice a familiar face on the news channel.

"Hey Chapman, turn that one up … I know that guy."

The bartender stopped washing glasses and pointed a remote control at the television displaying John Malek's mug shot. Some of the bar patrons paid attention as the volume grew louder.

XBC NEWSCASTER: "… Malek had resided in a garage apartment on the monastery grounds. Even though Sister Mary Clarita was cloistered, it is known that she had a close relationship with the accused. Police sources have hinted that they cannot find information on his past but that they suspect he is an illegal alien of middle-eastern origin. Anyone with information about this man is encouraged to contact Yashar Police …"

"I knew it!" Ricky exclaimed. "I gave that guy a ride. Man, what a loon!" Ricky swelled with pride, imagining his importance in a news story that was receiving national attention.

XBC NEWSCASTER: "Secretary Concepcion's press spokesman has issued this statement: 'Both as a Roman Catholic and as a citizen of the world, Secretary Concepcion is deeply saddened by the shocking news of the murder of Sister Mary Clarita. The Yashar Police Department has confirmed that the suspect is the same unbalanced agitator who disrupted the Secretary's recent speech in Washington, DC. Secretary Concepcion believes that this terrible tragedy reminds us that it is time for America to finally get tough on violent criminals and illegal immigration.'"

The newscaster continued, "In a moment we'll tell you about the controversial Russian oil billionaire who is, once again, under investigation and the impact that the new embryonic stem cell research bill might have on fetal farming..."

"I bet they were makin' out," came a voice from behind him. Ricky turned to see a confident young man. "You know, the killer and the nun … Aw, he's guilty as sin. Probably a terrorist."

Where did he come from? Ricky thought. It seemed to him that such an unusual looking man, with bright red hair and a colorless complexion, would have been hard to miss.

The stranger sat on the stool next to Ricky so he could see the television better. "Frrrrreaky … Was he hitchhiking?"

"Yeah ... I shoulda known he was dangerous. We drove for, like, three hours and all he wanted to talk about was pain."

"Oh, boy," the red head laughed. "Hey, everybody, listen to this." People gathered around Ricky and the bartender muted the news channel's audio.

The bartender leaned on the bar, "Were you scared? Come on, you were, right?"

Ricky liked being the center of attention, for a change. "No, not really. But I could tell he was strange, really strange, and kinda dangerous. He kept saying: 'Pain is good … I love pain.'" Everybody laughed. So, he repeated, "I just looove pain!"

"So, what did ya do?" the bartender asked.

"I dumped him at a gas station." Ricky chuckled. "But not until I fleeced him for twenty bucks on gas." With all the attention, Ricky felt like a hero.

The redhead suggested, "You oughta call the police and tell them what you know."

"Yeah, maybe I will."

"No, don't wait," the stranger insisted. "Do it now."

"That's okay. I don't have a cell, I'll call when I get home."

The stranger wouldn't take no for an answer. "No, look … here," the redhead held out his phone with an adrenaline-rushed smile. "Call directory assistance on my cell … Go ahead … Do it now … We need to nail that Jew."

Ricky found that comment odd and disquieting. *Who said he's a Jew?* He tried to ignore the phone in his face and watched the report on Haiti's sudden devolution into machete-wielding anarchy.

"Come on!" the redhead prodded. Then he started chanting, "Turn him in ..."

The drinkers around Ricky all joined in, pressuring him: "Turn him in ... Turn him in ... Turn him in ..."

Ricky took the phone and everyone cheered.

Only a virtuous people are capable of freedom.
As nations become corrupt and vicious,
they have need of more masters.
Benjamin Franklin

15

State Capitol
Albany, NY
June 3

The Secretary did not try to hide her doubts about the young man in her office. He had been able to maneuver his substantial connections to arrange this introductory meeting. However, the Secretary had not promised, nor was likely to offer, anything more.

This position is too important for a novice.

Under normal circumstances, she would not have given him a meeting but she had started to doubt the quality of her campaign advisors. They had not been able to tamp down the airing of the embarrassing video of her confrontation with John Malek at the ESAC breakfast. So, her staff mounted a shadow campaign to discredit him as a crazy Christian hypocrite: anti-abortion for babies and pro-murder for nuns.

However, when it became known that John also was a Jew, her advisors feared that she might alienate her Jewish constituency by attacking him so publicly. So, her staff arranged a highly-publicized lunch at a Jewish delicatessen. Privately, her campaign manager advised her to order a pastrami on rye. When she requested, instead, pastrami on white toast with mayo, journalists laughed at her when the waiter rolled his eyes and mumbled, *"Oy ve."*

Then after forgetting to leave a tip, Angela was cornered by an old

Jewish woman who begged, "My people are the canaries in the coal mine. When supreme evil pollutes our atmosphere, it is the Jew who is sacrificed first. Please do not turn your back on Israel. God gave us our land!"[1]

The next day, a picture of Angela's disinterested eye roll made the cover of a New York tabloid. Again, she blamed her staff.

"I realize my resume' may appear thin," the confident young man conceded, "but most of my work must remain confidential."

"So, Mr. Thas, you expect me to hire you," Angela ridiculed, "without knowing anything about you?"

"Of course not," he said. "My client has authorized me to answer any questions you have."

The Secretary could no longer control her laughter. "So, you have *one* client and you think that qualifies you to be my campaign strategist? I'm sorry but I'm running for President of the United States, not the Junior League!"

"My client is Huntington Cyst."

The smile left her face.

"What is your position on universal broadband access?" he asked.

She studied this self-assured young man who still must be in his twenties and realized he was no one to be laughed at for long. With his bright red hair and colorless complexion, he was not immediately attractive. His smooth, intelligent confidence, however, made him appear interesting, perhaps even enticing.

"I support it, of course, Mr. Thas."

"Please, call me Evan."

"Evan … so, how did you come to know Dr. Cyst?"

"When I was five, I was identified by the Cyst Foundation and moved from my home in Canada to study here on a Cyst scholarship."

"Oh, I didn't realize the Cyst Foundation gave scholarships."

"Just one … anyway, I proceeded rather quickly through my studies and received my PhD in Advanced Quantitative Analysis from MIT 12 years ago."

Angela's brow furrowed as she calculated in her head.

"I know," Evan smiled, "I was sixteen … anyway, by then I also had received degrees in psychology and sociology. My education, of course, was at the direction of my benefactor."

"So, with all due respect, what does this have to do with me?"

"Dr. Cyst has had an interest in you, has studied your career, for quite some time. We both thoroughly enjoyed your speech at the ESAC dinner." Thas chuckled, "Unfortunately, we missed the next day's breakfast when our limo broke down. We had to take the Metro to the airport." Evan shuddered, "Ooh … commuting with the masses."

Angela didn't laugh. "And?" she asked a bit impatiently.

Unperturbed, Thas got to the point: "Dr. Cyst wants you to be our next president."

Angela stiffened in her chair.

Evan added, "I'm sure you realize Dr. Cyst usually gets what he wants."

One of the most brilliant men in the world – the Prophet of Technology - wants me to be president!

She knew that the secretive Dr. Cyst was a founding father of the Internet and the engineering mind behind the most sophisticated search engine in the world. She remembered reading, recently, that he also was behind many biotechnology advances. His passion for his work had made him the first global "rock star" of modern science.

"All I can say is … Wow," Angela confided. "Where do you fit in?"

"You may have read that the CyBot search engine, in conjunction with our Cyst-Blanc supercomputers, mines the data that it processes. That's why when you send an email to a friend mentioning, for example, your old tennis shoes, shoe company ads soon appear on the side of the screen."

"Yes, I've noticed that."

"Dr. Cyst has always believed that knowledge is more important than money."

Angela smiled, knowing that Dr. Cyst was a multi-billionaire. However, she also realized that news reports had suggested that he could have become far wealthier if he had not pursued risky ventures, reinvesting all his profits into so many ambitious, cutting-edge projects. Recently, she had read of a Cyst Institute breakthrough in the field of biomechanics. For the first time, electrodes had been successfully implanted into a man's nervous system, allowing him to mentally control a prosthetic arm and hand. This kind of success – coupled with his almost evangelical fervor for finding a technological Promised Land – explained why he had become known around the world as "The Prophet of Technology."

Angela did not realize, however, the extent to which her young visitor's accomplishments had been shielded from the media. In fact, much of Dr. Cyst's success had originated with the ideas of this bold red head. Back when CyBot had numerous Internet search engine competitors, Evan suggested the brilliant stroke of offering free online backup. For CyBot users, the accidental loss of hard drive data soon became a problem of the past when all that personal information was conveniently stored in the data banks of XCyst Industries.

"So," Thas continued, "Dr. Cyst directed me to mine our user data, quantify it and develop a psycho-social demographic construct."

"I'm sorry, but you're losing me."

"May I show you?"

"Of course."

Thas picked up the leather bag next to his chair and pulled out what looked like a large but super-slim notebook computer. He placed it on top of Angela's desk and appeared to type for a moment on the screen. Immediately, a three-dimensional hologram projected above the device. It looked like a pyramid hovering up-side-down. The image had numerous colored bands of varying thicknesses and a variety of strange numbers and formulas floating in and around it.

Angela was underwhelmed by the colorful display, suspecting it to be a fancy gimmick.

Thas said, "Based on 1,476 personal characteristics, this is a graphical representation of the psycho-social demographic patterns of the 614 people who will be attending your speech at the State Rotary dinner on Monday."

Angela offered a puzzled grin. "You certainly do your homework."

"We were able to mine the attendance list. But, frankly," Thas admitted, "there are 16 more people attending. We don't have enough personal data to include them in our construct. What can you do? A few barbarians still don't use the Internet. With them, we rely on public information, which is only marginally helpful ... But, anyway, watch this."

Thas pointed a remote control device and clicked at three axis points. The pyramid suddenly cut a section away. Then data streamed in the air along the side of it with summary information at the end.

Angela read from one of the lines of summary data: "Moralists, 86% by 92% equals 79%."

"Right," Evan nodded, "that's a great rating. You see I just carved out of this chart your most populated sliver. Here we find that 86% of the attendees on Monday tend to fit the Moralist category 92% of the time. That gives the group a 79 Moralist rating."

"So?"

"Watch this." The young man pointed and clicked on that rating. Suddenly, words and data streamed for a moment. "Now look." He read, "Ranking from highest rated, the stock phrase 'vision for the future' has a 97 appeal rating … phenomenal. 'Cut waste, fraud and abuse' has a 94 appeal rating. 'Stand up for America' has a 91. And 'Change is on the way' hits 90."

"Sounds interesting," Angela admitted.

"It's more than that. It's power!" he said with the enthusiasm of a teenager inspecting a new skateboard. "It's the unified field theory of social control. Of course, this is just a simple one-step example I've given you. In addition to Moralists, there are another 136 psycho-social demographic categories. And, of course, we have only discussed a single iteration of the data. We recommend at least 2,000 iterations before any major speech. Our computer program automatically will evaluate each sliver with respect to each category and compile the net effects."

Evan paused to gauge the growing excitement in her eyes.

"You're a very bright young man, Mr. Thas."

"I hope you don't mind, Madame Secretary," he said as he handed her two sheets of paper, "but I took the liberty of running off these recommendations that will be best received at Monday's speech. These speech patterns, phrases and issues are lobbed softballs just waiting to be hit out of the park. Pack your speech with these and you'll get their undying support … guaranteed."

Angela scanned the list and read, "'Trust me, I will never lie to you.'" She frowned. "I'm not sure I feel comfortable making such a blanket statement."

“Madame Secretary,” he said with obvious disappointment, “it’s not lying when circumstances change … and circumstances always change. Don’t worry about it.”

She felt something mysteriously enticing in his advice, but wasn’t completely sold.

“Look,” he continued, “79% of this audience, and 52% of America’s likely voters, already believe you are an opportunistic liar.”

She recoiled at the statement.

“I’m sorry to be so blunt, Madame Secretary, but these are the facts. That is why you must neutralize this issue. Your surrogates must proclaim your honesty endlessly while pointing out, at every opportunity, your opponent’s dishonesty.”

“But what if a lie becomes necessary?”

“Madame Secretary!” he shouted, “Just do it!”

She found herself nervously laughing along with him.

“Let’s be honest,” Evan resumed, “we’re all liars, we’re all crooks! Again, it may be disquieting to hear it said out loud but everyone has his price. So, why should you handicap yourself by trying to be a saint? Honesty, in modern politics, is an overrated attribute. In the old days, information and entertainment were broadcasted via three television networks. Because each audience was so broad, the rules for dissemination of such information and entertainment were standardized in order to avoid conflict with the mores of the American public. A singularly identifiable popular culture developed.”

“I understand,” she said with a little impatience.

“Two of those mores were universal truth and traditional values. Step out of line and that lightning bolt from God might strike you dead. Now, however, Americans choose to rise above those traditions and superstitions. Right or wrong, true or false, good or evil are not carved in stone anymore; they can vary with the individual or the circumstances. That gives us more freedom to operate. We can mold truth. Now, via the Internet, we can discern 'digital tribes' and exploit their emotions, prejudices and addictions. We have entered the age of narrowcasting: information, entertainment and marketing delivered to an audience of one. The man who is capable of believing a lie can be targeted with a persuasive message, just as the woman who is angry about being lied to can be assuaged with another lie." He giggled. "It's quite amazing. They're like soft clay in our hands!"

"Hmmm."

"Tell them what they want to hear! If you don't, your opponent will! I'm sorry if that offends you. But the reality is that our CyBot search engine, along with our Cyst-Blanc supercomputers and our proprietary analytical software, have the power to engineer their perceived universe of options. We can nudge them in the direction we choose. The Internet controls the information flow and we control the Internet. No matter what the poor sucker believes, we can design a message that fits his psychological needs. Do you understand?"

"Not really."

"Look, I am going to tell you something that must never leave this room." He did not pause for a response. "CyBot handles over 900 million searches a day. A third of those can be tailored to generate results that directly or indirectly promote you, your strategies or your world view. That is 300 million hits a day! For anyone who depends on the Internet for news or entertainment, CyBot can scrub what we don't want him to know and steer him into whatever we do. We'll plant the seeds of your message wherever his mind wanders. How will that help your credibility both nationally and internationally?"

"Pretty impressive."

"And, as you've seen, regarding group audiences, we can form psycho-social demographic profiles that allow you to maximize trust by targeting the predominant prejudices, emotions and addictions of that particular audience."

The Secretary spoke more directly: "It all sounds great in theory but, with all due respect, how can I be sure that you really know as much about people as you say?"

Evan Thas' demeanor changed. He now looked upon her as if she may not be capable of learning, as if she may not be able to appreciate the platinum opportunity that he was offering her.

"Madame Secretary," he said with a condescending air, "there are things you do not yet understand."

She recoiled defensively.

Thas sighed deeply then asked her, "Pick a date, Madame Secretary, within … say … the next month."

He placed his computer in his lap.

"Oh, I don't know, uh, how about the fourteenth?"

Thas tapped on the screen for a short while, "Let me see … okay … on the fourteenth …" Then he started to read: "Your Delta flight 1601 will arrive in Zurich at 8:42 AM. You will have flown first class in seat 4A at a cost of $4,842 … round trip, of course."

A frown came over the Secretary's face.

"You are scheduled," he continued, "to meet at UBS with Mr. Heinrich Helm at 11:00 AM. Mr. Helm is forty-two years old, divorced, and has custody of his fourteen-year-old twin boys. One of the boys, by the way, is having trouble keeping up his grades."

Angela tried to hide her discomfort.

"Mr. Helm has been instructed to meet you when you enter the lobby so you will not be handled by any other employees. He will take you to the second floor where you will access your account with the pass code of ZR38…"

"Hey, shut up!" she snapped. Then regaining her composure, "Uh, I'm sorry … Please … I've heard enough." She took a breath and rolled her eyes. "Talk about Big Brother! You guys are worse than the IRS."

She paused to think about what she had just heard. Should she be afraid? Ecstatic? Annoyed? Then, fully grasping the power that this prodigy offered her, Angela asked, "So, how much will this cost me?"

"I'm sorry, but you can't afford our services."

Her eyes tightened with concern.

"For now, our relationship must maintain plausible deniability. Just think of me as a resourceful, but secret, volunteer."

Relieved, Angela slowly nodded with a smile.

"I take it we understand each other now?" the man asked.

Again, she nodded, this time with vigorous certainty.

"And one more thing, Madame Secretary: This is all confidential."

"Definitely," she agreed. As she clutched those two precious pages in her hand, she could hardly control her excitement. "Secret it is … It's been a true pleasure to meet you, Evan… Please convey my gratitude to Dr. Cyst."

After Thas left, Angela sat quietly at her desk. Here, in her own office, she felt like she just had been violated yet empowered, defeated yet ultimately victorious.

I do not want to tick these people off … at least not yet.

These signs will accompany those who believe:
In My name they will cast out demons ...
Mark 16:17

16

Holy Sacrifice Monastery
Yashar, NY
24 Years Earlier

After Father Alonzo completed morning Mass, he removed his vestments and left through the back of the chapel. When he pushed open the heavy wood door, his eyes immediately focused on a passing station wagon that was blasting rock music out its windows. Then he almost tripped over someone who was sitting on the steps.

"I'm sorry … Is there something I can do for you?" the priest asked.

The groaning young man rocked himself in a fetal position while gripping his stomach. "I … I need help."

"Of course … I'll call a doctor."

"No," the young man pleaded. Then quieter, he added, "I need confession."

"Yes, that's fine," Father encouraged as he leaned over and gave the man soft pats on the back. "Come with me… into the church."

"No!" he said. "I need it here … now!"

Father Alonzo looked around and realized that they had privacy. So, he sat next to the young man on the flagstone steps, suspecting that he was another drug addict, suffering from withdrawal.

"Okay. Are you well enough to do this?"

The young man nodded.

"What's your name?"

"Huntington Cyst," he grunted.

The name and face were unknown to the priest. "Go ahead, Mr. Cyst."

"I don't know what to say … I've never done this before."

"Confess your sins, repent and our merciful Lord will hear and forgive."

The young man rocked a few more times and then moaned, "Demons control me."

The priest mildly dismissed the statement. "Mr. Cyst, let's not jump to conclusions. Demonic possession is extremely rare. The fact that you are here, now, indicates to me that they do not actually control you."

"Sometimes I can fight them off, like now. But those times are becoming shorter and rarer."

"Did you invite them in?"

Cyst paused and then nodded. "They said they'd give me power and fame. But I got none of it. Now they say they'll still give it to me, but only if I completely surrender. I don't want to, Father. They lie!"

"Look," the priest sympathized, "Occasionally, we have … psychological disturbances that make us think things like …"

"No!" he shot back. "I am completely sane!" The young man rocked and groaned some more. Then started to cry. "I … I don't need a psychiatrist … I need an exorcist."

Father Alonzo felt a deep sense of discomfort. "It's okay … don't worry," the priest empathized, "don't lose faith." Undetected by the young man, Father Alonzo pulled a rosary out of his pocket and held it in his hand as he reached to pat Cyst on the back. "The evil one can only possess you when you consent and if you will just seek the love and forgiveness of Je..."

Suddenly, the man stiffened and shrieked a shrill howl. The priest's rosary-filled hand pulled away from the man's unnaturally cold back.

"Damn you, priest!" Cyst growled, sounding like a cacophony of wounded animals. The young man's face had whitened and looked as though his skin had been pulled taut. "Leave him alone!" the demonic voices screamed from Cyst's mouth.[1]

Father Alonzo backed up against the chapel door as he tightly clutched his rosary. He feared what he saw but, more profoundly, he feared the evil that he felt projecting from this stranger.

More sinister voices emerged from Cyst's mouth, "Go back to your happy thoughts, Priest! Don't mess with us. We'll tell your secrets. Yeah, we know about ..."

Just then, Pedro came running from the garden and Sister Liguori opened the chapel door.

"Are you okay, Father?" she asked.

The priest looked down at the young man who now seemed stunned, recovering his senses and emerging from his pain.

"Yes, I'm okay ...." Then he added urgently, "Sister ... Pedro ... can you stay with this young man a few minutes? Just watch him ... be careful. I have to call the Bishop."

HE HAD HOPED he would never have to do this again. Twice before, Father Alonzo had served as the junior priest in exorcisms. He had found that the successful results were fulfilling, but that the disturbing after-effects remained an unshakeable part of him. Now he understood, regrettably, that vicious spirits sometimes lay hidden beneath attractive veneers and that we live closer to evil than we realize. Alonzo suspected that Cyst was, at worst, only partially possessed.

The way the demon or demons came and went – as indicated by Cyst's alternating attitudes – led the priest to believe that he had a good chance for success. However, he knew the odds would be much more greatly stacked against him if Cyst ever reached the extraordinarily evil level of perfect possession.

Assisting Father Alonzo were Sister Liguori, Pedro and a particularly devout doctor who attended Mass daily at the chapel. Dr. Edmund Fitzpatrick was a former college football player who had the strength that might be helpful, as well as the medical knowledge that might be necessary to insure the safety of Huntington Cyst. Father Alonzo had fewer assistants than he would have liked but, as he had told the Bishop, "God needs to strike while the iron is hot." Alonzo knew that exorcism, like possession, is a choice subject to the free, but oppressed, will of the possessed. Delay might have allowed this willing exorcee to change his mind and remain forever in the clutches of the evil one.

So, with only a short time to prepare, the apartment over the garage on the monastery grounds was chosen for the ritual. Its Spartan furnishings included the table, chairs and a small bed that would be needed. Sitting on the table were a crucifix, a Bible, two candles, and a silver *aspersorium* containing holy water and an *aspergillum* for sprinkling the blessed water. In the corner, a running tape recorder sat on the floor next to a half dozen lengths of rope. The door would remain closed and the only window's draperies were drawn so, with five participants, the tiny room felt uncomfortably crowded.

Once the Bishop had given his authorization, the procedure was expedited. Huntington Cyst now was feeling and acting normal. So, with apologies and his consent, they locked him in a tool shed for a few moments in order to allow the exorcism team to privately prepare. During that time, Father Alonzo nervously instructed his assistants as they walked in the garden. He told them that they should prepare for obscenities beyond their imagination; that they might witness blood, urine or excrement; and that the smells might become overwhelming.

And, with that warning, he pulled cotton balls out of his pocket and handed some to them. "Here, stuff these in your nose if it gets too bad."

He told them that they must obey three cardinal rules: first, they were to obey his commands immediately and without question; second, they were to take no initiative on their own; and third, they were to avoid saying anything to the possessed person. To insure that they understood, he had them repeat the rules. Only meek Pedro seemed too nervous to remember.

The priest put his hands on the young man's shoulders, looked into his eyes and said, "Pedro, you're a good man. You'll do fine."

And, with that shot of confidence, Pedro calmed down and was able to recite the rules.

The priest warned them that this procedure may take twelve hours or more and that, while the exorcist is usually the focus of the demons, their sins and weaknesses also might be exposed and taunted.

"I need you, but if you do not feel up to it, I understand. The time to back out is now."

The three assistants remained anxious but committed.

"If you need a break, say my name," Father continued. "But remember, breaks can be dangerous times in which we lose everything that we have gained. So, please keep them to a minimum."

Then Father Alonzo instructed them to pray constantly and bring Cyst up to the apartment while he prepared. When they left, Father Alonzo dropped to his knees and prayed for guidance.

Inside the apartment, the exorcism team waited only a few minutes before they heard the priest's footsteps echoing on the wooden stairs. He entered the apartment wearing a full-length black cassock. Over it was a waist-length white surplice and, around his neck, was a narrow purple stole that hung down his torso. He handed each of his three assistants a small booklet. The cover of each read, "*The Roman Ritual of Exorcism.*"

During the wait, Huntington Cyst sat on the bed and had been surprisingly relaxed with the others. However, when Father Alonzo entered the room, Cyst's demeanor changed, the air chilled and a Dark Presence was perceived by all. The feeling was unnatural and disturbing for the three assistants. It was a combination of hopelessness and depression that oppressed their minds. Sister Liguori feared for her soul. Dr. Fitzpatrick worried that he may be endangering his family. Little Pedro fought hard against the Presence and filled his mind with repetitions of, "And lead us not into temptation, but deliver us from evil."

"I'm already feeling much better now, Father," Cyst commented anxiously.

With confidence that Jesus Christ had commanded his followers to "drive out devils," the priest began, "In the name of the Father, the Son and the Holy Spirit ..." Then he sprinkled everyone with holy water and ordered the tying of Cyst's hands to the bed.

"Father," Cyst cajoled, "is this really necessary? I'm okay now. You made me feel much better. At least leave the ropes long enough for me to keep my hands folded in prayer."

Father Alonzo allowed that request. So, Pedro and Fitzpatrick tied the man's wrists with one rope loosely stretched toward the headboard and the other toward the footboard. Then the priest kneeled and the others joined him.

Alonzo proceeded with the ritual that has been practiced for two millennia, using many of the translated words that are identifiable at least back to the third century.[2] First, he prayed that Cyst, the assistants and himself would be protected. He made the sign of the Cross and sprinkled holy water on them all. Then he recited a litany of saints, requesting God's grace through their intercessions.

Then the priest continued, "Oh, God, it is an attribute of Yours to have mercy and to forgive. Hear our prayer, so that this servant of Yours who is bound with the chain of sins, may be mercifully freed by the compassion of Your goodness. Holy Lord! All-powerful Father! Eternal God! Father of our Lord Jesus Christ! You who destined that recalcitrant and apostate tyrant to the fires of Hell; You who sent Your only Son into this world in order that He might crush this Roaring Lion ..."[3]

Cyst cried, "They're leaving me, Father. I can feel them fleeing." He started to gag.

The priest drew a sigh of relief at his rapid success. "Pedro, get the trash can ... over there."

The Honduran quickly grabbed the container and placed it under Cyst's chin. He immediately convulsed and brought up a horrible smelling vomit. Dr. Fitzpatrick stuffed the cotton in his nose as the odor filled the room.

When Cyst finally finished and regained his composure, he seemed much better. "Thank you, thank you everyone." His face had returned to its normal color and his demeanor was now relaxed. "I'm fine now, Father ... They're gone."

"I'm pleased to hear that, but we'll continue the ritual," the priest said as Pedro reached to take the trash can from Cyst.

Suddenly, with the reflexes of a cobra, Cyst snatched little Pedro and pulled him onto his lap. Everyone was shocked to see Cyst strangling the small man with one arm. However, in Cyst's other hand, they were even more terrified to see a large, rusted nail. Cyst menacingly gripped the crude weapon over Pedro's right eye. Belatedly, they realized it had been a mistake to lock Cyst in the tool shed.

A cacophony of voices erupted from Cyst's mouth. "Untie him or we'll poke it out!" Wide eyed, Cyst relished the fear he provoked when he repeatedly pretended to stab Pedro's eye.

"If you harm him," Father Alonzo warned, "I'll never let you escape … In the name of Jesus Christ, do not harm this man!"

Pedro trembled in Cyst's crushing, cold grip. "Untie him, now!" the demons growled.

The priest felt he had no choice. He held up a crucifix as he slowly moved closer and untied the ropes from the head and foot boards. Sister Liguori continued to kneel in deep prayer, afraid to look up at the turn of events. Fitzpatrick, too stunned to talk, backed into the farthest corner as Pedro watched the priest out of the corner of his eye.

Just as the last knot was loosened, Alonzo tossed the crucifix into Pedro's lap. The demon voices screamed "Noooo!" as Cyst hurled the Honduran across the room.

"We'll remember you, priest!" the voices growled as the demoniac bolted for the door. When it loudly slammed behind Cyst, Fitzpatrick jumped up and locked the deadbolt. Father Alonzo and Sister Liguori went to Pedro's side to assist him. They all remained quiet, anxiously listening for the echo of footsteps heading down the stairs. Strangely, they heard nothing. They feared that Cyst and his demons still waited outside, preparing for an ambush.

But, more deeply, Father Alonzo feared for Huntington Cyst's spiritual safety. He blamed himself for not completing the exorcism. He knew his failure could have devastating consequences. He could not stop thinking about Jesus' words: "When an evil spirit comes out of a man, it goes through arid places seeking rest and does not find it. Then it says, 'I will return to the house I left.' When it arrives, it finds the house swept clean and put in order. Then it goes and takes seven other spirits more wicked than itself, and they go in and live there. And the final condition of that man is worse than the first."[4]

After a prayerful delay, Father Alonzo finally found the courage to open the door. Cyst was gone.

THAT NIGHT, Huntington Cyst's demons celebrated their victory while he binged on Tequila and beer. Now, they had almost taken complete control. It was an eventful day in his life … followed by a more important night.

If we confess our sins,
He is faithful and just and will forgive us our sins
and purify us from all unrighteousness.
1 John 1:9

17

Tarbuwth Correctional Facility
Yashar, NY
June 17

Father Alonzo walked down the familiar corridor and up to the visitor sign-in window. Corrections Officer D.J. Jefferson sat inside the fortified room, on the phone. The small muscular, black guard signaled to the somber priest that he would need another moment. Father nodded and waited.

When he got off the phone, the guard slid a small bowl through a hole in the bullet-proof glass and Father Alonzo emptied his pockets into it. The big priest with the short, blond pony tail was dressed completely in black except for his white collar. He only had his car keys, a wallet and a belt to hand over. Today was the first time he went through this familiar procedure without offering a friendly or funny comment.

Through the glass, Jefferson leaned forward to see the priest's shoes. "You got shoestrings, Father?"

"No, I don't."

Jefferson retained the bowl and its contents and slid the standard form out the window with a pen. The priest signed under where it stated that he understood and would abide by all prison policies.

As a guard named Kevin limped up behind him, Father obediently spread his legs and raised his arms. The guard "wanded" him up and down, searching for anything metallic.

"Do you have your rosary on you, Father?" Kevin asked. "We

can't let 'em in anymore."

"No, I didn't bring it today. But I'd like to bring in my Bible."

The priest handed the book to the guard, who leafed through the pages and flexed the cover and spine. "Okay, Father. No problem."

Jefferson inquired, "I take it you're here to see the new guy … uh … Malek?"

The priest nodded.

"Kevin, you stay in the room with Father. We don't have a read on this guy, yet."

"No, I can't have that," Father Alonzo quickly responded. "I'm here for confession. We need a private conference room."

The sharp response from the priest surprised Officer Jefferson, but he approved anyway.

"Wow. The secrets you must know," Kevin wondered aloud. "Father, how can you ever forgive an animal like that?"

The priest didn't respond.

"Father Alonzo?" Jefferson inquired. "You're gonna be in there alone. Don't go getting close to him. You stay on your side of the table … You see how Kevin's limping here? Sometimes things get out of control."

Alonzo nodded.

"And Father?" Jefferson asked with a hint of embarrassment.

"Yes?"

"I'm sorry to have to ask this but … You're not gonna go in there and get some kinda revenge, are you?"

"No, no of course not."

"Okay, just checkin'. Kevin, take him to Conference Room C and stand outside the door … Father, you yell if you get into any trouble … Hey, and remember to sign out when you leave. You forgot last time."

The priest nodded and Jefferson watched through the glass as the two men walked to the steel gate. Though he didn't care much for Catholics, he admired Father Alonzo. He was a man who lived by his faith. Many Christians talk about helping the downtrodden but few ever showed up here. This man was different. Every week he came for Mass and confession. Some of the prisoners really respected him for that … others hated him.

The black guard pressed a button from behind the glass window. The electric deadbolt in the heavy barred gate unlocked with a buzz. Then, the two men stepped inside a holding area and the gate shut behind them. They waited patiently for the second gate to buzz and unlock. Soon it did and they passed through it and headed down a hallway that had prisoner cells on each side.

"Save me, Father. Save me!" One prisoner dramatically moaned.

"Hey priest," another one screamed, "I'll show ya what sin's all about!"

As he limped down the hall, Kevin told the priest what he already knew, "Don't listen to 'em, Father. They're gonna get what they deserve."

"I been healed!" A voice echoed, "Alleloooooia, I been healed!"

The priest suddenly stopped dead in his tracks, not from something he heard, but from something he felt. He looked into the cell on his left. There, a massively muscular bald man, with flame tattoos across his forehead, sat staring straight through the priest. He could have been any other prisoner just sitting there with a cup in his hand. However, the extraordinary evil in this man's eyes was unmistakable. The inmate suddenly jerked his hand at the priest and the cup's liquid splashed across his cassock. Father Alonzo immediately realized it was urine.

"Dammit Worthington!" The guard shouted. "I'm sorry Father. That rabid dog ... He's why I'm limpin' right now."

Father Alonzo did not feel anger or rage, but for the first time, in a long time, he felt fear. This prisoner inspired fear in everyone he met. Whenever the inmates were allowed to watch a big football game in the recreation room, the best seat was always offered to, or taken by, Worthington. No sane inmate bought or sold contraband without offering some to him. And no one ever spoke to him unless Worthington spoke first.

The two men continued down the hall and found that the last conference room had "C" on the door. They went in and the priest sat at the table.

"I'll be right back," and the guard left.

While waiting, the priest looked around the room. The table and two benches were bolted to the floor. The table had room for six and, on the sides of the table, six U-bolts protruded. The room had concrete block walls and no windows. The floor and ceiling were poured concrete. The door was steel, with a small reinforced glass window and two deadbolts.

The steel door squealed open and the guard walked in with John. Father Alonzo couldn't even bring himself to look at the prisoner. But he listened and could tell that the guard had handcuffed John to the other side of the table, through one of the U-bolts.

"Make sure you stay on your side, now," the guard warned as he left the room. "Yell if you need me."

When the door slammed shut and the two deadbolts slid into place, the priest's expression changed. He immediately violated the rule he had been given and slowly moved to John's side of the table. Standing over the prisoner, with eyes red and tormented, he folded his hands and suddenly fell to the floor. On his knees, the priest dropped his face to the floor and begged, "Bless me Father for I have sinned … I am sorry I didn't protect you. I am sorry I failed. Please forgive me. Please forgive me."

I know your deeds, that you are neither cold nor hot.
I wish you were either one or the other!
So, because you are lukewarm—neither hot nor cold—
I am about to spit you out of my mouth.
Revelation 3:15-16

18

Ricky Zipp's Apartment
Yashar, NY
June 17

Ricky pushed all the newspapers onto the floor. The television was tuned to a "reality" dating show. He poured a small amount of white powder onto the glass top of the cleared coffee table. He pulled an expired credit card and his last dollar bill out of his wallet and used the flat edge of the card to arrange the powder into a thin, neat line. Ricky rolled the bill into a tube and deeply inhaled the powder into his nose, as deeply as is humanly possible.

"Ohhhhh, yeah!"

Contented, he slumped back on his red leatherette sofa and gazed at the show he never missed. One of the female contestants made him mad and he shouted at the TV, "Get outa here, you skank!"

Ricky flipped through the channels and stopped when he saw an attractive young woman who was getting signatures on a petition to outlaw "dihydrogen monoxide" (otherwise known as H^2O). Her spoof encountered no trouble enlisting the support of concerned citizen environmentalists, especially when she warned that "Dihydrogen monoxide is now being found in our lakes and rivers and it remains on our fruits and vegetables after they have been washed."

Ricky chuckled, took a big swig from the vodka bottle on the table and burped. Then the phone rang … and rang … and rang. He ignored it.

Bill collectors!

Ricky glanced around at the messy apartment and realized how dirty it had gotten.

Man, I need to get me a maid.

The phone rang again.

"Crap! Leave me alone!" But he answered it anyway. "What d'ya want?"

"Ricky?" It was a voice he recognized. She was crying.

"Cindy? What's a matter? You okay?"

She was sobbing too much to respond. Suddenly, like a bolt of lightning, Ricky was hit with the words that John had spoken to him a month earlier: "He needs you, Ricky, and you need to go see him … Don't put it off … You mean well but you have a habit of putting things off."

"Jeremy!?" Ricky screamed. "Cindy, is Jeremy okay?"

He was barely able to understand her, and he prayed he heard her wrong.

"He killed himself, Ricky. I came home … from work … he hung himself. Why would he do that, Ricky? Why … would he do …"

Ricky gently hung up on her slumped back on the sofa.

No ... this is just a bad dream. It can't be true.

Then he remembered something else John had told him: "It may not be today. But one day – perhaps a month from now – you will think about it. And when pain forces you to start asking the right questions, you will realize they all have just one Answer."

There is always someone behind me
that torments me, pushes me, and cries to me,
"Go on, go on, destroy Rome!"
Goth Leader Alaric
410 A.D.

19

Fiumicino Airport
Rome Italy
June 22

When the little Honduran lined up at customs, he was proud to hold the American passport that proclaimed the citizenship he had earned nearly thirty years ago. This was not just his first international flight but his first flight. He worried about the language barrier but prayed that his Spanish would be understandable to an Italian. While waiting in line, he kept whispering to himself, repeating the detailed instructions he had received from Father Alonzo, who had received his instructions from John. Perhaps Pedro's unnatural mumbling was why the customs agent stopped him at the counter. But, after a long, searching stare, the agent waved Pedro through without further delay.

Father Alonzo had conveyed John's exact instructions verbally. Nothing was to be in writing except the name of Pedro's destination that he kept forgetting how to pronounce. This, he was told, was the way that the early Christians had to operate. During the persecutions, everything about the faith was committed to memory because confiscated writings produced a sure death sentence. Now that Pedro was no longer a suspect in Sister Clarita's death, he was free to travel.

The overnight flight had been uneventful, but still exciting.

Pedro made the most of the free food and drink but he experienced, for the first time, the painful ear pressure that sometimes comes with altitude change. Because of its precious contents, his one carry-on bag was near his feet, never out of view. Adrenaline kept him from sleeping.

After customs, Pedro rolled his bag through baggage claim and out the ground transportation door, just as he had been directed. There, he found a waiting taxi and slid into the back seat. Pedro was tired but he knew he had to get his mission accomplished immediately.

Looking into his rearview mirror, the driver asked something in Italian … something that Pedro could not understand.

Reading from a note card, Pedro slowly tried to pronounce, "*L'Archivio Segreto.*"

He cringed when the driver shook his head. Then the Italian offered, "*Vaticano?*"

"*Si, Si. Vaticano.*" Pedro smiled at his quick mastery of the Italian language.

Clutching the suitcase in his lap, Pedro could tell from the Italian billboards, the aging tile-roofed apartments, and the numerous umbrella trees that he was no longer in America. He tried to absorb everything as they zipped through the countryside toward Rome.

Mama Mia!

But before long, his eyes grew heavy and he eventually dozed off into a deep sleep. Even through bumps and abrupt stops, Pedro slept soundly all the way to town until a group of little scooters buzzed around the taxi, swarming like gnats. Then, a sharp turn fully woke him. He groggily opened his eyes to see, straight ahead and approaching, the focal point of the smallest country in the world: the largest church in Christendom.

Pedro knew nothing of the contributions of Bramante, Michelangelo and Bernini in designing the towering wonder of St. Peter's Basilica. Spanning an area that could cover six football fields, the cathedral's 40 altars welcomed spiritual pilgrims from around the world. This church was the most monumental undertaking of the High Renaissance, with construction spanning two centuries, 18 pontiffs and 12 architects.

The Vatican as a country, is as unique as its Basilica, with fewer citizens than the number of representatives in the U.S. Congress. Perhaps the tiny nation would have grown larger in population if not for its zero birth rate and the fact that each of its 1,100 residents must get special permission to return after the official 11:30 P.M. closing of the gates each night. The Vatican has no hotels, restaurants, or entertainment facilities. It has not a single school, hospital or even traffic light. Its only two industries produce just mosaics and postage stamps. Yet, it is one of the most vibrant places on earth with 10 million visitors each year.[1]

From this strange land, one man rules the country as its head of state, legislature and judiciary. He has no bank account because he receives no pay. Yet, for almost three quarters of a billion people, living in every country of the world, he is the leading defender of the Faith and Traditions that have been passed down for over two thousand years. Throughout those centuries, during the Sacrament of Holy Orders, each generation of Church leadership laid hands on those who would succeed them. Consequently, each pope, just like each Catholic bishop or priest, can still trace his ministerial lineage back to a specific apostle.

However, Pedro knew little about the popes, both good and bad, who had shepherded the flock from this unique land. Yet, he did understand – deeply – his faith in Jesus Christ and the Church He had founded.

The original St. Peter's Cathedral was christened in 326 AD with the endorsement of Emperor Constantine the Great. After two and a half centuries of persecution, Christianity was tolerated and Constantine even allowed religious matters to be decided by the pope. But, by the early sixteenth century, something needed to be done with this crumbling monument of Christianity. One ambitious man had a grand scheme.

Three times, Cardinal Giuliano della Rovere had failed to win the seat of St. Peter. Finally, however, after twenty years of rejection and papal infighting involving war, bribery, assassination plots and the suspicion, at least, of papal poisoning, della Rovere was elected Julius II, supreme pontiff of the Church of Rome. It was All Saints Day, 1503.[2]

Julius knew Church history and remembered the ambitious musings of a predecessor who had dreamed of constructing a new Rome and returning the Eternal City to its place as the world center of culture and religion. The center-piece of the grand plan would be a new St. Peter's Cathedral which would require hiring the greatest of the world's architects, artists and craftsmen. It would also require the scandalous destruction of the old St. Peter's Cathedral where 184 popes had been consecrated and dozens of martyrs and saints were buried within its walls.

The sad irony was that the construction of this monument to Christian brotherhood would ultimately divide the flock, drown the Church in a sea of red ink and, finally, light the spark that would ignite the Protestant Reformation and the devastating sack of Rome.

ST. PETER'S SQUARE was blocked off to vehicular traffic. So, once the driver reached as far as he could, little Pedro paid the man, hopped out of the taxi and headed past the blockades to the end of Bernini's colonnade. There, overshadowed by the towering Corinthian columns, he joined the faithful thousands who flowed to and from the Basilica. He felt like a small fish in a sea of tourists, as he rolled his luggage down the long curved portico.

At one point he paused to reflect on a nearby obelisk at the center of St. Peter's Square. Pedro knew that this monument marked the area where St. Peter had been crucified.[3]

Moved, but not slowed, Pedro quickly resumed his pace, with the suitcase rolling behind, singing *click, clack, click, clack, click, clack* over the cobblestones. But then the clicking suddenly stopped. Pedro had reached a line of tourists waiting to pass through metal detectors, and supervising the traffic flow were the colorful, but serious, Swiss Guards. Father Alonzo had told him to try to avoid having his suitcase inspected. However, it looked like every purse and bag were being opened and searched by the guards.

Around him, were thousands of tourists and clergy, speaking what seemed to be every language in the world. The guards, he thought, were too colorful to be intimidating. Watching them work the long line, Pedro smiled. *These guys look like they guard Cinderella's Castle.*

Finally, he heard English words in the air as two nuns passed by him. The line had stopped moving so Pedro set his bag down to reserve his place. He spoke slowly to the woman behind him, "I will be right back." She nodded as if she understood. Then, he quickly stepped over to the nuns and tapped one on the shoulder.

"Excuse me, Sister?"

They turned and asked, "Yes?"

"Can you tell me where this is?" Pedro pulled the card out of his pocket and showed them: *L' Archivio Segreto.*

"Oh, yes. That's the Secret Archives of the Vatican." Then, she asked with a smile, "Not much of a secret, is it?"

Pedro did not respond, fearing it would be impolite to agree. One of the nuns then directed him out a nearby gate and down a narrow side road, to an inconspicuous entrance. Pedro was relieved that the route would bypass Cinderella's inspection patrol. After thanking the Sisters, Pedro returned to his place in line ... *Where is it?*

The little Honduran frantically looked around. *Where's my bag?!*

In the distance, he could barely hear his suitcase calling for help: *click, clack, click, clack, click…*

Pedro looked toward the entrance barricades and saw a dark haired man rolling his suitcase away.

"Mister, that's my bag!"

The man picked up his pace and jogged toward a girl on a scooter. The suitcase screamed: *click, clack, click, clack, click...*

Pedro pursued as fast as his fat little legs could carry him. But he quickly realized it was hopeless.

Please, God, help me!

Suddenly, a colorful flash blew right past him. The sprinting Swiss Guard closed in on the thief as Pedro fell behind. The scooter girl's eyes flashed bright with fright and she instinctively zipped away just as the man with the suitcase neared her and then hopped onto the back. However, the guard still closed in on the slow-moving scooter. Suddenly, the thief heaved the suitcase at the pursuing guard. He caught the bag, but not the thieves. They safely disappeared into a nearby alley.

As the guard carried the bag back to Pedro, his stern expression melted into a smile as he watched the heavy, little Honduran dance with joy in the bright sunlight of St. Peter's Square.

* * *

A SMALL SIGN, displaying the name he couldn't pronounce, was posted outside the door. This was the Secret Archives of the Vatican. As Pedro entered, he was surprised to see that the interior was more austere and modern than he expected. Sparse furnishings were scattered around a large, heavy table that dominated the room. On it, he saw a sign-in book.

Standing there in his rolled-up jeans and flannel shirt, he waited as he admired the blond wood walls and sparkling white marble floors. A tall, skeletal priest in a black cassock soon came out and, seeing the small man with a suitcase in his lobby, loudly and disapprovingly said something in Italian.

Pedro responded, "Do you speak English?"

"*Si,* ahhh, I said this is a research facility. No tourists. You can get a hotel room down the road … to the right."

"Oh, no, I don't need a room. I'm here to see the Prefect."

The priest chuckled. "I'm sorry. The Prefect is a very busy man." Then, more seriously, he added, "He is not available."

"I was told to tell him that I have been sent by John Eben Malek."

The priest's face changed, staring as if he couldn't understand.

Pedro repeated, "John Eben Malek?"

The priest responded with extreme embarrassment and humility. "I'm so sorry. Please, please, come with me."

"Do I need to sign in?" Pedro asked.

"No, no, of course not ... I am Father Pirelli, the Vice Prefect. May I carry your bag for you?"

THE PRIEST LED PEDRO for quite a while down darkened corridors, up numerous narrow steps, and through circuitous passageways. In some areas his path opened wide with many thousands of volumes encased around him under beautifully ornate ceilings. Although everything appeared to be meticulously cleaned, he could smell the aroma of the aged collections.

To fill the time, Pedro tried pleasant conversation.

"This place is big. How many people work here?"

"Yes. We have about twenty five miles of historical documents. Unfortunately, some of them have never been researched. We only have seven people on staff. However, we do grant access to about two hundred researchers every year from all countries. We can't welcome more guests because our small staff must locate every volume that is requested. Here, you see, we don't allow private browsing." Father Pirelli smiled knowingly. "These books are too important."[4]

Pedro's suitcase tipped over when he rolled it around a narrow corner. "Sorry. It's pretty dark in here."

"Yes," Father Pirelli responded. "This area has no electric lighting. On cloudy days, it can get pretty dark. You see, the flicker of illumination alerts our guards to the presence of nighttime intruders. I'm used to it."

Pedro rolled his suitcase through maze-like corridors that were made even narrower by bookshelves on both sides. He was surprised at how few doors and windows he saw. "This place looks secure. I guess nobody ever stole anything from here."

"Oh, no," the priest laughed, "quite the contrary. The Goths, the Huns, and the Vandals all plundered our Archives. Later, we endured Norman and Saracen invasions. And when our documents were being transferred to Avignon, for safe-keeping, the Ghibellines plundered the collection. Our most recent raider was Napoleon himself. Actually, however, time is our greatest adversary. You know, natural deterioration and that sort of thing."

"Why would all those people want a bunch of books?"

"You see, in past centuries, rarely would copies of books be made. Written records were the life – the soul – of a people. So, to destroy an archive was to destroy a culture, a government, a preserved faith. Also, many of the most revered books had jewel-encrusted wooden covers." Father Pirelli gave a 'what can you do?' shrug. "Unfortunately, through the centuries, many precious works and records have been burned, thrown to the winds or even used as wrapping paper."

"That's really sad." Pedro said breathlessly as he prepared to lug his bag up the stairs. "Who is the Prefect?"

"Monsignor Bolaka, from Rwanda … a very dedicated man. He is appointed for life, by *Beatissimo Padre* … ahhh, Holy Father."

In deference to Pedro's sweating and panting, the two men climbed the rest of the stairs quietly. Near the top, the priest announced, "We are almost there."

"Father," Pedro confided, "I was praying you were gonna say that."

Finally, the two men entered a large area that was bright with natural sunlight.

"This is the Tower of the Winds," the priest said proudly.

The sweaty, gasping little man studied the impressive, bright room. Two walls boasted large, beautiful frescoes but Pedro's eyes were drawn to an interesting indoor weather vane on the ceiling that seemed to change with the direction of the wind outside. Pedro didn't realize it, but this was the astronomical observatory where the Gregorian calendar had been conceived in 1582. Though its miniscule error rate was just one day in 3,323 years, it took non-Catholic countries nearly two centuries to trust and adopt it. The delay was just one more indication of the deep Christian divisions that existed after the Reformation.

Bookcases and large tables filled the room. Researchers worked diligently at the tables. A thin black man with a long grey beard sat alone at one of the tables. The priest led Pedro there.

"Excuse me, Monsignor."

The monsignor looked up from his book.

"I have amazing news. This gentleman has been sent to us by John Eben Malek."

The black man rose to his feet and nearly gasped. "Wonderful! So nice to meet you. I am Monsignor Bolaka, the Prefect of the Archives."

Pedro responded, "Hello, I am …"

"No, no, that's quite alright," the monsignor interrupted. "Your name is not necessary. We prefer it that way. Father, please take our guest to my office where we can speak in private. I'll be there shortly."

Pedro feared that another two-mile hike might kill him.

THE PREFECT'S OFFICE was small, Spartan and filled with bookcases. Father Pirelli pointed at one of the two Savonarola chairs in front of the mahogany desk. Pedro rolled his suitcase over to it and gladly sat down to rest. Then the priest quietly disappeared.

Pedro listened to the church bells tolling the twelfth hour. He felt a rush of pride as he imagined what his parents would have said if they had seen him being treated like an important dignitary at the Vatican.

Studying the extensive collection of books around him, Pedro felt a little embarrassed that he was not allowed to introduce himself. Then, interrupting his thoughts, the elderly black man entered the room. Father Pirelli shut the door and stood quietly beside it.

"I am so pleased to meet you." They shook hands as Pedro studied this unusual African man with the long white beard that contrasted sharply with his black face and cassock.

Once he was seated behind the desk, the Prefect asked with great anticipation, "So … what do you have for us?"

Pedro thought, *These guys are going to be real disappointed.* He unzipped his suitcase, pushed aside his change of clothes, and pulled out an elongated clay jar that John had made. It was, perhaps, eighteen inches tall and six inches in diameter. From Pedro's viewpoint, it might best be used as a vase, if only it had a hole in the top. However, without an opening, it looked pretty worthless.

Sounding extremely satisfied, the Prefect said, "Oh, yes. Very nice." Both priests smiled broadly. Then, when Pedro handed it over, they quickly thanked him and the tall priest unceremoniously rushed him toward the door.

"Thank you. Thank you very much …"

"And … uh … there's one more thing," Pedro interrupted.

Father Pirelli took his hand off Pedro's back and stopped in his tracks. "Yes, go on," the monsignor inquired.

"John wanted me to tell you something. He didn't want me to write it down and I'm not quite sure why I'm supposed to …"

"Yes, yes, go ahead," Father Pirelli chided.

Slowly and clearly, Pedro recited, "They have my fingerprints now."

The two priests made serious eye contact with each other but remained silent for a moment. Then Father Pirelli resumed Pedro's hustle out the door.

"Thank you. Thank you very much. Good bye now."

"But how will I find my way out?" Pedro pleaded.

"Just, just, stay in that direction," the priest said as he pointed down a long dark hall. "Have a nice flight home."

Pedro rolled his black suitcase through the never-ending narrow halls and, finally, over the lobby's white marble floors. No matter how hard he tried, he couldn't quite understand what had just happened. *These people seem to have real authority.* For the first time, Pedro doubted the sanity of his Church's leadership.

WITHIN TEN MINUTES, the Prefect's office was abuzz. Fourteen select members of the clergy from around the globe crowded closer to his desk. All eyes were on the precious clay jar.

"Please close the door," Monsignor Bolaka began. A small, elderly nun shut it. "Some of you may be new here so, first, I want to say what must be understood. This matter requires absolute secrecy."

Mumbling rumbled through the room as translations were given to those who could not understand English. Looking around his office, the Prefect could see dedicated agreement in every eye.

"Now, let's take a look."

He slid open a side drawer and pulled out a towel. He spread the towel across the top of the desk and laid the jar there on its side. The Prefect then reached into another drawer, pulled out a hammer and smashed the jar. Carefully, he pulled the jar open at the crack and triumphantly held up its contents for all to see. An audible gasp could be heard as he raised a parchment scroll in the air. Some of the priests and nuns crossed themselves.

"Father?" The Prefect waved Father Pirelli to approach, and then rolled the scroll open on the desk.

Towering over everyone else, Father Pirelli stepped up and examined the text. "It is either classical Arabic or Aramaic. However, I will need more time to review it." The tall priest rolled the scroll open more. "Strange … it is not very long."

The Prefect announced, "I invited you in for the opening so that you will all be aware of our wonderful gift. You will see the translation after it is approved. Now, however, let us all prayerfully return to work."

The devout congregation funneled out the door. They were all quiet, but smiling with anticipation.

The tall priest remained with the Prefect, reviewing the scroll. "Yes … Yes … Aramaic it is ... I'll just need a couple of hours."

The Prefect added, "I will contact the Holy Father."

PEDRO PURCHASED A TOURIST MAP of Rome from a street vendor near St. Peter's Square. Then, congratulating himself for a job well done, he rolled into a *gelateria*. Pedro had heard of *gelato* but had never tasted it. Now, with his first lick of creamy green pistachio, he would never forget it.

Arriving at a bench, he sat down and admired the Square, the colonnades, the statues, the tourists, and even the pigeons. But, most of all, he studied the dome of the Basilica while he savored every lick of this heavenly dessert.

He regretted that he did not have much time for sightseeing. When he finished his treat, he slipped into one of the Vatican shops and bought a St. Christopher's medal. After all, Pedro was now a world traveler.

He rolled his suitcase away from the Basilica and paused to gaze at the foreboding , dark fortress before him. He knew nothing about *Castel Sant'Angelo* but realized that it must have played an important role in Church history. Then, hearing the bells toll twice, he hailed a taxi and hurried back to the airport for his afternoon flight home, regretting only that he had so little time in the Eternal City.

Daniel, keep this prophecy a secret;
seal up the book until the time of the end,
when many will rush here and there,
and knowledge will increase.
Daniel 12:4

20

Secret Archives of the Vatican
Vatican City
June 22

Monsignor Bolaka and Father Pirelli did not know what to make of it. For that reason, they had delayed sending the scroll through the normal channels. They sat across from each other staring at the Aramaic to English translation on the Prefect's desk. It was much shorter than expected and lacked specific instructions. It was a bit cryptic and they wondered if it could be an unfinished work. But then they noticed the dark red stamp at the bottom of the original which signified its end.

The Prefect read the translation one more time, aloud:

> "The living Church withers in parched, lifeless soil. If it were not so, the world's Shining Darkness could not have dawned. When My Church and My people are persecuted, be not afraid. The rise of great evil shall be confronted by the rise of the Greatest Good. Follow the beloved watchman who shall resolve the transcendent mysteries and crown the conquering monarch. Remain in Rome and prepare to carry your cross. When darkness prevails, victory is near, and no secret shall remain hidden."

They said a silent prayer and then crossed themselves before the Monsignor spoke up. "I will bring the translation to *Beatissimo Padre.* Please register the artifact and deliver it to the Archives."

FATHER PIRELLI GATHERED UP the treasured scroll and carefully carried it away. He went down many of the same halls that Pedro had wandered until he came to an inconspicuous steel door. He unlocked the deadbolt, went inside, and locked the door behind him. There, he was faced with a dark, winding staircase that seemed to descend forever into the abyss. His tapping shoes echoed, on one metal step after another, one flight after another, as he and his precious possession sank into the cool, dark depths.

At the bottom, far below ground level, far below where any fire or bomb could harm them, he found two Swiss Guards, standing at attention, on either side of a massive vault. Unlike the guards on the ground level, these were armed with sub-machine guns. Although he was well known, Father Pirelli still had to show his identification to one of the guards and sign in at a nearby desk. The record book had, "Johannine Vault" written at the top. On the next open line, number 1782, he listed the time and date of entry with his signature.

He then stepped up to a facial screen and also placed his hand on the glass surface next to it. When the retina scan and biometric palm print were approved, the massive bolts in the vault could be heard sliding. One of the guards then pulled open the heavy door.

Father Pirelli stepped inside the steel reinforced concrete bunker that was designed to withstand even a nuclear blast. Inside the vault, the filtered air smelled fresh and humidity was carefully controlled. He was in a room full of scrolls, neatly stored on shelves that rose to the ceiling. The only ornamentation in the vault was a wall with 15 framed photographs. Pirelli briefly stopped to glance at the historic pictures of the last 15 popes, dating back to 1823. He smiled as he, once again, appreciated that, in each photo, standing next to each pontiff, was the same 33 year old man.

The priest pulled out a tag, wrote on it 1782, and attached it to his scroll. He then placed his precious possession on the shelf next to the other 1781 scrolls that John had delivered to the Bishop of Rome over the past two millennia.

Honor no man
more than truth.
Socrates

21
Boaz, West Virginia
June 30

Elizabeta plucked three more tomatoes from the vine and put them in her apron. She was proud of the garden this year. The weather had cooperated. For twelve years now she had sought peace and anonymity in this small town.

She had not communicated much with her daughter over the past two decades. Elizabeta's phone calls were rarely taken and contact over that time amounted to nothing more than a handful of cards, from Angela, written in someone else's handwriting. Perhaps, their ancient history was just too painful to think about.

But the proud mother had one fond, recent memory. After she experienced flooding, three years ago, Angela sent her mother a check for $100. Elizabeta, however, refused to cash it and, instead, framed the treasure and hung it in her living room.

Her one bedroom cottage nestled into the narrow strip of land where the West Virginia hills abruptly meet the Ohio River. She had only an acre but farmland was fertile next to the river. Now, in her mid-seventies, she was very frail. Life had become difficult and physically demanding. Recently, she had fallen a few times and, once, had to lay there for six hours before a neighbor found her. However, she had suffered through tougher times and, all in all, she was not unhappy.

Elizabeta limped back to the house, cradling her prized possessions. She mounted the three back steps very slowly because her hands were unable to hold the rail. However, when she got to the top, she heard a strange noise, one that definitely was getting louder. She sat down on the porch and gazed over the garden, past the railroad tracks and the rolling green field that led down to the river. The noise was becoming deafening.

Suddenly, from the other side of the house, a shadow darkened her field. Then, a helicopter roared overhead close, very close, to her rooftop.

"What are you doing? You crazy fool!" She shouted at the aircraft as it made a tight turn and then descended onto her garden vegetation, "I just planted those beans!"

The propeller blast was blowing topsoil everywhere so Elizabeta had to cover her eyes with her hand as she protected her tomatoes with the other one. She could hear the blades slowing and eventually she peaked out ready to give somebody a piece of her mind. She ground her teeth as she watched the door open and a woman stepped out.

Could it be …? "Angela!"

The old lady nearly fell down the stairs as the tomatoes tumbled out of her apron and she hobbled over to her long-lost daughter. Suddenly, decades of hurt and disappointment melted away. After all these years of uncertainty, she finally realized her little *chiquita* did not hate her.

THE KETTLE WHISTLED and Elizabeta strained getting out of her white plastic dinette chair. She went over to the stove to make two cups of her daughter's favorite tea. Angela was surprised at how old and frail her mother looked as she limped around the kitchen.

"It must be difficult living alone," the daughter ventured.

"Oh, I do okay. I have Mr. Everling next door to help. He lost his wife last year. He's such a nice man. Says he likes when a woman needs his help." She smiled and lowered her voice, as if confiding a secret. "You know, sometimes I ask him to help me even when I don't need it. Makes him feel like he's still important."

As she set down the tea cups, they chuckled together just like they had done forty years before.

Then after the laughter died, the mother became serious. "Angela, I couldn't be more proud of …" But sobbing interrupted her sentence.

Angela leaned over from her chair and hugged her mother. "I know, mama."

Elizabeta collected herself and continued, "You know, I've been reading about you. Who hasn't? It's just amazing what you accomplished … And now they say you're running for president! My little *Chiquita* ... Amazing … You know, back in '61, you were supposed to be born before we left. But you were determined to wait until you reached America. You see, everything always works out for the best."

Elizabeta surprised herself with that expression, the one she had often said … until everything went wrong.

"Everything works out for the best," Elizabeta repeated, with childlike faith.

Angela knew she had to get down to why she had come. After a moment of quiet smiles, Angela's disappeared. "Mama, I have to talk to you about something. I'm not sure how to explain this so please forgive me if I'm not delicate enough." She took a deep breath. "Mama, I'm in trouble and I need your help."

"Oh, baby …" her mother lovingly reassured, "I'll help you any way I can."

"For a few months now I have thought I was being stalked. Whenever I'd show up at publicized events, I kept seeing the same fat, greasy man. He always seemed to be undressing me with his disturbing stares. Anyway, one day I was working my way along a rope line, shaking hands with constituents. Before I knew it, the man's hand was on mine. Mama, it was a large, sweaty hand. I almost jerked back but I realized he was passing me a note. So, I took it and moved down the line. When I finally found privacy, I opened the note. It had a name and phone number on it… Mama, it was Luke Skelton."

Elizabeta exhaled loudly. She closed her eyes and cried. "I knew it was him! I knew it was him!"

"Yes, mama, and I know you used to tell people it must have been him. But you can never say that ever again."

Years ago, Luke Skelton was the cute, older boy who had mowed lawns in their neighborhood. Elizabeta had never trusted him and had always warned her daughter to stay away from him. Now, just the thought of that fat, greasy pig turned Elizabeta's stomach.

The mother let out a howling moan, "Why! Why did you not admit it? Why did you let them blame your papa? Why did you let that boy get away with rape?" Elizabeta looked up at the sky, "Oh Fernando, you could never commit such evil!" Then she spoke with hatred in her heart: "I knew it was that boy!"

"Mama, I was just a kid. I didn't know what to say or who to trust. Luke told me they would send him to jail if I blamed him. He threatened me, mama. He threatened me."

"Why didn't you at least tell me?"

"I wanted to, mama. But every time I was ready to say it, you weren't ready to hear it. Then, when papa died, I just thought it would be best to keep Luke out of it. He always scared me, mama."

"Angela, why bring this up now? It was all dead. It was all buried."

"Mama, he's threatening me again. He knows the statute of

limitations for rape has expired. So he feels that he has nothing to lose. He wants money – a lot of it – or he says he'll tell everybody that I lied in my Supreme Court case."

"Let him tell! Let him admit that he's a rapist! Let him finally prove that your papa was not a bad man!"

"Mama, don't be emotional. This could sink my candidacy. That's why I had to talk to you. Think of what's best for America. He knows abortion is a major issue at the presidential level. However, it's not just abortion, the whole life question that will be debated. Mama, there are new biotechnologies that are coming out that will advance human health in amazing new ways. If he smears me, my women's rights leadership record and my reputation for honesty will be down the drain. Then he can take me out of the fight for all kinds of amazing new health advances ... But, on the other hand, if he gets his money, it can all be swept under the rug … Mama, let papa rest in peace. Let's just put this all behind us. Luke will go away if he gets the money."

Elizabeta mumbled, "I only have a few hundred dollars."

"No, I have all the money I need. But, mama, you are going to be asked a lot of questions in the coming months. I just want you to stick to the story. Do not defend papa. Do not mention Luke. If you do, you will destroy my chance to become president. Do you understand?"

Elizabeta could not speak.

"It's what's best for everyone, mama."

Her mother nodded.

"I'm sorry but I have to go now."

The two women rose from their plastic chairs and Angela hugged her mother tightly for the first time in decades. Elizabeta almost swooned from the affectionate embrace that she had craved for so long. Then Angela whispered in her ear, "You know, it's okay to tell the media about the loving relationship we've always had."

When Angela ended the embrace, she was back to business and headed for the door. Before leaving, she offered a simple, "Bye, mama."

Elizabeta returned a slight smile but her eyes remained sad.

Later, as she floated out of Elizabeta's life, Angela was relieved that everything was under control. Now, she had only one secret left – one that she would never reveal, and never forget: In the crash that had killed her father, it was Angela who had jerked the wheel.

Whoever believes in me will do the works that I do,
and will do greater ones than these...
If you ask anything of me in my name, I will do it.
John 14:12-14

22

Tarbuwth Correctional Facility
Yashar, NY
July 9

John was being held without bail and temporarily without charge because of the possibility that his hidden past signaled terrorist intentions. No one could understand how this seemingly simple man had so effectively remained off the grid.

John wondered why God would want him here, immobilized, ineffective and risking exposure. *What good can I accomplish in prison?* He had been jailed many times in the past, but this seemed more threatening, more permanent. Like a sprinter in the starting blocks he had waited … waited … waited for the starting signal that finally would hurl him against the dark forces of the world. Now, however, when evil appeared darker than ever, he was sidelined again. Looking back on all his years, he felt deep humiliation that he had been so ineffective at increasing the flock. He prayed that he had not disappointed God.

When his recreation yard break came around, Officer Jefferson and three other guards escorted John, and the other prisoners from his wing, out to the yard. This was the one hour a day when, corralled by chain link and razor ribbon, the inmates were allowed to get some sun and exercise.

When the steel door buzzed open John stepped out into the fresh air and inhaled deeply. It was a day as beautiful as he had ever seen.

The fencing was, perhaps, fourteen feet tall and buried deep into the ground. Along the fence lines, were black camera domes mounted every hundred feet, or so, recording everything. Rising above the east and west corners of the yard, were watchtowers with an armed guard in each one. The watchtower guards communicated with each other, when necessary, using walkie-talkies. They made no effort to hide their scoped rifles, which were always in their hands. However, on the ground, the four yard guards had only billy clubs.

Once out the door, John immediately headed away from the other prisoners toward a picnic table in the far corner of the yard. He sat down and observed the others separating into various packs. As usual, the Muslim prisoners stayed together and joined in a game of soccer. The biggest, most dangerous, men mostly went to the weight racks and began their workouts.

Then John heard someone behind him.

"Dear child."

He recognized the soft familiar voice. With a flood of emotion, he turned and fell to his knees. "Thank you Blessed Mother, thank you for coming to me, again." With ecstasy in his eyes, he gazed at what no one else could see: a sad young woman more beautiful than he could possibly describe.

"My Son's hand of justice will not be restrained forever," she warned. "The wolves are becoming stronger … smarter … hungrier. How I long for an end to their evil … Prepare your flock. From here you shall find your shepherds … Fear nothing. The Truth shall be revealed and, soon, everything shall change."

John waited, hoping for more words.

"My Son and I love you more than you can imagine."

Still kneeling, John suddenly felt a sharp kick in the back. Slowly, he turned and focused on the man behind him.

"I'm talkin' to you, asshole. What are you lookin' at?"

John slowly rose. Before him was the inmate named Worthington and two other thugs ready to back up his demands. Worthington alone, with his massive size and bald headed flame tattoo, could have intimidated any man, except John.

"I'm just trying to get along, my friend," John answered as he dusted off his knees.

"Friend?" Worthington asked while the men who flanked him laughed. "If I had a knife right now, I'd cut out your heart and eat it."

John responded, "Then, I must have failed."

"Failed at what?"

"I just prayed for your conversion."

Worthington smiled to his partners. "That's a good one." Then, angrily, he turned his attention back to John. "Why don't you just get back on your knees and pray I don't kill you?"

The east tower guard noticed the brewing conflict and radioed the other tower: "Hey, Oscar, keep an eye on the southwest corner." Through his binoculars, the guard could see that John was not intimidated, but was not acting threatening either. The guard whispered to himself, "Oh, no. Don't taunt the alpha-dog. Just back down and you'll go home in one piece."

John held his hands open, out near his waist, and did not back away. "I'm just keeping to myself … trying to get along."

Worthington twitched a couple times. "Look, this is my y…yard, asshole. You come into my yard, you better b…bring a gift. Did you bring a g…g…g…gift?"

John stepped closer to Worthington. The big man grimaced and brought his hands against his temples as if trying to massage away a piercing headache.

"Yes, I have a gift for you," John responded softly.

Worthington appeared to want to look away, but couldn't.

Then, compulsively twitching, he begged submissively, "W...what do you want f...from me?" Panic covered his tattooed face as his eyes rolled back into his head. "L...l...leave me alone!" He begged, "P...p... please... s...s...s...stop."

The men next to Worthington frowned with disbelief in their eyes. Keeping his hands outstretched, John moved another step closer.

"Hey, Oscar," the east guard radioed, "we got trouble."

Looking through his rifle scope, Oscar responded, "I see it. You better call 'em down."

The east guard picked up a bullhorn and blasted a warning, "Okay guys, back off." Then he pressed an emergency button on his tower desk.

The bullhorn always alerted the prisoners that a fight was breaking out in the yard so everyone ran over to watch the two combatants. As they circled around, some inmates tried to bet on the outcome. However, no one was willing to bet on John.

The four guards on the ground stayed far away, at the perimeter of the yard. The last thing they wanted was to be caught in the middle of a rec. yard riot. Besides, they knew that the tower guards had enough firepower to quell any situation.

"Don't make us open fire, guys," the bullhorn blasted.

Both tower guards viewed the pair through their scopes. The perimeter guards readied themselves, from a distance, with their billy sticks. The inmates shouted, egging on the two men. Alerted to the confrontation, additional officers streamed out of the building and took positions near the other guards on the ground.

John remained calm with his hands still open to his side, peacefully gazing into Worthington's distraught eyes.

John quietly commanded the demon he knew well. "In the name of Jesus Christ, come out of him, Asmodeus."

Worthington jerked and convulsed with a grimacing face and

frothing mouth. However, he still remained standing.

"Back off! Back off now!" the bullhorn blared.

John moved closer until they were face to face. The guards could see through their sights that Worthington was drooling, crying and trembling. However, the other prisoner had never even touched him. Worthington seemed to be experiencing unbearable pain but he didn't fall down or back away. Amazed, the ring of spectators became completely quiet.

"Back off now or we'll shoot!"

Oscar fired two shots near the feet of the two men in the middle. Only the inmates surrounding them retreated.

John inhaled, whispered "Receive the Holy Spirit," and then exhaled into Worthington's face.

The tattooed prisoner screamed an inhuman shriek of pain. He contorted and grimaced and finally collapsed to the ground where he groaned and flailed like a hooked fish. John stood above him, with his eyes closed, as if he hadn't even noticed Worthington's violent reaction.

The prisoners all backed away from John. Fear and confusion contorted their faces. They did not know what John had just done but, whatever it was, it wasn't good.

John went to his knee next to Worthington as the man convulsed on his back. He put his hand on the big prisoner's chest and said three times, "In the name of Jesus Christ, come out." Each time, Worthington responded with a cringing grimace and an exhale. Finally, all tension left the man's body and he laid there motionless.

"He's dead," a prisoner whispered. "He done killed him."

"No, he's not," John said. "He's resting."

"Looks like we lost one," the tower guard radioed.

"It's a shame," came the radio response. "It would have been more fun to shoot him."

"Everybody," the bullhorn blared, "head back to your cells, now!"

The guards rounded up the spectators and herded them back to the steel door. John remained behind, still on his knee, with his hand on Worthington's motionless chest. As they waited for the door to buzz open, every prisoner had his eyes on the two mysterious combatants; one supremely victorious, one completely destroyed. They looked like frozen statues until, slightly, Worthington's head moved … then his arm. Soon, he sat up and the prisoners exchanged baffled glances.

John gave a hand to help up the big man. Worthington rose to his feet, looked John in the eye, and wept. The surprised prisoners chuckled but were even more surprised when Worthington, tearfully and lovingly, hugged John.

He whispered into John's ear, "I saw Him … I heard Him ... He smiled and … and He said, 'Our Father loves us all … but He has His favorites.'" Worthington sobbed, "I think He meant me! I think He … He actually meant me!"

From a distance, Officer D.J. Jefferson had seen everything that John had done. He was fascinated by this mysterious man. In the hot summer heat, surrounded by prisoners who were cracking crude jokes, Jefferson felt a cool breeze caress his face. A deep sense of peace descended upon him and, just as quickly as it had arrived, the breeze was gone.

Jefferson was thrilled by what he had just seen and felt. He wanted to laugh but he knew he shouldn't. Still, he couldn't help but think, *That man doesn't belong here.*

You fools!
You know how to interpret the weather signs
of the earth and sky,
but you don't know how to interpret the present times.
Luke 12:56

23

Marriott Marquis Hotel
New York City
July 9

Standing in the hotel hall, Angela was surprised to see who opened the door. After all, Evan Thas had emphasized the importance of secrecy at this meeting and she had gone to great lengths to accommodate his wishes. She only expected Dr. Cyst to join them.

"Fred, what are you doing here?" she asked.

"Aren't you happy to see me?" Fred Whitehead quipped as he tossed back his abundant white hair. "Come in and join us."

Entering the penthouse suite, she saw Huntington Cyst sitting at a table in his motorized wheelchair, and Evan, at the marble bar, preparing a drink. Dr. Cyst flashed a wave but continued talking quietly on his iPhone.

Angela cast a studious glance at Cyst. He had a look of seriousness that contrasted with his bright flowered Hawaiian shirt and casual, white linen pants. But she knew they shared a spiritual relationship: born to the ruling class.

Angela admired his reputation. She planned to move cautiously with him. A man this brilliant might be volatile and she did not want to alienate the one person who could make all her dreams come true.

Suddenly, Angela was surprised to notice something she had never before realized. The mysterious Dr. Cyst was missing his feet. She knew he was wheelchair-bound but never knew why. Now she could see that his legs abruptly ended at the ankles.

She had thought she was coming into this meeting prepared. Not wanting to be caught short on informational resources, she had hired detectives to work up a background investigative report on Cyst and Thas. Missing feet seemed to be an obvious footnote, so to speak, that should have been included in the report.

Most of the briefing simply had provided more detail on the impressive broad generalities that she already knew. Cyst was the founder, visionary and largest shareholder of XCyst Industries, a multi-national conglomerate with interests spanning wide-ranging computer and biomedical technologies, aerospace, advanced weaponry, oil and gas, and even the media. One of their latest successes in the news was their algorithmic software system that had become the rage of today's stock brokerage houses. Now, 60% of all stock transactions were computer generated, controlling trades like a plane on auto-pilot, transacting billions of dollars in microseconds.

Years ago, Cyst had overcome a widely-publicized falling out with his partner, Henri Blanc, who had departed the company with $450 million and little gratitude. Blanc had been the brains behind the Cyst-Blanc supercomputer but left to pursue philanthropic ventures. It had been reported that Blanc's religious conversion irritated Cyst, leading to the breakup. Blanc went on to establish the internationally controversial and secretive brain-trust known as the Legion of Babylon. Members of that group included the world's most powerful policymakers, but Blanc's one-time friend, Huntie, had never been invited to join. It wasn't long, however, before The Legion had morphed into an organization that Cyst would love.

Cyst was widely respected as a master recruiter who attracted the world's top technology talent. Publicly, it was believed that his companies had exceeded normal standards of profitability because of his mastery of negotiating deals with states, the US federal government, and multi-national governing entities such as the United Nations. However, Angela believed that she had uncovered his secret. Almost all of Cyst's biggest deals, as he had once bragged, were with entities in which "everyone is guilty, but no one is responsible." He had his staff troll for large contracts in which "benefits concentrate around the few while costs spread among the many, particularly when politicians or bureaucrats are doing the spending." In short, he loved to do business with people who doled out other peoples' money.

The Secretary found it interesting that the relationship between the two men was more than Thas had admitted. In fact, Cyst was his adopted father. For an unknown monetary sum, Thas' Canadian parents had apparently signed away their parental rights when the boy was six years old. Reports told of the boy's angry resistance during the early years and of Cyst's intolerance for rebellion. However, by the time Thas reached his early teens, the two seemed to be a loving, father/son team. Now, the face of this twenty seven year old red head showed little evidence of his impressive experience. Discretely, for years now, he had travelled the globe representing Cyst in some of the most consequential trade negotiations in history. During that time, Thas had enjoyed Cyst's unwavering deference, even to the point of creating jealousies among Cyst's division heads. But, regardless of their resentments, they recognized that Thas was privy to every high-level decision.

As founder and Chairman of the Board of Directors of XCyst Industries, Cyst played a visionary rather than hands-on management role. The excellent talent surrounding Cyst allowed that luxury. Among top management, Thas had become feared, if not respected, as the unflinching hatchet man, ready to act whenever Cyst deemed the axe necessary.

On the other hand, Cyst had entrusted Whitehead's firm with leading the company's generous governmental relations efforts. Fred had an extraordinary talent for getting arcane legislative language inserted into bills. By the time he finished with a law, it would become so lengthy and tedious that the hidden goodies were rarely discoved by the media. So, while Evan Thas had become known as "The Angel of Death," Fred Whitehead had developed a reputation in political circles as "The Candy Man."

Evan called out, "How about a drink, Madame Secretary?"

"Yes, thank you. Kettle One with lime would be nice."

Angela walked to the window, parted the draperies, and looked down on the dazzling chaos of Times Square. Her heart beat faster as she soaked in the flashing lights, the brilliant colors, and the massive billboard images of beautiful, bare flesh. She always marveled at this sensual view of the great city that ruled over the kings of the earth. It was, she thought proudly, part of her kingdom.

"Please, Madame Secretary," Evan requested, "Dr. Cyst would prefer the draperies closed.... Ice?"

"Yes, please." She backed away from the window and sat on a leather stool at the bar, not wanting to intrude on the doctor's phone call. "Fred, come join me ... Where's your lovely sidekick?"

"Tonight's for real business. I left Amy behind to crunch numbers in Washington."

Evan handed her a drink. "I hope you don't mind that we invited Mr. Whitehead."

"No, of course not. It's always a pleasure to see an old friend."

"Now, don't make me out to be too old," Fred chuckled. "I prefer the word 'dear.'"

"Then 'dear friend' it is."

Angela sipped her drink and thought about how carefully she had worked to keep this meeting secret. She had spoken at a pharmaceutical conference earlier in the day. Then, after dining with a few select CEOs, she made her apologies to them and her staff, complaining that her headache demanded an early bedtime. She wondered if Fred's presence might complicate things ... or, maybe, new possibilities might open up for the future.

"So, how badly do you want it?" boomed a deep voice from the other side of the room.

Angela looked over at the balding man in the wheelchair who had finished his call and was now smiling at her. For an older gentleman, his goatee and bright blue eyes gave him a youthful look.

"Want what?" Angela toyed.

"Don't play games with me, Madame Secretary."

"Dr. Cyst, I want it more than you can imagine."

"I doubt that," he grumbled.

They both laughed as Angela walked over and shook his hand.

"I trust Evan has prepared a drink to your satisfaction," Dr. Cyst commented as he rifled through files on the table. "And I hope you don't mind that Fred is joining us."

"Yes and no… in that order," she quipped.

"Now, please," he waved them to come forward, "have a seat. I'm still jet-lagged from my Nauru flight and you're making me tired watching you stand."

As the three guests approached the upholstered chairs in the room, Angela asked, "Nauru? What were you doing there? I thought the only thing they have is bird crap."

She was referring the tiny Pacific island's infamous source of revenue: phosphate. It is a fertilizer ingredient derived from the island's abundant, but inconvenient, blessing of bird droppings.

"You're not the first one to suggest that, you know," he responded with a smile. "Madame Secretary, we have a biomedical engineering plant there and, I must say, because of that, we've done a lot of good for the Nauruan people."

"Excellent. Tell me more, if you don't mind."

"Of course. You may realize Nauru is the world's smallest independent island republic. For many years, the island had no more than 13,000 residents in an area a tenth the size of Washington, DC. The island had nothing of value to export except all that phosphate and, for a time, phosphate mining allowed Nauru the highest standard of living in the region. It was even called "the Kuwait of the South Pacific." However, mining experts had long warned that the supply of phosphate was finite. Yet, no one listened. Irresponsible over-mining eventually ruined the soil and exhausted the phosphate reserves. By the time we got there, mining had virtually ceased and the economy was on the brink of collapse. The country had a 90% unemployment rate and just about anyone who had a job worked for the government."

"That's awful," Angela sympathized. "Who gets the blame?"

"Everyone: corrupt politicians, greedy businessmen, and the fat, dumb and comfortable island residents.... Madame Secretary, never forget that comfort is the mother of ruin. Do you know what I mean?"

Angela nodded thoughtfully.

"But on the flip side of that," Dr. Cyst continued with a devious smile, "disaster is the father of fortunes."

For a few seconds, those words demanded quiet contemplation. Then, Evan Thas inserted, "But you should see Nauru now."

"That's right. It's come a long way since then."

"Tell her what you do there," Fred Whitehead prompted.

"There's plenty of time for that," Cyst demurred. "Anyway, we came in and built a longer airport runway – of course, I need that for my G550 – and we doubled the paved roads from 12 to 25 miles. Now, our biotech plant there offers employment with the highest wages ever seen on the island."

"Why don't you locate it more conveniently, like in America, perhaps in New York?" she asked, never missing an opportunity to market her state.

"I'm afraid that is not possible at the present time. You know, religious zealots have hijacked American politics and law. I'm sure I don't have to lecture someone as progressive as you about what a shame it is that the advancement of science and our quality of life have been held back by ignorant extremists."

"Yes," she sympathized softly, but without fully understanding his point, "that is a shame."

Then, with a smile, he added, "I anxiously await the day when science will be restored to its rightful place. Someday soon, we will show you Nauru and amaze you with the unlimited power of science."

"I look forward to it."

Thas added, "We've almost doubled the island's population, including almost a thousand doctors and scientists, who now live in an entirely new community with all the modern amenities. It's been quite a Renaissance."

"Perhaps, that's why they call Dr. Cyst 'The Renaissance Man,'" Angela praised sincerely.

"You're too kind," the doctor brushed away the compliment. "Now, enough about me, let's talk about your future."

As they settled back comfortably, Cyst asked, "Madame Secretary, who will be your greatest threat through the primaries?"

"Apathy," she responded confidently.

"Apathy?"

"Yes, I'm counting on running unopposed in the primaries. Lumpkin and Thompson have privately accepted future cabinet posts and Lowery is not far behind."

"Nicely done," Dr. Cyst approved, "but let's not get carried away. What do you say we get, oh, maybe, Derek Broughton in the race to stir things up? It'll give XBC News something to cover. Broughton will keep attacking you from so far left in the primaries that you'll look like a moderate by the time we get to the general."

"Sounds good to me," Angela said.

"You think you can arrange that for us, Fred?"

"No way," Fred laughed, "there's bad blood between us. Remember when I confronted him on getting your oil refinery approved in Louisiana?"

"I can get it done," Evan inserted calmly, as he took notes.

Dr. Cyst nodded at Thas and continued, "And what about the general election?"

"My research indicates that Senator Everson Blight is the biggest threat."

"Right you are." He smiled at her and clicked a remote control in his hand. On a nearby coffee table a large notebook computer screen came to life. "He has a lovely family, strong marriage and a straight forward approach."

She picked up the critique, "Yes, but his every solution is a knee jerk response. I mean, he acts like he's never read anything but the Constitution and the Bible. But I give him credit, he knows how to stay in the limelight and he sure knows how to attract right wingers."

"Like flies on a turd," Evan inserted.

Angela tried to conceal her giggle. "That's what makes him dangerous. But, actually, he is as dumb as a box of rocks."

Cyst continued, "Perhaps. But based on today's data, if both of you run the best campaigns possible," the computer screen displayed the election forecast, "you will only win by 4.8 percentage points. That's a rough estimate." Dr. Cyst smiled. "I may be off by as much as 0.2%. Now, let's take a look."

Cyst took them through chart after chart of demographic data emphasizing the best strategies and themes for each region of the country. Then he laid out a list of the corporations, unions and PACs that would contribute money, time and talent. Then he ran through lists – including thousands of various elected officials throughout the country – of endorsements and money tallies. He made staff and cabinet recommendations and showed her how to turn them into effective campaign surrogates. He also had run CyBot psycho-social profiles on all the major journalists who would be covering the campaign and was prioritizing their internet searches with results that bolstered Angela's positions.

Angela's data then was compared to correlating data on the Blight side. With each chart, an attack strategy – complete with internal tactics and external media themes – had been designed to best support her positions and weaken her opponent's.

Angela was impressed with the presentation. They certainly had done their homework.

However, after ninety minutes of dense but brilliant analysis, the conversation waned and Cyst's smile suddenly disappeared. He had a serious question on his mind. "Madame Secretary, I saw you looking down admiringly on Times Square," he observed. "Someday, those lights may go dark. If and when they do, are you up to the task? Will you have the balls to take control and set things right?"

With no hesitation, she responded firmly, "Absolutely."

"Because, if not," Cyst continued bluntly, "you can take your principles and uncertainties all the way to the unemployment line. I don't side with lovable losers."

"I understand."

"Madame Secretary, don't fail with half measures." He studied her response. "Even though you can always find something nuanced about your own side you don't like, and it's never perfect, you have to act in the end like there's simple black and white clarity between your side and the other side or you don't get anything done. Always remind yourself of that when you get confused."[1]

"I will."

Cyst studied her response with a careful nod as Thas added with a smile, "Well then, let's drink, drink and be merry."

Before long, everyone was ready to call it a night. Angela told Cyst what a pleasure it had been to finally meet him. She assured him that she would never forget his invaluable assistance and that the Oval Office door would always be open to him. He expressed his own gratitude for her principled persistence and then said, "Madame Secretary, I want you to have something." He handed her an iPhone. "Keep this within reach at all times. It is more important than it may seem."

A little puzzled, she thanked Cyst. Then she said goodbye to the other two men as they showed her to the door. She told them that she would be flying back to Albany tomorrow morning and, so, was ready for bed.

Before parting, Cyst added, "Madame Secretary, you have an upcoming trip to Australia planned."

"I do."

"If you will allow Evan to divert you for just eight hours, I promise he will give you a Nauru tour that you will never forget."

"I'll check my schedule. I hope to do it."

"Excellent."

As she stepped out of the door, Cyst added, "Oh, I almost forgot. Please keep all Nauru information confidential."

"Of course. No problem," she responded with a smile.

As they closed the door behind her, the three men briefly discussed the arrangements for their important meeting tomorrow night. It would be here, in the same room, at nine o'clock. Again, Dr. Cyst would inquire, "So, how badly do you want it?" They were anxious to hear how Senator Everson Blight would respond.

Why rent one politician when you can own them all.

Twenty minutes later, a confident knock was heard on another floor. Angela opened the door. Fred entered with a magnum of Dom Perignon.

"I told you, tonight is for real business."

I have set before you life and death,
blessings and curses. Now choose life,
so that you and your children may live...
Deuteronomy 30:19

24

Tarbuwth Correctional Facility
Yashar, NY
July 9

Remembering Worthington's demonic deliverance today, John rolled over in bed. Lights-out was a half hour ago but he still hadn't dropped off to sleep. The bed was lumpy and the nearby toilet smelled of bleach. He was thankful that, at least, he had a private cell. Safety and security were always a concern. But, the way some of these inmates snored, he was particularly pleased to be lying at a noise-deadening distance.

Still, John realized that he was in serious trouble this time. He felt like he had lost his guidance and his ability to maneuver. His mission had always been to save souls while deflecting the full impact of the Destroyer's blows against mankind. Led by the Spirit, he had always gravitated to the most important spiritual battlegrounds in the world. Now, however, he did not understand his purpose here in prison.

John just wanted to be released from this purgatory. He prayed that God would finally either unleash him against the growing Darkness or kill him. He could only take comfort in the fact that he was not now being pursued. Over the past two thousand years, so many times he had been hunted like an animal. He did not fear death but he could not say the same about pain. Of course, he obediently would carry his cross of pain whenever God willed it. However, he prayed fervently to be delivered from the suffering that was inflicted solely for the pleasure of evil men.

He had refused to cooperate with police questioning except to proclaim his innocence. He had not even requested a lawyer because he did not know what he could divulge to him. The police were now trying to determine John's identity and were baffled that he had been able to live in America without any public record of his existence. Because of his undocumented status and refusal to cooperate, bail had been revoked. Like it or not, this concrete block fortress would remain his home for the foreseeable future.

"Mr. John?" he thought he heard over the rumble of snores.

John listened carefully.

"Mr. John?" floated the unrecognizable voice again.

"Yes," John loudly whispered. "Who is it?"

"Worthington ... Mr. John, what happened today?"

"You received a Gift … the most important Gift."

The changed man thought for a moment and then added, "It's weird. I can think clearly, now. I mean, it's like the fog in my head is gone. My brain's not obsessin' about sex ...What do I do now?"

"You start by thinking about that question ... We'll talk tomorrow."

A moment later, "Thank you, Mr. John."

John knew the nightmare that Worthington had been living. He admired the humbled inmate for ignoring today's ridicule from some of the other prisoners and for remaining commited to conquering one of the most powerful demons in the world.

Now, comforted by the realization that he had delivered a favor, John rolled over, fell asleep, and dreamed another nightmare....

Anyone can begin a war,
the trick is to end it.
Niccolo Machiavelli

25

Papal Palace
Rome, Italy
May 6, 1527

John woke with a start. His heart was racing and his sheets were wet with sweat. Once again, a dream was foreshadowing evil at the door. In the dim dawn light, he scanned the extraordinary furnishings of his palace bedroom and cringed at the luxurious waste surrounding him. He was not accustomed to such ornamentation. Previously, he had been living outside Rome in quiet contemplation at Monte Cassino, a monastery founded by St. Benedict in 529 AD. However, six weeks ago, two Swiss Guards arrived on horseback and summoned John to a command papal audience. Since then, John had remained in this gilded cage, obediently translating correspondence for the Holy Father and awaiting the promised audience.

Just four years ago, Giulio de Medici had been elected pope, taking the name Clement VII. Perhaps never before had a man been so broadly welcomed to the papacy. Likewise, perhaps never before was a pope's reign preceded by such a decade of tumult in Europe and in the Church.

Giulio was a respected diplomat, with an unmatched pedigree. He had been raised and educated in Florence, the eye of the creative hurricane known as the Renaissance. His father had been assassinated one month before his birth and his mother had also died young. However, the boy's world-renowned uncle, Lorenzo the Magnificent, helped him overcome his troubles in style and raised him in an environment of art, literature and luxury.

His cousin, Pope Leo X, with whom he had grown up, had preceded his rise to the papacy by a decade. At that time, Leo wrote his younger cousin, offering, "Since God has given us the papacy, let us enjoy it." And enjoy it, he did. Leo was a popular, light hearted, *bon vivant* determined to experience and share all the pleasures that the high office could provide. Those ambitions proved to be so costly that the Church's coffers were empty within a couple years.

Soon after his ascendency, Leo engineered Giulio's rise, eventually naming him Archbishop of Florence, Cardinal, and the Holy See's primary minister and confidant. Leo had leadership qualities to offer. Unfortunately, he also had a deaf ear to warnings of financial disaster and the increasing complaints of an obscure but troublesome German monk.

Martin Luther's rise to fame coincided with the development of the printing press and its explosive impact on social traditions. Luther found that Church criticism was an immensely popular subject. Since posting his 95 theses, "Out of love for the faith and the desire to bring it to light," his subject matter, however, had become belligerent in the extreme. Luther was a man of rhetorical war and Pope Leo was in his crosshairs. His increasingly harsh rhetoric set tongues wagging across Europe and, the more famous he became, the more his publishing and vehemence increased.

Notwithstanding one papist theologian's call for the execution of "that pestilential fart of Satan whose stench reaches to Heaven,"[1] Luther's continuing freedom to criticize Rome was proof of Leo's moderation. Pope Leo attempted conciliation and, in 1518, issued a papal bull repudiating the extreme claims being made by Church clerics regarding indulgences. This accommodated Luther's chief complaint. So, by March of 1519, it appeared the rift was repaired. The wary combatants exchanged cordial correspondence in which Luther vowed complete submission. Perhaps now the wounds would heal.

However, a year later, Luther published, "… the true Antichrist is sitting in the temple of God and is reigning in Rome … the Roman Curia is the Synagogue of Satan … If we strike thieves with the gallows, robbers with the sword, [and] heretics with fire, why do we not much more attack in arms these masters of perdition, these cardinals, these popes, and all this sink of the Roman Sodom which has without end corrupted the Church of God, and wash our hands in their blood?" Also, that year, he wrote to a friend, "I am publishing a book in the German tongue about Christian reform, directed against the pope, in language as violent as if I were addressing Antichrist." By the end of the year, he proclaimed that no man could be saved unless he renounced the papacy.[2]

After Leo's death, the College of Cardinals deadlocked between Giulio and another candidate. As a compromise, a third man, a humble outsider, was elected. The new pope recognized additional abuses that Luther had complained about and launched extensive reforms. Clearly, he was serious about restoring the foundational principles that had always guided the Church. Soon, the frivolity of Leo's court had died. However, this pontiff also was dead within two years. Boisterous Romans made their feelings known when they declared that a statue should be erected … in honor of the papal doctor.[3]

In 1523, the Cardinals were happy to elect another Medici: Giulio. As Pope Clement VII, Romans felt that he could be counted on to return Rome to the good old days of Pope Leo. However, he was not the same man as his affable cousin. Clement was a canon lawyer and, by every account, a man of intelligence and high personal morals. He was sensible and God-fearing, but timid and slow to action. Unlike his cousin, he was abstemious and an avoider of luxury.[4] He quickly moved to bring order to the chaos that Leo had left and he responded to Luther's complaints by convening an international council of bishops. Nevertheless, he soon developed a tendency toward vacillation. As the Venetian ambassador observed, "He talks well, but decides badly."[5]

Amidst the jubilation of Giulio de Medici's rise, storm clouds were gathering, and that was why John had been ordered to Rome. God had not revealed John's true identity to the new pontiff. He only knew John was a man of faith and exceptional language skills. In fact, one of Clement's first initiatives as pope had been to send emissaries to help negotiate a peace between the warring kings of England, France and Spain. Those efforts had failed, possibly because of deficient communications. Now, considering the rising revolt of German Catholics, the delicate but dangerous balance of maintaining peaceful, non-preferential relations with England, France and Spain, and the rising tide of Islamic aggression, Clement found that he needed trustworthy, skilled linguists more than ever.

In recent years, fear had been spreading as Islam marched to its pinnacle of conquest. Suleiman the Magnificent had personally led his armies in a series of victories over the Christian strongholds of Belgrade and Rhodes and most of Hungary. He had annexed most of the Middle East from the Persians and conquered large sections of northern Africa. His ships dominated the seas of the Mediterranean, the Red Sea and the Persian Gulf. Under Suleiman, the Ottoman Empire had reached the apex of its military, political and economic power and it was only when he had penetrated into Europe, as far west as Vienna, that he was finally turned back.

However, more immediate threats lurked closer to home. Amorous King Henry VIII was in open rebellion against the Church because Clement had refused to grant the King an annulment from his first wife, Catherine of Aragon. Clement also had spent years juggling difficult relations with a warring duo who threatened to disrupt papal power in Italy. Francis I, the weak-willed, irritable and fickle French prince, had won early victories against Charles V, the young Holy Roman Emperor who had conquered or inherited an empire upon which "the sun never set." In fact, at its peak, Charles' empire was twenty times larger than Rome's. Parts of that Empire were the German regions where Martin Luther was most popular.[6]

Still, Clement chose the weaker partner and encouraged an Italian alliance against Charles's Empire. Feeling betrayed by his own Church, Charles directed his army against Rome. Along the torturous march through the Alps, his mercenaries suffered numerous privations, including the lack of pay.

Now, as the invaders neared the gates of Rome, the holy pontiff – a sophisticated diplomat – planned to meet and dissuade them from their ill-conceived plans. A man of war would have been better suited for the job.

Pope Clement had enlisted John's services, requesting that he translate and draft negotiation letters for all hostile parties. John realized that Clement's second guessing and mental turmoil had become well known in the papal court. He relied too much on his own power and not enough on God's.

John prayed for him, as he lay in bed, and thought, *Why does he have so little faith?*

Suddenly, with Spirit-filled urgency, John felt the need to warn – no, to command – Pope Clement.

Then, without knock or announcement, a Swiss Guard entered John's bedroom.

"Holy Father requests your presence."

At long last, this was the announcement that John had been

expecting for six weeks. Perhaps he would soon be allowed to return to the monastery.

John had slept in his woolen monk's robe so he quickly slid out of bed, slipped on his sandals and followed the guard. They jogged across the *Cortile di San Damaso* and into the Medieval Palace next to the Sistine Chapel. Then they hurried down one long, elaborately ornamented hallway after another as John straightened his hair with his fingers and wiped his face with his sleeve.

Eventually, they reached a massive, carved door. The guard knocked twice and another guard opened it. John entered, leaving his escort behind.

Standing at a window, with one advisor nearby, Pope Clement VII was reading from a small Bible. John immediately approached him, genuflected and kissed his ring. When he arose, they spoke in Italian.

"Brother John, I am so happy to finally meet you. I have heard many good things. You are highly regarded at Monte Cassino."

"Thank you, Your Holiness."

"Have your accommodations been…"

"Holy Father, I apologize for interrupting, but I am here with an urgent message."

"Yes?"

"We must flee, immediately, to the *Castel*."

"Brother," he calmed, "if you are worried about the Emperor's troops, it will be three days before they arrive. And, when they do, I will turn them back, not with guns, but just as the first Pope Leo turned back Attila: with God's words."

"Your Holiness, the barbarity of these men will exceed anything Rome has ever before experienced."

"Brother," Clement laughed, "I am disappointed. You sound ridiculous! Barbarian atrocities have been committed against the Church for many centuries. Rome has been sacked by Visigoths, Huns, Vandals, Saracens and Normans. However, the approaching troops march under the flag of the Holy Roman Emperor. Yes, he is upset with my recent alliances. However, his faith will not allow him to destroy his Church. Brother, he is an avowed enemy of Luther!"

"Again, I apologize, Holy Father, but if you are to live through the next hour, we must take the *Passetto di Borgo* now!"

"How do you know about access to the *Passetto?*" he asked warily. "Who told you to give me this message?"

"God."

"Prove it!" he demanded.

John calmly said, "How long will you refuse to humble yourself before Me?"[7]

"How dare you!" the aide jumped into the discussion. However, the pope waved him off as he considered those words. It was God's question that Moses had put to Pharaoh.

The verse stunned Clement. Just before John arrived, he had read, "Everyone who exalts himself will be humbled, and he who humbles himself will be exalted."[8] Then, he turned the pages to, "Humble yourselves before the Lord, and he will lift you up in honor."[9]

The aide continued, "Shall I remove this meddlesome…"

Just then a barrage of canon fire was heard and the room trembled as cannonballs smashed into their targets.

"Guards!" the pope shouted. Suddenly twelve of them rushed into the room. "We must go!"

One of them crossed the room and pulled a bookcase away from the wall, revealing a hidden passageway to a pedestrian bridge. John followed as they all sprinted to the protection of the *Castel San Angelo.*

* * *

FROM THE PARAPET of the *Castel*, Clement wept over the remains of smoldering Rome. What tragedies could have been avoided, what great things achieved, if only this indecisive pontiff had asked for God's guidance and acted with faith?

It had been six months since he, 13 cardinals and as many as 3,000 Romans had taken refuge in the fortress. Most of the Swiss Guards had been wiped out, many of them killed on the steps of the new Basilica.[10] The 5,000 defenders were no match against the 40,000 angry soldiers and mercenaries who had braved the Alps and other misfortunes for four months without pay. Now, ragged, shoeless and hungry their choices were to conquer Rome or starve.

It was time to settle old scores and a spirit of vengeance overwhelmed the city. Even the Italian Cardinal Pompeo Colonna had furnished forces against his enemy, Pope Clement VII.

The German and Austrian soldiers, as well as various other mercenaries, were unleashed on Rome like the biblical plagues of Egypt. Nothing was sacred, no one was spared. The orphanage and hospital known as *Santo Spirito* was overwhelmed and nearly all the patients were slaughtered. For protection, every *palazzo* paid a ransom and, whenever fortunes appeared to dwindle, children were flung from high windows to encourage further revelations of hidden stashes. The Papal Palace became a barracks, the Sistine Chapel a mortuary, and troops with their horses were brought into the Basilica. A priest was butchered for refusing to give a consecrated Host to a donkey. Roman countesses and baronesses were raped and forced into brothels. A cardinal was lowered into a grave and threatened with live burial until his ransom was delivered. Soldiers even broke into the reliquaries in the Basilica of St. John Lateran and reportedly played ball with the heads of Peter and Paul.[11]

A contemporary witness described the atrocities:

> "Many were suspended for hours by the arms; many were cruelly bound by the genitals; many were suspended by their feet high above the road or over the river, while their tormentors threatened to cut the cord … not a few were branded all over their persons with red-hot irons. Some were tortured with extreme thirst … many were cruelly tortured by having their teeth brutally drawn. Others again were forced to eat their own ears, or nose, or their roasted testicles, and yet more were subjected to strange, unheard of martyrdoms that move me too much even to think of, much less to describe."[12]

As many as 20,000 Romans were slaughtered and the stench of dead bodies filled the air as starving dogs fed on them. Then an epidemic of plague broke out.

Following John's urgings, Clement finally had melted down the papal jewelry and paid a ransom of 400,000 *ducati* in return for his life. He was also forced to cede lands to the Holy Roman Emperor. Venice then took advantage of Clement's weakness by snatching other Church lands for themselves.

During negotiations for Clement's release, John feared he might be killed anyway. So, John bribed Imperial officers and arranged for Clement to escape, disguised as a peddler. After six months of prayer and personal reflection, John was the only person Clement still trusted.

Charles V later mourned the atrocities, claiming his men had acted beyond his orders and out of his control. However, that did not stop him from still demanding Clement's ransom and keeping the Church's lands.

Regarding the defeat of Clement, the rape, torture and murder of Church clergy, as well as the desecrations, destruction and theft of sacred property, Martin Luther declared, "Christ reigns in such a way that the Emperor who persecutes Luther for the pope is forced to destroy the pope for Luther."[13]

As the years moved on, however, Luther found no solace in life. He became morbidly obese and suffered from a dozen diseases that prompted him to turn increasingly to alcohol for relief. He had, by now, slandered Erasmus and Protestant Reformers like "… Calvin … and the other heretics … they have in-deviled, through-deviled, over-deviled, corrupt hearts and lying mouths." And, while he could never accept the divine right of popes, he proclaimed the divine right of kings: "The hand that wields the secular sword is not a human hand but the hand of God. It is God, not man, who hangs, and breaks on the wheel, and decapitates, and flogs; it is God who wages war." Indeed, Luther's revolution had simply transferred religious authority from the Church that he had originally sworn to serve, to any king who had been bold enough to seize power.[14]

As death neared, Luther's vitriol continued to pour forth from his pen. The pontiff was new, but the attacks were the same. Luther's writings described him as, "the most hellish father," "this Roman hermaphrodite" and "Sodomite pope." Cardinals were "desperately lost children of the Devil … ignorant asses … One would like to curse them so that thunder and lightning might smite them, hell-fire burn them, the plague, syphilis, epilepsy, scurvy, leprosy, carbuncles, and all diseases attack them."[15]

However, it was Luther who suffered from such a wide variety of health ailments that, nearing the end, he wrote, "I am tired of the world and it is tired of me," and said "Rather than live forty years more, I would give up my chance of paradise." Indeed, even the supreme worry eventually haunted Luther: "The Devil assaults me by objecting that out of my mouth great offenses and much evil have proceeded; and with this he many times vehemently perplexes me."[16]

When John last saw Clement, the supreme pontiff was afraid and disguised as an inconsequential peasant. John lamented that this talented, well-meaning man had fallen so far. However, he realized that anyone who exercises authority over others shall be held accountable and, sometimes, that accounting occurs in this life.

Seven years later, John returned to Rome to visit his grave. During that interval Clement had remained in power, though as a much-diminished man. He had even made his peace with Charles V. He died from accidentally consuming poisonous mushrooms just days after commissioning Michelangelo to paint *The Last Judgment* in the Sistine Chapel. However, memories of his disastrous rein were not easily forgotten. At the gravesite John cringed when he saw that vandals had defaced the tombstone. It once proclaimed, *"Clemens Pontifex Maximus,"* but now read, *"Inclemens Pontifex Minimus."*[17]

Opportunity is a bird
that never perches.
Claude McDonald

26

Marriott Marquis Hotel
New York City
July 10

Angela rolled over and kissed Fred's bare shoulder. She was still giddy with the news of Huntington Cyst's strategic plan for her to take the White House. She spooned closer behind Fred and waited for a response. It was still early, and she could not see the clock, but the sun was starting to stream through the crack in the draperies. Angela nibbled on Fred's ear. He finally took a deep breath and twisted his head to see who was behind him.

"Oh, it's you, Angela," he said, feigning surprise.

"You rascal!" she said with a playful nudge.

Angela was very happy. She could not remember being this happy since Venice. After an amorous night together, she felt like she had just aced her final exam or breezed through the most important job interview of her life. She couldn't imagine that Fred had ever been more satisfied with a woman and she relished the memory of when she had total control over him. She had slept with many men and had developed a need for their acts of adoration, especially when it jeopardized their marriages. However, Fred was different. He came with strategic advantages.

Cheerfully, she popped up, with nothing but a sheet around her. "I'm hungry. Let's call room service!"

A half hour later they heard a knock on the door. They both threw on their terry cloth robes and Fred ran to hide in the bathroom. Angela let in the room service waiter and stared at him impatiently as he set up the breakfast and opened the draperies. When she confirmed that he had brought their favorite newspapers, she handed the waiter two bucks and then hurried him out the door.

"Come out, come out, wherever you are," she called.

When Fred emerged, she was pouring his coffee and nibbling on a strawberry. They enjoyed a leisurely breakfast together, rarely talking, but sharing her Washington Post and his Wall Street Journal. It was almost as if they had been living this routine together for decades, she starting with her Washington Society column and he with his financial pages.

"Fred?" she inquired as he reached for another section.

"Yes, dear?"

"I don't want you to freak out ... I mean, I'll understand and it's okay if you say no … But I … well, I'll use a sports metaphor: I would love to have you join my team."

He laughed. "I *am* on your team, Angela."

"No, I mean really on my team."

"What are you talking about?" he asked as he fumbled through pages of stock quotes.

"Fred … why don't we get married?"

His eyebrows rose in mild surprise.

She continued, "I don't want to be a lonely president, Fred. We'd make an excellent team. Your age, your interests, your looks are all perfect for me." Then somewhat sheepishly, "I hope you can say the same about me."

Her emphasis on "*my* team" bothered him but he responded with reassuring enthusiasm. "Well, of course, Angela! I'm, frankly, honored you would ask me. But what about all the baggage that I'd bring to your campaign, you know, the divorces and the lobbyist thing?"

The political tactician responded, "I've already had Evan poll on the issue."

Fred offered a friendly grimace.

"Now, Fred, you know that I'm always prepared. Anyway, it was all done very discretely. My numbers improve by 9.4% under the scenario that I marry and 6.9% even if my unnamed spouse is a divorced, former lobbyist."

"Twice divorced," Fred added. He wisely decided that mentioning the hundreds of additional girlfriends would belabor the point.

"Fred, the public wants me married … and I'm glad they do."

"Hey, that's great," he said, but not quite as enthusiastically as she had hoped.

"So, what d'ya think?"

He started nodding and thinking and smiling … and nodding … and thinking.

Last night he would have jumped off a cliff for me, she grumbled to herself. She realized she should have popped the question then.

"I think it sounds great," he finally responded, to her relief. "But it's just such a big question that I need to give it a lot of thought. I mean … if it was just up to me, I'd say 'hell yes!' I mean … I'm gung-ho about it. But I don't want to complicate your life, Angela. It wouldn't be fair to you."

"I've thought this through, Fred. It's what's best for both of us."

"I'm sure you're right. Let's just give it a little time, first."

"Of course ... I understand."

Angela reminded Fred of her morning meeting in New York and said she had to get moving. They showered together and shared loving embraces but the conversation careened, at times, from passionate to polite. He seemed to be very conflicted about the decision he had to make. When they were leaving the room,

Fred gave her a very loving kiss and said, "Thank you for an unforgettable evening … I'll be in touch."

THAT NIGHT, Cyst, Thas and Whitehead met with Senator Everson Blight. The drinks flowed more freely than on the previous night. Blight was in the mood to share his stories. He led with the one about when he won his Purple Heart medal for charging an enemy encampment in Vietnam. Then he described his days at the University of Alabama under Coach Bear Bryant. Whitehead did not realize that some of Blight's running records still stood in the SEC but everyone knew that his name recognition was high, and his reputation was respected, especially in the south. Yet he was also perceived by some critics as a spotlight grabbing blowhard. For that reason, after thirty minutes, Evan steered the conversation away from the glory days of college football. Soon, they were onto the business at hand.

"How badly do you want it?" Cyst inquired.

Even though Blight had not officially announced his intentions, his answer was as direct as usual, "I'm gonna give it everything I got."

"Well, sir," Evan asked parroting southern manners, "may we show you our presentation in which we have invested considerable time, talent and money?"

"Go right ahead. I've set aside ninety minutes for you."

Cyst and Thas initiated a slide presentation, again taking turns hammering home their messages. However, after only ten minutes, Blight interrupted. "Excuse me gentlemen," he drawled. "Maybe I'm misunderstandin' you. You think I'm gonna let you tell me what to say?"

"Oh, no," Thas said quickly, hoping to calm the senator's suspicions. Then he added another, "No!" with a chuckle. "We're just proposing to show you how to say it best … You know, Senator, some of your words and phrases tend to turn off significant percentages of the national electorate."

"Like what?"

"Well, for instance," Evan answered, "'War on Terrorism.'"

Cyst flinched and then adjusted himself in his wheelchair. "Now, let's wait a minute. We don't want to get ahead of ourselves. We'll get to that in just a …"

"No, I wanna know," the Senator insisted. "What's wrong with 'War on Terrorism'?"

Thas realized he had moved too quickly. He felt unprepared entering into this meeting because he had not been able to run a psycho-social profile on Blight. The Senator was one of those few remaining 'troglodytes' who still did not use the Internet. The only record Thas had to rely on was the public one and he refused to believe that the Senator actually said what he meant and meant what he said in public. After all, the men in this room could be honest now. They were behind closed doors.

Cyst gave Thas a regretful nod and Thas answered. "Senator, using different words can have a great impact on voter perceptions even when you mean the same thing. You see…"

"Okay, if you're gonna tell me you like the term 'War on Radical Islamists,' or 'War on Jihadists,' or even 'War on Everybody Who Wants to Cut My Head Off Just for Bein' a Christian or a Jew' then I'm with ya. But, somehow, I don't think that's what you're gonna say."

"Well, no," Thas answered uncomfortably, "Our research shows…"

"What do ya want me to call it?" he demanded.

"Senator, if I may say, only 10% of Muslims are Jihadists. To focus, in any way, on their faith, smacks of prejudice and bigotry."

"That 10% is 130 million enemies who want to cut your head off, son! I'm not angry with peace lovin' Muslims. God bless 'em! But they need to realize their faith is being hijacked by terrorists … Now, answer the question!"

"Well …" he looked over to Cyst and Whitehead who remained firmly committed to the sidelines. "I don't really have an exact …"

"Yes you do. I can see it in your eyes. You're just dyin' to tell me how your research shows I can change the world just by calling it a different name. Come on!" He demanded loudly, "What d'ya want me to call it? Tell me, so I can save the world."

Thas took a deep breath and then blurted out, "Overseas Contingency Operations."

"Are you friggin' kiddin' me? Son, when I'm president, there ain't gonna be nothin' contingent about my War on Terror. I'm gonna kill 'em before they kill us. Next, you gonna tell me I'll lose votes if I don't call a swamp a wetland? You gonna tell me I gotta call a jungle a rain forest? You're dealin' with word games, son. I'm dealin' with people's lives! We're at war no matter what you call it. Weak words signal a weak will and only encourage the belligerence of our enemies."

"Look, I'm just talking about your campaign rhetoric. Your actions in office can be whatever you want."

"Damn right, my actions will be what I want. And I don't need no punk-ass advisor sayin' it's okay. That's the problem with Washington, these days. We got too many Ivy League kids tryin' to advise politicians how to scam their way to the top. And we got too many spaghetti-spined politicians listenin' to 'em!"

Senator Blight stood to signal the meeting was coming to a close. "Our world is becomin' a more dangerous place every day and, unfortunately, people like you aren't makin' it any safer."

"Senator," Cyst tried to smooth his ruffled feathers, "I am certain that we can still develop a mutually beneficial relationship. Please stay and let us tell you what we have to offer."

"What guys like you have to offer comes at too steep a price for me and my country. I wanna be president, but I'm not willin' to purchase or sell the office. So, I'm gonna tell ya what you ain't never heard before: I don't want your support."

Moments later, after Blight had left without shaking hands, the men planned a letter of extreme apology that would blame Evan Thas' inexperience and misspoken intentions. They would try to mend the hard feelings with the senator at any cost. After all, the race still had to be run, and he might win. However, Blight's loose words would not be forgotten. Now, with focused effort and intensity, Evan would develop a file that contained every incriminating and unflattering detail of the senator's life. He knew Blight would have to learn his place.

TWO WEEKS LATER, Angela received a polite "Thank you, Madame Secretary" note from Fred Whitehead, again promising, "I'll be in touch."

Not even handwritten! she thought as she dropped it into the waste basket. She remembered the frenzied lust in his eyes that night. She wished she had popped the big question then. Sitting there alone, in her immense office, Angela promised herself that she would never forget the lesson she had just learned: In politics and love, timing is everything.

For I could have supplied each of you with all your needs, both spiritual and material. But I wanted to make you dependent on one another so that each of you would be My minister, dispensing the graces and gifts you have received from Me. All I want is love.

Words of God the Father,
as reported by St. Catherine of Siena

27

Tarbuwth Correctional Facility
Yashar, NY
July 10

As 50 prisoners – one eighth of the inmate population – filed into the recreation yard, one spoke up, "What the hell did you do to Worthington, yesterday?"

"I didn't do anything," John responded, with emphasis on the word "I."

The questioner persisted, "Hey Worthington, what'd he do to you?"

"I'm not sure," the big man answered as they walked toward the picnic table. "I fell down and then it was kinda like I was looking down at myself, watching me jerkin' and twitchin' on the ground. It kinda felt like something was being pulled out of my chest but I was too scared to let it go. I was grabbin' at it like it was the only thing that could keep me from fallin' off a cliff. I was holdin' onto it and it was holdin' onto me. Then, somehow, we broke free of each other and I looked down and saw this black, shadowy kinda cloud come out of my body and float away … What was that, Mr. John?"

"One of the Destroyer's demons; he no longer controls you," John answered.

For the first time, the inmates heard Worthington chuckle.

John sat on the picnic table. Seven inmates joined him, with four sitting on the ground around him and three standing. The other prisoners wandered off to play soccer or cards.

Like an inquisitive child, Worthington asked, "Is the Destroyer the Devil, Mr. John?"

John responded in a roundabout way. "You have more important things to focus on. For example, here in prison you are all familiar with shackles. You know what bodily restraint can do to a man. However, there are other shackles that are far worse."

John paused to gauge their response and then he continued.

"Everything we see in the physical world can be measured in three dimensions: length, width, and height. Our lives are also measured in three dimensions: Spirit, mind, and body. However, the greatest of these is Spirit, because to refuse the Spirit is to choose death.

"For example, the body of a man may be shackled and jailed. Still, his Spirit praises God continuously. Another one may be materially rich and free, but his oppressed Spirit curses his miserable existence. A child's mind may be humble, but glorious in love and faith, while a genius may be too proud to appreciate the humility and simplicity that fruitful faith requires. And regarding the body, even beautiful people are oftentimes unhappy and unfulfilled. It is the Spirit of Love that fulfills us. Jesus was very clear when He said, 'My command is this: Love each other as I have loved you. Greater love has no one than this, that he lay down his life for his friends... I have called you friends, for everything that I learned from my Father I have made known to you. You did not choose me, but I chose you and appointed you to go and bear fruit—fruit that will last. Then the Father will give you whatever you ask in my name. This is my command: Love each other.'"[1]

John changed the subject slightly. "Our Lord taught us to pray to the Father, 'Lead us not into temptation.' How many of you have prayed those words?"

All seven hands went up in the air.

"And how many of you would be moving closer to drugs, alcohol, violence, or promiscuity if you were free?"

Most hands rose again.

"You see. God answered your prayer. The greatest gift God can give you, in this life, is to make you uncomfortable in your sin."

One inmate mocked, "So, this shit's an answer to my prayers?"

Ignoring the comment, John continued. "Even though your body is shackled now, you have been given the place and time in which you may free your Spirit forever. Use this time wisely. To refuse God's call is to choose death."

The mocking prisoner walked away as John continued. "Always remember: the Spirit is humble. The body and mind, on the other hand, are proud, loud and domineering. Indulge your body and you become promiscuous, vain, addicted or lazy. Indulge your mind and you become proud, hateful or fearful. In each of these cases the Spirit will withdraw until you make It feel welcome again."

"Yeah, man," an inmate on the ground agreed.

"Your soul is like a garden in which the Spirit has planted beautiful, fragrant flowers. But, if you are too lazy to tend the garden, eventually the weeds will overrun the flowers and strangle the life out of them. Faith requires continuous tending. For the lazy or distracted, however, it withers away."

A tall black man standing at the back of the group professed confidently, "I don't believe in God."

"Booker," John responded, "He believes in you."

Booker felt very uncomfortable that John somehow knew his name. "Prove it!" he blurted out.

"Do you really want to find truth, or do you just want to argue?"

Booker answered tentatively, "The truth."

"Then, let's start here." John held up his Bible. "There are over 300 prophecies in the Old Testament that were fulfilled by the life of Jesus Christ. In fact, 29 prophecies were fulfilled just on the day of His death."[2]

"Oh, come on. Like what?"

"For centuries, the Old Testament prophets predicted that the Messiah would be betrayed by a friend;[3] that He would be sold for thirty pieces of silver;[4] that the money would be thrown into God's house;[5] that the blood money would be given for the Potter's Field;[6] that He would be forsaken by His disciples;[7] that He would be accused by false witnesses;[8] that He would be silent before His accusers;[9] that He would be wounded and bruised;[10] that He would be struck and spat upon;[11] that He would be ridiculed;[12] that He would reach the limits of His endurance;[13] that His hands and feet would be pierced;[14] that He would be executed with criminals;[15] that He would ask God's forgiveness even for His executioners;[16] that He would be rejected by His own people;[17] that He would be hated without cause;[18] that His friends and family would watch from a distance;[19] that spectators would shake their heads at Him;[20] that they would stare at His suffering;[21] that His garments would be divided and lots cast for them..."[22]

The inmates listened closely, amazed at John's memory.

He continued, "... that His passion would include great thirst;[23] that He would be offered gall and vinegar;[24] that He would feel forsaken;[25] but that He would still remain faithful to God;[26] that, even after all the abuse, none of His bones would be broken;[27] but that his heart would not withstand the torture;[28] that His side would be pierced;[29] that darkness would blanket the land;[30] and that He would be buried in a rich man's tomb."[31]

John paused to allow the men to absorb the evidence he was offering. He silently prayed that they would open their hearts and minds.

One of the bearded Muslim men, Qurban, had stopped to listen. He said, "Jesus – peace be upon Him – was a good man. He was a prophet but He was not God."

"That is not possible," John countered. "If Jesus is not God then He was lying when He proclaimed, 'I am the Way and the Truth and the Life. No one comes to the Father except through Me.'[32] If He is not God, He was blaspheming when He said, 'Anyone who has seen Me has seen the Father.'[33] A good man is not a liar and is certainly not a blasphemer."

Qurban realized he could not disagree.

Samir, a small Indian man who had once been a pharmacist, asked, "What about fraud? Maybe the apostles were all in on it, scamming for money."

"Liars don't make good martyrs," John responded. "Historical records - even those outside the Bible – show that in the early Christian Church, believers submitted themselves to the most heinous tortures imaginable rather than simply deny their faith. The apostles, for example, those men who knew Jesus best, endured horrible deaths for refusing to stop preaching.[34] James the Great was beheaded in Jerusalem after evangelizing in Palestine and Spain; Matthias, Judas' replacement, was stoned and beheaded in Jerusalem after preaching the Gospel in Palestine, Scythia and Armenia; Nathaniel Bartholomew was flayed and crucified in Iran after evangelizing in Palestine, Asia Minor, Armenia and central India; James the Less was stoned to death after spreading the word in Palestine; Andrew was crucified on an X-cross in Greece after evangelizing in Palestine, Asia Minor and Scythia; Simon Peter spread the Gospel in Palestine, Syria, Asia Minor and Rome before being crucified upside down on Vatican

Hill; Thomas, the doubter, evangelized in Palestine, Osroene, Armenia, Egypt and India before being stabbed to death by a Hindu mob in Burma; after spreading the Word in Palestine, Egypt, North Africa, Britain, Osroene, and Armenia, Simon Zealotes was mutilated and sawed to pieces, while Jude was impaled on a spear, by an Iranian mob led by pagan magi; James, the son of Alpheus, was beaten to death with a club after being crucified and stoned; and Matthew was hacked to death with a halberd. In fact, it was not just the apostles who suffered. It has been estimated that in the first three centuries, over a million Christians were martyred.[35] They were so dedicated to their beliefs that not only were they willing to be martyred but they raised their children knowing that they, too, might die for their faith."

"Yeah, I guess," Samir said, "but we just keep seeing stories about religious hypocrites. Some of them are worse than us."

"That's right. There are religious hypocrites out there. Some are inspired by the evil that hopes to encourage widespread prejudice against the faithful. However, the vast majority of believers choose the narrower path of righteousness. You'll hardly ever read about them. When a sinner commits evil, it is the person who is discredited, not God, not his Church."

Samir said, "Yeah, I guess."

Seeing he still had their interest, John continued, "Jesus instructed: 'Do not judge, and you will not be judged. Do not condemn, and you will not be condemned. Forgive, and you will be forgiven. Give, and it will be given to you …[36] Love your enemies, do good to them, and lend to them without expecting to get anything back...[37] Do good to those who hate you, bless those who curse you, pray for those who mistreat you.'[38] Is this the kind of lifestyle that attracts selfish frauds and liars? Of course not. Still, the evil one is a ravenous lion, seeking to devour anyone who gives him the opportunity. Even among the apostles, one denied and one betrayed Jesus.

Still, only one asked forgiveness. So, pray that God will deliver you from evil, but when you fail, always seek forgiveness."

"Mr. John, what should we do?" Worthington asked.

"It is different for each man," John responded. "God reveals Himself in so many ways. But start with reading the Inspired Word of God, the Bible. Then talk to Him. That's what prayer is, a conversation with God."

"He never answered my prayer," Booker complained.

"Yes He did," John responded. "His answer was 'NO.'"

Most of the inmates smiled and nodded as a few more prisoners joined the group.

"Then, with Scripture and prayer as your foundation, build your faith as God leads. You may find that you are drawn closer to God praying in the wilderness, in a cathedral, feeding the poor, nursing the sick, or even ministering to prisoners. Ask God to lead you and then find your personal path in life. I pray you will all find this peace. Remember that the story of Jesus does not end on the cross. Likewise, your lives do not end here. This is a beginning for you."

A voice on the PA system announced: "Officers, please bring John Malek to Conference Room C … Malek to Room C."

"Do not forget," John said pointedly, "if I have said anything that has planted into your heart, the Destroyer will soon try to uproot it and kill it. Be ready, and don't let him."

John left to meet D.J. Jefferson at the steel door.

"You doin' okay, man?" the guard asked sympathetically as he handcuffed the prisoner.

John answered, "I've had better days." Then he added with a smile, "But it's all good, brother."

As the steel door opened, John looked back at the distant table where Booker was still complaining: "Man, is he full o' crap, or what?" Some of the other men nodded their agreement.

* * *

WHEN THEY REACHED THE DOOR of Conference Room C, John made an unusual inquiry: "Officer Jefferson?"

"Yes?"

"I will pray for you daily, if you allow me to escape."

Jefferson responded with a broad smile. "Oh, you would, would you? And why would I do that?"

"Because you love mankind."

"And if I let you go, you can save us all."

John was serious. "I'm sorry … I can't do that."

Jefferson erupted with a belly laugh that brought tears to his eyes. He opened the door to where Father Alonzo was waiting and warned, "Watch out for this one, Father. He's a real jokester."

Jefferson attached John's handcuffs to the table. "Give me a yell, Father, when you're through with confession," the guard said as he left the room. Then the deadbolts grinded shut.

John's calm smile returned. "It's good to see you, Father. How did it go?"

"No problem. It was quite an adventure for Pedro, though. He was excited … really excited." The priest smiled, "He had so many stories, you'd think he had been in Rome for a month. He just can't stop talking about…"

"Let me guess: *gelato?*"

Alonzo grinned. "Right!"

The two men sat quietly for a moment as the smiles slipped away. Then Father Alonzo continued, addressing John with the title he always used in private: "Father, where do we go from here? Just tell me what to do and I will do it. I fear we must act boldly or circumstances will get the better of us."

"Fear nothing," John responded. "That was my message. After all this time, everything will soon change."

Even prisoners in the gulags cried
when they learned that Stalin had died.
Anonymous

28
Cyst Estate
Jupiter Island, Florida
July 10

After dinner, Evan Thas sat on the edge of the infinity pool with his feet in the water. Over the rumble of the foamy green waves crashing on the nearby beach, he heard Huntington Cyst motor up behind him with their usual Hennessy cognacs. They clinked their Baccarat tumblers then Cyst rolled his water-proof wheelchair down the pool ramp until he was waist-deep in the warm water.

The French cuisine, tonight, had been excellent. The chef had left. Now, as usual, they were alone together.

A distant child's laugh caused both men to notice someone on the beach taking sunset pictures of his son, near the rocks. Huntington fondly remembered doing the same with Evan almost a quarter century ago.

However, Evan's memories, as always, were more melancholy. Swirling his feet in the pool water, Evan thought about the parents that he had never really known and no longer wanted to know. He was pleased to imagine them spending their winters shivering on some icy Canadian tundra. The $220,000 that Cyst had paid for Evan's adoption rights had become ancient history for him, rarely remembered. But Evan would never completely erase the pain he felt from his heartless parents' greed and indifference.

Good riddance.

The two men quietly savored their sips while the day's last rays dimmed over the ocean. A distant pier began to blend into the horizon as the clouds turned blood red. Each day, this was the time they most looked forward to ... the coming of darkness.

The doctor had taught his student that nighttime invigorated the normally suppressed senses. "And there is nothing more sensual," he claimed, "than darkness accompanied by terror. The senses of smell, taste, hearing, and touch are most elevated when fearful eyes are blinded."

Dr. Cyst had experienced the ultimate blind terror only once. He was a reckless young man who had binged, one night, on Tequila and beer. As he headed to another bar, he came to a roadway intersection not far from railroad tracks. With drunken exuberance, Cyst listened to the approaching train and then bolted through the stop sign. Out of nowhere, a tractor trailer appeared. The truck T-boned his car and sent it twirling, ejecting him through the windshield.

Bloody and battered, Cyst quickly regained consciousness on the tracks. He heard the roar of the approaching train. He felt the ground tremble. He could even smell the rocks against his face exuding the odor of engine exhaust from days past. However, he could not move himself out of danger. His back had been broken. He closed his eyes and desperately tried to drag himself out of harm's way. As his violent destruction neared, he twitched and convulsed with terror and cried out, "Save me!" At that moment – a moment he will never forget – the Shining Darkness enveloped and consumed him.

Many times, Cyst had told this story to his adopted son to teach him lessons in perseverance and negotiation. Cyst was proud of his bargaining prowess, and this one was the ultimate. As the train bore down on him in the darkness, Huntington Cyst offered everything in exchange for his life.

"Never give up," he taught Evan Thas, "you always have something left to trade."

Huntington Cyst lost his feet in that accident. He should have lost his life. However, he had purchased more precious time and, in exchange, now and forever, he would be perfectly possessed by his savior.

These days, the risks Cyst took were every bit as dangerous but much more consequential and lucrative. At least, now, the deck was stacked in his favor.

The doctor's cell phone rang, jarring the two men from their poolside thoughts. He motored to the side of the pool, clicked on the speaker and answered it with the same verve that cognac usually put into his voice. A man with a strong Russian accent was on the other end of the call and, immediately, Cyst cut him off in mid-sentence. He angrily scolded the Russian for calling him at home and quickly hung up.

Evan realized, however, that Cyst's hot temper always melted away quickly. After all, there is little room for anger whenever pleasures are soon to be found.

Soon, Cyst slipped out of the wheelchair and drifted to the middle of the pool. He never ventured into the deep end because of his limited swimming ability but he always insisted on at least one full immersion at this time. It was his daily ritual of washing away Florida's bright, warm sunlight.

Moments slipped past. The light was dying. When it was time, the two men emerged from the water and headed into the house.

Thas reflected on what a great team they had become. For the brilliant doctor, Evan had made himself indispensable, excelling at every task assigned to him. And for years, now, Cyst had demonstrated a deep appreciation for Thas' intellect and judgment. The deference he had shown this young man was envied throughout the company.

This was the life Evan wanted. The perks were nice, but it was the adrenaline rush that drove them both. When their brilliant minds focused on conquest, adrenaline was never in short supply.

Their technological genius had made them apex predators in a global jungle. Like great white sharks in a sea of humanity, they thrived on the frenzy of blood in the water. They were at the top of the food chain and lived for the kill.

Around the dim home, the air smelled of salt and seaweed, and the crashing waves could not only be heard but felt. Silently, as darkness prevailed, they drifted inside, dripping here and there on the Carrara marble floors. Then, after one last look at the mysterious, dark ocean, Thas followed Cyst through the living room and into the bedroom, just as he obediently had done since the age of six.

My opinion is that all those who lack knowledge of God
are those who refuse to turn to Him...
[T]hey refuse because they imagine
this kindly disposed God to be harsh and severe,
this merciful God to be callous and inflexible,
this lovable God to be cruel and oppressive.
St. Bernard of Clairvaux

29

St. Francis of Assisi University
Yashar, NY
July 21

"Pray and love without ceasing. That is the most common theme of Marian apparitions in modern times," Father Alonzo instructed the class. "If we do not change our ways, if we do not learn to pray and love, a great chastisement will come, because it is the only hope left for changing hearts in order to secure eternal salvation."

Most of the students showed renewed interest in this obscure subject.[1] Their course, *Revelations from God,* was building in intensity and the students' enthusiasm reflected it.

"At Medjugorje, for example," he continued, "the Virgin Mary asked us to, '*Pray for perseverance. Pray for patience. Pray for endurance. The fire of love is strongest when the way is dark; then the fire of love guides you. Love untested is no love at all.*'"

"That chastisement thing's pretty scary," one student said.

"Look at it this way," the priest explained, "what if I told you, 'I have laid out this magnificent banquet for you. But, if you do not eat, you will starve.' Would you then focus on how terrible it will be when you starve? No! Listen, eat and live! Listen to Mother Mary's words: '*Do not think about wars, punishments and evil because, if you do you, are on the road toward them. Your task is to accept Divine Peace, to live it, and to spread it.'* That is our mission."

The girl in the front row asked, "What exactly is Medjugorje, Father?"

"Medjugorje is a small rustic town in what was once communist Yugoslavia. There, starting in June of 1981, the Blessed Mother appeared to six children. Her apparitions and messages to those children, who have now grown to be adults, have continued regularly since then. Three of the visionaries are visited daily and three see the Virgin at least monthly. In Medjugorje, miracles are commonplace."[2]

"Why," the girl continued, "doesn't everybody know about this?"

"Actually, most of us really don't care."

A boy asked, "What else has Mary said?"

"Highlighted among the many Medjugorje messages is a list of ten secrets. Since they are 'secrets' we don't know a lot of the details except the following: Some of them have to do with chastisements for the world; the third secret will be a visible, lasting sign that will miraculously be placed in Medjugorje; the third secret will be permanent, indestructible, and beautiful; two of the visionaries have stated that part of the seventh secret has been eliminated because of the prayers and fasting of people responding to Our Lady's call; the ninth and tenth, however, are most serious chastisements."

"Does that mean war?" a boy asked.

"Possibly that and more. Scores of prophecies from over hundreds of years describe the following scenario: At least one chastisement, the predicted 'minor' chastisement, will be both man-made and heaven-sent. If mankind fails to heed the call to change, the Church will be afflicted with heresy and schism; civil wars will simultaneously break out in France and Italy; and wars, famine and pestilence will spread around the world. Natural disasters will become widespread and Muslims will cause great trouble for Europe and the Church in general. When everyone thinks it is impossible, the Russian army will invade Western Europe. Civil war will spread to England. The pope will flee Rome and go into hiding, but will be found cruelly murdered. A saintly new pope will be elected and will be instrumental in bringing a Great French Monarch to power. This King will defeat the Russian, Prussian (northern Germany) and Muslim forces with the help of a miraculous event. And, near this time, the earth will be plunged into three days of total darkness, in which even electric lamps will not light. Finally, after the miraculous darkness, much of the world will convert and an Age of Peace will be established. Then, Spiritual and material prosperity shall reign."[3]

"What else do we know about the Medjugorje secrets?" a student inquired.

"Our Lady gave one of the visionaries, Mirjana, the responsibility of revealing the secrets at the proper time. She knows the day and date of each of the secrets. Three days before each event takes place, her chosen priest will announce it to the world. These Revelations will be a confirmation of the apparitions and a stimulus for the conversion of the world."

One girl said, "It makes me feel kind of helpless that I can't stop what is going to happen to the world."

"Never forget," the priest answered, "Our Lady assures us that '*through prayer and fasting we can avert wars and even suspend the laws of nature.*' However, let me read for you another message, one that almost sounds like a fairy tale, if only it weren't from Mirjana: '*The Virgin told me God and the devil conversed, and the devil said that people believe in God only when life is good for them. When things turn bad, they cease to believe in God; then people blame God, or act as if He does not exist. God, therefore, allowed the devil one century in which to exercise an expanded power over the world, and the devil chose to start at some point in the twentieth century.'*[5] Considering that global war broke out in 1914 and, since then, we have witnessed mankind's most violent century, it may be a tale to take seriously. If the prophecy proves true, the seeds of Satan have been sown and the fruits of his efforts will continue to flourish."

A boy blurted out, "But that could all be bogus. Are there any prophecies that have already come true?"

"Yes, many prophecies of a personal nature have come true, along with many miracles," Father answered. "One prophecy, for example, was fulfilled after a Croatian friar requested Mirjana to ask the Virgin if Croatia would ever be independent and free. Mirjana reported that the Blessed Mother answered that the country would gain independence after a war. Soon, war broke out and at least 300,000 lives were lost. Croatia is now free."

"How do we know that the Medjugorje apparitions are from God?" a girl asked.

"Good question," the priest responded. "I believe they are but the Church has not yet ruled. Of course, it is hard for them to pass judgment until the last chapter is revealed. Still, Pope John Paul II spoke favorably of the 'Fruits' resulting from Medjugorje which has generated such a renewed hunger for the Sacraments that the small village has become know as the world's confessional. Beyond that, however, I can tell you that pilgrims have claimed many thousands of miracles that they credit to God. These miracles include documented physical healings; Spiritual healings; rosaries turning golden; and witnessing the spinning and dancing of the sun there. On the top of what is called 'Cross Mountain,' there is a 33 foot concrete cross. Many witnesses have seen it spinning, changing into a column of light, or transforming into a silhouette of Our Lady. These are just a few of the many miracles."

Another student asked, "What about scientific investigations?"

"Yes, there have been exhaustive studies. The visionary children themselves, for example, have been repeatedly and extensively studied during their ecstasies by experts from all over the world, including neuropsychiatrists; cardiologists; neurologists; eye, ear, nose and throat specialists; and numerous other doctors. During the visionaries' ecstasies, these children had no physical response to shouting, jabbing and pinching. Their highly dilated pupils would not constrict even when a 1,000 watt bulb was shone into them. No response to pain was observed even when one of the girls was stabbed repeatedly in the shoulder with a long leatherworking needle. In fact, one psychopharmacologist concluded that they experienced 'complete analgesis,' in other words, the total inability to feel pain. While in ecstasy, their electrocardiograms and electroencephalograms all indicated they were not in any known state of consciousness. Based on the EEG beta and alpha cycles that were monitored, it appears the best term for their state of consciousness is 'hyper-awake.' Repeatedly, scientists and doctors have concluded that they could find no hint of deceit and no scientific explanation."

The boy in the back asked, "Could it be that these doctors simply tried to prove what they already believed?"

"Let me tell you a story: A neurophysiologist from Milan, named Dr. Marco Margnelli, went to Medjugorje to expose the phenomenon as a fake. He was an avowed atheist. After his studies, he returned home with a lot of 'unscientific' questions in his head. He concluded that the ecstasies were extraordinary phenomena that he could not understand. But, more importantly, he could not explain the synchronous eye movements of the children, within one-fifth of a second of each other, or the healing he saw of a woman with leukemia. Finally, what affected him the most was watching the hundreds of wild birds that showed up each afternoon and noisily chirped, that is, until the apparition began. The 'absolute silence of the birds' haunted him, the doctor admitted. A few months after returning to Milan, Dr. Margnelli became a practicing Catholic."

One know-it-all chimed in, "But don't forget the most important question: What is the message?"

"Right!" Father Alonzo approved. "Based on the study of apparitions, visions and locutions over two thousand years, we know that any spiritual manifestation that denies the Lordship of Jesus Christ is not from God. So, we have to ask, is the Medjugorje apparition professing that Jesus Christ is our Lord and Savior? Absolutely and relentlessly. She is modern mankind's 'voice crying out in the wilderness' warning us to repent and accept God's love. These years, in which she has communicated to us, are a time of Grace granted by God. Do you understand what I am saying? Do not ignore this Gift!"

The priest looked out at some intense nods and some blank stares.

Then he continued, "In the fourteenth century, St. Vincent Ferrer revealed, 'By revelation it is manifestly shown that the whole duration of the world rests on a certain conditional prolongation obtained by the Virgin Mary in the hope of the conversion and correction of the world.'" The priest added, "Don't just hear what she says, listen! She pleads with us, 'I have come to tell the world that God exists. He is the fullness of life, and to enjoy this fullness and peace, you must return to God.'"

Some students were starting to doze.

"Okay!" Father Alonzo shouted, loud enough to startle them awake. "See you next time!"

Come, let us build ourselves a city,
with a tower that reaches to the heavens,
so that we may make a name for ourselves.
Genesis 11:4

30

Republic of Nauru
South Pacific Ocean
July 30

The XCyst Gulfstream 550 approached Nauru International Airport. At first glance over the wing, the island's landscape was exactly what Angela had expected: harsh, barren, and an almost monotone grey moonscape. It was nothing like what Evan Thas had promised. However, when the pilot announced they would have to circle the airport for a few minutes, she was given a surprisingly different view. As the north end of the island revealed itself, she could see what looked like a large Mediterranean resort that had been dropped onto the island. The golf course was deep green, the crowded beaches dazzling white. Plentiful palms accented the yards of colorful new homes and commercial buildings that had been architecturally coordinated with pastel stucco and red clay tile.

"It's beautiful," she remarked.

Evan raised his hand to indicate that he did not want to be interrupted. Wearing headphones and mesmerized by the satellite-delivered XBC News Special on the cabin's flat screen, he just mumbled, "Wait a second."

Angela put her headphones on and listened as the aircraft circled.

XBC NEWS CORRESPONDENT: "...In ancient times, ritual human sacrifice occurred in almost all regions of the world.

However, the three great faiths descending from Abraham – Judaism, Christianity and Islam – all strongly condemned the ritual. Because of that, many casual observers have mistakenly assumed that human sacrifice is no longer practiced. But in Uganda, for example, 29 ritual murders occurred in 2009 alone. This prompted the establishment of an Anti-Human Sacrifice Taskforce and a public awareness campaign to 'Prevent Child Sacrifice.' Even though it is the highly-visible Ugandan witch doctor's who are likely to be behind the murders, there have been no convictions since 2007. Many Ugandans believe there is no political will to protect the children."

"That's awful," Angela shouted over the drone of the engines.

Thas ignored her.

XBC NEWS CORRESPONDENT: "Ritual murders are also still practiced in India, Indonesia, South Africa, Gabon and Tanzania. Recent popular, but violent, Nigerian films are believed to have enticed an increase in the murders. The films promote the myth that drugs made from human organs can bring riches and..."[1]

Suddenly the audio and video cut off and Lindley, the pilot, announced that they were beginning their landing approach. The two passengers took off their headphones.

"It's beautiful," Angela repeated.

"That's why we call it Eden. You know why we had to circle for so long?" Thas asked.

"Too many birds?" she quipped.

"No, too many jets."

"Why is the island suddenly so popular?"

"You'll see," he answered.

As Angela observed the fascinating resort below, she worried that this trip would take longer than planned. She had been attending a Global Warming conference in Australia and was willing to shoehorn this quick detour into the schedule only because

Cyst, who had stayed behind, and Thas had promised she would not be disappointed. They had assured her that, on this trip, she would witness the next quantum leap forward for scientific human advancement.

They had already done so many invaluable things for her campaign that she felt she could not turn down the invitation.

When they finally landed at the small but new airport, Thas cursed when he saw the limo was not waiting on the tarmac for them. He never tolerated imprecision. However, the short delay gave Angela a few minutes to observe that he had not exaggerated about the heavy amount of air traffic. Planes were constantly taking off and landing. She marveled at the professionalism and efficiency of the tarmac crews, a rarity for isolated island airports. Except for the XCyst Industries' Gulfstream, all the aircraft seemed remarkably similar. They appeared to be designed to ship cargo. Silver metal boxes, numbering into the thousands, were being conveyed onto the jets as refueling took place. Then, with little more than a few minutes on the ground, the planes were back in the air.

"Very impressive," Angela said.

"You ain't seen nothin' yet," Evan hinted.

When the black limousine pulled up next to the plane, Evan curtly informed the driver that his service would no longer be needed. Angela thought it was odd that Lindley immediately circled the car with an extendable mirror, inspecting under the chassis. Then he popped open the hood and inspected the engine. Soon, the dignitaries drove off in the limo, leaving the co-pilot in the plane, and a disappointed Nauruan limo driver standing on the tarmac.

Thas and Cyst had deliberately kept Angela in the dark about this tour. They wanted to surprise her. She rarely liked surprises but realized, this time, she would just have to go along with it.

Soon, the limo pulled up to an extravagant wrought iron gate with steel bollards in front of it. Red vertical lines of light scanned the vehicle and its occupants. Then the bollards automatically retracted into the ground and the gate opened. Two young armed guards smiled and waved them through as they passed palm trees, flowers and a sign that announced, “Welcome to Eden Village.”

“Friendly people here,” Angela commented.

Evan responded, “Yes they are. After just ten years here, they will be able to retire comfortably.”

“Excellent.”

They drove past six massive warehouse buildings. They were so large that Angela thought they looked like the ones NASA used to house the space shuttles. She could see that two more were under construction.

“What are those for?” she asked.

“We’ll see those last.”

As they drove through the residential community, she realized that they were the only ones using a car. Everyone else was in a golf cart, riding bicycles or walking.

“As you can see,” Thas said, “we’re a very eco-friendly community ... very health conscious, too.”

The residents, she noticed as they drove past the tennis complex, were all similar in many respects. They were of different races but it seemed they were all young, educated, fit, outgoing and friendly. None seemed over thirty. It was almost like a large college campus where all the fraternity boys and sorority girls congregated.

Thas took Angela through the fitness center with its variety of swimming pools; tennis, basketball and racquetball courts; and strength and cardio equipment. It was the largest exercise center she had ever seen. She noticed that everyone here seemed to take their health regimens very seriously. The place was crowded and the residents of Eden treated Thas like a celebrity: “Hello Dr. Thas,” “How are you today, Evan?” “Did Dr. Cyst come with you this time?” He was accustomed to being treated special and took it all in stride. Then Thas took her through the spa facility with its seemingly endless corridors offering saunas, mud baths, masseuses, hair stylists, manicurists and body waxers.

"These services," Thas commented, "are free of charge."

"Amazing!" she said.

"We find that perks such as these help our staff meet their quotas."

"So you actually expect some kind of work from these *prima donnas?*" She asked with a smile.

"Yes, of course. After all, we do have a business to run."

As they returned through the cardio center, she observed that one thing seemed to be missing."

"No TVs?" she asked.

"That's right. On this island there is limited television access. We just have two channels that broadcast mostly local programming. We find that traditional television shows distract the staff from their work."

She laughed. "Come on. What work? It looks like all-fun."

"Actually, it is, in a way."

They drove past hundreds of attractive, but very small, bungalows.

"They're so cute," she observed. "Can I see one?"

"Sure … Lindley," he instructed the driver, "pull over at this one on the corner. I think it's empty."

They parked in front of the bungalow and Thas led her to the door. When he reached for the door knob, Angela heard thedeadbolt automatically slide to unlock the door and he walked into the house.

"That's odd," she observed.

"Here at Eden, we have bio-metric access. My clearance level gives me unlimited authorization."

When she entered, she was surprised to see a gaudy, small apartment. It was clean and new but it almost resembled a *bordello* with its red satin sheets on a king size bed that dominated the small room.

She grimaced at the large ceiling mirror over the bed. She saw little space for additional furniture and, toward the back, noticed just a bathroom and a walk-in closet.

"No kitchen?" she asked.

"No, we prefer our staff to dine together. We have excellent cuisine in our dining..."

The ringtone of Thas' iPhone interrupted him. "Excuse me," he said as he stepped outside the building.

With little to do while she waited, she picked up the remote and clicked it at the large flat screen television at the foot of the bed. A second later she was embarrassed when a pornographic movie came into view. She quickly changed the channel but immediately realized it, too, was pornographic. She clicked the TV off, dropped the remote on the bed and wiped her hand on her dress.

Outside, she could hear Thas getting angry and loud. He soon ended the call and yelled, "Okay, Madame Secretary, we need to move on."

"Any problems?" she asked as she left the bungalow.

He responded with a frustrated smile. "It's always something."

Lindley next drove them to the restaurant where the two were seated at a corner table with stunning views of a rocky cliff that plummeted down to the azure Pacific. Evan assured Angela that The Garden – as the residents of Eden called it – had attracted some of the best chefs in the world.

Before they sat, however, Thas compulsively began adjusting the silverware placement.

"Excuse me," he said as he reached in front of her and rearranged the knife and fork that had been set on her plate in a cross pattern. He placed them parallel to each other, and then did the same for his own.

"I liked the placement," Angela suggested, with a smile.

The maitre d' offered, "Chef Francois thought ..."

"No," Evan interrupted with finality.

"Yes sir, Dr. Thas." The waiter's head nodded a submissive bow. "We will make the changes immediately."

Later, while enjoying a light pinot grigio, they ordered from a menu of excellent culinary offerings and, soon, were feasting on filets of Dover sole, duchess potatoes and roasted asparagus.

The conversation, however, kept a serious edge as Thas explained that the greatest threat to mankind's fulfillment is the mortal sin of forcing science to take a back seat to religion.

"How so?" she asked with interest.

"Before today is over," he predicted confidently, "you will see that science, not superstition, will elevate mankind to a new level of comfort, a new level of enlightenment. Imagine if we were able to extend our productive life expectancy to two, three or four hundred years. We would become like gods. What if Nietzsche, Machiavelli, Freud, Marx or Darwin had had that kind of timeframe upon which to expand their theories? Indeed, what if Huntington Cyst could build upon his accomplishments for four centuries? Think of the awesome benefits that mankind would realize. For humanity to reach its ultimate potential, we must focus on sustaining human life in terms of quality, not quantity. Quality of life is our salvation."

"I guess I see what you mean," she responded with some uncertainty.

"Madame Secretary, you are about to witness the greatest humanitarian venture in history."

Just then the attractive waitress that Angela had barely noticed spilled some water on Angela's napkin as she set the glass next to her plate.

"Oh, I am so sorry," the waitress said.

"Quite alright," Angela responded. "No damage done."

The waitress replaced the wet cloth napkin with a paper one and clumsily spread it on Angela's lap. Angela looked down and silently read the words scribbled on it: *Please help me escape.*

Collect plenty of food during the happy days of your spiritual summers. You will then be able to endure the difficult days of temptations during the winters of your soul.

St. Augustine of Hippo

31

Tarbuwth Correctional Facility
Yashar, NY
July 30

Handcuffed to the table, John quietly waited for Detective Tim Lassiter. He had not been in this conference room before today so he entertained himself by trying to find one thing that was not identical to the other conference rooms.

The deadbolts on the door slid open and Lassiter entered with another man who was carrying a large briefcase of some kind. The two men did not say anything to John as they sat down, opened the briefcase and started to adjust some pieces of equipment inside it.

Lassiter was still seething at John's refusal to cooperate and his inability to find any significant information on John's past. At first, he had been optimistic when, after being Mirandized, John refused a lawyer. However, the only thing the detective had learned, from those who knew John best, was that everyone thought it was impossible that John had committed the murder. The only hint of scandal was that Father Alonzo had arranged for Sister Clarita to spend long hours, alone in the chapel, with John. That had been forbidden by Mother Liguori but overruled by the priest. It was no secret that she resented his interference since that moment. The clashes started about the time Sister Clarita's *stigmata* appeared and that led Mother to doubt the authenticity of the apparent miracle.

As soon as Lassiter clicked on a recording device, John opened the conversation with, "I'm ready to cooperate."

Lassiter was stunned. He didn't expect a reversal this easy and this soon.

"Mr. Malek, for the record, I just want to be clear," the detective cautiously proceeded. "I have read you your rights. You realize you have the right to remain silent and that anything you say can and will be used against you."

"Yes."

"You realize you have a right to an attorney, but you have refused."

"Yes."

"If you can't afford an attorney, one will be appointed for you."

"I understand. No thank you."

Lassiter was ready to move ahead. "Okay, well, it's good I have Mr. Stemson here. If, as you say, you're cooperating, I'm sure that you won't mind if we verify you're telling the truth. Right?"

John affirmed, "No problem."

"Go ahead Tony," Lassiter directed.

The assistant set up the polygraph and voice stress analysis machines and then proceeded to ask John a few control questions that had obvious answers. "Mr. Malek, are you a man? Are you now in Yashar New York? Are you standing on your head? Do you have two hands?"

John's responses allowed Stemson to gauge truthful responses while Lassiter wrote questions on a piece of paper.

"Okay, we're ready," Stemson announced.

Lassiter handed him the page of questions.

Stemson asked, "What is your name?"

"John, son of Zebedee and Salome, brother of James."

"But what's your last name?"

"I don't have one."

"Then what's this John Eben Malek stuff?"

"In Hebrew, it means John, servant of the King."

Lassiter stepped in, "Come on, what's your last name?"

"In my culture, we don't have last names."

Lassiter frowned and then added, "So, where are you from?"

"Today, it is called Israel."

"Tony," the detective asked, "he's lying, right?"

The two officials made eye contact and Tony almost imperceptibly shook his head.

"Okay," Lassiter barked, "What year were you born?"

"You would call it fourteen."

"Fourteen what?" the detective shouted. "What the hell does that mean?"

"It was the Hebrew year 3775."

The detective didn't try to hide his frustration. "Come on. Quit playing games!"

"Uh, Tim," Stemson interrupted, "can we have a word outside?"

He clicked off the recorder, slid the equipment out of John's reach and the two men stepped outside to talk privately.

Stemson began, "This is the weirdest thing I've ever seen. His polygraph readings are rock solid."

"Tony, his answers don't make any sense."

"Yes they do, Tim. This guy thinks he's an apostle."

"What d'ya mean?"

"John… Jesus Christ's apostle!"

"Well now we know he's nuts."

"Yeah, pretty good chance of that," the polygrapher answered with a tone of sarcasm. "But he doesn't act insane… There is one other possibility."

"Yeah?"

"Hypnotic regression therapy explores what are called 'deep memories' and has been criticized for occasionally planting false remembrances. Perhaps, this man doesn't know the truth. Hypnosis has implanted fantastic memories that he actually believes."

"So," the detective concluded, "this guy may be sicker than even we thought.

"Could be."

THE QUESTIONERS RETURNED with the strategy to entice John to talk as much as possible in order to catch him in a lie or to trick him into divulging incriminating evidence. That plan required that they first make him comfortable by indulging him in his delusional fantasies. Stemson clicked the recorder back on and proceeded with new questions that the detective had written.

"So, Mr. Malek," the polygraph expert began politely, "I take it you are saying you are John, the apostle of Jesus."

"I am."

"So, what have you been doing all this time… I mean, since the Bible?"

"I have gathered the flock, one-by-one; I have protected mankind from the full force of Satan's fury; I have delayed the inevitable."

"Why haven't we heard anything about you?"

"Exposing my identity had not been asked of me."

"Asked by whom?"

"By God, or His messenger, Blessed Mother."

"You mean Mary?"

"Yes."

The two questioners stared at each other, fearing a roadblock.

Then the detective jumped in once more. "Come on, stop jacking us around. We've got a dead nun on our hands. I'm not in the mood for games."

John responded calmly, "Mr. Stemson, does your machine say I'm playing games?"

Stemson glanced up from his polygraph and at the detective. His blank look indicated that he could not dispute John's sincerity.

Lassiter continued, "Mr. Malek, I don't know if you're fishing for an insanity defense or what but..."

"I am not insane, detective. I have complete clarity. That is why I am hated."

"Look, spare me the pity party. If you want us to believe you, you have to give us some kind of proof. It's just a little hard to believe that you're fortunate enough to still be alive after two thousand years."

"I would prefer not to be alive today," John grinned as if at gallows humor. "But I do what is asked of me."

Lassiter didn't appreciate John's calm demeanor. He tried a different approach. "Look you maggot puke! You're not going to live much longer if you keep this up! I've got your life in my hands, you idiot!"

No response.

Exasperated, Lassiter yelled, "Come on, you freak... let it out. You despise me, right? You sick pervert! You want to kill me, don't you?"

"No"

"What are you thinking?" Lassiter demanded. "Come on, what are you thinking?"

"I'm praying for your salvation."

That took the wind out of Lassiter's sails. He sighed deeply, glanced at Stemson's nod, and paced across the room twice.

"Okay, then," Lassiter prodded more calmly, "give me some proof. Tell me something that I don't already know about you."

"I'll try." John thought for a moment and then began. "Because of my language skills, many rulers have employed my services through the years. So, if you like, I could describe for you Emperor Hadrian's Villa Adriana in the 2nd century; or the royal residence at Sigiriya Sri Lanka in the 5th century; or the original Imperial Palace at Kyoto Japan in the 8th century."

"That won't help. You coulda seen pictures in a book."

"No, those buildings have been gone for centuries. But I can describe 3rd century horse racing and gladiatorial games in the Aphrodisias stadium in Caria, Turkey. I was there with 30,000 spectators. Or … if you just pick any major monastery, I'll probably be able to describe it … I've lived in a lot of them."

"No, no, none of that works," Lassiter complained. "We need some kind of proof that can be scientifically verified."

John nodded, thought for a moment and then added, "Oh, what about this? For many years after my exile on Patmos at the end of the 1st century, I travelled through the countries that border the Mediterranean Sea. Mostly I walked or sailed. While doing that, I became fluent in many languages and, consequently, was able to preach the Gospel everywhere I went."

The detective interrupted. "Can you be specific about a particular event at a particular time?"

"For example, about the year 310 AD, I was captured by one of the most powerful rival powers competing for control of the Roman Empire. My captors scheduled me for immediate execution because I was identified as a Christian Jew and, consequently, useless to them. However, I convinced them that my language skills could be valuable to their leader, Maxentius. Hoping to be recognized for having found and delivered an accomplished linguist, they had me before Maxentius within days."

"Mr. Malek, do you have information that can be verified?" Lassiter pushed.

John continued. "Maxentius brought me and his five linguists before him for a test. Each of them specialized in two or three languages. While he watched, they tested me in each language they knew. In every language, to their amazement, I responded fluently. Then, Maxentius did what I cannot forget. He complained that he previously had to feed five linguists, but now, only one. So, he ordered and enjoyed the immediate beheading of each of them."

"Excuse me," Stemson interrupted. "I need to flip the tape." He did so, and when he clicked the recorder back on, John continued.

"This confirmed my concerns regarding the evil nature of the man and reinforced in my mind that I could not serve his ambition to rule Rome. But I also could not make my feelings known. So, in general matters I loyally served, translating and interpreting for months."

"We need something provable," the Detective reminded John, "not just a history lesson."

John ignored his prodding. "At that time, the Roman military leader, Constantine, was advancing on Rome to fight and remove Maxentius from power. They had both served as leaders of the Empire in a four-man tetrarchy. However, now, they had reached a point where only one would live and lead. When Constantine reached the Milvian Bridge at the entrance to Rome, I was sent out with a stern and intimidating message. However, when I came face-to-face with the man I was surprised to see that he had a *chi* and *rho* on his helmet, the first two Greek letters in the word Christ. Then, I delivered Maxentius' belligerent message of certain defeat for Constantine if he did not retreat. Constantine refused to respond to such a threat. As I prepared to depart,

I looked around and saw that each of his soldiers had a Cross on his shield. So, I asked Constantine what these symbols meant to him. He explained that he had received a message from the Christ, in a vision, who told him that by the symbol of the Cross he would conquer. Then I realized where my allegiance would be well-placed. I told Constantine, 'In the name of our Lord and Savior Jesus Christ, believe your vision, and not my threats.'"

"Something provable, please!" Lassiter begged.

"I returned to tell Maxentius the truth: I had delivered his message and had received no response to it. So, he began the attack that led to the decisive battle of the Milvian Bridge. During the course of the conflict, Maxentius grew very angry at me for not convincing Constantine to retreat. So, he slashed me across the forearm. You see … I still have the scar."

John pointed out the slash across his arm and Lassiter snorted, "Big deal."

"I was injured so badly that I had to flee the fighting. I was fortunate to find a hidden alcove under the bridge. Built into the northern bridge support was a hole, not easily accessible, almost like a man-made cave, hidden away from rain, sun and wind. With much difficulty, I was able to crawl down into the alcove and hide until the battle was over."

"This is ridiculous," the detective interrupted. "We're wasting our time. Nothing you say is provable."

"The bridge still stands."

"So what!" the detective shouted. "There's a lot of ancient Rome that's still around! It proves nothing!"

"And I bled profusely in there."

The faces of two questioners suddenly changed. They realized what that might mean.

Stemson raised his eyes from the polygraph, looked at Lassiter and mumbled, "Rock solid."

Detective Lassiter slowly shook his head at John, marveling that this crazy story actually might be worth investigating.

Could his DNA still be in there?

Could it be Carbon dated?

A rat is a pig is a dog is a boy.
They're all animals.[1]
PETA Founder
Ingrid Newkirk

32

Eden Village
Republic of Nauru
July 30

After lunch, the tour of Eden continued as Thas led Concepcion through one bio-metric scan after another. Finally, after a long series of checkpoints and armed guards, they entered the enormous central warehouse.

"It's so hot in here," she complained.

"Ninety eight point six," he responded.

She looked up, wide-eyed, as if dwarfed by skyscrapers. All around her were countless glass tanks that towered, perhaps, a hundred feet high.

"What is this?" she asked with amazement.

"Let's look around and you tell me what you think it is."

He led her through the narrow passages between the tower tanks. Inside each she could see a clear solution and numerous black sacks, in a variety of sizes, each connected to black hoses. The liquid had a constant flow of bubbles rising as if to oxygenate the fluid.

"Is that water in there?" she asked.

"No, it's an amino acid, single-chain polypeptide hormone. Normally, it is synthesized, stored, and secreted by the somatotroph cells within the lateral wings of the anterior pituitary gland, but we manufacture our own."

She frowned.

He tried again. "Perhaps the easiest way to think of it is that it functions like how Miracle Gro® works on plants. It nourishes and accelerates growth and development."

"So, there are plants in those sacks?"

"No Madame Secretary," he said without the least bit of hesitancy, "those are embryos."

"Human?"

"Of course."

Her eyes scanned the warehouse and the thousands upon thousands of black sacks around her. She was startled when she noticed the sack closest to her. "That can't be an embryo," she blurted. "It's bigger than me!"

"Like I said, we have learned how to nourish and accelerate growth and development. That was one of our earliest. We've been nurturing it for three years."

"Why?" she asked with some exasperation. "Why are you doing this?"

"For the good of mankind, Madame Secretary … For the good of mankind."

"Just wait now … maybe we better back up a little … I mean … what is this, *in vitro* fertilization?"

"No, Madame Secretary, it's *in vivo* fertilization. We do not combine an egg with sperm in a Petri dish to achieve fertilization. Conception at Eden occurs naturally. Then we just remove and incubate the embryo in a synthetic uterus so our staff member can get back to the fertilization process."

"So, your staff here, they … they just … screw?"

"That's not how I'd describe it. They have scientific responsibilities."

"And the quotas you mentioned, they are for …"

"Embryos. Yes, that is correct."

Baffled, she shook her head. "But why?"

"Madame Secretary, right now, just in America alone, the demand for organ, eye and tissue donation still vastly exceeds the number of donors. More than 100,000 men, women and children currently need life-saving organ transplants. And that doesn't include the far more whose lives can be improved with organ transplants. Every 11 minutes another name is added to the national organ transplant waiting list. An average of 18 Americans die each day from the lack of available organs for transplant.[2] The need is far worse in most other countries. From this little island paradise, we will now be able to meet the organ, eye and tissue needs of the entire world. Think of how much good we can do from here … And you wouldn't believe the profit that can be made from an operation like this. Think about it. To a rich man, how much is his quality of life worth to him? I'm sure we can bring you in on the initial public offering … if you like."

"Those silver boxes I saw being loaded at the airport, what were they?"

"That was our first crop of organs being shipped worldwide. That's why we asked you to take our tour now. Soon, along with the scientific community's praises, there may be some not-so-flattering press from religious circles about these shipments. We want our allies prepared if the shit storm hits." He chuckled amiably but she was still serious.

"So, you plan to use the organs in these embryos like spare auto parts?"

"Again, I wouldn't put it that way."

"Come on, Evan. Are you serious? I mean, look at it." She pointed at the large sack near them. "That's not an embryo in there. That's an adult human being!"

"Don't be silly, Madame Secretary. It's never been born."

She felt sick to her stomach.

"Madame Secretary, you're not going to get all preachy on me, are you? Come on. I thought you were progressive. Surely, you don't want to hinder scientific progress. Join us, Madame Secretary. Let's change the world for the better."

He could see that she still wasn't buying it. "Look, Madame Secretary, the Chinese are happy to execute prisoners so they can take their organs. In some parts of the world, people are kidnapped and killed for their body parts. This is certainly more ethical than those alternatives."

She stared at the large black sack in front of her. It was so big that she thought it had to be a man. She flinched when she noticed a sharp movement from inside, like a punch or a kick. Then she saw two more. Though she had often talked about empathy, for the first time she felt it. And she felt shame for mankind's selfishness.

What was that jab? Is he trying to break out?

What did he do to deserve this?

This is wrong!!!

As her eyes scanned the thousands of black sacks around her, she noticed that many, perhaps even most, were displaying sharp, punching movements. Angela felt overwhelmed, as if she were drowning in one of those tanks or suffocating in one of those sacks. She wanted to demand to be taken away, to condemn what she was seeing, to put a stop to it!

It was her moment to choose salvation ... but the moment slipped away.

ON THE FLIGHT BACK to Australia, Angela was very quiet. She could not stop thinking about the words the waitress had written: *Please help me escape.* The images of the punching and kicking from inside the black sacks weighed heavily on her mind.

However, Evan Thas was not concerned about her silence. She had been shown what good would come from the Eden Project. She seemed reassured when he reminded her of Dr. Cyst's logical proposition that, when it comes to the human population, quality is much more important than quantity.

Still, Thas realized that it was best to cut the tour short. So, he did not include the warehouses where human mutation and cloning experiments were being studied, or where immortal synthetic organisms were being developed.

When he arrived home, he predicted to Huntington Cyst that, within days, she would be fully back on their team. He was confident that her wave of compassion would soon subside and that she would then float on to more immediate concerns, opportunities and pleasures.

He was correct.

Revenge is a dish
best served cold.
Afghan Proverb

33
Secretary of State's Office
Albany, NY
August 4

The newspaper flew across the office, hit the door and fell to the floor. Angela had just read the Washington Society column that she never missed. In it, the political marriage of the year had been announced. Fred Whitehead had become engaged to *that little tart.*

Angela's assistant asked over the intercom, "You okay, Madame Secretary?"

She picked up the phone and responded flatly, "Yeah, Betsy, I'm fine … No problem."

The assistant continued, "Your mother is on line two."

"Tell her I'm in a meeting. See what she wants and take care of it."

"And Mr. Whitehead is on line four."

Dammit.

"Do you want to take it?"

Angela thought for a moment. She realized this was not the time to alienate anyone from Cyst's camp. She had grown to value the priceless aid that Cyst and Thas had been giving her campaign. Every evening, before dinner, she would sip a chardonnay while reading from her iPhone the latest recommendations for strategy, tactics and talking points in her campaign. She knew that it was with no small expense that Cyst secretly kept his polling division on the phones and his CyBot search engine data mining for her. That timely information, combined with his unprecedented analytical capabilities, had steered her words and actions brilliantly. With little effort, she would delete the "for your eyes only" section of the daily emails and forward the remaining information to her new team of managers, strategists and speechwriters. Thinking these were her words, Angela's campaign staff members were amazed at her brilliant grasp of campaign issues. They soon followed her directions religiously. Quickly and smoothly, those words, phrases and concepts were transcribed to her teleprompters and, at each campaign appearance, Angela proved to be an exceptional reader.

"Madame Secretary?" the assistant pressed.

"Uh, I guess … Yeah ... I'll take it." She contemplated her options, punched the button and spoke with unbridled happiness, "Fred, where have you been hiding? When are you coming to see me again?"

"Uh, hello, Angela. I take it you haven't read the paper today."

"No, why?" She feigned alarm. "Did something happen?"

"Angela … we were just kicking it around … there was no real commitment."

"Fred, what are you talking about?"

He laid it out directly: "The Washington Society column is reporting that I'm engaged to Amy Laugherly."

Angela laughed, "Yeah, good one, Fred. She's young enough to be your … what? Granddaughter?"

He didn't respond.

"Fred, you're not laughing … Is it true?"

"Well, not really," he hedged, "but kind of."

Angela sensed his ambivalence. So, she pitched, "Fred, I'm sure she's wonderful as the flavor of the month but you can't be serious. You have nothing in common. You two won't last a year. Fred, don't make the mistake of falling into one of those mid-life crises. Buy a Maserati, get a Led Zeppelin tattoo but, Fred, don't marry a child!"

"I'm sorry, Angela. I don't want to hurt you … I didn't mean for it to get out this way. No hard commitment had been made … I'm gonna kill whoever leaked it."

Angela quietly marveled at his ignorance: *She leaked it, you idiot!* But Angela had begun to learn how to control her temper.

"Look, this is easily fixable. Just issue a press release saying no commitment has been made," Angela pressed. "Say the two of you are dating but there is no commitment yet. You hear what I'm saying: no commitment."

Angela waited for Fred's response. "It's too late, Angela … It's too late."

The Secretary sat back and heaved a sigh of disappointment. "Well, Fred, it's your call to make. I'm hoping you will straighten out this mistake. If not … well … I'm sorry it had to work out this way."

"I just want you to know, Angela, I am torn … very torn."

"I know, Fred," Angela responded with an end-of-the-conversation tone. "Whatever you decide, I'll understand."

"Please don't hate me, Angela."

"Nonsense. If this is what you want, then I wish both of you the best. You'll make a beautiful couple."

He knew she was the ultimate professional, but still offered, "I hope this won't harm our working relationship."

"Don't be silly, Fred. I never let personal matters interfere with serving the people. I understand. Believe me, I'm okay. It just wasn't meant to be. You stay in touch now." And then she hung up the phone.

This, she thought, was like salt in a sore wound. Her critics had already mocked her for being in love with humanity in general, but no one in particular. Maybe, they were right.

After a few quiet moments, Angela regrouped her emotions and buzzed her assistant. Her words were unplanned.

"Betsy, arrange a meeting for me, here, this afternoon, with the Speaker. Tell him I need to discuss some problems that I have with Green E."

Give me your tired, your poor,
your huddled masses yearning to breathe free,
the wretched refuse of your teeming shore.
Send these, the homeless, tempest-tossed to me...
Inscription on the
Statue of Liberty

34

Tarbuwth Correctional Facility
Yashar, NY
August 8

Out of respect, the inmates chose to sit on the ground. John would have been more comfortable on the picnic table but refused to place himself above the others. He sat with them, on the dusty prison yard.

Some of the prisoners talked about the crime that had landed them in prison. Rodney, a Californian who looked older than his sixty years, told of his remarkable financial rise and tragic personal crash. He had been raised by devout Catholic parents and seemed to have led a charmed life. He had been a football star, an Army veteran and a Las Vegas hotshot before the pursuit of wealth and ill-defined success led him to real estate brokerage in Hollywood California. There, he became a multi-millionaire with many celebrity clients. One night, at a party in Hollywood, he met an attractive young woman who asked, "Do you want to meet my best friend?" So, he enthusiastically followed her to an upstairs bedroom. Rodney expected to meet another woman there but, instead, she opened her purse and introduced him to cocaine. Within a year, he had lost all of his worldly possessions: his millions, his Ferrari, his home in the Hollywood hills. He became homeless and the many friends he once had quickly deserted him.[1]

"But your life is on track now, isn't it?" John asked.

Some of the prisoners laughed.

Rodney thought for a moment and answered, "Strangely, yeah … actually you're right."

"Tell them why," John encouraged.

"Well," Rodney proceeded uncomfortably, "one night I was sleeping in a vacant home ... Actually, I had broken into it ... In the middle of the night, a beautiful, shining young woman woke me and told me, 'Roddy' – that's what my mother always called me – 'you shall do great things for my Son.' I know it sounds crazy but it had to be the Virgin Mary. At that moment, she broke the back of my cocaine demon."

Jin, the thin Asian-American doctor quipped, "If she's so powerful, you'd think she would have kept you out of jail."

"No." Rodney thought for a moment. "I think this is where I'm supposed to be right now … Anyway, that night I got busted for breaking and entering. But that's okay. I'll be out of here in a few months, and I'll be leaving a better man than before."

"She's right, you know," John said. "You will do great things, Roddy."

A tall, blond computer hacker from Australia had been standing back, listening, but Ozzy the Aussie could not hold his tongue any longer. "Come on, mate. Everybody thinks he's got the best faith. Religion's done nothing but divide people and cause wars."

"True Christian faith is a shield, not a sword." John responded. "Our Lord was a sacrificial Lamb and He is the example we must follow. If we are persecuted for our faith and God wants us to die, then we die. If He wants us to live, no matter how dire the circumstances appear, a miracle will be provided. Our Lord never advised us to attack those who believe differently. It is an unfortunate reality that in every man, whether faithful or not, Satan attempts to stir up hostilities. He is the father of lies and a murderer from the beginning. So, don't confuse defending the faith with harming others who believe differently. Your Christian acts of mercy and love are your most powerful weapons against evil. Therefore, trust the Word of God, not the words of men. Life is a test for us all and, as long as we live, the evil one will seek to mislead us."

Rodney asked, "But what about the people who say they're born again?"

"It is true that you must be born of water and of Spirit to enter the Kingdom of Heaven.[2] However, Jesus warned us that even when the Spirit is willing, the body is weak.[3] We are each engaged in a life-long test to prove we are worthy to spend eternity with God. Remember the words of The Lord's Prayer: 'Lead us not into temptation but deliver us from evil.' We are all to pray these words. Those who are born again are not immune from temptation and evil. Look at the apostles. Every one of them deserted Jesus in his hour of need."

"No," Rodney corrected him, "the Apostle John was faithful to the very end."

"That's not true!" John snapped, startling his listeners. "He was a spineless coward at Gethsemane! He fled with all the others and he hid in the bushes, watching, as they took Jesus away. When a soldier snuck up on John, he ran so fast that the soldier ripped the cloak off his back. John fled into the darkness, naked and crying.[4] He spent a very long time atoning for his cowardice. If he could not forgive himself, how could he expect God to forgive him?"

Most of the inmates felt uncomfortable with John's uncharacteristically harsh words, leveled against a revered saint.

John added, "We prove ourselves worthy of eternity with God whenever nothing is more valuable to us than His love."

"I agree with Ozzy," the Asian-American doctor said, abruptly changing the subject. "I'm a man of science. I don't believe in God."

"But for science to exist there must be order. Otherwise, there is only random chaos. So, who or what established that order? How can chaos lead to order? As a doctor, you realize how amazingly complex we human beings are. Surely, when you walk in the woods and come upon a minimally complex structure, like a log cabin, you don't assume it just fell together by random chance. You realize it must have had an intelligent designer. Science is the study of cause and effect and while God has established an order, he still controls all effects." Then John asked the doctor, "For example, Jin, tell me why you are here."

Jin responded casually, "The IRS got me … tax evasion."

"That's not true," John said. "Why are you *really* here?"

"It was tax evasion. I'll be out in three months."

"Jin," John said softly, almost pleading, "you will never be free from your prison until you confess what you've done."

"Look," Jin barked, "I'm not going to argue with you. You have me confused with somebody else!"

John sighed and his tone began increasing in intensity. "It is true you evaded taxes. You insisted on being paid in cash so you wouldn't have to declare your true income. But that is not why you are here. Jin, you are here because you murdered 5,127 unborn infants. You are here because you supervised another 17,458 murders at your clinics. You are here because you had your staff dispose of most of the bodies by stuffing them in garbage bags, flushing them down toilets and grinding them through garbage disposals. And, for those 147 babies who were mistakenly born alive, you ordered your staff to asphyxiate them. You are here, Jin, because you trained your counselors to befriend vulnerable and naïve young women in order to convince them that abortion was their only reasonable option, and that it would be easy, painless and forgettable … Do I still have you confused with someone else?"[5]

Jin was afraid to respond. He knew that child molesters were treated horribly in prison. He wondered if abortionists might receive the same fate. He felt another wave of depression coming over him.

Jin mumbled, "It's the woman's choice."

John asked bluntly, "Are you lying to me or yourself?"

Jin's brow tightened. He appeared bewildered.

"The woman's choice," John repeated as he sighed and looked up to Heaven with exhaustion in his eyes. Then he focused on Jin. "You know the studies that show two-thirds of women after abortion reported that they had felt pressured. You know that over half reported that they had felt rushed or uncertain. You know that four out of five said that they were not informed of all the available options. You know that homicide is the leading killer of pregnant women. You know that the suicide rate climbs six-fold after abortion. What kind of choice is that?"[6]

Jin looked at the ground, nervously dragging his toe in the dirt.

"Look at me!" John demanded.

The doctor's scared eyes raised slowly, but his head did not.

"You paid your staff a bonus for every dead baby. You trained them to offer no alternative to abortion and even to side with the menacing boyfriends who came along just to make sure the girl did not change her mind and choose life." John shouted, "You gave her no choice!"

Jin's eyes had returned to the ground. He remembered how, once, he had been rich and flamboyant. Now, all he had and all he was, amounted to nothing.

Jin exhaled long and hard. "What do you want me to do?"

John said, "The spoils of Satan's war against God are those souls that refuse to admit that the battle has begun. It will be very difficult for you to overcome your sins and to change your life … much more difficult for you than for any of these other men. Your pride is your worst enemy."

"I'm not proud of what I've done," Jin said with an air of self-loathing.

"Still, you are too proud to reach out to God with true humility. I tell you, if you do not humble yourself before God and beg His forgiveness, you will never overcome your sins and you will never escape your prison." John could see he still had not fully gotten through to him. "Jin, you have only one precious possession that no one can take from you. It is the same treasure that you are willingly giving away."

Jin quietly contemplated those words as Booker spoke up. "John, why would God send anyone to hell?"

John appreciated that Booker had come so far. His question was sincere and it calmed John down.

"Booker, the real question is: Why would God want to spend eternity with anyone who rejected Him for a lifetime?" Then John continued with one of Jesus' parables: "The lord of the vineyard had a fig tree, and he went to look for fruit on it, but did not find any. So he said to the man who took care of the vineyard, 'For three years now I've been coming to look for fruit on this fig tree and haven't found any. Cut it down! Why should it use up the soil?' 'Sir,' the servant replied, 'leave it alone for one more year, and I'll dig around it and fertilize it. If it bears fruit next year, fine! If not, then cut it down.'"[7]

None of the prisoners seemed to comprehend the message.

John explained, "I am that servant, praying for more time. If fruits are not produced, the tree will be destroyed."He examined their blank stares and voiced his frustration. "If I appear angry today, it is because time is running out. I cannot save the fig tree on my own. Will you help me?"

Most of them nodded but, still, had confusion on their faces.

Worthington asked, "Why do you tell us stories? Why don't you just give us simple answers?"

"I want you to think about what I am saying. If I give you an apple, do you expect me to chew it for you first?"

Henry, the Jamaican with the dreadlocks, asked, "What can we do, man? We're stuck here, just like you."

"Henry, the time of your test is coming," the teacher said. "Be ready for it."

"How? How can I get ready?" the Jamaican asked sincerely.

"Do you all want to hear?" John asked the group. Most of the men nodded and none objected. So, he continued, "In every man's life, there are precious opportunities to choose eternal life. But the more one chooses to surround himself with sin, the fewer chances he will have. Pride, materialism and selfishness are pollutants of the mind. A sinful mind is incapable of discerning purity, and is even repelled by it. Like the arrogant, tone-deaf music critic, he mocks and condemns what he cannot comprehend. Today, however, you have been given one of these precious opportunities. Start your journey now, not tomorrow, not next week."

"But what do we do?" Henry insisted.

"Life is a jigsaw puzzle. To put it together takes time and effort. Ill-conceived shortcuts, like forcing pieces to fit, don't solve the puzzle for you. But there are some practical shortcuts you can take."

"Yeah," the tall, quiet Canadian spoke up. "I always find the four corners first and then all the side pieces."

"Right," John said. "Then you can build the frame within which all the other pieces will fit. I tell you all, if your life is framed by the teachings of Jesus Christ, life will make sense to you and you will be able to fill in life's pieces. If the frame of Jesus' guidance is missing, you will struggle, and most likely fail, to complete life's puzzle. Jesus leads us to God the Father, and 'No eye has seen, no ear has heard, no mind has conceived what God has prepared for those who love Him.'"[8]

Still embarrassed from being singled out, Jin blurted, "So, you're saying only Christians should go to heaven?"

John answered, "No, Jin, I didn't. God knows your heart ... Jesus said, 'I am the way, the truth and the life. No one comes to the Father except through Me.'[9] However, He also recognized the ignorance of the men who tortured Him to death and asked His Father to forgive even them. Jesus gave us an insight into God's judgment when he said, 'To whom much is given, much is required.'[10] Yet, he repeatedly warned that we are not to judge.[11] The horrible execution of our Savior – this harmless, sinless, loving man – proves that we are not always capable of judging righteously. So remember, we set a high standard for ourselves when we ask God to 'Forgive us our trespasses as we forgive those who trespass against us.' Live life forgiving and loving, and leave the judging to God."

Henry pressed again, "So, specifically, man, what do I need to do?"

"Pray, pray, pray. If you realized the true power of prayer, you would never stop praying." Henry pondered that statement and John continued. "Faith is not about feeling good it is about being good. And being good is not an act it is a habit. First, you must take control of your mind. If you do not take control of your mind, the Destroyer will. Your mental habits will make or break you. So, whenever you need something important, ask God. Whenever you don't, thank God… Let me ask you, are your thoughts sometimes filled with profane music, images and words?"

Many of the prisoners nodded slightly with embarrassment.

"And how many of you have filled your quiet time here with thoughts of anger, revenge and hate?"

All of them nodded uncomfortably.

"The Bible teaches: 'As he thinks in his heart, so is he.'[12] Like an athlete training his body, or a singer training his voice, each of you must learn to train your mind. When you lay in bed, instead of letting violent lyrics run through your head, contemplate the words, 'Thank you Jesus' over and over again while reflecting on the tortures He endured for your salvation. When you wake up in the morning, instead of dwelling on revenge plans, meditate on the words, 'Lord, forgive me' as you remember that He even forgave his executioners. Do you see what I mean? Helpful thoughts must replace harmful ones. Every night before you fall off to sleep, ask yourself three things: 'What bad things did I do today?' 'What good things did I fail to do?' And, 'How can I do better tomorrow?' Prayer does not have to be complicated but it must become a habit for you and, over time, it will bring you to a deeper and deeper understanding of God's love and wisdom. Whatever is true, whatever is noble, whatever is right, whatever is pure, whatever is lovely, whatever is admirable—if anything is excellent or praiseworthy—think about such things."[13]

Some of the inmates shared approving glances.

John continued, "Once you have started to train your mind away from destructive thinking, you must learn to die to self. This step sounds scary and unpleasant, but it is actually the most blessed gift you can receive. You will never regret it. Jesus said, 'I tell you the truth, unless a kernel of wheat falls to the ground and dies, it remains only a single seed. But if it dies, it produces many seeds.' So, God has called you to seek the death of your fallen nature - the death of your slavery to the god of this world – and to share in the wealth of His Kingdom. To thoroughly understand evil, one must hack through its thin attractive veneer. Ask God to kill your proud selfish nature, kill your anger and hatred, and kill the evil within you. Like Jesus, seek to serve, not to be served. You will be surprised at how much happier and fulfilled you will become if you follow God's Word. Let God purge the addictions, ambitions and harmful emotions out of your life. Become a soldier for God like the soldier who is obedient and willing to sacrifice for a greater good, even if he sacrifices his own life. Take up your Cross. Serve God and your fellow man humbly, obediently and without complaint. And, if you fall short, get on your knees and pray that God will strengthen you so that you will not fail again. Sincerely ask forgiveness, and He will forgive, love and reward."

Big Worthington, who was sitting closest to John, nodded. His conversion was what drove most of these men here. They wanted in their lives the same amazingly positive change they had seen in Worthington's.

"Gentlemen," John continued, "we have entered the entrepreneurial age of evil... Let me ask you, what was the tree in the Garden of Eden called?"

Booker answered, "The tree of good and evil."

"Not exactly," John corrected. "It was the tree of the *knowledge* of good and evil. Think about it. Modern man is constantly immersing himself in movies, books, music and television that have a primary attraction of teaching new presentations of evil. Rarely do we find a popular story that does not focus on promiscuous sex or creative murder. And with the Internet, never before has each individual possessed so much power to destroy lives. Because of the knowledge found on the worldwide web, the terrorist bomb-maker, the crystal meth manufacturer and the porn star will be inciting mass murder, addiction and lust long after each dies from an explosion, an overdose or AIDS. Racists, pedophiles, radical atheists and anarchists can now access the stored knowledge of like-minded destroyers from around the world and throughout history. Nuclear, chemical and biological secrets will find their way into the hands of those whose goal is to bring suffering. It is truly a worldwide web, a spider's web. And the more man uses it to learn evil, the more he becomes entangled in it. Yes, this is the information age, the age of knowledge. Will you seek the knowledge of good or of evil? Pray that you will be ready for the coming test and remember that – with God – all things are possible."

"Mr. John," Worthington asked, "can you pray over these guys like you did me?"

The men all seemed to be agreeable, so John glanced over to D.J. Jefferson, who had been keeping an eye on them.

"Is that okay with you, Officer Jefferson?" John asked.

Once before, at a revival meeting, Jefferson had been "slain in the Spirit." He had found it to be a wonderfully positive experience. He did not object.

One by one, the inmates walked up to John. Worthington stood behind each man ready to catch him if he fell. As John prayed over them and laid his hands on them, some stiffened like a board and fell back, others went limp and collapsed, some didn't fall but remained standing in prayer, a couple dropped in twitching convulsions as demons fled from their bodies, and others were overwhelmed with joy and uncontrollable laughter. When the inmates had finished resting in the Spirit, they all rose and began telling each other of their experiences. All twelve of John's followers found it to be a profoundly Spiritual encounter, all of them except Jin.

Injustice is relatively easy to bear,
what stings is justice.
H. L. Mencken

35

Yashar Police Station
Yashar, NY
September 29

Tim Lassiter had been summoned to the Police Chief's office and had been warned that it would not be a friendly visit. The young detective was worried that he had now gone out on a limb by refusing to dismiss John Malek's story as the ravings of a lunatic. He had been able to keep John's fantastic tale from the press, but the office was buzzing with smirking disbelievers. He would even classify himself as a smirking disbeliever but, with a man's life on the line, he felt no stone should be left unturned. He just didn't have enough evidence to book John for murder. Lassiter had been allowed to hold John this long, without charges, because his identity and past were still a mystery. Could this man without a past be an illegal alien? A sex offender? An enemy combatant?

As soon as he spotted Lassiter approaching, the chief bellowed, "Get your ass in here, Tim."

Lassiter obediently went in and sat down. The chief tossed an opened envelope at him and asked, "What the hell is this?"

Lassiter pulled out an Italian invoice. He cringed.

"Chief, I had to check out Malek's story. This was for the investigation and DNA testing in Italy."

Chief Morrison picked up his mug. He had an annoying habit of stirring his coffee whenever he was mad. *Tink, tink, tink, tink...*

"Read it ... out loud," the chief grumbled.

Lassiter read, "For the following services rendered: DNA specialty team (two men) drove to site, located north alcove on the Milvian Bridge, repelled down to alcove, observed floor discoloration that appeared to be blood..."

Tink, tink, tink, tink, tink...

Lassiter continued reading: "... Conducted numerous scrapings of stone floor, returned to lab and conducted DNA analysis on scrapings. Conclusions: No DNA found. Area was discolored by a non-human source or the DNA has deteriorated by age or contamination. Radiocarbon dating not applicable."

Tink, tink, tink, tink, tink...

The detectives words became almost inaudible. "...2.5 hours driving time, 4.25 hours site time, 4 hours lab time. TOTAL: $5,375. Due upon receipt."

Tink... "Ya know, I oughta make you pay this ridiculous bill?" the chief growled.

"Chief I was proceeding on a hunch. Everything Malek has said..."

Chief Morrison shoved his mug onto the desk, spilling some of the coffee. "You haven't been around long enough to have hunches!" he shouted. "When you've seen as much as I have, then I'll let you play your hunches. But don't waste taxpayer dollars on them. We'll all go broke if you do."

"Yes, sir."

"Now, where do we stand? How many suspects have you got?"

"We've checked out a number of possibilities, but..."

"How many?"

"Just one," Lassiter admitted.

"Okay, time to turn the case over to the prosecutors. We got our man. It's foolish to waste more money on the investigation."

"Chief, it's just that there's no hard evidence that links him to the crime except that rosary."

"That's good enough for me."

"He's passed every polygraph test and voice stress analysis."

"Lunatics believe their crazy stories."

"No one who knows him believes that he did it."

"So? He's a charming lunatic. You got any witnesses who can vouch for his whereabouts at the time of the crime?"

"No, sir. It was the middle of the night."

"You got even an inkling of another person of interest?"

"No, sir."

"Then come on, man, grow up! The Devil didn't pop in there and kill her!"

Lassiter was blushing from embarrassment. The chief studied the young detective and felt a tinge of guilt for being so hard on him.

"Look, Tim. You're trying to do a good job. I appreciate that. In fact, you remind me a little of myself when I was your age. But you're too damn gullible for your own good. Enough! You're costing my department time and money. Hell, I've even got the Secretary of State's office breathing down my back on this one!"

"Secretary of State?"

"They got a burr up their butt for this guy."

"Hmmm."

"So, charge him. You got your man, and he ain't no apostle."

The ultimate test of a moral society
is the kind of world that it leaves to its children.
Dietrich Bonhoeffer

36

Greenbrier Hotel
White Sulfur Springs, WV
October 1

Evan Thas adjusted the Secretary's hair under the electro-encephalographic cap. He then maneuvered each of the 63 electrodes to try to insure that each one was secure against Angela's face and head. He realized cutting her hair would enhance connectivity but, under the circumstances, that was not practical.

Notwithstanding some of her occasional reservations, she had grown to trust these two men. She respected their determination to get things done no matter what obstacle confronted them. Their campaign assistance had proven to be priceless and their wisdom regarding human nature was remarkable. She thanked her lucky stars for their support and pitied whoever chose to side against them. They did not trifle with small favors and, once they offered to assist, one's choice was between trusting or fearing them.

The men had spent the first hour, this morning, explaining the importance of this exercise and the years of research that had formed the foundation for the top secret program called Titan. Cyst began by quoting Sun Tzu: "If you know the enemy and know yourself, you need not fear the result of a hundred battles. If you know yourself but not the enemy, for every victory gained you will suffer a defeat. If you know neither the enemy nor yourself, you will succumb in every battle."[1] He explained how the first step toward conquest was to develop an understanding of the enemy's way of thinking and he assured her that the dominant role of the Internet in this age of information allowed his proprietary technology to gain that advantage. But, just as important, Angela's innate leadership skills would have to be evaluated and, where necessary, improved upon. That was today's goal.

"Absolutely no pictures," the Secretary quipped as she adjusted her cap. "I look like a monster."

Sitting at the window, Cyst had been in deep thought while viewing the lush green golf course nestled between the Allegheny Mountains of rural West Virginia. He smiled and rolled over to the Secretary.

"Are you ready for this?" he asked.

The Secretary thought about how alone and vulnerable she was without staff or security. She had told them that her mother was sick and that she wanted to be alone with her for a couple of days. Then she diverted her trip to meet privately with Cyst and Thas under an assumed name. She had even donned a wig and enjoyed being a blond for a change.

"Just don't give me any electrical jolts," Angela responded.

"Okay, Madame Secretary," Thas took charge and opened a notebook computer on the table in front of her. "This will take about forty five minutes of concentration. Titan tracks brain wave stimulation in the limbic system and frontal cortices of your brain. That is where memory and emotional thoughts occur. You will be witnessing an audio/video presentation. Stay focused on the computer screen. Now, in your hand is a slide device. Push the lever up to register your degree of love for what you see and hear, down if you dislike or hate something. Stay towards the middle if you are indifferent. You see what I mean?"

She tipped her head as she slid the lever up and down.

"Okay. All the way up: love it. All the way down: hate it. Just slide to the level that matches the intensity of your feeling. Are you ready?"

She nodded without enthusiasm.

He placed headphones over her ears and pressed a computer key. Images and words streamed across the screen. Sounds, voices and music flooded her ears. She quickly started sliding the lever, trying to keep up with the frenetic pace of images.

For almost an hour, the two men quietly watched her reactions to sights and sounds of motherhood, faith, violence, leadership, sex, war, love, patriotism, sacrilege, punishment, family, race, fame, poverty, wealth, police, greed, hate, marriage, persecution, sloth, death, control, lust, power, abortion, rage, history, and on and on as the minutes passed. Angela's hand frantically jerked the lever, while the computer on the table, and its associated equipment, compiled and analyzed the data.

When the images finally stopped streaming, Angela took a deep breath. Within seconds, the printer that was attached to the computer started spitting out page after page.

"That was exhausting," she playfully complained.

"I find the exercise enlightening," Dr. Cyst suggested. "Don't you?"

"I'll let you know when my mind stops whirring. Holy cow! What a rush!"

The two men laughed as Thas began removing the electrode cap. "Madame Secretary?" Evan asked, "We'll need time to analyze the report. We have room service coming in an hour. Would you like to relax in your room while we go over this?"

"That would be great."

* * *

ALMOST TWO HOURS LATER, lunch was finished and the two men had not brought up the results yet.

"So, how did the test go?" Angela asked.

Thas and Cyst looked at each other and the doctor took the lead. "Well, Madame Secretary … not as good as we had hoped."

"Oh? What do you mean?"

"Madame Secretary," Thas responded quickly, "we think you're just great. And, if it were up to us, we wouldn't have you change a thing."

"But?" Angela nudged.

Cyst laid it out bluntly. "Your responses indicated a self-imposed limit on your leadership effectiveness."

"A 'self-imposed limit'? Gentlemen, I can assure you, I do not intend to hold myself back."

"Yes, Madame Secretary," Cyst remained blunt, "we all tend to believe that about ourselves, but it is usually not true. Based on your test results and our research, you will not accomplish much in the White House. Titan's assessment is that you will be your own worst enemy."

Angela laughed scornfully, "Are you joking?"

"Madame Secretary, please don't take this personally," Thas tried to soothe her.

"But I am!" she insisted. "Your little machine is saying I will fail as president!"

"No," the young man insisted, "it is saying you will fail as president if you do not change your leadership instincts. Madame Secretary, education is the answer… if you are willing to learn."

"Then by all means, gentlemen, educate me."

"Okay then," Cyst said confidently, "buckle your seatbelts."

The three of them pulled up around the table, ready for the long haul.[2]

Cyst began, "Madame Secretary, circumstances change but human nature remains constant. Thus, human history is a vast reservoir of examples on how to gain and retain power."

She nodded her agreement and he continued.

"The world consists of scarce resources and unlimited human wants. So, social conflict is inevitable. Never make the mistake of seeking to be loved. Being feared is much more important. Love is fickle and forgetful. The dreaded fear of punishment, however, never recedes. Since men love as they will and fear according to the will of the leader, it is better to govern by factors you control rather than those controlled by another. Seek not the love of the people. Seek only to avoid arousing their hatred. You cannot govern effectively with a sympathetic heart. For your purposes, it is the ultimate vice."

Cyst paused for Thas to take the lead. "Madame Secretary, you can never be a great leader without mastering the art of deceptive self-promotion. Those of us who understand the world from a pragmatic perspective realize that deception is the one essential ingredient for political success. Surely, Madame Secretary, you believe in the vital importance of your programs for the benefit of the people you represent."

"Of course."

"So, there is nothing wrong with a lie that furthers your agenda for the greater good. Speak with certainty, but act opportunistically. And never be caught without a good excuse for changing your story. Frankly, men are so controlled by their present wants that the one who deceives can always attract those who are willing to be deceived. People don't want truth, they want comfort."

Cyst jumped back into the discussion, "At least by appearances, try to walk in the path of good. But, whenever necessity dictates, never fail to detour into what the simpleminded call 'evil.' Am I making you uncomfortable, Madame Secretary?"

"No," Angela responded cautiously, "go on."

Cyst continued, "Appear to possess kindness, mercy, faith and integrity. People judge more with their eyes and ears than their minds. Everyone sees what you appear to be, not what you are. So, preach peace and faith but never let them get in your way.

"Generally, as long as you do not deprive a man of his property or honor, you can live in peace with him. The only exception to this rule is the man of ambition. The man of ambition is always a major opponent and must be controlled or destroyed. Control him by learning his vices. Destroy him by exposing those vices. But, once he is defeated, test your enemy with offers of patronage. His defeat will have afforded him an understanding of a future without power. If he has been properly humbled, he will remain your servant as long as he understands that all power is on loan from you.

"Seek neutrality from opponents, but avoid giving it. Irresolution leads to ruin. Let it exist in the mind of your opponent, not your own."

Thas resumed the lesson, "There are three types of intelligence: one can decipher complexity on its own, the second can learn what others have discovered, and the third neither understands by itself nor through the intelligence of others. Seek to monopolize the talents of those rare individuals in the first category, seek to control and educate the second, and seek to learn the addictions and emotions of the third to exploit their weaknesses. Like lemmings off a cliff, you may lead them wherever you want. In fact, the third category of mankind is the most valuable to a leader because they may be counted on to disrupt or even riot, whenever necessary.

"Forget the dream of eliminating political hostilities. Inevitably, there will be friction between those who wish to maintain and those who wish to acquire. Rely on the fact that people will always turn out badly for you unless some necessity makes them good. And remember that they are much more pressed by current needs than by favors of the past."

Again, Cyst took the lead. "There are only two ways to treat men of power: either pamper them or dispose of them. Middling efforts will allow them to avenge themselves for minor offenses.

"Injuries should be inflicted all at once for one big blow does less damage to your repustation than ten moderate ones, over time. Benefits, on the other hand, should be distributed by piecemeal so that they may be savored more fully at a leisurely pace.

"It is relatively simple to satisfy the masses. Their desires are modest. More difficult, is the goal of satisfying the powerful. Their desires are unlimited. The former group seeks little more than not to be oppressed; the latter, requires oppression.

"One can never go wrong advocating change and reform. People desire novelty to such an extent that those who are doing wellwish for change as much as those who are doing badly.

Thas bounced back in on the lesson. "History does not move in a linear direction but, rather, in a circular one. Nietzsche wrote, 'Extreme positions are not succeeded by moderate ones, but by contrary extreme positions.' So, it is important that our entire communications effort focuses on branding everything our opponents say and do as having extreme and evil intentions. Thus, when the time is right, we may impose whatever measures that we deem necessary as a response to the extreme policies of the past.

"Never play by your enemies rules. It is said, the man who does not know how to fence confuses one who does. So, do not limit yourself to 'fair play.' Play to win. Play for keeps. Confuse your enemies by writing your own rules.

"Madame Secretary, you say you won't hold yourself back. Let me ask you something: Are you willing to lie, maybe even violate the law, to get what you want?"

Angela responded hesitantly, "Well, uh, yeah, I guess so."

"No!" Cyst barked. "Never admit an incriminating truth to more than one witness. Whether in a court of law or of public opinion, someone of your stature will be believed contradicting one traitor, but not two."

Embarrassed, she responded, "I just thought I could trust…"

"You can't!" Cyst interrupted. "Trust only one person at a time. If you must have an incriminating talk, do it one-on-one. In larger meetings, listen, hedge, or defer, but never incriminate yourself."

Thas continued, "Madame Secretary, Machiavelli once wrote, 'If a prince truly seeks worldly glory, he should hope to possess a corrupt city.' So, Washington, DC is perfect. Possess it! Don't make the mistake of most presidents who retire finally realizing that they should have loved less and deceived more. If you want love, get a dog. Instead, seize control. Seize it viciously, if necessary, or seize it viciously just as a warning to enemies. But seize it!"

Cyst added, "Your surrogates must personalize everything, Madame Secretary. They will not be 'government' programs, anymore. They will be 'Angela's' programs: 'Angela's college tuition tax credit,' 'Angela's low-income housing assistance,' 'Angela's school lunch program,' 'Angela's Social Security cost-of-living increase.' When Senator Blight proposes to restrain or oppose your programs, your allies should never hesitate to attack personally: 'Blight must hate the homeless … Blight believes only the rich deserve higher education … Blight wants school children to go hungry … Seniors will suffer and die under Blight's right wing schemes.' By the time we're through with Blight, his own mother will despise him."

Angela hadn't budged throughout that tag-team match. After a moment of thought she said, "Wow, you've given me a lot to think about.

It's … it's really a new way to think about governing effectively. I mean … I'm playing with the big boys, now. This is the White House we're talking about. If I play by my old rules … I'll lose."

Cyst asked, "Are you comfortable with what we've said?"

"Yeah," she nodded, "I get your point. It's time to play for keeps. I'll make the rules … or should I say …" as she changed to an attitude of role-playing, "I have some strong misgivings with your ideas. I'll talk to you about it, one-on-one, tomorrow."

"Exactly," Thas applauded.

When they parted, Angela was ebullient. It was as if she had been given the keys to the kingdom. She now realized that no love, no rules, and no truth would bind her anymore. She would love whoever served her purposes. She would write her own rules. She and her public relations team, alone, would establish what would be true.

And, as the two men closed the door behind her, they too were excited. They had gained her complete confidence. But, more importantly, Titan had developed a psychological profile of Angela that mapped even the darkest recesses of her mind. They now would know her every fear, desire, hatred, pride, shame, prejudice, love, disgust, envy, rage, torment, sympathy, longing and lust. Like her, Cyst and Thas realized that no love, law or truth would limit their actions and, like a lemming at the cliff, they would lead her, now, wherever they wanted.

SIX DAYS LATER, fat and greasy Luke Skelton left his new condo to walk his new puppy. He was in a very good mood, for a change. While watching the dog sniff around a fire hydrant, Luke hummed an old tune from a happy song. He stopped when a 9 mm hollow-point bullet entered the back of his head.

Two Years Later

The destructive capacity of the individual,
however vicious, is small;
of the state, however well-intentioned, almost limitless.
Paul Johnson

37

White House
Washington, DC
June 8

Hundreds of times, predictions of the imminent end of life as we know it have gained a popular following. Of course, none of those forecasts proved true. Still, this time, a pervasive pall had shrouded the globe causing widespread concern that mankind might be beginning a chaotic and bloody crescendo of conflict.

Under the masterful, but invisible, direction of Cyst and Thas, Angela had won a close victory in last November's election. The two strategists discretely rode both horses during the race, assisting their campaigns and sizing up not only the candidates but also their staffs. Then, just as Blight opened up a seemingly unstoppable double-digit lead in the polls, he seemed to become hopelessly uncooperative with Evan. Within a week, XBC News interviewed one of Blight's young male interns who revealed the sordid details of an affair. Blight was so stunned by the bogus tabloid allegations that his entire campaign was knocked off track.

While Blight was playing campaign checkers, Thas was playing chess.

As Election Day neared, Angela had almost pulled even with the senator. However, her running mate, a ticket balancing southern preacher, had been no help at all. Then Angela had a stroke of good luck. It was that stroke that killed her running mate.

Scrambling for a replacement that would dazzle the American imagination, Evan hatched a brilliant scheme. At her running mate's funeral, Angela announced that, if she won, she would heal the nation from this divisive political contest and name Senator Blight to serve as her vice president. The offer was reported as a gracious gesture that symbolized the post-partisan politics that her administration would give to the American people. The move also would effectively muzzle Blight - a man who knew where all the skeletons are buried on Capitol Hill - and keep him on the sidelines.

Check and mate.

Blight's staff and financial supporters realized that the alternative was the political wilderness and so they welcomed Angela's offer. That momentum carried her into the White House.

The election year had seen unprecedented economic turmoil and predictions of civil unrest and war. In fact, news coverage now seemed to be an unending commentary on wars and rumors of wars.[1]

Most analysts were starting to understand that America's mortgage lending policies had triggered the meltdown that expanded into the broader American markets and then globally. Like a virus, the contagion spread from sub-prime loans, to prime, and even into sovereign debt guarantees. However, it appeared to some at the time that unprecedented government spending had stimulated the economy and saved the day. The trumpeted and expensive "economic jump start" was short-lived, but the additional national debt burden was not. Soon, in addition to waves of home foreclosures, condominium complexes were collapsing from Miami to Seattle. Then declining mall sales caused high-end anchor stores to refuse to renew their leases, so, smaller mall stores fell like dominoes. Many of America's previously most thriving areas now looked like ghost towns and ghost malls.

True to form, the largest banking institutions again were claiming that the global economy would collapse if they did not receive the new bailout that they sought. But unstoppable deficit spending, this time, caused the demand for American Treasury Bonds to dry up. The Federal Reserve Bank was caught in a rate trap in which raising interest rates would further slow the sick economy, but keeping rates stable was crushing the value of the dollar. In fact, the dollar had already declined drastically and precious metals had shot up in value. Regardless, the strategy of stimulating economic growth with rate cuts was now impossible to implement. For too many years, the Federal Reserve Bank had kept rates at record lows, enriching their banking friends as asset bubbles inflated. Now, however, Central bankers had no more bullets left in their arsenal for monetary stimulus.

Internationally, one country after another had developed unsustainable debt burdens in recent years. Of particular concern were the European countries known in international financial circles as the PIIGS: Portugal, Ireland, Italy, Greece and Spain. They first sought European Union support from the stronger EU economies. Then, appealing to the lender of last resort, the International Monetary Fund, the PIIGS found themselves forced to initiate such draconian cutbacks in government spending that civil unrest, riots and strikes were becoming common. From Athens to Bangkok, urban warfare was breaking out and even the IMF alternative had become depleted. Everyone was forced to realize that long-standing financial backstops had collapsed and the EU was on the verge of breaking apart.

The Chinese communist leadership was becoming increasingly belligerent as the global economy slowed and their historic construction boom ended. Unemployment for young Chinese males had skyrocketed and, magnifying that problem, was the shortage of women that had resulted from the country's family planning and forced abortion practices. Now, hundreds of millions of men had no jobs and tens of millions would never find a wife. The Chinese leadership feared that this excess of testosterone could soon be channeled into a new revolution. They knew that they could never survive if the unemployed rural masses started flooding into the cities. So, finding an enemy to demonize, and sacrificing 50 million young men to the god of war, had become not only a practical but, perhaps, even a desirable strategy for the regime.

The unending growth of governments, both foreign and domestic, had foreshadowed the inevitable day of fiscal reckoning. Like shameless credit card hucksters, politicians had learned the "buy now, pay later" pitch and Americans loved them for it ... until it became time to pay. Mirroring the eventual but inevitable exhaustion of phosphate on Nauru, the money just ran out. Americans had been gambling that future generations someday would figure out how to solve the problems. They had bet wrong.

Even states, cities and counties were now failing. Pension plans for retired government employees had proven impossible to honor. Tax increases to meet those obligations were negated by higher rates of tax evasion, business closings and job losses. The same retirement uncertainty was being discovered by many union retirees. Regulators had exposed that union pension plans were 13 times more likely than their nonunion counterparts to have alarmingly low funding of 65% or less.[2] With a tsunami of entitlement spending soon engulfing America as the "baby boom" generation prepared to cash in on retirement, everyone was finally beginning to realize that the "if it feels good, do it" lifestyle ultimately comes with a price.

Everyone under 50 now complained about the high cost of providing for an aging population, but few realized that the 50 million Americans who had been aborted could now have been supporting those senior citizens. No easy choices were left. American retirements, it seemed, had been built on a vast array of Ponzi schemes.

Those who most hungered for centralized power over others, found an ally in chaos. Radical environmentalists, Islamists, neo-Nazis, communists and other opportunists, at home and abroad, were using the global recession as a pretext for taking their fight to the streets. Western European democracies were particularly at risk. Especially in the big cities, crime had become ubiquitous. Some sections of towns had become so hostile to the local police and firefighters that they had little choice but to declare them "no-go zones." Consequently, they were being transformed into violent urban jungles. For businesses that remained open, bosses were now being kidnapped and held for ransom. Banks and even grocery stores were rarely open. In response, right-wing groups organized to burn Qur'ans and harrass or attack anyone who did not look or act like themselves. People resorted to growing their own food whenever they had access to a back yard or a rooftop garden, but night-time thefts of produce brought most of those efforts to naught.

On the geopolitical front, an alliance of communst and oil-rich Muslim countries were putting unprecedented pressure on America and Israel, especially at the United Nations.

By Election Day, voters had been ready for a fresh face from outside Washington. The common refrain of the Angelistas was, "It can't get any worse."

Today, however, many of her supporters had become disheartened because the economic slide had continued, unabated. Still, tonight, those problems would not be the most pressing. Things were about to get worse … much worse.

***

PRESIDENT CONCEPCION had called a midnight emergency security meeting at the White House because of the alarming reports coming out of the Middle East. In attendance were White House staff, Congressional leaders, Cabinet Secretaries, the intelligence hierarchy and the Joint Chiefs of Staff.

The President spoke from the head of the table. "I know we all have a lot of questions and very few answers. I also know that time is pressing. However, I want us all to be reading from the same page. Carla, what do you have for us first?"

The Director of National Intelligence, Carla Perkins, was Angela's old roommate from their Berkeley years. She had been one of the President's most controversial appointments because of her lack of experience in intelligence gathering and analysis. However, the President insisted on having someone in the position that she could trust.

Cyst and Thas had screened and recommended every member of her staff and every political appointment. Each had been profiled by the Titan battery of tests, the psychological screening device that XCyst Industries was still operating in secret.

"Madame President, ladies and gentlemen," Carla began as she opened her documents. "We have pulled together the following assessment of the situation in Saudi Arabia. Credible reports indicate that, over the last twenty-four hours, there has been a massive personal security breach in the Kingdom. Mysterious biological agents appear to be attacking every Saudi palace. Of the seven thousand Saudi Royals, we believe that half have been seriously infected, and a third of them are dead."

Audible gasps filled the room.

The DNI continued, "As bad as that sounds, we believe this bio attack is in its early stages."

Stunned silence prevailed until Angela remembered that she was leading the meeting. "Dr. Willoughby, what about what you've seen?"

The Director of the National Institutes of Health stood and offered this summary: "We have very sketchy information but the symptoms appear to point to a highly potent biological agent in the *Filoviridae* family. These viruses cause viral hemorrhagic fevers characterized by bleeding and coagulation abnormalities, often leading to hypovolemic shock and death. This particular virus shows signs of being linked to the Ebola virus but has demonstrated a lethality exceeding even that of the Zaire Ebola strain. In terms of symptom development rapidity, I have never seen anything like it. Also, it is baffling to me how a biological agent has been so narrowly and effectively targeted at the Royal Family. These things can take years to incubate and reach this level of lethality."

"General Brodderick," Angela inquired, "what do you have for us?"

The Chairman of the Joint Chiefs grumbled, "We don't have much to go on, yet. However, a focused, simultaneous attack on the palaces, that spares all surrounding buildings and civilians … that's just mind boggling. I don't see a rationalization for this being a state-sponsored attack, and I don't see how a non-state-sponsor would have the capability to pull it off. Hell, I don't even know how we could pull it off. But we're working on it. I promise you, we'll get to the bottom of it in short order."

Vice President Blight jumped into the debate, pleased that his opinion might finally be needed. "What about securing the oil? We have to assume the motive here is oil."

"Mr. Vice President," the general responded to his friend, "it will take a little time to mobilize, but we can seize control of those oil fields and that country, with two divisions, in … two weeks."

"Hell, this could be a blessing in disguise," Blight added.

The general looked at the other Joint Chiefs and they

nodded their agreement. Then his cell phone vibrated and the General turned in his chair to quietly answer it.

"Hudson, what do you think?" the President asked.

The Secretary of State responded, "We know there are a lot of people who would like to see the Princes dead … oppressed women, immigrant workers, even the Shi'ite minority have plenty of reasons. And that horny Abdullah has had over fifty wives. So you have at least fifty prime suspects right…"

"Son of a bitch!" The general shouted into his cell phone. "Are you sure? Have you verified this?"

The conference room suddenly became completely quiet, except for the excited, muffled voice on the other end of the General's call. Then he responded, "Listen, you contact me the second you know more."

He ended the call and growled, "Twenty minutes ago, those Saudi bastards triggered Petro SE!"

Around the room, Angela studied how each face reacted with either an ignorant frown or sheer terror. She heard people mumbling words that she had never before heard in one of her meetings: prayers. Suddenly, she sensed a spirit of impending doom in the room and, perhaps, in the world.

The President was embarrassed to ask, but had to know, "What is Petro SE?"[3]

PRESIDENT CONCEPCION HAD CALLED a fifteen minute recess. During that time, everyone was to report back to their departments for updates. She requested an immediate briefing on Petro SE from General Brodderick. But, hoping to stay on top of new developments – and inwardly chafing at having to report to an ignorant neophyte – he demurred, asking if she would allow his assistant, a Middle Eastern specialist, to brief her instead. She agreed and escorted the young aide into a side room.

"Okay, Corporal Simmons," she directed, "General Brodderick says you're his go-to guy on the Middle East. We have fifteen minutes. Bring me up to speed on the Saudis and Petro SE."

"Yes Madam President," he said, somewhat nervously. "If I may begin with some background … Saudi Arabia has about a quarter of the world's oil reserves. They produce about eight million barrels of oil a day. Because the oil there is close to the surface it can be drilled much more cheaply than in places like the United States. Through most of the 1990s, a barrel could be drilled there for about fifty cents. It costs more now but is still well under three dollars a barrel. Eventually, as much as a trillion barrels will be recovered from under the Saudi sands. The unique, porous limestone under the Arabian peninsula is the richest oil-bearing rock on the planet."

"Okay," she said, "but what about the relevant geopolitical history?"

"The defining moment in America's relationship with Saudi Arabia came on October 6, 1973. In Israel, it was *Yom Kippur,* the holiest day of the Jewish calendar and the day that Egypt and Syria chose to launch a massive military strike on Israel. Because of the holiday, Israel was caught off-guard and the previously ineffective invading forces made surprising gains in the first week.

"Consistent with the religious politics of what is sometimes called 'Muhammad's Gold,' Arab nations – particularly Saudi Arabia – and the major oil companies in bed with them, demanded that the Nixon Administration deny assistance to Israel. With the sole exception of the Netherlands, Western European nations buckled to the pressure and froze previously scheduled military shipments and refused to grant over-flight access or refueling rights in any effort to resupply Israel.

"Despite the extreme pressure, within a week America was resupplying the Israeli cause and, after three days of receiving help,

Israel turned the tide. Israel retook the Golan Heights and, with clear-momentum in their favor, was marching toward Damascus and Cairo. Then, in an effort to placate the Arab states, America demanded that Israel halt their offensive. Israel had no choice but to comply.

"However, saving the provocateurs from a devastating defeat was not enough to satisfy the Saudis. Immediately, OPEC raised the price of oil by seventy percent. Then they adopted a proposal to cut oil production in monthly increments until Israel withdrew from the occupied territories. For even greater effect, the Saudis and other Arab countries announced an embargo on their oil shipments to the United States. The embargo precipitated America's deepest recession since the Great Depression.

"Oil cost three dollars a barrel in October of 1973. Within a decade, the price had shot up ten-fold and Saudi profits had zoomed fifty-fold. Yet, the Saudis still felt extremely insecure, both from internal revolt and external attack. Considering the value of oil in the U.S. economy, they had always counted on the protection of American forces if and when they ever needed it. However, they had also witnessed how a turn in American politics had caused an abandonment of the Shah of Iran. So, the House of Saud reasoned it needed an insurance policy that would make the abandonment option unthinkable. They decided to make an internal revolt or an external attack pointless."

"Petro SE?" she inquired.

"Yes, ma'am. Petro SE stands for 'Petroleum Scorched Earth.' It was given that name in American classified documents after the NSA intercepted communications in 1986 of Saudi diplomats describing their secret plans. For all these years, many of our intelligence analysts have not taken the threat seriously and have even scoffed at the idea as a brilliant Saudi scam.

"The name was taken from Hitler's Plan B apocalyptic fantasy. Rather than allow the Allies to take his homeland, Hitler would leave them only 'Scorched Earth.'

"The idea came about in the kingdom after the Saudi Royal Family heard rumblings, in diplomatic circles, that America would never allow another oil embargo. Instead, America would simply invade the lightly protected kingdom and take the oil fields. Whether that was a bluff or not, I don't know. However, it certainly got the Saudi's attention. So, contemplating the possibility of an attack, and after rejecting more modest defensive countermeasures like setting the wells on fire or destroying infrastructure, the House of Saud chose to concoct a massive network of devices consisting of Semtex, and rubidium, cesium 137, or strontium 90."

The President interrupted, "Corporal Simmons, are you saying dirty bombs?"

"Yes ma'am … Radioactivity will contaminate each site for at least a decade … probably more like two or three … The area will become a dead zone. The oil will be worthless."

She pieced it all together, "So, the Saudis must have concluded a leadership decapitation strike was in progress. Rather than give up their resources, they detonated Petro SE."

"Yes ma'am. I'm no oil trader, but my guess is that oil will trade tomorrow north of six hundred dollars a barrel."

Angela sat quietly staring at the aide. Her mind was racing with the implications of one quarter of the world's oil supply now radioactive. She considered the economic consequences of oil trading overnight at two hundred times its 1973 price. She could see that military contingency planning was now in order but so much was still unknown.

One question would not leave her head: *Who did this?*

This is what the Lord says,
"Do not learn the ways of the nations
or be terrified by signs in the sky,
though the nations are terrified by them."
Jeremiah 10:2

38

NASA Heliophysics Division
Boulder, Colorado
June 8

The two young physicists sat across the table from each other. For almost an hour, now, she had been studying his card playing technique while he studied that her large, green eyes and full lips contrasted with her anorexic-thin body. Around them some of the world's most sophisticated equipment hummed and buzzed, even at this late hour. Monitoring solar plasma, solar radiation and how the Earth's magnetosphere responds to solar activity required this facility to operate 24/7.

Dr. Tilda Lars was dressed as if ready for a snow storm, with a hat, scarf, coat and gloves. Chad Boyle, on the other hand was down to his boxer shorts and undershirt.

"You got any..." he ventured, "queens?"

She smiled. "Go fish."

He picked a card from the deck and grumbled a profanity.

She looked over the one card in her hand and asked, "You got any fours?"

"Crikey! How do you do that?" He reluctantly passed her three fours and she laid her entire hand on the table.

She gave him a probing stare and said, "Okay. Next."

He started to pull his T-shirt over his head but was interrupted when an alarm buzzed loudly. Both physicists quickly moved to the other side of the room and when they got to the monitors the alarm stopped.

"What was that?" he asked.

"I don't know. I think we just lost our satellite connection."

"That's weird. I never heard of that, before."

"Check the STEREO charts," she directed. STEREO stood for Solar Terrestrial Relations Observatory. The program consisted of two solar satellites that monitored the sun's surface activity from opposite sides, giving mankind a thirty minute "heads up" whenever severe solar activity occurred.

He grabbed a printout and studied its seismographic lines. "Whoa! Look at this."

She cast her more experienced eyes on the chart squiggles that suddenly indicated a burst of activity on the surface of the sun. "Coronal mass ejection … X-class solar flare … Holy cow, X28!" She reviewed more data and whispered, "That's scary." Then Tilda sat in front of another computer and tapped the keys. "I'm gonna see where that was."

She knew that the sun was moving into the more active phase of its 22 year solar weather cycle and that a surprise century-class solar storm could disrupt smart power grids, satellites, air travel, financial services, and even emergency communications. One of those bursts could cause more damage than twenty Hurricane Katrinas.

"I guess we've been living right," she said with a scared smile.

"What?" he asked impatiently.

"We're not in the line of fire ... It's headed out into space."

They nervously grinned at each other, pumped to have experienced their first near-miss.

"How big was it?" he asked.

As she continued to study the data streaming across her screen, she tried to recollect the details of the so-called Carrington event of 1859 that fried telegraph lines across Europe and the United States. Her smile disappeared. She couldn't believe she was answering with the words: "Millennium-class."

Everything that exists
deserves to perish.
Mephistopheles
in Goethe's Faust

39

Oval Office
The White House
June 9

The intercom buzzed and Angela jolted awake. She did not answer it immediately. As she raised her head from the desk, she reoriented herself, noticing that she had drooled on a document.

She had been dreaming the same nightmare that had been interrupting her sleep more and more. She was trapped in a black sack, trying to kick and punch her way out to freedom. Over and over, she screamed, "Please, help me escape!" But no sound penetrated the dense liquid around her. No one came to her aid.

The intercom buzzed again and she answered, "Yes, Betsy."

"I'm sorry Madame President, there's been a tragedy."

"What?" Angela asked angrily. "What!?"

"Your mother … she passed away. She must have fallen in the shower. A neighbor found her a couple days later."

Angela breathed a sigh of relief. "Okay. Make sure you look after the funeral arrangements. Send a large spray of flowers and my condolences. Make sure you contact the media about my 'tragic loss,' 'extreme shock,' you know what I mean."

Angela hung up the phone. She rubbed her eyes and fingered through her hair. After sleeping all night at her desk, it was now mid-morning on Sunday.

The full extent of the Petro SE damage had not been determined. But, here in America, a fringe Christian group had enflamed passions by publicly burning Qurans.

Overseas, all that was known, so far, was that the Royal Family infection rates and deaths continued unabated. Food and air contamination had been ruled out, so, doctors in the kingdom surmised that the biological agent must have been sprayed on objects such as door knobs, silverware and royal telephones. With nothing else to go on, they could only recommend frequent hand washing to minimize the spread of the virus.

The President had communicated her condolences through diplomatic channels to the Saudi Royal Family on behalf of the American people and pledged her support for finding the perpetrators of the biological attack. She received no response.

Now, her primary concern was in trying to narrow down the list of potential terrorists or terrorist organizations. She felt that she could not determine criminal intent until she had a criminal in mind. And, until she knew the intent behind this heinous act, she could not know what apocalyptic game America was entering into this time.

She had ordered her tutor, Corporal Simmons, to report to the Oval Office and he had just arrived.

"Okay Simmons," she hurried, discarding with formalities, "I can give you about twelve minutes but I need a lot of information. Specifically, I want to know what groups have the means and motive for this mass murder."

"Madam President, I may be a little disorganized but here's the way I see it. If the plan was to take control of the Saudi oil supply, it failed miserably. If, on the other hand, it was to create global chaos, this diabolical plan succeeded brilliantly. Unfortunately, I believe we are dealing with the latter scenario.

"At any one time the Saudis have up to thirty thousand guards protecting their oil infrastructure. They even constructed a multimillion-dollar, state-of-the-art war bunker, for the Royal

Family, that is capable of withstanding nuclear, biological and chemical weapons. Consequently, it would be foolish for an enemy to believe he could overwhelm the Saudi defenses and protections. A successful plan would require the House of Saud to actually choose to annihilate their oil fields themselves. However, finding the perpetrators will not be easy because so many groups have one or more motives.

"The biological attack could have been inspired by the kingdom's Shi'ite minority that is concentrated in the oil rich province of Hasa. It accounts for 98% of the country's oil production. Whenever Shi'ite/ Sunni tensions flare, as they did when Shi'ite dominated Iran went nuclear, the kingdom gets nervous about its oilfields. Authorizing flyover rights for Israel to attack Iran was a major slap for the ayatollahs. Further, there is a powerful Shi'ite faction controlling the Iranian government that seeks the speedy return of the *Mahdi,* the Twelfth Imam. He will lead, they believe, a world-wide bloodbath in which the infidels will either convert to Shi'ite-style Islam or die a violent death at their hands. The global chaos sparked by the Saudi tragedy could be the pretext they need for initiating this apocalyptic war."

"You think they actually believe all that stuff?"

"I do. Suicide bombers are a good indication of how strongly they believe it. President Ahmadinejad insists, 'Our revolution's main mission is to pave the way for the reappearance of the Twelfth Imam.'[1] His chief strategist, Hassan Abassi, has said, 'We have a strategy drawn up for the destruction of the Anglo-Saxon civilization … There are twenty-nine sensitive sites in the U.S. and the West. We have already spied on these sites and we know how we are going to attack them.' Ahmadinejad is clear about his intentions. He says, 'We don't shy away from declaring that Islam is ready to rule the world. We must prepare ourselves to rule the world.' In their eyes, America is the Great Satan.

Israel is the Little Satan.

"Yes, but that's just bluster. What would placate them?"

"Madam President, Hussein Massawi, the former Hezbollah leader probably described their sentiments best when he was asked about Israel. He answered, 'We are not fighting so that you will give us something. We are fighting to eliminate you.'"

"Hmmm … go on."

"The point I want to emphasize is that this is not just philosophical for Ahmadinejad. He claims that he has been in contact with, and instructed by, the *Mahdi.* He believes that the end of the world is rapidly approaching."

Angela sighed deeply. "Oh boy."

"Also, I don't believe we can rule out the kingdom's female population. The attack might have been internally conducted by a conspiracy including women who are either on staff or in the Royal Family itself. The religious rules against Saudi women have always been among the strictest in the world. On March 14, 2000, for example, a fire broke out in a girls' school in Mecca. While the girls were attempting to escape the burning building, the religious police showed up and stopped many of them from exiting because they were not wearing the head scarves and black robes required by the kingdom's laws. One witness reported seeing three policemen 'beating young girls to prevent them from leaving the school…' Fifteen girls died, that night, and more than fifty were injured. No disciplinary action or prosecutions ever resulted from the incident.[2] By the way, the purchase of wives is still condoned in the kingdom. However, I believe that the women in the kingdom would lack the capabilities to pull this off alone. Consequently, if they are involved, they must have conspired with one or more other parties.

"A third possibility is that it could have been an Israeli attack. In every way the Saudis have supported the destruction of Israel. The hatred that the House of Saud has had for the Jews is fanatical. King Faisal, for example, was a believer in, and promoter of, the widely discredited anti-Semitic forgery, *Protocols of the Learned Elders of Zion.* Among many other fabrications, he believed that the Jews murder Christian and Muslim children so they can drain their blood and use it in their religious ceremonies. Perhaps, the Israelis were ignorant of Petro SE and believed that, with the House of Saud eliminated, America would have no choice but to take the oilfields. In one blow, the Israelis would have transferred the ownership of the world's most valuable asset from their sworn enemy to a friend.

"Fourth, it could be from zealous Saudi Wahhabis, similar to Osama bin Laden, who have rebelled against the decadent ways of their rulers. Wahhabism is the strictest sect of Sunni Islam and the branch upon which the kingdom was founded. There, the slightest deviation from accepted religious custom is punished severely. However, it is no secret that many members of the Royal Family travel extravagantly all over the world and are known to have lifestyles when they travel that are, to put it mildly, inconsistent with Wahhabist teaching. Around the globe, thousands of Saudi funded *madrassas,* or religious schools, have infused their students with the intolerant, radical teachings of the Wahhabi sect. A 1996 CIA report concluded that one third of all Saudi charities were linked to terrorism. Many still are today. I don't think it is too far of a stretch to suggest that radicals who are trained to seek the destruction of Christians and Jews may seek the same for those rulers who, they believe, denigrate their faith.

"Fifth, it could be an internal power struggle in the Royal Family. At the death of King Fahd, Crown Prince Abdullah rose to the throne. However, he does not have the unequivocal support of Fahd's six full brothers and their sons. It is well known that severe divisions have occurred in the House of Saud from time to time. Even among the princes, there are extremists who despise the pragmatists. But, until now, money has always bought peace. In 1998, for example, the Saudi Royals approved a $10 million "donation" to Osama bin Laden with the understanding that he would henceforth focus his attacks on America and not the kingdom. Don't forget that fifteen of the nineteen 9/11 hijackers were Saudis. Six of them went through religious recruitment while living in the kingdom. Have the extremists now attempted to commandeer the moral pulpit and levers of power? Did their plan, perhaps, backfire?"

"Jeez, no short list," she interjected. "What about Russia?"

"Yes, ma'am, it could have been a Russian/Iranian conspiracy. The new Russian hard-liners may be stepping up their nuclear parnership combining Russian nuclear supply with Iranian nuclear demand. They are allied for the first time in their long histories. Taking out a large part of the Sunni supply of oil would give the Iranians and the Russians a strangle-hold on the planet's life blood. Perhaps, they calculated the risk that enemies might declare war on them, but how would they move their troops, fly their planes, or sail their ships without oil? The Saudis have long angered the Russians by financing Sunni rebellion in southern Russia, particularly in Uzbekistan and the war-ravaged region of Chechnya.

"Or, it could be from a corrupt deal gone bad. The days, during the embargo, of suitcases filled with cash being passed around Riyadh hotels may no longer exist. But, to this day, bribery is widespread in the kingdom. Perhaps a viciously sophisticated enterprise like the Japanese *Yakuza* or the Russian *Mafia* paid for a deal that was not honored. Keep in mind, these bribes are not inconsequential. An American company once paid a Saudi middleman over $106 million in 'commissions.'

"Finally, and perhaps scariest of all, is the possibility that this has been orchestrated from American soil. Either it could be originating from rogue elements in the CIA or from private interests who have something to gain."

"Why is that the scariest?" the President asked.

"It just hate the thought that we may have an enemy in our ranks and I fear the convulsion if America is blamed. Half the Islamic schools and mosques here were built with Saudi funds. It may not be politically correct to point this out but the facts speak for themselves. In 2000, a survey of 1,200 mosques in the U.S., undertaken by four Muslim groups, found that 70% of *imams* were favorably inclined toward fundamentalist teachings and almost a quarter taught strict Wahhabism. Radicals, even here in America, have preached that it is the duty of every Muslim to wage *jihad* against infidels, Zionist crusaders, and apostates.[3] Something like this could ignite the holy war. Who knows?"

President Concepcion asked, "Of course, this is a devastating blow to their country. But is there any element of society there that can exert a stabilizing force?"

"I don't think so. Despite the common misconception that Saudi Arabia is a wealthy country, the kingdom has been running deficits for over two decades. A third of the children are not in school. A water shortage is beginning to take its toll. Fundamentalists, like bin Laden, are continually increasing in number. The youth population has doubled in the last twenty years and the standard of living and quality of life has drastically dropped. In fact, per capita income has collapsed to one quarter of what it was in 1981. There are no freedoms of speech, press and assembly, or right to a speedy trial, in the kingdom and elections are so rigged that only 10% of the population vote. Acting 'suspicious' regularly can place you in jail and, often, subject to horrendous torture[4] … No, Madame President, I don't see any stabilizing influences."

"What about the Saudi people?" she asked.

"For over a thousand years, the only thing that held the Arabian tribes together was Islam. In some ways, I can't help but admire their dedication to their faith. They get on their knees and pray five times a day, fast throughout the holy month of *Ramadan* and, sometimes under extreme hardship, make their pilgrimage to Mecca. Islam is not just a faith – it is their way of life. Too bad most Christians don't truly live our faith. However, there is also the dark side of Islam.[5] Slavery, for example, flourished in Saudi Arabia even until the 1970's. Children were routinely sold into slavery and prostitution. The annual pilgrimage to Mecca was the primary source of human chattel particularly from poor Sudanese and Nigerian pilgrims who had to sell their children in order to finance their return home. Saudi textbooks teach: 'It is compulsory for Muslims to be loyal to each other and to consider the infidels their enemy.' But, by 'enemy,' they even mean Muslims who do not follow their Wahhabi teachings. American black Muslims, for example, have often been denied entrance into the kingdom because..."

The President's telephone intercom buzzed and a voice announced, "Madame President, the Secretary of Defense has arrived." And with that interruption, they thanked each other and the corporal departed.

As he left the Oval Office, Angela reflected on how much she had once wanted this job and how quickly things had changed. Transforming the world was infinitely more difficult than she had ever imagined. Her economic initiatives were floundering. She had tried her old crystals and channeling techniques but they offered her no relief. Campaign promises were now the burdens she had to carry. Angela tried to pump her optimism up, but she still felt traumatized from the Rose Garden ceremony, two days ago, when a resentful ESAC board member pelted her with a large handful of Gulf Coast Jaguarundi dung.

The hour is coming when everyone who kills you
will think he is offering worship to God...
I have told you this so that when their hour comes
you may remember that I told you.
John 16:2-4

40
Tarbuwth Correctional Facility
Yashar, NY
July 9

Officer Jefferson had been so impressed with the cooperation of the inmates, in recent months, that he had arranged a reward for them. Tonight, the world heavy-weight boxing championship would be decided and those who had shown self-restraint would be allowed to watch. This incentive never would have been offered, in the old days, because there had always been too much fighting and too many contraband violations. Now, however, a Spirit of Peace had somehow made its way into many of the prisoners' lives.

The journey had not been easy, particularly in the wake of the rabble rousing preaching of Brother Daniel Mitchum.

Ten years ago, Mitchum was an unknown, white taxi driver in Atlanta. One day, thugs opened fire on his cab. Within hours, a picture was shown on front pages around the world. It was of a tearful Mitchum, holding in his arms his passenger, the country's most respected civil rights leader, bleeding to death.

Not one to miss an opportunity, Mitchum decided to bestow upon himself the civil rights leader's mantle of sainthood. It was a heavy-handed self-promotion that reminded John of Mahatma Gandhi's quip, "I like your Christ, I do not like your Christians."

After that, the mainstream media couldn't get enough of this charismatic agitator. The fascade of his sermons were always laced with

Christian themes. But the fruits of his ministry were resentment, blame, envy, and violence. Prisoners, in particular, were drawn to his "redistribution of wealth by any means necessary" philosophy. From either end of the political spectrum, no one could listen to his tirades without enflamed passions.

Tonight, however, preachers were not on the minds of the inmates. A half hour before the match, the prisoners were released from their cells. Forty seven men had qualified for the reward and all of them were loud and boisterous as they shuffled into the rec. room where twelve chairs had been placed in front of the big screen television.

In jail, a clear pecking order is always established. It is one of the efficiencies of prison life. Unlike life on the outside, inmates quickly know their priority in the hierarchy, or are taught their place with a violent lesson.

Here, at TCF, the twelve biggest and baddest prisoners had always claimed their seats early. The rest of the inmates would watch standing... with one exception. Whenever he chose to watch, Worthington would typically straggle in at the last minute and stare at one seated man. Without a spoken word, that inmate would get up and Worthington would plop down in his seat. No one dared complain about the tradition that had been irrevocably established.

Tonight, as usual, twelve men claimed their seats and the others stood behind them. Chatter filled the room, as cigarettes or candy were wagered on the outcome. Even the officers were excited about the fight. Then, shortly before the match, Worthington walked in and stared at the man in the middle of the front row. The target quickly got up and moved to the side.

"Hey John," Worthington called to the back of the room. "I got a place for you, up here."

John did not respond.

"John?" the big inmate persisted.

Some of the others at the back encouraged the timid prisoner, "Yeah, take it, man!" "Go for it!"

"No, no," John finally answered, "let someone else."

"Don't be crazy, man," Worthington insisted, "I want you to see the fight."

"Please, brother," John begged as others stared at him in disbelief, "anybody but me."

Worthington was embarrassed but, more importantly, he was humbled. So was everyone else in the room. The focus was no longer on the television. Except for the sound of a commercial, the room full of men was quiet.

Then, a bearded man in the second row stood up. It was Qurban, the big Muslim who was serving a life sentence after being implicatedin an unsuccessful bombing plot. He had recently prayed privately with John and, now, professed a Spiritual transformation. Rumors were circulating among the Muslim prisoners that he was planning to convert to Christianity.

Qurban shuffled to the side of the room and mumbled,

"Somebody can have my seat." But nobody took it.

One by one, each seated prisoner gave up his spot. No one was quite sure if it was because of the intimidating glare of Worthington or the humble example of John. Perhaps both played a part. However, regardless of why it happened, such a display of selflessness had never before been seen here. Also, standing around twelve empty seats, never before had these men so thoroughly enjoyed a boxing match.

THE NEXT MORNING, when Officer D.J. Jefferson made his rounds, he found Qurban's cell mate kneeling on his prayer rug, softly reciting *"Allahu Akbar,"* next to Qurban's lifeless body.

***

JEFFERSON WAS ANGRY when the ambulance finally arrived. After such a long delay, he had no hope for resuscitation. He resented that the prison run was always the lowest priority. However, the medics still conducted CPR for twenty minutes and even zapped Qurban with a defibrillator six times. They declared him dead at 7:42 AM. Suffocation was determined to be the cause of death.

When they rolled the gurney out of the cell, Jefferson escorted the medics. In the hallway, as they passed inmates heading out to the rec. yard, John asked, “May I?” Jefferson nodded, stopped the medics, and uncovered Qurban’s face. With the other inmates looking on quietly, John bowed his head and, with his thumb, drew the sign of the Cross on Qurban’s forehead. He then whispered some words that the observers could not understand and returned the sheet over Qurban’s face.

As they rolled the dead man out, one prisoner quipped, “Great way to shorten a life sentence.”

Later, when the ambulance pulled out of the prison sally port gates, the driver saw no need for the siren to sound or the lights to flash. While the medics argued over last night’s Giants game, the vehicle merged into morning rush-hour traffic and blended in with the other slow-moving cars.

Suddenly, a rush of wind and noise filled the ambulance. The driver swerved into the emergency lane and hit the brakes.

“Dammit!” the passenger medic shouted, looking back at the gurney.

The back door was open.

Qurban was gone.

If you had known what these words mean,
'I desire mercy, not sacrifice,'
you would not have condemned the innocent.
Matthew 12:7

41

Holy Sacrifice Monastery
Yashar, NY
July 30

In the darkened confessional booth, Mother Liguori kneeled across from Father James Alonzo. He had been hearing confessions for two hours and believed this was the last one for the day. The priest slid the privacy door between them open, and she began to speak very softly.

"Bless me Father for I have sinned. It has been one week since my last confession. These are my sins."

Then she paused. In the shadows, he could not see that her eyes were red from crying and her face pale from lack of sleep.

"Yes, go on," he urged.

"Father, I am struggling with wicked thoughts and suspicions."

"Please explain, Sister?"

She blurted it out: "Father, I believe you had something to do with Sister Clarita's murder."

"Sister!" he answered a bit too loudly. Then he whispered, "What makes you say a thing like that?"

"Father, I am discussing this with you privately so that you may right your wrongs, confess your sins."

"What wrongs have I done, Sister? What sins are you talking about?"

"It's been going on for years, but I kept quiet. Now I feel this horrible murder never would have happened if I had spoken out in the beginning."

"The beginning of what? What are you talking about?"

She gathered her thoughts and then attacked, "I'm sure you remember that skinny blond woman from three years ago, Miss Berne."

The priest's silence was his admission.

She continued, "I always noticed how you paid special attention to her whenever she was around. She was always very friendly, very helpful, but I never trusted her. Then one day, you were hearing confessions, right here as a matter of fact. I noticed that she was deliberately waiting to be last. I know I shouldn't have, but she was acting so suspicious that I knelt in a pew close enough to hear her when she spoke up. I heard her so-called confession. I heard how she taunted you with descriptions of her sexual sins. You let her go on. She continued her vulgarities for far too long before you finally told her to leave."

"But I told her to leave."

"She went on far too long, Father."

He didn't deny it.

Mother Liguori continued, more forcefully, "Then, I watched her face as she came out … Father, she left with a smile! She enjoyed saying those things to a supposed man of God. Father, I cannot understand why you did not cast that foul woman, like a demon from hell, out of this holy House of God."

"You're right … Sister ... I should have stopped her sooner."

She continued, "That was about the time John arrived … Father, I believe you opened the door to demons and one came through by the name of John Malek. You have sown the wind and we have reaped the whirlwind."

"Sister, Sister, no, now you are so wrong. Please don't say things that you don't know. Please don't persecute the innocent."

No longer whispering, she said, "Suddenly this stranger arrives and you become totally in awe of him. You give him a place to live, you spend tremendous amounts of time with him, and you even make him Sister Clarita's Spiritual Director. Father, you have obviously been under his spell! You have not been thinking clearly!"

"Sister, you don't know all the facts."

"Then, once this strange man started supposedly praying with Sister Clarita, she mysteriously developed the *stigmata*. It's all too diabolically clever. Just like with you and Miss Berne, his sessions with her in the chapel went on far too long. Did you know that the afternoon before she died they were together for hours? Nobody saw her after that. He could have killed her before he left for Washington, or he could have come back in the night."

"Sister!"

"It's true! I hate that I have to say it but I can't think of anyone else who could have killed her. Who else could have done it?"

"Sister, please stop this madness. Please don't say what you don't know."

"He's not even a priest but you made him her Spiritual Director! Father, you know the demon can deceive, even dressed as an angel of light. Why were the rules broken for him? Why was she allowed to spend so much time with this layman? Why didn't you support my leadership in this convent? Tell me! I have a responsibility to keep these sisters safe."

"Sister, I am sorry but I cannot tell you everything that I know."

"Father, you leave me no choice but to believe that there is something dirty, something evil, in your relationship with this man."

"Sister, please! Your imagination is running away with you. Someday all will be revealed. Let's not succumb to gossip. I forgive you for any anger or resentment that you have had toward me and ..."

"You forgive me," she interrupted. "You forgive *me?!* The question is not whether you forgive me, but whether I can ever forgive you!"

She rose abruptly and slammed the door behind her as she left the confessional and then stormed out of the chapel.

Father Alonzo sat in the quiet darkness, the same quiet darkness he remembered after his last encounter with Miss Berne. At that time, it was true, he had not stopped her soon enough. He felt helpless to stop her, and she knew it. It was not until she left that he was able to regain his Spiritual senses. He felt like he had been violated, even raped. Here, where he wanted to do nothing but please God, she had filled him with an uncontrollable urge to sin with her.

The priest remembered how he had rushed back to the rectory to make phone calls and get her off his mind. As he approached the house, he saw a strange man sitting on his lawn. He looked like he might be travelling but didn't have any bags; just jeans, a T-shirt and sandals. The man rose as the priest approached.

"Father Alonzo?"

"Yes?"

The stranger said, "Peace be upon this place. I have nowhere to sleep. Our Lord has led me to you."

The priest remembered how he surprised even himself when he mumbled, "Sure … you can stay here."

The man approached closer, put both of his hands on each side of the priest's face, and then whispered, "God bless you."

Father Alonzo remembered that, as he collapsed onto the grass, he experienced an amazing Spiritual rush of joy, love and pleasure. Then he heard the comforting words that would forever change his life: "James, this is My beloved apostle, John. Together, serve Me."

A jury consists of twelve persons
chosen to decide who has the better lawyer.
Robert Frost

42
Yashar County Courthouse
Yashar, NY
September 29

John's court-appointed lawyer did not inspire confidence. He had popped the top button on his shirt, his collar had separated under his tie, and a display of curly chest hair was available for all to see. A thin brown mustache crawled across his lip and, for the observant juror, a smear of mustard accented his coat sleeve. This was the man, nevertheless, who held John's life and freedom in his poorly manicured hands. Perhaps Teddy Tipton was a good father or a good bowler, but a good lawyer he was not.

At the other table, the tall, smooth prosecutor offered a study in contrast. Ben Gatwick's appearance and demeanor exhibited his confidence that this courtroom was just a pit stop on the race track from frat house to Congress. Every female juror loved him, just as every female voter would, some day.

However, drawing from many years of experience, the judge, an older African-American woman, had resisted jumping to conclusions. She understood that many lawyers aren't as bad as they first appear, and many others aren't as good as they think. But still, initially, she did not have high hopes for either. Her pessimism would not be disappointed.

Two years ago, following the strategic advice of Cyst and Thas, Candidate Concepcion had transformed this trial into a media event. The ESAC breakfast confrontation had prompted her enemies to launch a bumper sticker and billboard campaign, mocking Angela's focus on endangered species, using the slogan "Kill Bugs, Not Babies." So, her team retaliated with the highly edited recording of John's words, portraying him as a lunatic.

Cyst's private research had indicated that emphatic pronouncements regarding Sister Clarita's murder would bolster her wavering support in the pro-life Catholic community and silence the critics who felt that she was too soft on crime. So, Angela had proclaimed that, as New York Secretary of State, it was her responsibility to insure that justice won out for this horrible crime. That comment baffled many of the political pundits. But, for the first time, she supported the death penalty, just as her focus groups had dictated.

Heavy demand for seats in the courtroom had necessitated a lottery system. But, as soon as the drawing was over, journalists offered whatever it took to buy the winning lottery tickets. The locals were becoming hostile to the media employees as they monopolized courtroom seating along with all available parking. During the deliberations, simultaneous translations in nine languages were electronically delivered to foreign reporters, causing a distracting rumble of noise in the courtroom.

The trial had dragged on for weeks. Previous defense witnesses had little to offer except glowing admiration for John. Ricky Zipp, however, was the star witness for the prosecution, based on his telephone call to emergency services reporting that John "had an obsession with inflicting pain." On the stand, however, Ricky disappointed everyone by admitting that he changed his mind and now believed that he had been mistaken about what John actually meant. Yet, Tipton had not established a credible alibi for John. Because of that, picketers outside uniformly demanded both justice and death. It was John's word against the world's prejudice.

At trial, no evidence of forced entry was presented. So the murderer must have been trusted, he must have been an insider. No money or possessions had been stolen. So the motivation could not have been financial. Suspicion naturally fell on John, who was admittedly a friend of Sister Clarita's, and his lack of any public record indicated to the jurors that he had been hiding his true identity all these years. In short, the jury found no hard evidence against him but no reason to acquit. The charge was first degree murder and, considering the special circumstances involved, the death penalty was now almost certain. Only one conclusion could save John's life: a verdict of not guilty by reason of insanity.

When a defense psychiatrist testified that the accused had exhibited symptoms of schizophrenia, such as hallucinations of demons and paranoia of evil forces, a disbelieving listener had to be ejected from the courtroom when he shouted, "You're pretending to be crazy!" On cross examination, however, Gatwick made it clear that other symptoms of schizophrenia were totally absent. John had not exhibited signs of depression, confusion, lack of motivation or strained personal relationships. In fact, his leadership of his fellow prisoners was inspiring. Many of them had gone on to lead exemplary lives after their release and credited John's loving guidance for their success. Ironically, testimony regarding John's admirable leadership skills established his sanity and reinforced the likelihood of a death sentence.

Today, satellite trucks surrounded the courthouse. The star witness was about to testify. Tipton had felt that the only way to save his client's life would be to let him demonstrate, in his own words, how insane he really was. However, the lawyer's greatest worry was that Malek's testimony would be so ridiculous that it would appear obvious to the jury that he was fishing for an insanity defense.

When John mounted the witness stand, he placed his right hand on the Bible, raised his left hand, and calmly but deliberately recited, "I swear to tell the truth, the whole truth and nothing but the truth, so help me God." Everyone who heard those words, stated with such firm sincerity, now had to wonder about their earlier prejudices. Journalists from around the world filled the courtroom and, for most, these were the first words that they had heard the defendant speak.

Tipton approached the stand and, after a few introductory questions regarding where John was at the time of the murder, ventured into John's life story. "So, Mr. Malek, where did your name come from?"

"In Hebrew, it means John, servant of the King."

"Tell us about your life, Mr. Malek."

"I am a servant of my Lord Jesus Christ."

Some of the viewers could be heard grumbling.

The prosecutor rose. "Objection, your Honor. This is not the Inquisition. The defendant's faith is not at issue here. Can we be a little more precise with our questioning?"

The judge ruled, "Mr. Malek, please keep your testimony focused on answering the question and, Mr. Tipton, you better have more specific questions than 'Tell us about your life.' I expect to grant some latitude here but my patience is not unlimited."

"Yes, your Honor," Tipton fumbled along. "Uh, Mr. Malek, you have no criminal record. So, you've always stayed on the good side of the law. Right?"

"No, that's not correct," John stated flatly.

The startled lawyer remembered his Evidence professor's warning: Never ask a question without first knowing the answer. But this question had seemed so innocuous.

Before Tipton could regain control, John was elaborating. "Ohhh, where do I start? My earliest venture was to Rome. However, I was forced to flee in order to avoid religious persecution. After that, I lived in Ephesus for a while. The authorities did not like what I was teaching, so they exiled me to Patmos. After a few years, I escaped on a small boat and headed north to Smyrna and then on to Pergamos. There, I was nearly imprisoned for healing a demoniac. Word of this got around. So, after that, I had to stay on the move. Over the next few years, I fled to Thyatira, then Sardis, then Philadelphia and on to Laodicea."

"Objection, your Honor," Gatwick interrupted. "The defendant sounds like he's just making up names. The only cities I recognize are Philadelphia and Rome. I'd like to check out whether he ever really lived in Pennsylvania or Georgia but he's not even telling us when he was there."

Over the sound of whispers in the courtroom, the judge told John, "Mr. Malek, we need to know the time-frame of the events you are describing."

John responded softly, "It would be in, what you call, the first century."

The courtroom was immediately filled with shuffling and murmuring. The judge asked, "Please, everyone, quiet down. What was that, Mr. Malek?"

John spoke more loudly, "The first century. These things happened in the first century."

The roomful of international journalists took this testimony the same way as the jury: a brazen lie to establish an insanity defense. To them, this proved beyond any doubt that the mysterious Mr. Malek was more concerned about concealing the truth than taking his chances with a murder conviction. Even a lunatic would not come up with such a ridiculous story. Regardless, the Saudi oil crisis had eliminated any tolerance for potential terrorists. Whether he commited the murder or not, surely this drifter must be some kind of nefarious fiend.

The court proceedings moved along, in short order, and the jury deliberated only two days. World public opinion was divided between those who despised John for murdering a holy nun and those who mocked him for thinking that anyone would be fool enough to believe he was John the Apostle.

International media reported that the verdict was guilty and the penalty was death. Easily dismissed or forgotten, however, was the extraordinary fact that John's entire testimony was understood, without translation, in the native tongue of every foreign journalist.

"Come," they say, "let us wipe out Israel as a nation.
We will destroy the very memory of its existence."
Psalm 83:4

43

Oval Office
Washington, DC
October 12

Fred Whitehead entered the Oval Office with a look of dread. Normally, Angela would greet her visitors at the door. This time, however, she didn't even rise from her desk chair. With all that was going on, she was in no mood for idle chit chat. Still, he pasted on a brave smile when their eyes met.

"Hello, Angela. It's been a long time."

They shook hands across the desk. She didn't suggest that Fred take a seat but he did anyway. To her, he looked heavier, perhaps even unhealthy. For the first time ever, she noticed his black roots were showing.

Times must be tough.

"Hello Fred. How's your lovely bride?"

He hadn't wanted to get into it this quickly. He responded without enthusiasm, "She's okay." Then he audibly sighed, put his face in his hands and groaned, "Ohhhh, she made me sell the *palazzo*." Angela cringed as he continued. "You were right. We have nothing in common. I made a big mistake. I should have listened to you."

But she was not ready to let him off the hook. "I'm sorry to hear that, Fred," she droned.

Angela knew that Fred was on a run of bad luck. After the Green E bill had collapsed in the New York legislature, a domino effect took place and it was rejected in state after state. That caused XCyst Industries to move on to another lobbying firm, putting Fred's company under pressure to find new deep-pocketed clients. So, they took on an Indian casino gaming company that turned out to be more Russian than Indian. For six months, Fred's minor role in the fraud caused his name to be continually dragged through the newspapers … particularly those papers that followed Angela's direction.

"So, what can I do for you, Fred?" she asked, quickly getting down to business.

Before he could answer, the President's receptionist interrupted on the telephone intercom: "Madame President, excuse me, it's the DNI. She says it's urgent."

"Sorry Fred," Angela signaled the meeting was over. "I have a lot on my plate today."

He nodded reluctantly and made his way to the door. "Angela, I just wanted to apologize. You were right."

"Sure … yeah," she responded without emotion. As he walked away, Angela could see that this was a beaten man. She was pleased that he had been humiliated and humbled. She resented how he had led her on and rejected her offer. However, he, like she, was a fighter who knew how to claw back to the top, and she liked that about him. Actually, she preferred a man who had learned his place, a man she could now control. Perhaps, the relationship could be rekindled. She would have Evan Thas focus group the issue and then decide.

Before he left, she recited Fred's line that had always made her cringe: "I'll be in touch."

THE DIRECTOR OF NATIONAL INTELLIGENCE sounded distressed on the phone.

"Madame President, can you talk privately?"

Angela answered a bit warily, "Yes, go ahead, Carla."

"We've learned details on the delivery system used for the Saudi bio attack."

"Yes? Where did it originate?"

"America … Specifically, New York state."

"Ohhhhh," Angela groaned.

"It has been tracked to a contaminated shipment of a hand soap manufactured by Luxuriant Cleansing Company in Yashar."

"Accidental contamination?"

"No, had to be deliberate. The strain of *Ebolavirus* is simply too potent and rare to have occurred naturally. It requires laboratory conditions to produce and a lot of time to incubate. NIH and CDC are working on it. I'll get back to you when they report."

"What about the people involved?"

"Get this … that Jew Malek worked there."

"That's interesting."

"Very. We've been questioning Clarence and Jamal Porter, the soap company owner and his son. They seem to be clean but we had to scare the hell out of them before they'd give us much on Malek. They defend him, but Jamal suspects three illegal aliens who worked there around the time the contaminated batch was manufactured ... They were Saudis."

"Sunni or Shi'ite?"

"Shi'ite, we believe. We're still checking on it. We think they were probably the three Semitic John Does that were floating in the Hudson River a couple years ago."

"It figures. If they were Shi'ite, I wonder about Iranian involvement."

Carla Perkins exhaled, "We're lucky the Porters saved a note that was left at the soap plant the night their Saudi employees disappeared."

"Yes?"

"It just said, 'Remember Abolhassan Hamdim.'"

Angela remembered that name well. Hamdim had been an internationally recognized religious rights activist in Saudi Arabia, a country where that sort of subversion is not tolerated. As a member of the kingdom's Shi'ite minority, he was already viewed warily. However, when his message became religious tolerance of even Christianity, the government cracked down and imprisoned him. Angela had briefly met him at a human rights conference in London and was very impressed with the charismatic calm with which he led his nonviolent movement. Rumors had circulated that he had converted to Christianity while imprisoned and, even there, refused to stop evangelizing. The thirty-year-old man was eventually released and, soon after, was found dead, without a tongue. It was a public relations miscalculation and became a highly publicized embarrassment for the kingdom.

Angela shook her head. "I don't think Hamdim's supporters would resort to violent means of revenge."

"I agree. Our analysts think that name was used to throw us off the trail."

"So," Angela asked, "ruling out the Christian revenge angle, you suspect this bio attack could have resulted from a conspiracy involving Saudi Shi'ites, probably with Iranian support?"

"No. That is what they want us to conclude."

"Who are 'they'?"

"The Israelis."

"Whoa, Carla … I realize that Malek guy is now in the picture but you're making quite a leap."

"Madame President, there was a fingerprint on the note. We matched it to Ariel Golden."

"Never heard of him."

"An undercover Mossad agent, stationed in New York."

"What's your level of certainty on Golden's print?"

"100%."

Angela groaned and pounded the desk. "So, it was that damn Malek!" She rubbed her eyes to concentrate. "What the hell is Israel doing? They've really screwed up this time! I guess they thought we'd just snatch up all that Saudi oil once the Royal family was losing control of it! I am not gonna be played like this! They just dug their own grave."

"We've checked out the Malek angle on it."

"What have you found so far?"

"We strongly believe he was involved."

"Why is that?"

"XCyst Industries offered us computer forensics assistance on the condition that their role would be kept secret. Their CyBot search engine detected incriminating biological weapons information on a computer hard drive at the monastery."

"That evidence won't hold up in court."

"I know but the bio virus information was from the same *Filoviridae* family as the Saudi strain. It's too obscure to be a coincidence."

"Keep those cards close to the vest. I want to control events, from here. I'll decide when the tsunami of shit hits Israel."

"Too late. XBC News is already reporting the story."

"Dammit! Then, grab Golden and squeeze some answers out of him!"

"We can't do that."

"He fled to Israel?"

"No. He also drowned … in his bathtub."

People like me want to... satisfy our hearts to the full,
and in doing so, we automatically have
the most valuable moral codes. Of course,
there are people and objects in the world,
but they are all there only for me.
Mao Tse-Tung

44

Cyst Estate
Jupiter Island, Florida
December 2

Just as he did almost every working morning, Evan Thas pulled the custom black van up to the front of Huntington Cyst's oceanfront estate. And, like clock-work, Cyst rolled out the door at precisely 7:22 AM. The van's powered door opened, the ramp rumbled into place, and Cyst rolled up and into the vehicle. Once the ramp came up and the door closed, Thas drove to their offices in West Palm Beach.

If he could have it his way, Evan would rather ride his motorcycle to the office and let Lindley – Cyst's pilot, bodyguard and driver – take the boss to work. But only on rare occasions, when Cyst was sick or decided to stay home for the day, was Thas allowed that luxury.

Someday, Evan dreamed, *I'll do whatever I want.*

Cyst always insisted that he and Evan spend the forty minute drive productively, on their cell phones barking orders, giving directions or schmoozing potential business partners. However, this morning, for some reason, they were both quiet. There had been an unusual reserve in Cyst's attitude toward Thas, lately.

After a while, Cyst spoke up. "I've been thinking, Evan. We'd enjoy more company around the house. How about if I got you a little brother?"

Evan laughed, "A brother … are you joking?"

"No, I'm serious."

Evan didn't like this idea at all. "You mean a baby?"

"No," Cyst answered as if he had no ulterior motive, "a little boy."

Thas didn't respond.

"Don't worry, Evan," Cyst said. "You're my boy and always will be. No one can replace you."

Thas' cell rang and he answered it. It wasn't a very important call but one he welcomed so he could gather his thoughts. However, when the call was over, the two men sat quietly for a while.

To cover the awkward silence, Cyst changed the subject. "By the way, I have an important business matter that I need you to handle."

"Sure. No problem."

"It's in Russia."

"Ahhh, Huntie. You know I don't like Russia this time of year."

"Can't be helped. We have a deadline to meet. I'll brief you at the office."

"How long will it take?"

"No more than a week."

"What about the Gulfstream?"

"I'll need it here. Don't worry, you'll fly first class."

"Of course."

For the rest of the drive, nothing more was said.

Discontent is the
first necessity of progress.
Thomas Edison

45
Dollar Store
Yashar, NY
December 4

The new and improved Ricky Zipp stood outside the store window watching Cindy at the cash register. She was ringing up the customers and making them feel welcome. He had always admired her grounding in life. She had been a good mother and a good wife. These days, he often remembered her strength of character and her simple beauty. Unfortunately, he had foolishly driven her away.

His hair, was now short and his face clean shaven. He was even wearing a collared shirt for the first time in years. He held a single rose in his hand. It was yellow, her favorite color.

When the line of customers receded, Cindy shouted to someone in the back, "Hey Benny, goin' on break."

Ricky panicked. He wasn't ready yet. So, he quickly slipped into the pet shop next door. From there, he watched Cindy as she breezed out of the Dollar Store, lit a cigarette and sank down on a bench.

He paced at the window and kept repeating to himself: *It's now or never. It's now or never. It's now or never.*

Cindy pulled one final drag off the cigarette, got up from the bench and snuffed the cigarette out before flicking it into the parking lot.

Behind her, she heard, "Cindy?"

Immediately irritated, she turned around to face him. “Ricky, what are you doin’ here? I ain’t got no money for ya.”

“I ain’t here for money, Cindy,” he said with his hands behind his back. “I come to say I’m sorry. I know I let you down. I let Jeremy …”

He couldn’t finish the sentence.

“Here,” he said as he thrust the flower in front of her.

She stared at it with a puzzled look. “I don’t want that, Ricky. That doesn’t change nothin’.”

He tried not to show his disappointment. “I understand, Cindy. I don’t blame ya.”

She studied how much his look and attitude had changed. He seemed more mature, more open.

“What are ya doin’ these days, Ricky?” she asked a bit warily. “Ya got a job?”

“Yeah, I’m workin’.”

“Good,” she answered without passion. “You gonna yell at me if I ask about drugs?”

“No, Cindy. I changed. I ain’t doin’ em any more.”

“You still protestin’?”

“Yeah, kind of …”

She frowned.

He quickly countered, “But it’s all good. It’s not like what I used to do.”

“Protestin’ is protestin’. Gets you all worked up, blaming all your problems on everybody but yourself. Protestin’ doesn’t do anything but make people mad.”

“No, this is different ... Cindy, I’m different.”

“Yeah, sure.”

Ricky reflected on his mistake-filled life. “Ya know, I been protestin’ for forty years and I never changed anybody’s mind, never saved anybody’s life ... until now.”

"Until now? Right."

"Cindy, you know how I used to love the adrenaline rush of a riot with all the screamin' and breakin' windows. I loved throwin' marbles on the street and watchin' the cops come crashin' down when their horses slipped. I never told you this, but I was drawn to …"

"I know."

"Drugs, easy women ... I done a lot I'm ashamed of now."

She shrugged. "That's your problem, not mine, anymore."

"Cindy, I know I caused you a lot of pain. You didn't deserve me."

"So?" she asked with a disgusted tone.

"I been attackin' greedy capitalists for global warmin' and protestin' for everything from the delta smelt to the blue whale. But I finally realized that my anger wasn't accomplishin' anything. I was just letting all that pain fester in me. Then, when Jeremy … ya know … I got to thinkin': How can I save the world when I can't even save my own family… the people I'm supposed to love? I wondered, how many babies did I create?"

"Come on."

"Please Cindy, please listen … Maybe another Jeremy is out there; maybe a bunch of 'em. But then I thought about what really must have happened and I knew they were all gone. I had to ask myself: How many abortions have I caused? I honestly don't have a clue."

"Ricky," she interrupted, "I don't wanna hear this."

"I even wanted you to abort Jeremy … Thank God you didn't listen to me. I had no idea how much I'd love him."

"Please stop."

He continued, anyway, "I can't blame American foreign policy, or capitalism, or polluting companies, or even the greedy rich for that. And, I started to realize, it ain't just the women's fault. I blame me ...

It took a lot of pain to wake me up, but I realize that now."

She snorted a suppressed chuckle. "Ricky, you feelin' alright?"

"I don't mean to sound like a nut, Cindy, but I go with a group now, twice a week, to protest abortions."

He could see her face tighten.

"No, it ain't what you think. We're not screamin' and breakin' things. We just get on our knees and pray in front of the clinics. You wouldn't believe it. That simple, humble act has changed more minds than I could have imagined. We offer these girls love and prayers. We offer them a place to live until their baby's born. And if they want to put it up for adoption, we help. I've saved lives, Cindy. I'm serious. All the screamin' I've done at protests has not only been worthless, it's been counterproductive. I realize that now."

Cindy was so baffled that she didn't know what to say. *Is this one of Ricky's scams?*

"Ya know, Cindy," he said with an increasingly guilty tone. "In the past, I still woulda been hittin' on those scared young women … I targeted vulnerable girls."

"I know."

He continued, "And I used to think I could solve my problems by makin' other people hurt. When I was mad, I'd break things … somebody's things … anybody's things."

"Ricky, I know all this."

"And every time I dished out hate and violence, I got hate and violence back. The world wasn't a better place."

"Look, Ricky, I gotta get back to work."

"Cindy, please listen. Now I realize love is the only way to change people's minds. I want to show you love. I can only hope I get it back. But, if I don't, I won't be mad at you."

This was all too much for her to comprehend, at the moment. She looked inside the store window and saw a customer approaching the counter. Ricky nodded his understanding. It was time to go.

As she opened the door, Ricky blurted out, “Cindy?”

She stopped and looked at him sadly.

He mumbled words he had never spoken before, “You look real good today.”

She paused in the door and for the first time sounded warm, “You do too, Ricky. You really do.”

She went inside and he trudged off with the flower that he would never throw away.

And in that day will I make Jerusalem a burdensome stone
for all people: all that burden themselves with it
shall be cut in pieces, though all the people of the earth
be gathered together against it.
Zechariah 12:3

46
Air Force One
Over Kansas
December 14

Angela sat alone in her plush leather recliner as she watched a midnight moon from 35,000 feet. She was deep in thought, contemplating whether the rising tide of violent rebellion around the globe would soon wash up on American shores. She looked at her watch and pulled out the encrypted iPhone she used for every difficult issue. She hit the only number that was programmed into speed dial. After a few rings, the call was answered by a sleepy voice.

"Evan, I'm sorry to be calling you so late but I have research work that must be done ASAP."

"Sure," Thas responded as he turned on his bedside lamp and reached for pen and paper. "Go ahead, I'm ready."

"Here's the gist of it. First," she started rattling off, "I need a benchmark public approval rating of my handling of the oil crisis, so far. Are they blaming me?"

A staffer walked past and Angela responded curtly, "Excuse me? Get out ... everybody out." Four aides quickly evacuated to the forward cabin.

Then she continued, "Second, do my numbers move if it is determined that Israel caused the crisis?"

Thas interjected, "Dammit! You think Israel did this?"

"Yeah, we have the evidence."

"Those bastards!" Thas growled.

"Third, if conventional forces invade Israel in retaliation, and I do not assist Israel, how will that play?"

"I can tell you that, right now. Defending Israel would be your Vietnam times ten."

"Yeah, that's what I'm thinking. They've been a thorn in my side from day one." She continued, "Fourth, if nuclear weapons strike Tel Aviv, I need a P.R. plan for staying neutral. Fifth, if we see genocide in Israel, will I have to do anything about it, other than lip service? You know what I mean?"

"Yes ... yes, I do. We'll just combine inaction with a lot of speeches about what a vital ally Israel is." Then Thas seized his opportunity, "Madame President, if I may speak freely..."

"Yes, I need your honest advice," she urged.

"Economically, America is teetering. Banks, insurance companies, and even entitlements are on the brink. If this all goes badly, it's not overly dramatic to say that our country could descend into Haitian-style anarchy. The only difference will be that our gangs will be roaming the streets with more than machetes."

She interrupted, "What if we get that Brother Mitchum guy on our team? Maybe, make him inter-faith outreach Czar, or something. We'll give him a platform and somebody to blame. "

"Sure ... we need the streets under our control. I'll check him out." Thas went on, "But it will take more."

"I need suggestions."

"Madame President, a great woman once proclaimed 'When mankind creates a problem, fearless government leaders must find the solutions.' Do you still believe that?"

"Of course."

"Nobody can blame you for this oil crisis. You have cover. It's time for fearless leadership to force the centralization of power. Half measures will be dangerous."

"We'll get a lot of push-back on that."

"That is why we have to get control of political speech, and not just on the streets. We need choke points for disruptive comments on radio, TV and even the Internet. How about we push through new Espionage and Sedition Acts?[1] Congress will be too timid to challenge your leadership during a crisis like this. Can I get our operatives moving on that initiative now?"

"Yes … yes, that makes sense … but, do you really think it's necessary?"

"It is going to get rough so, bottom line, we need legislation that will stop criticism of your administration. With technology today, free speech is out of control. It's not like it used to be. We can't allow your irresponsible opponents any kind of platform. With those laws in place, you'd be able to shut up your opponents on the streets and in the suites. Let them reflect on their troublemaking in prison. They criticize your policies, they go to jail; simple as that. But, hell, we don't want to be too obvious so, for good measure, we'll also prosecute any criticism of mom and apple pie."

She offered a suppressed chuckle. "I see what you mean."

"That's the spirit! There is no reason to get our spirits down. This crisis is an opportunity! It's an opportunity to get things done that we couldn't have accomplished otherwise."

She admired Evan's upbeat take on events.

Then he cautiously added, "But, look, I hope you won't mind if I really open up."

"Please."

"Israel … that's the root of your problem. I don't mean to kill the buzz, here, but that little speck of land has caused more troubles for more people than any in history. How many more decades do we need to be floundering with the problems they create? If Israel jeopardizes our oil trading relationships, I not only fear for our country, I fear for your safety. We've got extensive research on the subject. You can't afford to appear weak. Somebody has to be sacrificed."

Angela sighed, "I understand."

"Internationally, you've got to get above this thing. You'll have to throw the Arabs a bone."

"Like?"

"Give them their Palestinian state."

"And divide Jerusalem?" she asked.

"Of course. Just shove it down their throats. What can Israel do about it, now?"

She pondered the suggestion. "That would probably placate the Arabs, and maybe even Iran."

"You've got to seize control of the situation. Seize it quickly. Seize it ruthlessly, if you must, but seize it no matter what."

Angela started to back away. "Evan, it's not that simple. There are other countries' interests at stake, here. They won't just sit idly by as one country starts moving pieces on the geo-political chess board."

"It will be a globally coordinated effort."

"Evan, come on! You think too much of yourself."

"Madame President, over the past twenty years, why do you think that you have been the only major U.S. Presidential candidate who did not belong to the Legion of Babylon?"

"I assumed that they suspected my relationship with you and Dr. Cyst. I just figured Henri Blanc still held a grudge after his angry departure from XCyst Industries. Anyway, the Legion can't have more than 6,000 members at any time. The world's a big place. Maybe they were maxed out."

"First of all, Dr. Blanc was pushed out years ago. The man is a religious burnout. He walked away from everything he had."

"Why?"

"Who knows? He's nuts. But, more importantly, you have not been associated with the Legion of Babylon for the same reason that we have kept your relationship with me secret: public disclosure does not serve our purposes."

Her brow furrowed as she mulled over his words.

"Madame President, I promise you. This is a slam dunk. The central committee of the Legion of Babylon has spent years developing this plan in secret. When the right time comes, the Legion's members will be ready to fall in line."

She privately wondered how the Legion could have been so far ahead of this crisis. She tentatively offered, "It's just that you are starting to sound so extreme."

"If you're worried about your public image, don't. We'll package it so that you're the good cop and Vice President Blight's the bad cop. He lives for the limelight and loves to talk tough. After all, Homeland Security will justify your actions since Jewish terrorists might strike at any moment."

She offered an incredulous chuckle. "Are you kidding?"

"Look, Angela," Evan said, dropping the formalities and hardening his tone. "The world is poised for another purge. Throughout human history it has happened regularly. People are going to die, no matter what you do. It's just a fact. The only question is: Will you choose the right people to live?"

She mumbled, "And choose the right people to die."

"Oh, come on!" he barked. She was taken aback by his blunt and aggressive attitude. "You chose this job. Now, man up! What do you think war does? What do you think abortion does? Frankly, it's about time somebody steps up to the plate with an unemotional evaluation of who gets to live. We've just got too many people on the planet. We can't afford them all. We can't feed, clothe or house them all. They're bankrupting us! Imagine how much better the world would be if half the people were gone!"

She sighed deeply and reflected on his dire assessment. "Okay … maybe … I don't know." She kept shaking her head, but then added, "Go ahead and get me talking points on denying all forms of assistance to Israel. They precipitated this crisis. We'll stay out of it. We can't afford to alienate the Islamic world. Our oil is at stake." Then, sounding panicked for the first time, she pleaded, "We can't lose our oil!"

He realized she still did not understand the extent to which he expected her to take control. "Madam President, before you go ..."

"Yes?"

"As I mentioned, our strategists at the Legion have been gaming various disaster scenarios. I have a briefing available for you on martial law."

"Martial law? Here in America? You really think it'll be necessary?"

"Unfortunately, yes. We're not going to have the time or manpower for lengthy court proceedings just to lock people up. You've got to establish a command and control framework in which to operate effectively. Article 1, Section 9 of the Constitution gives you the authority to declare martial law in cases of rebellion, invasion or public safety. Madame President, this public safety situation is critical. You may have no alternative but to assume dictatorial powers."[2]

"Yeah … yeah …" the President whispered to herself. "I guess you're right …" Then decisively, she ordered, "Be here tomorrow afternoon at three. We'll meet one-on-one."

THAS HUNG UP the phone. Next to him, in bed, Cyst grumbled, "So, how far have they traced it?"

"They're focusing on Israel."

"Good. They'll probably stop there." Cyst smiled. "I love Israel. They're such an easy target."

"She is completely freaking out," Evan chuckled.

"You think she'll defend them?"

"Of course not."

"Well, either way, tomorrow call Albertine in Advanced Weaponry. Tell him to bump production to three shifts, around the clock ... You can't stop a rising tide ... And tell Albertine to focus on ERW output."

"Which ones, neutron bombs?"

"Right. Titan isn't quite ready."

Thas smiled, remembering Cyst's favorite saying: "Disaster is the father of fortunes." However, he was disappointed that Cyst did not seem as excited about the developments as Evan had expected. After all, the seeds they had been sowing for years would soon be ready for harvest. *Maybe Huntie's just tired.*

Along the way, they had rigged far more clues, in this amusing who-done-it game, than anyone would ever fully appreciate. The obvious Hamdim tip pointed the finger of suspicion at vengeful Christians or Saudi Shi'ites. Then, digging just a little deeper, the planted Israeli spy fingerprint was found. However, if the investigators had bothered to check, those lightweights would have found that the note paper was manufactured in Iran. If they had inspected the phone records of the Saudi suspects, they would have discovered lengthy, mysterious calls to North Korea. Other hints included unexplainable flights to Egypt, packages to China, emails to Venezuela, and large sums wired to Switzerland. In short, a cornucopia of clues pointed in every direction except the right one.

Russia is a riddle
wrapped in a mystery
inside an enigma.
Winston Churchill

47
Aeroflot Flight 3214
Approaching Moscow, Russia
December 19

True to his word, Cyst's administrative assistant had booked first class tickets. However, Evan was miffed when he discovered that he would be flying Aeroflot. The jet was barely a third full because ticket prices now reflected the stumbling global economy and the cost of fuel, these days. But Russia, as the world's second largest oil exporting country, and XCyst Industries, as the world's sixth largest oil extraction company, were two of the biggest winners in the global oil market turmoil. Just a year ago, when oil was trading at $70 a barrel, Russia had been struggling. However, now, at $700, Moscow could flex its muscles around the world again.

The flight had been long and boring for Evan. However, it allowed him time to muse over the irrelevant meeting he had just concluded with the President. For an hour and a half, he had listened to a desperate Angela drone on and on about the situation. *Blah, blah, blah.* She had no idea that she was no longer in control.

On board, he had been pleasantly distracted by the charms of an attractive Russian woman. However, she soon alerted him to the fact that she was a high-priced hooker who wanted to meet him in Moscow. That had never slowed him down in the past but he decided to keep his visit short and professional, this time.

Cyst had only recently mentioned this trip. Evan wondered what the big rush was all about. For some reason, Dr. Andrei Spasky, the Russian aeronautical scientist, could not wait. So, just as always, Evan did not question his orders and fulfilled them to the letter.

Thas knew Spasky well. The thin, methodical Russian scientist had previously been the point man for the Russian space agency, *Roscosmos,* when XCyst Industries' three satellites had been launched by them. In deference to the scientist's valuable assistance, Cyst had named the satellites after horses, the Russian's favorite creatures. Though he rarely demonstrated evidence of a pulse, the dour Spasky was thrilled when he learned that he would be responsible for launching "White Appaloosa," "Red Thoroughbred," and "Black Arabian."

Certainly, this new deal with *Roscosmos* was important. They had reached the stage of negotiations in which a letter of intent was to be drawn up regarding the technology coalition that Cyst had been working on privately for three years. It sounded like a mission that should be handled by Cyst and the lawyers by teleconference. But, perhaps, the secrecy issue was still paramount for the boss.

This fourth satellite launch would marry the technologies of Cyst-Blanc supercomputers, for hardware; the software analytical capabilities of the CyBot search engine; and the top-secret Titan technology in which even Evan felt he was not fully versed. This was such a major undertaking that even XCyst's Advanced Weaponry Division had been a part of it. "Glass Andalusian" was the code name given to the project.

Certainly, U.S. and Russian technology waivers again would have to be obtained before the deal could be executed. Yet, however much Huntington assured Evan that government approval would not be an obstacle, this time Thas had his doubts.

Regardless of how amazing the potential for this partnership appeared to Cyst, Evan felt the execution plan seemed half-baked.

Russia was mysterious and enticing for Thas, at least on warmer days. Looking down from the sky, he couldn't help but marvel at the seemingly endless icy forests in which Napoleon's retreating army had been frozen. He appreciated the cunning ruthlessness of the Bolshevik Revolution. Lenin and Stalin, to him, were interesting role models. *They understood how to get things done.*

But, once he arrived, Evan wished that he could be studying this country from afar. Today – as always, it seemed – the sky was leaden and the ubiquitous snow was grimy with road salt and covered with a thin layer of industrial soot. At Sheremetyevo 2 Airport he was pleased to see that his driver was waiting for him outside baggage claim, just as it had been arranged. The hulking bald Russian, a former CIA informant named Anatoly, would serve as his driver, translator and protector on this trip.

Unfortunately, things quickly went downhill from there. The car was not parked near the door so the men had to walk a good distance through the heavy snow. Evan was forced to carry his big suitcase when initial efforts to roll it in the snow proved impossible. Anatoly did not offer to help but, instead, led the way almost too fast for Evan to keep up with him. Never one for physical fitness, Evan had to stop occasionally to catch his breath. Then he would resume his staggering footsteps, crunching through the snow, while gasping the frozen air.

This was nothing like the treatment he had received on his first trip to Russia. Then, shortly after the breakup of the Soviet Union, every Russian had been dreaming of cutting deals with the Americans. His hosts had always treated him like a Czar. He had been graciously escorted to performances at the Bolshoi and Kremlin Palace Theaters. He had toured the restricted areas of the Kremlin including the Armory where a vast collection of historic jewels were kept. In the Tretyakov Museum his guide had even showed him the important stored works that were not on display. Most of all, he had enjoyed the private casinos near Moscow. He remembered how amazed the struggling locals had been at his seemingly unlimited financial resources. The only sour note on the trip that year was his visit to St. Sergei's Monastery at Zagorsk, an hour's drive from Moscow. The fabulously decorated onion domes had been beautiful to behold as Evan approached. But, once inside, he was put off by the devout Russian Orthodox priests who had described decades of persecution by the communists. Listening impatiently, Thas remembered a saying from Nietzsche, his favorite philosopher: "After coming into contact with a religious man I always feel I must wash my hands."

The Russians that Thas and Cyst worked with these days were the new *kleptocrats.* They were the powerful former communists who had deviously maneuvered their way through the country's political and economic transition to become the world's boldest and bawdiest billionaires. Russia – a country that spans eleven time zones and consists of one sixth of the world's land mass – had allowed its abundant natural resources to fall into the hands of a privileged few.

When the two men finally reached Anatoly's car, Thas asked, "What is this? I was told it would be a new Mercedes."

Instead, it was an old white Lada, covered with road grime.

Anatoly shrugged, "As you Americans say, 'It is what it is.'"

Having no other choice, Thas stepped to the back of the car, where Anatoly was standing. As he handed him his suitcase, Evan slipped on an icy patch and nearly fell. He tried hard to keep his cool as he regained his footing. However, when he opened the passenger door, he groaned, "Son of a bitch."

"Problem?"

The back seat was filled with tools and equipment. The front seat was covered with a dirty towel in order to hide its worn fabric. Left with no other convenient option, Evan got into the front seat. Then, with Anatoly constantly puffing on unfiltered cigarettes, they sputtered into Moscow.

When they reached the Hotel Metropol, Anatoly pulled over near the front door. The Metropol was the largest hotel in the city built prior to the revolution and definitely catered to a high-end clientele. Thas felt at home, here, with its eclectic style and its great location, a short walk from the Kremlin and across from the Bolshoi. He wasn't much for ballet but he loved Russian ballerinas who were attracted to available American men.

The driver removed Evan's bag from the trunk and placed it on the sidewalk while they discussed plans for dinner. Suddenly, someone grabbed the nearby suitcase and another man hit Evan over the head. When the dazed American came to, seconds later, Anatoly was standing over him. "You okay?"

Thas raised his face from the frozen concrete with a stream of curses. "Did you catch them?"

Anatoly laughed, "You want me to risk my life?"

Evan angrily inventoried his possessions and was minimally comforted when he realized that at least they had not taken his wallet, passport or cell phone. Other than those items, he now had only the clothes on his back. Then he cursed again when he realized that all his briefing papers were in the stolen suitcase.

Anatoly passed it off with a shrug. "Moscow these days … the wild, wild west."

***

THE NEXT MORNING, Anatoly pulled the crusty Lada up to the front door of the Metropol. Evan had just checked out and, embarrassed to be picked up by clunker, quickly darted across the opulent lobby, through the revolving doors and into the car.

"Let's go. Move it," Thas urged. "Come on!"

The two men rumbled off to find where Thas could buy luggage and replacement clothes before they caught a train out of town. The American was still jet lagged, hung over from emptying his room's mini-bar, and fuming mad.

Once inside the car, Thas laid down the law: "Look, we hired you to do just a few things for me. One of your absolute responsibilities is my protection."

"You do not look injured."

"They took my luggage!" Thas shouted.

"Yes but you are alive and healthy. I cannot be expected to stop what is impossible to stop. This is not West Palm Bay."

"Beach… West Palm *Beach,*" Thas grumbled.

Anatoly stopped the car in the middle of the road. Horns honked as cars forced their way around them on the highway.

"Mr. Thas," the driver said, looking his passenger directly in the eye. "If you do not want me to work for you, then I will let you out here. And if you expect me to do the impossible, you will have to pay me more."

Surrounded by the sound of skidding tires, honking horns and revving engines, Evan responded flatly, "No … We'll stick to our original agreement."

"Good … Now, let's go get your clothes before we catch the train."

Clearly, Anatoly did not realize that he had picked an unfair fight.

***

THIS WAS THE PART OF THE TRIP that Thas dreaded. He and Anatoly were sharing a first class cabin on a 19 hour train ride into north-central Russia. By Thas' standards this was hardly first class, but he felt lucky to get it. When the train station lady snapped, "Impossible!" to his emphatic request for first, or even second, class tickets, Evan realized that he might end up sleeping in a rail car with forty other passengers. Then Anatoly quietly recommended a $20 bribe and, suddenly, all things became possible.

As they pulled out of Yaroslavsky Station, Evan sat on his cabin bunk and looked out the hazy window. The cabin smelled of cigarette smoke and some kind of meat – perhaps salami – from the previous occupants. Evan's new suitcase and ill-fitting clothes were stowed away. He was shocked at how much they had cost him. Moscow had become a city with an impossible cost of living.

As the two men sat quietly, Evan wondered why he was being sent to such a desolate meeting place in Arnietsk – a small town that was unknown to him and most of the world. The Russian space agency, *Roscosmos,* was headquartered in Moscow, and its launch sites were in Kazakhstan, to the south, and near Arkhangelsk, to the north. Evan felt that this extreme detour into oblivion was inconvenient and unwelcome. Perhaps, that was why Cyst had seemed so distracted during his unusually superficial briefing.

As the train rumbled on, Evan turned his cell phone off. Where he was going, it would be useless. Anatoly dug around in his bag and pulled out four bottles of vodka along with pickled cucumbers and pumpernickel bread bites. He placed them on the small table between the two men. Then Anatoly poured two stiff shots of vodka into coffee mugs.

"Here, in Mother Russia," the suddenly pleasant Russian toasted, "may you conduct your negotiations with the wisdom of Peter the Great."

Smirking, Evan countered with another old Russian toast, "To Stalin."

"May God fry his soul," the Russian added without missing a beat. The two bunkmates clinked their mugs and Evan took a sip.

"Do dna! Do dna!" The Russian shouted.

Evan knew what that meant: "*To the bottom!*" This was the tradition that he should have remembered.

Like all Russians, Anatoly threw the alcohol down in one gulp and then chased it with the black bread. Realizing resistance was futile – and numbness was welcome – Thas gulped big.

"Remember," the Russian warned with mock paranoia, "the sober one at the table is usually the stool pigeon." Then he quickly refilled the mugs and saluted, "Between the first and second toasts, may a bullet never pass."

Again, the American countered with, "To Stalin!" They clinked mugs and chugged.

The toasts and shots, mingled with the finger food, continued through the night until the two men were deeply engaged in *vodka veritas.* Certain truths were rarely told, in Russia, without the blessing of vodka. However, no Russian ever drank without food accompaniment. That was considered the mark of a man with a problem.

The train had emerged from the crowded city and passed numerous small *dachas* — vacant summer homes of Moscow residents. Now, they were rolling through frozen hilly terrain. Evan observed that the sky was steel grey and everything steel was rust red. Just then a golden setting sun revealed itself on a hilltop and Thas appreciated today's first glimpse of breathtaking natural beauty.

"You see those rolling hills?" Anatoly inquired.

Thas nodded.

"That is where Catherine the Great famously rode her stallions."

Evan frowned. "Didn't she die trying to have sex with one of them?"

"Mr. Thas!" the Russian pleasantly scolded as he took a drag on his cigarette. "Is that the sort of history they teach you Americans these days? It is vicious lie."

Evan now poured two shots and toasted, "To Catherine the Great!"

Anatoly added, "If she had known me, she never would have needed her stallions."

It were better for him that a millstone
were hanged about his neck,
and he cast into the sea,
than that he should offend
one of these little ones.

Luke 17:2

48

Cyst Estate
Jupiter Island, FL
December 20

In the darkened office, Cyst sat at his computer and scanned through one profile after another. The CyBot analytical software had been screening options ever since Evan left for Russia. Now, it had narrowed down the top twelve candidates. Each one was highly intelligent, male, under six years old, and living in an underdeveloped country.

Like a loving father, he slowly savored every picture.

Beautiful boys. How can I choose just one?

However, Cyst knew that even one might upset Evan. Two or more would positively freak him out. So, one it would be … at least for now.

Methodically, he scanned the biographies and made his eliminations, one after the other. The last three rejections were very difficult choices. But, finally, he chuckled when he arrived at the picture of little Javier Esposito, the smiling four year old with the big brown eyes. His home was in Las Piedras, a small town in southern Uruguay.

Dr. Cyst congratulated himself for his choice. He smiled, thinking about his Eden Project and how he and this new friend might spend hundreds of years together.

Lucky boy.

Cyst printed out the report on the child for his pilot, Lindley, whom he always trusted with his most difficult assignments. Then, he casually jotted notes on the biography sheets, marking that Montevideo would be the closest airport at which his Gulfstream could land. He printed out directions from the airport to the boy's house. He also scribbled a variety of notes including how many people lived at the house, how isolated it was and the best time for the kidnapping.

Not necessity, not desire – no, the love of power
is the demon of men. Let them have everything –
health, food, a place to live, entertainment –
they are and remain unhappy and low-spirited;
for the demon waits and waits
and will be satisfied.

Friedrich Nietzsche

49

Arnietsk, Russia
December 21

After a restless nineteen hours, the train rumbled into Arnietsk Station. Evan and Anatoly were waiting at the door and hopped off with their luggage as soon as the train came to a stop. Evan immediately felt the bitter cold on his face but was mostly struck by the beautiful snow covered mountains surrounding the small station. Here the snow was pure and beautiful.

"Anatoly," a male voice called out to him.

Evan turned and watched Anatoly icily greet the stranger and exchange a few words in Russian. While they talked, Evan sized up the new Russian. He was dressed in black, from his *shapka* fur hat to his military style boots. Only the brown wood of his Kalashnikov rifle strapped over his shoulder offered any contrast. Though he was not a big man, he looked fit, serious and deadly.

"Evan," Anatoly introduced, "this is Sergei Nikolaevich. He will take us to our meeting."

Thas extended his hand and responded, *"Ochen priatna"* as the two men shook hands.

"It's okay," Anatoly advised, "he speaks English … but he does not talk much."

The armed Russian led the two visitors through the heavy snow to a large black Mercedes Benz. Sergei threw their bags into the trunk and the men began a long, silent ride up a narrow, winding road. After rising to a beautiful plateau, well above the train station, the frozen road seemed to be nearing a dead end.

"We'll soon be there," Anatoly assured Evan. "Mr. Melnikov is expecting us."

"Wait, wait. You mean Dr. Spasky, don't you? I'm supposed to meet Dr. Spasky."

Anatoly didn't respond. Evan studied his bodyguard and could tell he was worried that he had exposed a secret.

Thas felt very uncomfortable, here, in the middle of Frozen Nowhere. "You said 'Mr. Melnikov.' Are you talking about Vasily Melnikov?"

The Russian tried to undo the damage. "Don't worry, Mr. Thas. Everything will be okay. You will know everything in a little while. Trust me."

"Trust you?" Evan growled. "Your job was to follow my directions, to protect me and to lead me to a meeting with Dr. Spasky. I've come halfway around the world to this God-forsaken ice cube and now I realize you've been jerking me around. You've been lying all along!"

The driver stopped the car and stepped out with his Kalashnikov at the ready. He opened Evan's door and instructed, "Get out."

"Mr. Thas, please don't cause problems," Anatoly begged. "This is not a man that you mess with."

As the two visitors emerged from the car, the driver popped open the trunk. They grabbed their bags and the quiet Russian nodded toward a nearby gondola on a ski lift. With the armed man bringing up the rear, they boarded the enclosed gondola and, after a push of a button, they lurched forward and then slowly glided across a deep ravine. Around them were breathtaking jagged mountains stabbing into the blue sky, but Thas hardly noticed them. With Anatoly next to him, he sat across from the armed Russian and pondered his immediate fate. Perhaps, he was being kidnapped and held for ransom. If so, Evan doubted Huntington Cyst would pay up … even if it meant saving his life. Maybe he was about to become the victim of a revenge murder. After all, Cyst had made plenty of enemies around the world. Whatever the scenario, Evan felt he had been unforgivably deceived by his bodyguard and betrayed by who knows who else. Because of that, he now feared for his life.

After crossing the chasm, a palatial mountaintop estate appeared in the mist. The enormous whitewashed stone castle – with a steeply angled clay tile roof – had a medieval appearance. It sat on a plateau that was surrounded by cliffs. Studying the view for his possible escape routes, Thas was disappointed to see only one way for him to leave the property, and he was sitting in it. The premises were fortified with armed guards patrolling the perimeter with dogs and surveillance cameras scattered about the property. He noticed what looked like a heliport at the rear of the castle.

Evan thought: *Whoever owns this estate must have serious money … and serious paranoia.* And, from what he had read, that fit the description of Vasily Melnikov.

Melnikov was Russia's richest man and, with the recent explosion in oil prices, might well have become its most powerful. Shortly after the breakup of the Soviet Union, he had ruthlessly gained a stranglehold on the country's oil and gas industry. He was one of the shadowy members of the Legion of Babylon. But, as far as Thas knew, he had no financial interests regarding the technology contracts that Evan was here to negotiate.

The gondola slowly glided toward the castle and, finally, ground to a stop. The men silently stepped out into the bitter wind as two small Asian men quickly approached. They took the luggage and led the men to a side door. Once inside, the visitors shook off the snow and were instructed to remove their coats, gloves, hats and boots. One of the Asians handed them plush sheepskin slippers, sized appropriately. Then, without a word, the other Asian led them through the castle's hallways. Sergei followed with his ever-present rifle.

From somewhere ahead, Evan heard women giggling. Then, suddenly, the dark, narrow hallway ended in a bright new wing of the building. Before them, was a massive room with an indoor, Olympic sized swimming pool. The walls and ceiling were made of glass, allowing not only abundant lighting but also exposing one of the most scenic mountain views on the planet. It was jarring for Evan to feel the comfortable, warm temperature of this pool room while realizing how bitterly cold it was outside. In and around the pool were at least a dozen beautiful women all making the most of their scanty bikinis.

"Mr. Thas, I'm glad you could join me." Evan turned and saw a short, fat man with a coal-black comb-over leaving the sauna and coming his way.

That is one ugly guy, Evan thought as he noticed a small wart on the Russian's large nose and a larger one on his second chin. Evan appreciated that, at least, the little man had the decency to cover the rest of his distorted body with a terry cloth robe.

"I am Vasily Melnikov," the troll said as he extended his stubby-fingered hand.

Thas kept his arm down. "Mr. Melnikov, I do not appreciate being brought here under false pretenses. This is a very disturbing turn of events. Dr. Cyst will also find this to be an unforgiveable diversion from my responsibilities here in Russia."

"No, no, nonsense," the host dismissed the complaint with a wave of his hand. "Dr. Cyst knows exactly what is happening. Ask Anatoly, he tell you."

Evan ignored the broken English and turned to see his bodyguard standing behind him. Embarrassed, Anatoly nodded in agreement.

"You can't be serious. I was briefed for technology meetings. I came with a file full of briefing documents. They were stolen."

"Yes, necessary diversion. We knew your papers would be compromised. It is better for us that Russian and American governments think you are here for that purpose. I am sure you understand."

"No I don't! You mean, you knew that I would be attacked?"

"No, usually they quietly microfilm or remove them from hotel room. Perhaps the government operatives saw the opportunity and jumped a little too hard. Russians can be that way. But it is good that they now will be wasting time on a wild … how do you say … a wild duck...?"

"Wild goose chase."

"Precisely … Now, Mr. Thas, I want you relax and enjoy your stay here. Please make yourself a home." Melnikov glanced at the smiling beauties around the pool and suggested, "Our staff can be very accommodating."

If you gaze for long into the abyss,
the abyss gazes also into you.
Friedrich Nietzsche

50

Melnikov Estate
Arnietsk, Russia
December 22

Thas moved around his luxurious bedroom with the suspicion that he was being watched. He did not know where the video cameras were hidden but he was confident they were there. He slid his slippers softly over the wood plank floors but, occasionally, heard a loud creak. Cautiously, he opened his door, looked into the hall and cursed when he saw Sergei standing there with his Kalashnikov.

"What do you want?" the guard asked.

"I want you to stop treating me like a prisoner."

The Russian didn't respond and Evan slammed the door. Thas walked across the room and opened the French doors. He stepped out onto the small balcony, braving the cold air. The view was breathtaking but the escape route, unfortunately, would require a forty foot fall. Even if that were possible, *then where would I go?*

Evan realized that he would be staying here for as long as his host required. So, adapting to his confinement, the unhappy prisoner strode to the heavy, carved wooden door, opened it, and ordered, "Hey, why don't you make yourself useful and get me a bottle of vodka?"

The guard answered, "That is not a problem." But he did not budge. The response confirmed Evan's surveillance concerns and, sure enough, within three minutes he heard a knock on the door. When he opened it, one of the smiling pool beauties entered holding a tray of caviar, black bread and vodka. Evan admired her string bikini, and everything in it, as she delivered the tray to a small table in the room. Normally, he would have been all over her. But, today, he made a point to show no interest. He was more concerned about regaining his freedom and safety.

After curtly seeing her out the door, Evan angrily threw back a few shots of vodka and cursed Cyst for keeping him in the dark. Evan had always done everything he was asked, no matter how difficult, humiliating or unnatural it felt. However, this was too much. Never again would he allow himself to be deceived like this.

DINNER CONSISTED OF the Russian foods that Evan liked least: beets, cabbage and a bit of ground steak accompanying his generous serving of gristle. Except for the meat, the food was probably high quality, but just very different than what he preferred. He thought the *solyanka* – cold soup with fish and vegetables – was almost inedible. However, Evan had decided to be an agreeable guest, hoping that a charade would get him out of here fastest. And after finishing off most of the vodka in his room, a cordial attitude now came easier to him.

Melnikov and his guest sat at a small table in a cozy old dining room. This couldn't have been the main dining hall but, still, it was beautifully furnished and perfect for intimate dinners next to the roaring fireplace. Except for the occasional intrusion of a waiter, the two men spoke privately.

"*Na zdorovie!*" Melnikov toasted as he raised a shot of vodka.

Thas responded with, "*Nu,*" and both men downed their alcohol, exhaled loudly and nibbled on their black bread.

The host apologized for the unusual circumstances that drew

Thas here. He assured his guest that all would be explained to his satisfaction and that he hoped this would be remembered as the most important and profitable night of the young man's life.

After the toasts and the apology, the conversation soon became personal.

"How much are you worth, Mr. Thas?" the Russian asked boldly.

"Not a lot. But I have everything I want."

"Really? I would think Dr. Cyst should be more generous with you."

"He's my adopted father," Evan answered with irritation. "Whatever is his, will be mine, someday."

"Yes … someday," the Russian nodded, and then added, "perhaps."

Evan let that odd word pass.

"And you are here to negotiate with Dr. Spasky for a Russian-American joint venture that will feature the technology you call Titan?"

"That's the plan."

"No," Melnikov stated with emphasis. "That is the ruse."

Evan grew even more irritated. "Look, I've watched Dr. Cyst commit Cyst Institute resources on Titan for three years. He is hardly a man who wastes his time and money."

"He has not wasted it," the host answered as he poured more vodka. "The aerospace application of Titan is not only theoretically possible, but now practical. However, your ignorance on the details demonstrates that Dr. Cyst does not trust you as much as you think. Perhaps I should not be discussing this sensitive information with you." Melnikov smiled and then added, "Do you agree?"

Without a response the Russian continued, "Titan scares hell out of your government and mine. They are afraid someone – other than themselves, of course – will control it." He passed the alcohol over to Thas. "Is this all news to you?"

"Yes ... and with all due respect … I don't know whether I believe you." Evan corrected himself. "In fact, I don't. Why does Huntie need you?"

"If Titan is ever to become something more than a theory, he needs a financier to put him over the top. But if he works with a government, he will lose control."

"Oh, come on. He's a billionaire."

Melnikov chuckled. "Mr. Thas, there are billionaires and then there are *billionaires*. Your Dr. Cyst is truly brilliant, but I can buy him twenty times over."

The Russian raised his glass and toasted, "To true genius, true wealth and true power, Mr. Thas."

Evan refused the gesture. "I have to talk to him before I say anything more. I'm sorry."

"That can be arranged but he will be angry. It is two in the morning there and he does not like when I call his home."

"Do it."

The pudgy host pushed his chair back and slowly rose from it. He walked over to a table, picked up a satellite telephone and dialed a number. He handed the phone to Evan.

On the other end, Thas could hear a sleepy Cyst grumble, "Yeah."

"Huntie?"

"Yeah … Evan … I hope you're not calling me from …"

"Listen, now. Am I supposed to be with Mr. M. and not Dr. S.?"

"Uh ... yeah … yeah … that's right. It had to be done this way. You'll be bringing back information … unwritten, of course."

"And I am completely safe?"

"Yes," Huntington assured. "Don't worry."

"Huntie?" Evan continued, realizing that the man on the other end might be an imposter, "Can you authenticate?"

"Yes, of course." Cyst recited the code that had been established for this trip, "D3869F1B6."

Disappointed that he had been used as a clueless pawn in an elaborate chess game, Evan mumbled, "Okay," and pressed the off button.

"You see Mr. Thas, I am completely trustworthy," the Russian bragged, and then added. "for those who are cooperative."

When they had finished the last course of sweet dumplings and coffee – Evan's favorite part of the meal – Melnikov laid out the grand plan that had brought Evan to this remote place. He shared with the young man Titan secrets that Cyst hadn't yet revealed to his apprentice. For an oil man, Evan could see he certainly had a broad understanding of the technology issues inherent in this project.

Titan, he explained, was a technological breakthrough that enabled the tracking of human brain waves. Like the way a Radio Frequency Identification (RFID) tag tracks a product in a store, or a car moving through the EZ Pass lane, the Cyst Institute had discovered that electrical activity in the brain, produced by firing neurons, is uniquely identifiable. Consequently, electroencephalographic brain waves could now identify each person as effectively as a fingerprint. Driver's licenses and access cards would become a thing of the past. More importantly, every commercial transaction would automatically be credited or debited to a certain individual's account. Thus, there would be no more waiting to pay at the grocery store, the bar or the movie theatre. With Titan's short-range scanners, every security clearance would be attributed to a unique brain wave pattern. This would allow authorized individuals to avoid delays at airport security, military bases or even entering the White House's West Wing. Terrorists and criminals could be tracked continually and, consequently, terrorism and crime would become impractical. In fact, with long-range satellite surveillance, every human on earth could eventually be tracked.

Evan immediately realized that the profit potential of this plan was staggering. Combining Cyst-Blanc supercomputers with the analytical capabilities of the CyBot search engine, the power that such a breakthrough offered was mind-boggling.

Melnikov continued: "But Dr. Cyst's dilemma is finding a partner to finance this massive project. Of course, governments have the deepest pockets, but they also expect complete control. And assistance from financial institutions would compromise confidential information with their reporting and oversight requirements. I, on other hand, have a lot of spare change in my pocket since the oil shock, and Dr. Cyst knows a relationship with me is, necessarily, discreet."

Thas reflected on what was said and waited for more.

"Mr. Thas," the Russian leaned in toward him and confided softly, "I appreciate what you did for me."

Melnikov was a man who typically played his cards close to the vest, but Evan immediately knew what he meant. No person had benefitted from the oil crisis more than Vasily Melnikov. Thas resented that his veil of secrecy had been lifted. He thought that the takedown of the Saudi Royals had been a secret operation based on Cyst's shifting investment portfolio. He had not realized Melnikov had been dealt into the game. It made Evan squirm to realize that he had been playing blind in a no-limit poker game with the ultimate stakes. Cyst obviously had shared too much information with the Russian.

Thas wondered, *How much does he know?*

Cyst had participated in the Saudi operation but Thas and Lindley were the only ones who got their hands dirty. Thas had arranged for the hiring of the Saudi soap workers and their eventual demise. He had planted the string of dead-end clues. In fact, Thas felt that he deserved prime credit for orchestrating the entire crisis and its eventual opportunities.

The Russian interrupted Evan's mental calculations, "Young man, please don't act so shocked. I know more than you think and, apparently, a lot more than you. Why does Dr. Cyst choose to keep so many secrets from you?"

Thas, slumped back in his chair, grumbled, "Perhaps, you can fill me in."

Melnikov explained that he had contacted Cyst after his sources had informed him of the Titan project that Cyst was pitching to the Russian government. Melnikov said that he was actually the one who came up with the Saudi strategy. He also had procured the biological agent, with the help of corrupt Russian laboratory officials. Thus, the mutually-beneficial partnership of Melnikov and Cyst had allowed the Russian to become obscenely wealthy in order to privately finance Cyst's Titan project that, eventually, would make both of them obscenely powerful. These revelations reduced Evan to feeling like a bit player.

"And my briefing papers?" Evan asked.

"We knew they would be stolen. The schematics were very close to the real thing, but critically flawed. Once Dr. Spasky inspects the documents, the Russian government will quickly conclude the project is a pipe dream and drop it. I'm sure Cyst has already received a call from Dr. Spasky, feigning alarm, asking why you miss meeting. Dr. Cyst will act concerned for you and Dr. Spasky will act concerned for you. However, neither side will seek another meeting.

Evan exhaled loudly and grumbled sarcastically, "I'm gonna kill Huntie when I see him."

The Russian smiled and then abruptly declared, "Enough for this evening. We talk more at breakfast."

Evan nodded.

The Russian offered a devious grin. "You did not seem to like Svetlana, Mr. Thas."

Evan understood he was referring to the beautiful woman who had delivered vodka to his room earlier. "Oh, no, *otleechna!*" he responded with the Russian word for "excellent."

"I think I understand. I send someone you like best."

For the first time, the two men smiled. They shook hands and retired.

AS EVAN CRAWLED UNDER the plush down comforter and plumped up his pillows, he wished that Melnikov would change his mind and send Svetlana to his room. He felt bad for making her feel unwanted. Now, he was ready to be more charming.

With his bedside lamp still on, he thought about how it was only when travelling that he was able to pursue his natural inclinations. That was one of the main reasons he enjoyed being sent all over the world to represent Cyst's interests. Otherwise, his monogamous lifestyle in Florida would have been suffocating. He realized his relationship with Cyst was weird, but mutually beneficial. It was the only life he had ever known … and not a bad one at that.

Evan heard a knock and shouted, "*Da*" from the bed. Sergei opened the door and, looking at Evan with an expression of disgust, shoved someone into the room and closed the door. It was a small boy, perhaps eight years old. The child had a broad smile plastered on his face, but fear in his eyes.

"I want be your friend," he recited his memorized lines in broken English.

"No, no, no. This isn't what I want."

"Yes, mister. I be your friend tonight."

Haunting memories flooded Evan's head. He remembered his own boyhood: lost, alone and powerless. Those first few years in America were terrifying. It was only with Cyst's daily regime of rewards and punishments, year after year, that he had learned to hide the hurt and accept the inevitable. However, he was not like Cyst and did not want to be.

Now, a manifestation of his childhood pain stood before him.

"Hey, it's okay," Evan tried to comfort the boy. "You don't have to do anything for me … You can leave now. Okay?"

"No," the boy insisted, "I make you happy."

"Look, I'm not interested. Please go."

"I can stay. You not be sorry."

"No," Evan objected. "Leave!"

The boy looked at him blankly and then started sobbing. But still he didn't leave.

Thas was disgusted, realizing that his secret relationship with Cyst was known. Suddenly, he felt dirty. He resented Melnikov for this presumptuous "gift" and for putting this boy through the degradations that he, himself, had endured.

"Look, you're a nice young boy," Evan assured the child. "Don't be upset. You don't have to do anything with me tonight. That's good, right?"

"Mister, if I go…" the boy choked out between sobs, "he will beat me... Please, I stay."

Evan got out of the bed, walked toward him, took the boy's hand and brought him to the bed.

"You sleep here," Evan said as he lifted him up and tucked him in. "No one will bother you tonight."

Thas took two pillows, turned out the lamp and curled up in the corner on the wood plank floor.

* * *

IN THE DARKNESS, the tormenting demons returned. Vague memories of Evan's cold, faceless parents flitted through his consciousness. He remembered children mocking him for his appearance but, when he rushed crying to his mother, he suddenly realized that he didn't look like her either. He remembered two more dark skinned boys.

Were they my brothers? Were they the favorites?

Deeper and deeper the voices brought him.

I wish I could smother the life out of them ... I hope death rains down on all of them.

He remembered his mother putting him to bed in a darkened room, but could remember no expression of love and no facial characteristics, except those strange, exotic eyes.

Bitch!

Then the sights and smells changed. It was Cyst during those first days with odors of tequila and sweat on that hairy body that wouldn't stop pressing down on him ... suffocating him ... burying him. He was only a child, powerless. No matter how much he fought it, he could not control it.

As he laid there on the castle's cold wooden planks, Evan's entire being burned with rage, vengeance and hate. He despised his parents for giving him up so easily.

How could they just sell their son? That pathetic $220,000 is probably long gone, by now. Did they regret what they did? Did they cry over it? Why didn't they try to contact me? It's their fault I only know hate.

Hidden deep within his soul, Evan's anger became a consuming furnace. The growing fire could not be contained much longer. Evan Thas suspected that he would soon release the pressurized conflagration within himself. It had to be vented ... but at whom?

* * *

THE NEXT MORNING, the sun peaked through the wooden shuttered windows. When the light hit him in the face, Thas rolled over and rubbed his sore back. He could hear the soft sound of deep breaths. Evan shuffled over to the bed and gently shook the boy's shoulder. He jolted awake with a gasp.

"It's okay," the man whispered. "You can go now… Tell him I was very happy."

The boy nodded enthusiastically, hopped out of the bed and bolted out the door.

Evan cleaned himself up, using the wash basin that had been left in the room, and changed clothes. When he left the room, the ever-present Sergei led him down the old, dark hallway back to the small dining room where Melnikov was reading a newspaper next to the fireplace. Evan wondered how difficult it must be for the paper to be delivered each morning.

"Where has Anatoly been hiding?" Evan asked with barely concealed resentment.

"Good morning, Mr. Thas," the Russian greeted. "We sent him back to town last night. He will pick you up later. Please, join me."

Evan plopped down at the table, resenting that his own bodyguard was taking orders from Melnikov. But, then again, *Maybe they killed Anatoly.*

The dour waiter poured coffee and placed blintzes and fruit in front of the guest.

"So, I can leave today?"

"Of course."

"Mr. Melnikov, I still don't understand why I had to make this trip. Why am I here?"

"You are here because I requested a face-to-face meeting."

"Why?" Thas demanded.

"We are talking about lot of money. I always want to meet my potential partners."

"Your partner would be Dr. Cyst. Why don't you fly to America and meet him in person?"

"Your government would not treat me hospitably on their soil," the Russian frowned. "We have our differences."

Melnikov did not seem to mind the questions. In fact, it appeared he was studying Thas as the interrogation proceeded.

"So, what good is it to meet with me? I follow Dr. Cyst's lead."

"I believe in long-term relationships. If it is true, what you say, someday, you will have the power." The Russian changed the subject. "Did you sleep well last night? Did you enjoy your visitor?"

"NO I DIDN'T!" Thas snapped.

"Yes, yes, I understand," Melnikov nodded with mock sympathy. "It is terrible thing when a boy is put through that kind of life."

Melnikov studied Evan's face then added, "Isn't it, Dr. Thas?"

Pride goes before destruction,
a haughty spirit before a fall.
Proverbs 16:18

51

Russian Railways Car
Western Siberia
December 23

The old train rumbled, squealed and screeched through the snow-covered birch forests of central Russia. Thas had said little to Anatoly since they left the castle eight hours ago. He had too much to think about, too much to absorb. Sober, Anatoly didn't care much for talking, anyway.

When the Russian lit up his tenth cigarette in the cabin, Evan took a walk through the train. He saw few people onboard and all of them appeared to be Russian. He found no food car and the only form of entertainment seemed to be smoking. Occasionally, he would pass a Russian carelessly standing next to an open door, admiring the passing scenery and puffing his smoke out into the brisk air. One cabin had a group of men getting loud and drunk as they played cards.

When Evan returned to his cabin, Anatoly had pulled out vodka and food.

"Mr. Melnikov sent us off in style," the Russian bragged as he held up the bottle. "This is not just Russian vodka. It is *Jewel of Russia* … the best."

Evan did not respond. He felt as if he was suffering from Post-Traumatic Stress Disorder. He could not stop remembering how vulnerable he had felt when he realized his secrets had been exposed and his safety compromised. So, he comforted himself, killing his pain the traditional way. The first few shots were consumed without toasts as both men watched the endless forests pass by, outside the train. Evan remembered how, twice now, his bodyguard had failed to protect and inform him. The theft of the briefing papers might not have been avoidable, but the unexpected diversion to the castle was inexcusable.

Evan wanted to lash out at the Russian. However, he was still on foreign soil and out of his element. He forced himself to remain calm.

"Anatoly," Evan said, "you really let me down. I could have gotten killed back there."

"No, you were safe," the Russian reassured. "Vasily Melnikov would not murder you… at least not in his home. Besides, Dr. Cyst told me to keep the details secret."

"Well, I just wish I hadn't been blindsided by you. Can I trust you now? Am I in control now?"

"Of course. Everything goes smooth from here. We can relax."

And, with that, Anatoly passed another shot of vodka and lit another cigarette.

Evan asked, "Do you have to smoke that in here? Your cigarettes are giving me a headache."

"No problem," the Russian responded. He downed his alcohol and stepped out of the cabin.

Thas stared through the grimy window, into the frozen darkness. He had seen no signs of civilization out there for over an hour. His spirits were low and the demons were still nagging at him, stoking the fires. But he wasn't giving in easily. Perhaps, he thought, Melnikov had been trying to sow seeds of dissent, hoping Evan would mastermind a mutiny at XCyst Industries. However, Evan knew that that pipe dream would never happen. He had excelled at whatever role Cyst had assigned to him, be it right hand man, son, student, or even lover. He was pleased with being Cyst's indispensible assistant.

Before they parted, the ugly Russian had expressed his desire to review and execute a detailed contract as soon as Cyst's lawyers could send it. "I can work with you, Mr. Thas," were some of Melnikov's last words to him. "If anything happens to Dr. Cyst, can I count on you to follow through?"

What did he mean by that? Was that a threat against Huntie? But, maybe, he's just a cautious man, eliminating any long term uncertainty. After all, he'll have a lot of money on the line.

Evan left the cabin to get some fresh air. Down the hall he found Anatoly standing next to an open door, puffing his cigarette. His emergence from the hot stale air of the cabin, into the cold brisk air near the doorway, stimulated Evan's senses. The air did not seem as bitterly cold as it had been and Evan breathed deeply as he slid next to the Russian.

"You still mad at me?" Anatoly asked.

Thas said, "Yeah."

"You were lucky I was there," Anatoly bragged as he took a puff. "You do not realize how much I protect you,"

"No I don't," Thas snorted.

"It is true. This is Russia, not West Palm Bay."

"*Beach*, it's *Beach*, dammit!"

Anatoly shrugged, "Beach, Bay, it makes no difference here. The only thing that is certain in Russia is that you need me."

"Need you for what?" Evan asked.

Anatoly frowned as he glanced up and down the unintimidating American. "You Americans," Anatoly's vodka sneered, "so typical! When oil was cheap, you treated us like dirt. Now, we will see who has to beg. Soon, we will own you. We hold all the cards."

"Thanks for your concern," Evan dismissed, "but we'll be okay."

Anatoly laughed. “You are not as smart as you think you are, little errand boy. You complain about how I do my job, but I brought you back alive. You don’t know how close you came to being disposed of like yesterday’s trash.” Anatoly turned to dramatically flick his cigarette out the open door. “We are not men you want to mess w…”

Thas shoved the Russian into the frozen darkness. The opportunity was too perfect to ignore.

All that is necessary for evil to triumph
is for good men to do nothing.
Edmund Burke

52

Tarbuwth Correctional Facility
Yashar, NY
December 24

Prison officials were amazed at the kooks that John brought out of the woodwork. Since the internationally publicized trial had concluded, TCF had been flooded with letters addressed to him. People from all over the world claimed they had known John years, even decades before. They all expressed their love for the man that they said hadn't changed a bit.

But, among the inmates, more pressing concerns were on their minds, these days. In the cafeteria, John's followers sat around the lunch table with him, bowed their heads and gave thanks for the slop they were about to eat. However, they did not gobble down their lunch like in days past. With the day of John's execution approaching, none of his friends was in the mood to eat. They only wanted to hear John speak.

"Remember what I have told you," John reminded them. "The story of Jesus does not end on the Cross. Likewise, your lives do not end here. This is a beginning for you."

The men all nodded in agreement.

"What about Qurban?" Booker asked. Gossip was rarely believed in prison but all the inmates had heard that the dead Muslim had miraculously resuscitated in the ambulance and escaped.

John responded, "For a man of faith, it is not a hard thing to die, and it is not an easy thing to live. Qurban now has true life more abundantly than he has ever imagined it. Whether his body is alive or dead, be happy for him. He chose to hear. He chose to see. However, for the man who refuses to hear and see, it will be worse for him than if he were deaf and blind." John paused, thoughtfully, and then added, "I will be leaving you soon and..."

Worthington interrupted, "Mr. John, please don't go. We're praying for a miracle. You told us our prayers have power."

"Everything is good, brother. It is God's will that I go. But you will see me again … And between now and then, I pray that you will bear much fruit for the Lord."

The men at the adjacent table erupted with laughter when one of them turned and deliberately spat, hitting John on the shoulder. John's companions instinctively jumped out of their seats, ready to pound the life out of the aggressor. The attacker's friends also stood, bracing for a fight.

But John kept talking calmly: "From now on, whenever you see Christ's Cross, remember that He allowed His hands to be nailed down because of His love for you."

Except for the sound of John's voice, a tense silence prevailed around the tables as the twenty adrenaline-rushed combatants faced off against each other.

John, the only man still sitting, ignored the passions and continued, "He needs your hands, now, to continue His work. He wants your hands to bless, your hands to heal, your hands to Spiritually transform."

Worthington's clenched fists slowly loosened and, for the first time in his life, he withdrew from a fight and sat down again. One by one, the men at both tables followed his lead.

"Worthington," John added, "you say that you are praying for a miracle … He will give you many. However, do not think in terms of me against you. For each of us, the ultimate challenge in life is me against me. Not until pleasure and pain, praise and insult don't matter anymore can Spiritual perfection be achieved."

Worthington offered a weak smile but John could tell he was not reassured.

John sniffed over his food. “The mashed potatoes don’t smell right.”

Worthington lifted his plate up to his nose and took a big whiff. Just then, John reached over the table and gently shoved the plate into Worthington’s face. Everyone gasped at John’s rash provocation. As the big inmate lowered the dish, John sat across from him, grinning. Worthington’s potato-smeared face showed shock and his chest started twitching and trembling until, to everyone’s relief, the giggles he was holding back burst into a thunderous laugh.

As they all hooted, the prisoners wondered at John’s invincible calm, even as his execution approached. They could not understand why John had refused to appeal the verdict and had even assisted to fast-track the process. His cooperation, along with the behind-the-scenes manipulations of the White House, insured a record setting pace for an American execution in modern times.

John smiled at each one of his twelve followers and said, “Rejoice in the Lord always. I will say it again: Rejoice! Let your gentleness be evident to all. The Lord is near. Do not be anxious about anything, but in everything, by prayer and petition, with thanksgiving, present your requests to God. And the peace of God, which transcends all understanding, will guard your hearts and your minds in Christ Jesus.”[1]

That evening, the men all rested comfortably in their bunks, finally starting to fully appreciate John’s “insanity” and realizing how good it felt not to be recovering from the cuts, bruises and breaks that their vicious prison fight would have caused.

Strangely, however, John’s thoughts were drawn to someone he hadn’t seen in decades.

Now learn this lesson from the fig tree:
As soon as its twigs get tender and its leaves come out,
you know that summer is near. Even so, when you see
these things happening, you know that it is near,
right at the door. I tell you the truth, this generation will
certainly not pass away until all these things have happened.
Mark 13:28-30

53

St. Basil's Convent
Outside Beirut, Lebanon
31 Years Earlier

John quickly surveyed the damage, flagged down a passing truck on the dark street, and recruited two dazed men to assist him. Just moments earlier, an errant missile had slammed into the east wing of St. Basil's Convent, leveling three sleeping quarters. He suspected that nuns were buried under the rubble and that their time was running out for them.

"You!" John barked in Arabic, "get over here. Watch your step … And you, start on the far corner."

As the morning light dawned, the three men frantically removed the collapsed stones that had trapped the moaning survivors beneath the debris. One by one, they freed each varying chunk and rolled or hurled it away. The process was slow moving.

By now a crowd of men and women had gathered in the street.

"Please, help us," John begged.

Two women and a man joined in while others simply watched and cursed the Israeli missile attack.

"Be careful," John advised. "It's unstable … There are survivors underneath."

They worked for twenty minutes, under the increasingly warm

morning sun, until John displaced a stone that revealed a small part of a nun's face.

"Can you see me?" he asked as he looked into the hole.

He watched the young woman's eye open, and she whispered, "Yes" in Syrian Arabic.

John felt a stab of emotion, jarred by the incongruity of the beautifully exotic, almost cat-like eye that helplessly beckoned from under the crushing debris. Perhaps, he could save this one innocent victim.

"Everyone, over here!" he shouted.

Under John's direction, the six workers focused and intensified their efforts over the survivor. Proceeding cautiously, but deliberately, they removed one stone, one beam, after another. Soon, John managed to lift her out of the enlarged hole as she quietly stared into his eyes. Under the circumstances she seemed unembarrassed to be seen with her close shaven hair exposed and wearing only a modest cotton night gown. She also did not show any outward signs of serious injury. Inwardly, however, she was damaged.

John's heart raced, not only from the strenuous work he had just finished, but also because of the effect this beautiful woman in his arms had caused. He had not felt this emotion in many, many years and, when he carried her to the arriving Red Crescent ambulance, some spectators cheered. However, one man grumbled at the indecency of their actions. Perhaps that was because John could not turn his gaze from her mesmerizing eyes.

As they approached the ambulance, he held her head close when she whispered in Syrian, "You saved my life."

He returned a blushing smile.

Then, almost inaudibly, she asked, "Why?"

He did not know how to respond. So, he didn't. As he turned to lay her on a waiting gurney, she saw the leveled wing of the convent. Her thin jaw tightened, her eyes narrowed. She whispered something he could not understand.

"What?" he asked as he moved his ear closer.

She turned her beautiful eyes his way and repeated, "Damn Jew pigs."

JOHN HAD ARRIVED in Beirut the night before the missile strike. He had been given a job and a room, across the street from the convent, at *Caritas Internationalis,* the Roman Catholic international relief agency.

Immediately, when he heard the pre-dawn crash, he bolted from his bed, and raced to the scene. John knew that Lebanon had been ripped apart by civil war for seven long, destructive years. The hostilities, however, were only half spent. Eventually, there would be fifteen years of civil war, 250,000 people killed and a million more wounded.

Primarily because of his language skills, *Caritas* had assigned John to help the diverse range of victims in this war-torn region. Specifically, he was to assist with the physical needs of the suddenly vulnerable, including refugees, migrants, needy children, orphans, widows and the elderly. He also hoped to bring at least some small hint of Spiritual peace to this devastated community, even if only delivering it one-on-one. While trying to get to Beirut, he had encoundered one delay after another. Suddenly, however, his ministry was starting sooner than expected.

Southern Lebanon was now controlled by the Palestine Liberation Organization which was vehemently anti-Israel and, increasingly, under the domination of the terrorist mastermind B. Abu Ladin.[1] He was widely regarded as the most ruthless of the Palestinian leaders but his dark, charismatic deportment easily enticed one's eyes away from the blood on his hands. In addition to seeking the destruction of all Israel, B. Abu Ladin had planned and executed terrorist attacks in 20 countries. Each of his atrocities was autographed with his extreme, but random, cruelty. One publication summed him up as, "... a patriot turned psychopath. He served only himself ..." Proudly, he once boasted, "I am the evil spirit which moves around only at night causing ... nightmares."

Even though he was busy fomenting civil war in Lebanon, it was his leadership that introduced regular rocket launches into northern Israel. Ladin realized that no country would tolerate continued shelling from a neighbor. However, he also knew that any military response from Israel would only serve to advance his primary goal: to galvanize the region's hatred for the Jews.

Israel, on the other hand, had demonstrated its willingness to seek peace by returning control of the Sinai Peninsula to Egypt just three years earlier. That initiative, however, had increased Arab hostilities against Israel and, in retaliation, the Arab League suspended Egypt from its ranks. On the streets, Arabs and Persians reiterated their claim that peace is not possible with Israel. Iraq stepped up its nuclear weapons development threat and Egyptian President Anwar Sadat was soon dead, at the hands of Muslim extremists.

So, it became clear that Jewish peace overtures and restraint were only encouraging belligerent responses. After waiting twenty five centuries for the prophesied return of the Jewish state, after enduring all manner of discrimination and persecution, the Israelis were in no mood to allow further missile attacks on their homeland.

That was the chain of events that had brought unintended death to a small convent outside of Beirut.

* * *

JOHN'S TEAM HAD SAVED one nun, but lost two that day. The rest of the residents had escaped without injury.

Now, three days later, John went to visit the woman he had rescued. He was still bothered by the nun's distressing comment. He knew she must have been furious, perhaps even incoherent. Apparently, she even wanted to die. But surely, by now, she would have recovered from despair and regretted her repulsive remark.

At the hospital, he asked to see Faridah Shaaban, the nun's birth name. An unfriendly, skinny nurse signaled him to follow her. Walking down the hall, he became more uncomfortable with each echoing step of the nurse's clunky shoes. He considered turning to leave but he wanted to see this woman again. He could not get her off his mind. John admitted to himself that he had felt an extraordinary attraction to her. But her appeal had to be more than just the physical. He had long been celibate and had no lust in his heart. Surely, a Spiritual dimension motivated this fascination. It couldn't be caused by her beauty alone.

"Sister?" he asked softly in Syrian after the nurse showed him in and left the room.

The nun opened her eyes and blinked at John. She had bandages on her arm and around her forehead.

"My name is John Malek. I pulled you out of the debris the other day."

"Yes, I remember," she said without any indication of appreciation.

"How are you doing?"

"I'll be fine."

She seemed discomforted by his visit, so an unsettling silence endured for a moment. John had planned to say more but, now, could think of nothing. Like a father aching for an injured child, he felt helpless. So, when she silently turned her head toward the window, he ended the visit.

"Well, Sister, I just wantedto check up on you. I hope you get well soon."

She nodded.

John turned to leave, embarrassed and wondering whether she was depressed, still mourning the loss of friends or, maybe, resentful that she had been saved by a Jew. Just as he reached for the door, she said, "Mr. Malek?"

He stopped, pleased that he might finally get a response from this mysterious, silent woman. Flatly, she revealed, "I know who you are."

FOUR DAYS LATER, John led a group of men in a salvage operation on the damaged wing of the convent. They hoped to sift through the wreckage and save personal possessions, particularly sacred objects and sacramentals, before the rest of the debris was hauled away. They set up a table for all the items that might be claimed by survivors and relatives of the deceased. John looked down on the collection, disappointed that more items had not been found. They had only collected two rosaries, four Bibles, one crucifix and several sets of religious vestments. But, then again, these women had all taken a vow of poverty.

Then one of the workers tossed a torn and dusty book on the table and said, "I don't believe it."

John grimaced when he recognized the black book with a red pentagram on its cover. It was *The Satanic Bible* by Anton Szandor LaVey. It had been written only thirteen years earlier but had gained a surprisingly strong, international following.

How did this get into the convent?

John picked up the book and tossed it to a nearby trash heap. With clear disappointment in his voice, he suggested that everyone should stop for lunch.

He and his workers had spent the last four hours without a break and the surviving nuns had brought a modest lunch out to them. When John sat to eat with the men at the makeshift table, he soon tried to lift their spirits with small talk and occasional jokes. He felt the circumstances around them were dire enough without contributing to the gloom with self-pity and blame.

As they finished lunch, he noticed the hospitalized nun observing them from a distance. She was not wearing her habit. John wondered how long she had been watching and, when she realized she had been spotted, she slipped back into a shadowed alley. However, John smiled and waved her to come join them. Reluctantly, she stepped into the light and approached their table. The only sign of injury that John noticed was a large bandage on her forehead.

"You seem to be recovering nicely, Sister."

"Call me Faridah," she responded cautiously.

The men had finished lunch, so they returned to their work, leaving John and the woman to speak in private.

John pointed at the religious items on the table and asked, "Do you want to claim any of these?"

She barely glanced at them, "No."

"Please, Sister, take whatever you want."

"I said don't call me that."

"Why? I don't feel comfortable calling you by your given name."

"I left the Order."

"Oh, I'm sorry to hear that … Is there anything … anything I can do for you?"

"No, you are too late."

That struck John as an odd phrase. *Too late for what?* He could not hold his curiosity back any longer: "Faridah, what did you mean when you said you know who I am?"

"I know more than you think," she responded, standing over him as if in a position of superiority.

"Apparently not," John tried to make light of her remark, "or you wouldn't have made that racist comment to the Jew who saved you."

"I knew exactly what I was saying."

"So, you hate all Jews?"

"Don't be ridiculous," she barked, finally, with emotion. "I *am* a Jew." Faridah paused and, for the first time, studied John's reaction. Then she added, "You see, we are more alike than you realize. We are two sides of the same coin. I ran from my Jewish roots just like you."

"I did not!" John answered with surprise. "I am proud of my ancestors. My faith is the fulfillment of my Jewish heritage."

She sneered, "And what pleasure has that faith brought you?"

"Sister … I mean, Faridah … I hope you are not saying that you have lost your faith … I can tell you, God does exist."

She dismissed his statement with, "You are such a fool. Of course, God exists."

"Then, what did you mean when you said I am too late?"

"Year after year, I waited, but you never came. If you had come, even a day earlier, things might have turned out differently."

"I don't understand anything you're saying. I couldn't have stopped a misguided missile."

"What makes you think it was misguided?"

"That's ridiculous. Who would want you dead? Why?"

"As I said, we are two sides of the same coin."

John's irritation finally showed. "You are nothing like me!"

"Two sides of..."

"What coin?!" he shouted.

She quietly relished his anger for a moment, then added, "We both know God … You choose to love Him … I choose to hate."

John frowned and shook his head as he tried to fathom what she was saying. "Why are you so angry?"

"I am not angry," she responded in a monotone. "I am numb."

John had reached his limit. Exasperated, he stood and left, returning to his salvage work. When he looked back after fifteen minutes, she was still there. Then, twenty minutes later, she was gone.

Throughout the rest of the afternoon, John worked harder than ever, trying to drive her disturbing words out of his head. When the workers finished for the day, John wiped the sweat off his brow and lined up with the men to rinse his filthy hands in a bowl of water. He made arrangements with the other workers to return the next morning, collected the saved items off the table and headed towards his room in the *Caritas* building.

However, he soon stopped and retraced his steps back to the table. There, studying the nearby trash heap, he realized that the black book was gone.

A WEEK EARLIER, the mysterious nun had retired to her sleeping quarters at dusk. She removed her habit and changed into a modest cotton night gown. Then she knelt beside her bed. But, instead of praying, she slid her hand under the mattress and removed the black book. She got up, slipped under the covers, and started reading.

Throughout her life, Faridah had strived to be special. She had always rebelled against the established order, in the most unusual ways. Descending from a long line of Syrian Jews, she not only converted to Catholicism but insisted on becoming a nun. Soon, however, she was again disenchanted and sought out ways to rebel. For four years, she had concealed her book and had meditated on and accepted its enticing messages. Finally, she was truly special. She had even challenged God to stop her. But He didn't.

After reading for a few hours, she put the book down, slid out of bed and changed back into her religious vestments. She crawled out of her window and, with her book in hand, wandered down the darkened back roads of Beirut. A half hour later, she was drawn to an inconspicuous house. She knocked on the door and a man answered it with a gun in his hand. Oddly, it did not take much explaining and, soon, she was led to a back bedroom. There, she offered her body on the bed of B. Abu Ladin.

Three hours later, just before that fateful dawn, she returned to the convent and crawled into her cell through the window. Tonight she had accomplished what she had once only imagined. Without emotion, she changed back into her gown, slid her book under the mattress and extinguished the light.

No friend ever served me,
and no enemy ever wronged me,
whom I have not repaid in full.
Roman Dictator Sulla

54

Palm Beach International Airport
West Palm Beach, FL
December 25

Soon after Evan exited the baggage claim area through the ground transportation doors, Cyst's van pulled up to the entrance. Lindley hopped out, threw Evan's bags into the back and the two of them drove away from the airport. The two men normally didn't converse much but they knew each other very well. Lindley had worked for Cyst since before Thas had been adopted.

"Welcome home," Lindley offered as he clicked off the radio's Christmas music.

"Oh, man. I feel like I've been in a time warp," Evan said as he gazed out at the palm trees under the mild Florida sun. "It's as if I've been transported from bitter winter to early spring in twenty hours."

"Everything go okay?"

"It was a friggin' disaster … Never again … I'm done with Russia … I can't tell you how pissed I am at Huntie for putting me in that kind of danger."

Lindley did not continue the conversation. As Cyst's pilot, driver and bodyguard, he maintained the image of a quiet, mysterious man. Still, his lean muscularity and short haircut made him an imposing presence, even at 65. He looked like a tri-athlete who had won numerous Iron Man competitions … and he had. He also had been an Air Force Special Operations Commando in

Vietnam. His unwritten job description occasionally called upon some of those old skills. He was Cyst's go-to guy whenever secrecy, skill and *cajones* were required.

"Where's Huntie?" Evan asked as they headed north on I-95. "I thought he would be with you."

"He couldn't get away. We've been really backed up. He's even had me doing some of your stuff."

Thas didn't like the sound of that. "Like what?"

"Ahh … just gopher stuff."

He liked the sound of that even less. Evan cranked his seat back and closed his eyes.

After a while, Lindley spoke up. "We've had some new developments since you left."

Thas cracked his eyes, "Yeah?"

"You've got a little brother, now."

Evan shot up in his seat. "What? What are you talking about?"

"The adoption went through."

"What adoption?"

"Dr. Cyst was hoping that you'd be happy about it."

Thas could not accept the news. "No, no. There was no adoption going on. I would have known about it if there was."

"It was a … uh … quickie adoption."

"Bull shit! There is no such thing as a quickie adoption!" Thas studied the driver's face. "You're lying to me, man."

Lindley turned onto State Route 708. However, instead of heading east, Thas' belligerence confirmed for Lindley that they must go west.

"You dumb shit, you're going the wrong way!"

Lindley remained calm, "We have to pick up papers at a client's house on the lake."

"Oh, man, you are so friggin' fired if you don't take me straight home."

"Your plane was late. I can't make it in time if I take you home first. Sorry, I just do what I'm told."

As they headed toward Lake Okeechobee, the largest freshwater lake in the south, Evan remembered that Cyst had taken him there many years ago. The area's snakes and alligators, soaking themselves under moss covered oaks, had creeped him out so much that he promised himself he would never return.

Thas demanded answers from Lindley. "How old is he?"

"I don't know. Maybe, six."

"What's his last name?"

"I don't know."

"Where'd you pick him up?"

He did not respond.

"Come on!" Evan now knew that he had Lindley cornered. "Huntie can't drive. So, where did you pick him up?"

"Look, you talk to Dr. Cyst about it."

"Why? What's the big secret?"

"I don't want to talk anymore."

Evan tried to assemble the pieces, but the puzzle didn't make sense. *Why did Huntie need the jet while I was away?*

Evan leveled an extreme accusation: "You kidnapped the kid, didn't you? You probably flew to some pathetic third-world country and just snatched him!"

Lindley didn't respond.

"Did you!?"

Lindley's silence was his admission.

Evan growled, "you sadistic bastard!"

Lindley remained calm but firm, "I just do what I'm told."

"Bull shit!" Thas erupted as they bounced down a dirt road. "You're a liar! Huntie wouldn't ask you to do that!"

"Why not?"

"Are you insane? He wouldn't destroy that kid's life!"

Suddenly, Lindley's attitude turned hateful. "You stupid … spoiled … rich brat! Your life wasn't destroyed, was it?"

At that moment, Evan's world flipped and the demons returned.

"Yeah," Lindley attacked with venomous rage, "But I didn't have to kidnap *you*. Your mother ordered us to take you! And there were three before you. They just didn't last very long."

Forgotten nightmares exploded in Evan's mind: flames dancing on candles … organ strains rumbling in a cave … a jarring buzz and then a woman – *My mother?* – demanding, "Take the boy, now!"

Suddenly, Lindley slammed on the brakes and skidded to a stop next to a lone wharf on the lake.

"What are you doing?" Evan asked with alarm.

Silently, Lindley got out of the car and circled around to the other side. Evan locked the door but Lindley unlocked it with the key remote and quickly jerked the young man out by the collar.

Thas closed his eyes and begged, "Please, please don't hit me."

"Give me your wallet," Lindley demanded.

Evan handed it over with a sense of relief. *Maybe he just wants to rob me.*

Unfortunately, Lindley was more interested in concealing the identification of the body. He stuffed the wallet into his pocket, kneed Evan in the crotch and threw him over his shoulder. A helpless paralysis overwhelmed Thas, who was now hearing squeals of delight from the demons.

His senses elevated. The smell of this man … it was the same sulfuric odor of the one who had carried him away from his mother! His parents' dark features suddenly became clear in his mind. *They don't look Canadian!* Unable to open his eyes, Evan felt the vibration in his throat as he groaned from the acute pain in his groin. He heard Lindley's quick, heavy steps on the dock and the sound of crickets welcoming the approaching dusk. He breathed in the swampy smell and realized it would be his last. Even the saliva in his mouth tasted of death.

He knew he was nearing the Abyss, so he bargained just as Cyst had taught him.

Like a sack of potatoes over his shoulder, Lindley lugged Thas to the end of the wharf. There, he saw three alligators resting in the shallow water. As Lindley adjusted the young man's body for the toss, Evan heard the words, "The piling." He opened his eyes and saw a wharf piling barely within reach. He grabbed it with all his desperate strength. When Lindley staggered, off balance, Evan kneed him in the head. Lindley lost hold of Thas, dropped him on the hard dock, and stumbled to the edge. Teetering at the brink, Lindley's panicked eyes turned to Thas as if crying out for assistance. Evan offered nothing, not even a smile.

Seconds later, as he watched the alligators feast on Lindley, Evan received a revelation. He suddenly understood – more clearly than he had understood anything before – that the demons were now a part of him and that, this time, they would never leave.

Evan Thas had been born again, on Christmas Day.

TEN DAYS LATER, the police investigation accepted Evan's version of events and concluded that two masked men had broken into the Cyst estate shortly after Thas returned from Russia. One held Evan at gunpoint while the other dunked Cyst in the pool, trying to force him to divulge the combination to his safe. When Cyst refused to comply, the over-zealous interrogation resulted in his drowning. Thas, however, was able to convince the robbers that he did not know the combination and, instead, offered them his wallet that still held a large amount of travelling cash. The men took the wallet, hit Thas over the head with a vase – causing a concussion and the need for seven stitches – and fled in Cyst's van.

In the hospital emergency room, Thas had warned the police that one of the masked men sounded like Dr. Cyst's pilot. He couldn't identify the other man.

Two days after the incident, a man's partial remains were found in Lake Okeechobee near Cyst's abandoned van. His pants pockets held Evan's wallet and, among other things, Lindley's driver's license. The police concluded that the two culprits must have had a falling out. For two days, the police dragged the bottom of the lake searching for the other perpetrator. They only found the partial remains of an unidentified young boy from an apparently unrelated drowning.

Perhaps, now, Thas would never find out the extent to which Cyst and Melnikov had manipulated him like a laboratory rat. Prior to the trip, Cyst had shared Evan's psycho-social Titan profile with the Russian for the purpose of proving the program's predictive and manipulative capabilities. Cyst had plotted every unexpected turn in Evan's journey and predicted, for Melnikov, Evan's every response. Cyst suspected that Evan would never have tolerated a new boy in the house. So, the plan was that, once Melnikov was satisfied with Titan's powers, he could do with Thas whatever he wished, as long as Thas never returned home.

The brilliant Dr. Cyst, however, did not count on Melnikov working Thas for his own purposes. The young man who returned to Cyst was a ticking time bomb, ready to explode, and the news that Cyst had been immediately dispatched upon Thas' arrival was Melnikov's validation of Titan's predictive power to control others. Melnikov believed that, compared to the head-strong Cyst, he would now have a more malleable and submissive partner.

Back in America, it was not easy for Thas. He endured numerous lengthy meetings with accountants, probate judges and lawyers but, eventually, the $14.2 billion estate transferred with surprising speed. In recognition of Evan's lengthy experience as Cyst's right hand man – along with Thas' promise to support existing Board members and to use his clout to improve Board pay and perks – Thas was elected Chairman. His pride swelled with the realization that no one would ever again think of him as an errand boy or boy toy. He was now the man that everyone sought to meet and befriend.

During a meeting with one of Cyst's former lawyers, an envelope was handed to Thas. The front of it read, "For Evan Thas, upon my death, read in private and burn." The attorney left the conference room as the young man ripped open the letter. It was dated only days before he had left for Russia. The letter should have astonished him but, instead, Thas was not surprised.

Evan,

When you read this I will be dead. So, I must now tell you of your past and, indeed, your future.

Your father died eleven years ago. Your mother lives in Syria. When you were young, they nurtured you in safe-houses, from Corozain to Bethsaida to Capernaum,[1] *before releasing you to me. Once I am gone, she will attempt to find and control you. Do not trust her.*

You see, I eventually came to regret my pact with Satan. The prophets had predicted that the Chosen One would gain full power at the age of thirty. So, I knew my mission was coming to an end. I had foolishly hoped you were replaceable. I wanted to buy myself more time.

Once before, I tried to back away and lost my feet. This time, I lost more.

My purpose has been to smooth the path ahead of you, to prepare your way. That, I have done.

Your knowledge and skill have been prophesied for centuries. Use them. Your enemies shall try to divert you from your awesome task. Destroy them. You are the one for whom mankind waits. Serve your god and, with him, rule the world.

Huntie

Later, outside the law offices, Thas headed straight for an alley. He found a vagrant and offered him a hundred bucks for his lighter. Evan admired the flames as he burned the letter and destroyed its ashes.

He walked across the street, hopped on his motorcycle and gunned the engine through town as he remembered the adrenaline rush of that fateful evening: Cyst had been treading water in the infinity pool when Evan surprised him; the poor swimmer was no match for Thas when they struggled in the deep end; Evan found the young boy asleep in Cyst's bedroom and easily smothered the life out of him with Cyst's pillow; he returned to the lake in the van, with the dead boy in the passenger seat and the motorcycle in the back; he rode home on the motorcycle after dumping the child's body in the swampy waters; and he slammed the vase against his own head shortly before calling 911.

Every sin and blasphemy can be forgiven—
except blasphemy against the Holy Spirit,
which will never be forgiven.
Matthew 12:31

55
Holy Sacrifice Monastery Chapel
Yashar, NY
January 17

The satellite uplink trucks stretched a quarter mile down a narrow two-lane road. Due to the lack of space, many celebrities and dignitaries were left out of this invitation-only event and the limited seating in the chapel was filled mostly by journalists. No one was quite sure why the funeral of the famous "Prophet of Technology" had been delayed so long and had to be held in a small town's little-known chapel. It seemed an odd request because Cyst had not been Catholic and hadn't even attended a Christian Church service for half a century.

But, as requested, Father Alonzo presided over the ceremony, assisted by two altar servers. The priest did not remember meeting Cyst, decades ago. He only knew him from his later successes. Thas had directed that the funeral be kept simple, and the funeral Mass be skipped. Also, he asked the priest to avoid a sermon or eulogy and, instead, defer to those who knew Cyst best. In fact, the ceremony was so controlled that the priest and altar servers began to feel like insignificant stage props for an Evan Thas production.

During the ceremony, one speaker after another announced admiration and acclaim for the man of accomplishment in his closed, golden casket. However, no tears were shed and none of Cyst's relatives attended. Perhaps, the only person there, who might be considered a friend, was Thas himself. The rest were business associates, politicians or financially-interested clingers.

Soon, it was time for the eulogy everyone awaited.

"It is fitting," Thas began, "that Huntington Cyst's last tribute be broadcast around the globe. His early work on geosynchronous orbital research, indeed, paved the way for global satellite communications. Likewise, his visionary commitment to bioengineering is preparing the path for what, before now, was almost unthinkable: the immortal human body. Just imagine, someday, body parts will be replaceable, eliminating all human concern for death and disease. That dream will be accomplished because of the vision and commitment of Huntington Cyst.

"You may wonder where he received these inspirations. Only now do I feel at liberty to reveal to you Huntington Cyst's long kept secret. Will you reject the truth when I tell it to you? If so, you will join the ranks of those who always doubted Dr. Cyst and, consequently, ended up embarrassed and on the wrong side of history. The secret of his inspiration is hard to believe but, nonetheless, true. He was visited by an Angel of light."[1]

Chuckles, snorts and whispers softly filled the chapel.

"Yes, an Angel inspired him, many times. The greatest technological genius of our age was guided by an Angel. Is it that hard to believe? Why shouldn't it be an Angel who protects mankind from the dangers of global warming, overpopulation and religious radicalism? Why shouldn't inspired leaders, like Huntington Cyst, show us the scientific path to perfecting this flawed world of ours? It is only through political and scientific leaders like him that we can find enlightenment, social justice and the collective salvation upon which our individual salvation depends."

Father Alonzo wanted to stop the eulogy, but when Thas looked over at him and offered an eerie smile, a shiver went through the priest.

Suddenly, he remembered that unusual name, from many years ago, and the final words that Cyst's demons had said to him: "We'll remember you, priest!"

"Still," Evan continued, "even after all that Huntington Cyst accomplished, many of you will doubt that he was inspired. Yet, doubting my words, you will enter that room," Thas pointed toward the Adoration Chapel, "and worship a piece of bread." A few members of the congregation gasped but most were stunned silent, including Father Alonzo.

"Huntington Cyst was 'the voice crying out in the wilderness, preparing the way.'[2] He was the 'Prophet of Technology,' declaring that the age of superstition is dead and the age of science has arrived."

Over the rumbling mumbles of irate listeners, Thas continued, "Huntington Cyst's work is not done. In fact, it has just begun."

Thas paused for a moment to study the confused reactions of those in the pews. Then, he opened the Bible in front of him and proclaimed loudly: "'The Spirit of the Lord is upon me, because He has anointed me to preach good news to the poor. He has sent me to proclaim freedom for the prisoners and recovery of sight for the blind, to release the oppressed, to proclaim the year of the Lord's favor.'"[3]

The cameras and the eyes of everyone in the chapel were fastened on him. Then he closed the Bible and proclaimed: "Today this scripture is fulfilled in your hearing."[4]

Again, uncomfortable shuffling rumbled in the pews.

"Do you doubt me? I tell you, there will come a day, soon, when all will doubt me. But, before long, I will triumph beyond your wildest dreams. How do I know this?"

Thas stepped down from the podium and over to the closed casket. Then, to everyone's surprise, he opened it. The cameramen rushed forward to take the last pictures of Huntington Cyst.

Standing over the cold, white body, Thas declared, "He's just sleeping."

Evan glared at the disbelieving audience. He paused to gauge their shock, as if he had something else to say. Instead, he turned and quickly exited through a door behind the altar. The stunned congregation quietly sat before the open casket waiting for the service to continue but, a moment later, they heard Thas' helicopter rumbling overhead.

The funeral had ended unceremoniously and, within moments, the casket was closed and loaded onto a cargo jet for a direct flight to Nauru.

For it is in giving that we receive;
it is in pardoning that we are pardoned;
and it is in dying that we are born to eternal life.
St. Francis of Assisi

56

Holy Sacrifice Monastery
Yashar, NY
May 16
32 Months Earlier

Sister Clarita knelt on the hard tile floor beside her bed. She had been praying there for hours. It was now almost midnight but she was unaware of the time. Surrounded only by God and the golden glow of one dim lamp, she reveled in her ecstasy and pleaded with God to let her swim in this ocean of joy forever.

That afternoon, with Father Alonzo's permission, she had spent hours with John in the chapel. There, kneeling at a prescribed distance from each other, they had prayed together, meditating on the sufferings of Jesus Christ. This time, however, was different than their previous meetings. She seemed more confident, more sure of herself, while he seemed almost Spiritually adrift. He was worried for her safety.

In the past, John had always been shown the direction in which to proceed. Obediently, he had followed wherever God led him and, for two thousand years, he had opposed and prevented the Destroyer's attempts to prevail against the Holy Catholic Church and to ignite the final conflagration. Now, however, John felt uncertainty. Something was being hidden from him. Something was going to happen … something big … but what?

He knew he could stop the Destroyer as long as he walked with God and God willed it. He was ready to continue the fight against the evil one. He was not afraid because more souls, so many more, still needed to be saved. But, for some reason, a veil had descended between God and himself. Unlike before, he was not sure if the coming changes would be for the good … at least not initially. So, he prayed for more Spiritual strength to effectively oppose the Destroyer and to protect the innocent.

In the chapel, he had whispered, "Sister, something has changed. I sense that we are both involved in God's plan but that it is His will that I remain in the dark, for now. I have always wanted to protect you, Sister. But now I must say: Protect yourself. I may be of little help."

Perhaps to assuage his melancholy, she opened up, as never before, about some of her personal history. This, he found very interesting because it reminded him so much of his own remarkable life. Her Religious Order, she told him, had been established almost two hundred years ago. Those daring Sisters were missionaries who worked in the most impoverished regions of the world. They served the poor, mostly, as nurses and educators. Many of them braved weeks and even months on the high seas, and then they travelled into the jungles of South America, before they finally reached their destinations. Sister Clarita, herself, had served sixteen years at an orphanage in Bolivia.

"And my time in Bolivia is what I would like to tell you about."

"Yes, Sister. Go ahead."

He expected her finally to tell him the story of which no one ever spoke, about how she had been forced to leave her beloved, impoverished Bolivians after being brutally raped and left for dead in a shallow grave. But then she giggled and blushed as if she was embarrassed to indulge in a happy story.

"I remember one Christmas, especially. I had asked for two volunteers to help me make a little Christmas tree out of whatever greenery we found. Only one child volunteered: a sweet, eight year old, named Enzo. The scraggly tree wasn't much but we enjoyed having it around, anyway. Then, on Christmas morning, I invited Enzo to come over. Below the tree, I showed him two small wrapped gifts. I handed him one and told him to open it. Inside, he found a little plastic airplane. He was thrilled. Enzo kept waving it through the air as he hummed like a plane. Then I handed him the other gift. He refused to open it. He gave it back to me and shook his head."

"He wouldn't take it?"

"No, he wouldn't."

"Why not?"

"He was satisfied, Father … Isn't it wonderful when we encounter someone who is simply happy and wants nothing more?"

"Yes it is … and it is so rare."

They meditated for a few moments. Then John asked, "You're not going to leave me … are you sister?"

It was the one inevitability that he had always found the hardest to accept. She did not answer.

"Please sister. Especially now, I need your strength ... your prayers."

A tear rolled down her cheek. "You will always have them."

"Sister … don't leave me … Please sister."

"Father John," she smiled, "I understand why you were His favorite.... Do not worry for me. God's Will be done. I have never sacrificed anything for which I was not rewarded a thousand fold."

John realized that, like Jesus Christ, Sister Clarita had been willing to offer her own suffering — the pain of her *stigmata* — for the good of others. Perhaps it was because of this that she had detected John's concern for her. So, she assured him with the words he well knew: "Be not afraid."[1] Like clay on a potter's wheel, shewould be pliable in the hands of God.

John's heart was broken … again. But he would not question or complain. Sensing that he could do no more for her and realizing that it was time for him to leave, he offered her a sad smile, grabbed his backpack, genuflected, and departed for Washington.

Once gone, Sister Clarita noticed he had left his rosary behind.

THAT NIGHT, before the golden dawn had shown its light, Sister Clarita prayed on her knees for hours. At the peak of her ecstasy she heard the gentle Voice, this time, beckoning her home. It was a request like no other, for a time like no other.

She asked, "How, Lord?

She waited for a response, but discerned none. Perhaps, she did not wait long enough.

I will rise to my Lord.

With peace and joy in her heart she removed the white coif and royal blue veil from her head and placed it on the bedside table next to the lamp. She reached into the pocket of her woolen dress, removed John's ancient rosary and reclined on the bed.

She reflected for a moment and then put the rosary around her neck. She crossed her forearms over her chest, reaching her right hand to the left side of her neck and the left hand to the right side. Then she clutched the rosary with both fists as tightly as she could and jerked. Her legs instinctively kicked, but her disciplined will would not allow her arms to release. She pulled even harder as the rosary cut into the skin, veins and tendons of her neck. Her violently thrashing feet pushed the bed away from the wall and, as she fell to the floor, the bed fell over on its side.

While her body fought, her mind was peaceful, her Spirit joyful. Like Isaac in the hands of Abraham, she believed she was placing herself in God's hands. Then on the floor, between the bed and the wall, she lost consciousness and bled to death.

Sister Clarita did not understand God's purpose but she believed she was obeying Him unquestioningly, just as she had done when He first sent her to Holy Sacrifice Monastery.

It was God's will that John be blamed for Sister Clarita's death so that, for the first time, he would be powerless to delay the coming chastisement. John's incarceration prevented him from thwarting the biological attack that would trigger the great conflagration and God's final warning to mankind.

How many warnings were necessary for men finally to change their ways? From the prophets of holy Scripture to the holy visionaries of modern times, mankind had been admonished to love, pray and flee evil. The choice had been between God's Love and God's Judgment.

The true Light of God's Love – the only thing that can bring true Peace and Joy – had become eclipsed by the Shining Darkness. The descent of man had required an end to God's merciful patience. No longer content to destroy their own lives, people, in their arrogance, thought themselves masters of all life, tampering with and destroying it according to their own pleasures.

The floodgates were opening and every living soul would soon be swept up by the torrent. Within reach, each would be thrown a life preserver and every one would be free to choose whether to accept or reject it. God's prophesied Day of Judgment would soon bring everlasting ecstasy or eternal punishment.

For Sister Clarita, her sacrificial intercessions for the salvation of others had come to an end. In imitation of her beloved Savior, she had lived and died for God and mankind. Now, she would pass through the doorway to the Father's palace of eternal reward.

Her life had been her sacrifice.

Her Life had just begun.[2]

For our struggle is not against flesh and blood,
but against the rulers, against the authorities,
against the powers of this dark world
and against the spiritual forces of evil
in the heavenly realms.
Ephesians 6:12

57

Wynn Hotel and Casino
Las Vegas Nevada
February 28

After spending a few moments proclaiming an era of unlimited potential, the new Chairman of the Board of XCyst Industries allowed questions from shareholders and reporters. Evan's sunny demeanor seemed disconnected from the mood of the country. After all, over the past week, violent and destructive riots had broken out in Detroit, Atlanta, Miami, Seattle, and Los Angeles – all cities that recently had been visited by Brother Daniel Mitchum.

Since Cyst's death, uncertainty surrounding the future of the company had caused its market capitalization to slide. Evan Thas' erratic behavior and Messianic proclamations at Cyst's funeral had seriously damaged his credibility. Even Angela had been wondering about the young man's sanity and whether she might begin distancing herself from him.

Everyone realized that this shareholder meeting was Evan's chance to win back a suspicious public. He needed to be at his best. Perhaps, his optimism was appropriate during these challenging times. But there is a fine line between being visionary and delusional.

Typically, whenever controversial issues are discussed at shareholder meetings, the performance of the Chairman is a subject of heated debate. However, by the time this meeting ended, the quality of Evan Thas' leadership was not debatable. It was obvious to those attending that he was in hot water and completely over his head. In fact, he almost sounded irrational when he responded to the question, "Are you concerned that some of your management talent may leave now that Dr. Cyst is no longer at the helm?"

"Let them leave," was his curt response. "I can run this place without them."

From that point on, a seemingly endless stream of hostile questions proceeded and Evan's responses – filled with *ad hominem* attacks on the questioners – rarely addressed the substance of the inquiries. The meeting evolved into a public relations disaster and the financial media reported it as such. Within days, shares were trading at half their fifty-two week high.

For a few days, Thas stayed out of the spotlight, making no public appearances. However, the stock continued to slide. The future of XCyst Industries evolved from a drama on arcane financial pages to a joke on late night comedy shows. Everyone realized that Thas was out of his league, at best, and insane, at worst. It now seemed that the company was crashing without the controlling genius of Huntington Cyst.

Then, at the worst possible time, even XBC Television News appeared to be piling on Evan's P.R. problems. They reported that Thas had cracked under the pressure and had threatened to fire hundreds of top managers. He had reportedly locked himself in his Las Vegas hotel suite and cancelled all private meetings. One witness claimed Thas had suffered a nervous breakdown and that he was surviving on a diet of Twinkies and Wild Turkey.

However, a mysterious press release was quickly issued insisting that Thas was "as brilliant as ever," had "a date with destiny," and "for the good of all mankind" refused to relinquish control or sell any shares. The release ended by stating that Thas demanded to be addressed as

"Doctor" from now on and that he will stay the course "no matter how bad it gets."

It was the last straw.

Wary investors thought they had protected themselves with stop loss orders. But, within seconds, the market dipped and a wave of programmed trading algorithms on computer platforms in major brokerage houses triggered a cascade of sell orders. When matching buy orders quickly dried up, a tsunami of stop loss orders were converted into market sell orders as the computers took control. The stock suffered a "flash crash." Market analysts worried that the stock exchange trading platforms might break down under the strain of the volume. By the end of the day, the biggest corporate slaughter in market history had occurred and shares of XCyst Industries finally stabilized at one-twentieth their fifty-two week high.

Perhaps the bottom would have been lower if not for a major investor who unexpectedly swept in and gobbled up every available share, except those stubbornly held by Thas.

XCyst Industries, once America's most respected publicly-held conglomerate, would soon become a shadow of its former self, reduced to a private company in the hands of two men. A Wall Street Journal headline proclaimed, "A Fool and His Money are Soon Parted" when it reported that the eccentric new investor would keep Thas at the helm. With good reason, the company's 140,000 employees feared the inevitable job losses to come.

A FEW HUNDRED MILES AWAY, Fred Whitehead knocked on the door of a penthouse suite at the Fairmont Hotel. Again, he was holding a magnum of Dom Perignon. Even though the visit had been prescreened by the Secret Service, Angela seemed pleasantly surprised to see him.

After a few drinks, Whitehead explained that he had done some much-needed soul-searching in recent months and that he had determined he needed Angela more than he had ever before realized. (That part was true.) He told her his days of womanizing were over and that he could never feel for anyone else the love and adoration that he had for her. He said he was now ready to follow her wherever she led him and would no longer let his foolish male pride stand in the way of loving service to her interests. These were the words she had longed to hear since that magical visit to Venice.

Fred Whitehead had recited his lines exactly as Evan Thas had scripted them.

Within days, the White House Press Secretary announced the engagement of President Angela Concepcion to Mr. Fred Whitehead. Just as Thas had predicted, the stunning surprise overwhelmed the news outlets and journalists started scrambling to find every angle on this attractive pair's relationship and the upcoming details of their White House wedding. Finally, journalists had something positive to report. After a seemingly endless diet of stories on job losses, foreclosures, global rioting, Islamic terrorism, and geopolitical instability, this was the cotton candy that America had been craving. Angela reveled in it all. Even the tabloid stories that exposed Fred's playboy past were okay with her. They portrayed her sympathetically and, better yet, sometimes even as a victim of an opportunistic cad.

In fact, journalists around the globe were so fascinated that most didn't even cover the Treasury Secretary's announcement that day. It was just one more government bailout that now blended with all the rest. XCyst Industries had been officially declared "Strategically Vital" by the Commerce Department and, consequently, was now eligible for an immediate infusion of previously-approved economic assistance.

The dominoes had all fallen exactly as planned. Even the Green E Bill – such a loser at the state level – was now on a nationwide fast track in congress.

LATER, ON THE PHONE, Evan laughed so hard that he almost choked on a bourbon-soaked ice cube when he explained that the agreed upon bailout was $40 billion. The emergency assistance package had been structured as a loan. However, Whitehead had worked out a private deal in which, as long as a face-saving quarter of the funds were repaid prior to the next election, the rest of it would be written off as an investment in job growth. Of course, that debt forgiveness was implicitly conditioned on XCyst continuing to work its magic to get Angela re-elected.

In an uncharacteristically jovial mood with Evan Thas, Vasily Melnikov realized that he had underestimated his resourceful new business partner and the power of the Titan technologies that he controlled.[1]

Evan had become so absorbed in playing the role of the crazy hermit that he forgot the importance of this special day. Then the Russian congratulated him with, "Happy 30th birthday, my friend."

I know not with what weapons World War III will be fought,
but World War IV will be fought with sticks and stones.
Albert Einstein

58

Tarbuwth Correctional Facility
Yashar, NY
June 12

Today, John's purgatory would end. He had been removed to a special "death row" cell in preparation for his execution and had just rejected his last lunch. Death by lethal injection would occur shortly before midnight.

In recent weeks, John had not seemed to recognize his impending doom. Some of the inmates speculated that he had been comforted by the fact that the news coverage of his coming execution had highlighted the saintly sacrifices and qualities of Sister Clarita. Perhaps, he appreciated the international revival of Spiritual self-evaluation that her gruesome death had prompted. So, he had continued teaching, preaching and loving as if nothing of importance was about to happen.

Even until this morning, the prisoner had seemed calm, quietly praying and meditating. But now, for good reason, his stomach was churning. Periodically, he would hunch over the small toilet in his cell and vomit loudly.

The inmates and guards who had come to know John were visibly shaken. Many of them, who were some of the toughest men alive, shed tears privately. Of all the many prisoners who claimed innocence, John was the only one who was universally believed.

At the visitors' gate, Officer D.J. Jefferson signed in Father Alonzo, and Kevin, the limping guard, prepared to escort him back to John's cell. Because of the solemn occasion, the priest was wearing his black cassock and hat. He also had brought his black leather bag containing holy water and holy oils for administering the Last Rites on John. Considering the finality of the circumstances, Officer Jefferson was not going to deny his friend this one last blessing.

Jefferson's eyes were red and his attitude was somber. But, trying to find some way to ease the tension of the moment, he commented, "I see you've been getting a lot of sun lately, Father. You been hangin' out at the beach?"

Mustering a faint smile, the big, tanned priest adjusted his long blond hair under his hat and simply responded, "No."

Kevin led Father Alonzo as Officer Jefferson buzzed the electromagnetic locks, allowing them to pass through the metal gates. As usual, Kevin did all the talking while he shuffled through the hall on the way to the cell. He was the kind of person who never permitted a thought to remain unspoken.

"Listen to the difference, Father," Kevin commented as he held a hand to his ear. "Used to be everybody was shoutin' and cussin' every time we brought somebody down this hall. I tell ya … John really made a difference 'round here. We're all gonna hate to see him go. Most of these prisoners won't tell ya, but they're pretty shook up about it."

Approaching the cell, Father Alonzo could hear the echoing grunts of John throwing up.

"I guess," Kevin ventured, "John's pretty shook up too."

When they reached the prisoner, the guard unlocked the gate as John pulled his head up from the toilet.

Kevin asked, "You want me to stay in here with you, Father?"

"No, thank you. Part of the Last Rites includes hearing Confession. We'll need privacy if you don't mind."

"No problem. I'll just be down the hall."

Kevin locked the two men in the cell and stepped away. From a distance he could hear mumbled prayers being recited. He wasn't quite sure what to do during the prayer session. He wasn't a praying man, himself, so he walked down the hall. On each side, he saw that every prisoner was quiet and deeply contemplating the tragedy that was about to transpire.

Finally, after ten minutes, or so, he heard Father Alonzo announce, "Kevin, I'm ready to go."

When the guard limped back to the cell, his eyes were drawn to poor John, again on his knees and vomiting. The suffering man's long black hair was a mess, almost dangling into the toilet. Still, the priest gathered his bag and led the way as Kevin locked the cell door and followed behind him.

The gagging sounds followed them down the hall. "Man, I'm surprised he still has food left in his stomach." As they walked, Kevin chattered aimlessly, to cover the sound of John's suffering. "I wish he wouldn't let it upset him so much… That's awful … I hate throwin' up … That's one of the worst things in the world for me ... especially when I'm hung over." Then, when they reached the gates, Kevin called out, "Hey D.J., open up."

One after the other, the deadbolts on the two gates slid open. Kevin let the priest through and, seeing his head bowed deeply in prayer, allowed him to exit alone. Seemingly oblivious to his surroundings, the praying cleric slowly walked toward the prison exit.

But then, as Kevin disappeared, Jefferson shouted, "Father Alonzo, you forgot to sign-out."

Adjusting his long blond hair under his black hat, the priest turned and slowly walked back to the plexi-glass window. His tan hand reached through the hole in the glass for the sign-out clipboard.

Then D.J. Jefferson offered, "Here's a pen for you, Father."

He slipped the pen through the hole and, as he raised his gaze, he suddenly realized that this big, blond priest's eyes were not blue. They were brown.

His mind screamed: *Malek!* Officer Jefferson's hand instinctively jerked toward the red emergency button, but he did not push it. He could not take his eyes away from John's calm, deliberate face. He saw no fear in those brown eyes, only acceptance of whatever might come.

Jefferson's mind raced. He was sworn to uphold the law. However, he deeply believed that John Malek's execution would be the greatest miscarriage of justice that he had ever witnessed. For a moment, the two men stared at each other, contemplating a suddenly revealed choice between life and death. Jefferson knew he could save John's life by letting him through, but he feared he would be fired or even prosecuted for the escape. He realized that the poor priest in the cell had sacrificed himself for this man and that Father Alonzo would spend the rest of his life in prison for his crime.

Jefferson was torn with indecision. It would have been easier for him if he had realized that all mankind would be affected by his choice.

The guard retraced the events in his mind and realized that Father Alonzo must have smuggled in blond and black wigs in his leather bag. The two men must have changed clothes inside the cell. Then, since they were about the same size and, now, both were tanned, all that was needed was a hatted head, lowered in prayer. The deception was complete … almost.

John waited patiently for Jefferson's response.

Lowering his eyes, the guard slid the pen through the hole and spoke deliberately, "Next time, Father Alonzo, remember to sign out."

John took the pen and scribbled something – much more than a name – and then Officer Jefferson watched John as he casually walked through the lobby and out the glass door.

Once again, John would be a hunted man. However, this time, his most important work was just beginning. Now, he would be unleashed.

John knew that the time had arrived for the fulfillment of what had been foretold for centuries. He must now find the two prophesied men of greatness – one of leadership and one of faith.

John had finally become strong enough to endure with the Lord to the very end. Someday, he would meet his twelve disciples again. They would still have to learn, however, to remain humbly obedient to the Spirit, even with the realization that on the road to Christ's glorious resurrection a crucifixion came first.

As the glass door slammed shut, Jefferson turned the clipboard around and read what John had written: "Without love, there is no sacrifice. Without sacrifice, no trust. Without trust, chaos prevails."

The guard looked out again and saw that, instead of running, John was patiently standing on the sidewalk, looking to Heaven. He seemed peaceful in the light of freedom. But Jefferson understood, somehow, that John was returning to a darkening world.

Hurry! the guard thought.

Suddenly, down the hall, Jefferson heard Kevin scream, "Escape! Malek's escaped!" Jefferson's fist instinctively punched the red alarm button and the prison entered into extreme lockdown. Sirens immediately pierced the calm day. Electronic deadbolts grinded into place and cantilever gates automatically closed around the perimeter. Officers, holding shotguns, sprinted out onto the grounds and the tower guards readied their rifles.

Looking out through the lobby doors, Jefferson grew angry, wondering why John stood motionless, as if in prayer. With no other choice left, he quickly turned to unlock the gun cabinet and pulled out a shotgun. He ran out of his office, through the lobby and out the front door, into the summer heat.

Where'd he go?

Jefferson studied the area. The parking lot around him had been closed for repaving. No car was within a thousand feet. John was not hiding, he was gone.

The shrieking sounds of alarms, sirens and frantic activity stabbed through the warm air and another roar reached a crescendo. It was the unified applause and cheers of the prisoners, rejoicing as the news quickly circulated.

In the midst of the tumult, Jefferson's mind raced with confusing, angry thoughts. Then, as the guard stood alone in the empty parking lot, a cool, gentle wind caressed his face. It was the same blessed breeze that he had felt before, with John. This time, however, it flooded his senses with a vision of Christ's glorious return.

Exchanging anger for awe, Jefferson dropped to his knees, let it all go, and laughed until he cried.

If I want him to remain alive
until I return,
what is that to you?

John 21:22

For the secret power of lawlessness
is already at work;
but the one who now holds it back
will continue to do so
till he is taken out of the way.

2 Thessalonians 2:7

If My people, who are called by My name,
will humble themselves and pray
and seek My face
and turn from their wicked ways,
then will I hear from heaven
and will forgive their sin
and will heal their land.

2 Chronicles 7:14

The Trials and Triumph Trilogy:

The Rise
The Rebellion
The Return

For reports on

Christian miracles in modern times,

please join the author's blog at:

MiraclesAndProphecies.com

NOTES

CHAPTER 1:

1. In 1990, Zdenko "Jim" Singer, a Croatian visionary who immigrated to Canada, claimed Jesus Christ told him: "Dear children, be alert, for you are now entering into the age of great viciousness by the Shining Darkness." The prophecies in this chapter can be found in the books that are listed in the Sources section and preceded by an asterisk.

2. In the 14th century, St. John of the Cleft Rock predicted, "… twenty centuries after the Incarnation of the Word, the Beast in its turn shall become man." Sister Bertina Bouquillon, a *stigmatist* also known as the Nursing Nun of Belay, prophesied in the 19th century, "The beginning of the end shall not come in the 19th century, but in the 20th for sure."

3. St. John Dascene, who died in 770, prophesied, "He will reign from ocean to ocean. Antichrist shall be an illegitimate child, under the complete power of Satan … The devil [will] take full and perpetual possession of him …"

4. In 1846, in LaSalette France, the Virgin Mary said to two shepherd children, "… the Antichrist will be born of a Hebrew nun, a false virgin who will communicate with the old serpent, the master of impurity and his father will be B." There is no explanation for what this initial represents.

5. St Irenaeus (130-200) cites Jeremiah, writing, "We shall hear the voices of his (Antichrist's) swift horses from Dan… This, too, is the reason that this tribe is not reckoned in the Apocalypse along with those which are saved." Also, St. Hippolytus predicted in "*The Antichrist,*" around 200 A.D., "[W]e find it written regarding Antichrist … as Christ springs from the tribe of Judah, so Antichrist is to spring from the tribe of Dan..."

6. St. John Chrysostom (d. 407) prophesied, "The world will be faithless and degenerate after the birth of Antichrist. Antichrist will be possessed by Satan and be the illegitimate son of a Jewish woman from the east."

7. After Jesus Christ predicted that the Antichrist would come from the people who destroyed the Temple, most scholars assumed he was referring to a successor to the Roman Empire. Rarely pointed out, however, is that the battalion that destroyed the Temple was comprised of Assyrian subjects of the Roman Empire. Keep in mind that the two legged statue of Daniel's prophecies, fits the description of the two capitals of ancient Rome, one of

which was Constantinople, or modern day Istanbul, the former capital of the Islamic Ottoman Empire. Also, Lactantius, a fourth century Christian apologist, predicted, "[A] king shall arise out of Syria, born from an evil spirit, the overthrower and destroyer of the human race, who shall destroy that which is left by the former evil, together with himself … But that king will not only be most disgraceful in himself, but he will also be a prophet of lies, and he will constitute and call himself God, and will order himself to be worshipped as the Son of God, and power will be given to him to do signs and wonders, by the sight of which he may entice men to adore him … Then he will … persecute the righteous people." ("Divine Institutes" 7:17 [A.D. 307]). Also, Isaiah 10:5-7 reads, "Woe to the Assyrian, the rod of my anger, in whose hand is the club of my wrath!" And, finally, Origen (d. 254) prophesied, "… another king shall arise out of Syria, born from an evil spirit, the overthrower and destroyer of the human race…"

8. "He will be raised at different secret places and will be kept in seclusion until full grown." (St. Hildegard, d. 1179). Other prophets have maintained that Antichrist will be nurtured in the towns around the north of the Sea of Galilee that Jesus condemned: "Woe to thee Corozain … Woe to thee Bethsaida … and thou Capharnaum, that are exalted up to heaven, thou shalt be thrust down to hell." Luke 10:13 Capharnaum is moder-day Capernaum.

9. Revelation 17:9 reads, "This calls for a mind with wisdom. The seven heads are seven hills on which the woman [who was drunk with the blood of saints] sits."

10. "… power will be given him to do signs and wonders, by the sight of which he may entice men to adore him … by which miracles many, even of the wise, shall be enticed by him." (Origen d. 254).

11. "… power was given him over all kindreds, and tongues, and nation …" (Revelation 13:7) "… then shall the deceiver of the world appear, pretending to be the Son of God, and [he] shall do signs and wonders, and the earth shall be delivered into his hands." ("Didache" 16:3-4, ca. 70 AD) St. Cyril of Jerusalem, a fourth century theologian and Doctor of the Church, prophesied, "Having beguiled the Jews by the lying signs and wonders of his magical deceit, until they believe he is the expected Christ, he shall afterwards be characterized by all manner of wicked deeds of inhumanity and lawlessness, as if to outdo all the unjust and impious men who have gone before him. He shall display against all men, and especially against us Christians, a spirit that is

murderous and most cruel, merciless and wily." Also, St. Irenaeus, in the second century, foretold, "The Antichrist will deceive the Jews to such and extent that they will accept him as the Messias and worship him." ("Adversus Haereses," Book 5, Chapter 25) St. Anselm, a Doctor of the Church, said "Towards the end of the world, Antichrist will draw the hearts of the Jews to him by his great generosity and sympathetic attitude so much so that they will praise him as a demi-god. The Jews will say to one another: 'There is not a more virtuous, just and wise man than he to be found in our entire generation. Of all men, he certainly will be able to rescue us from all our miseries." (Franz Spirago, "Details Concerning the Antichrist According to Holy Scripture, Tradition and Private Revelation," Prague Pub.)

12. "The temporal lords and ecclesiastical prelates, for fear of losing power or position, will be on his side, since there will exist neither king nor prelate unless he wills it." (St. Vincent Ferrer, "The Angel of Judgment," Ave Maria Press, p. 105)

13. Revelation 13:16-17; Also, St. Hippolytus (d. 235) predicted, "Antichrist will reign upon the earth … and by reason of the scarcity of food, all will go to him and worship him."

14. "In those days and at that time, when I restore the fortunes of Judah and Jerusalem, I will gather all nations and bring them down to the Valley of Jehoshaphat. There I will enter into judgment against them concerning my inheritance, my people Israel, for they scattered my people among the nations and divided up my land." Joel 3:1-2

15. St. Hildegard prophesied, "At that period when Antichrist shall be born, there will be many wars and right order shall be destroyed on the earth. Heresy will be rampant and the heretics will preach their errors openly without restraint. Even among Christians, doubt and skepticism will be entertained concerning the beliefs of Catholicism."

16. In the eighth century, St. John Damascene prophesied: "There is also the superstition of the Ishmaelites which to this day prevails and keeps people in error, being a forerunner of the Antichrist."

17. See Fatima prophecies regarding Russia as reported in William Thomas Walsh's "Our Lady of Fatima" (Image Books, Doubleday) and Renzo and Roberto Allegri's "Fatima, The Story Behind the Miracles" (Servant Books). In one example, just months before the 1917 Russian revolution, the Virgin Mary

said, "If My requests are not granted, Russia will spread her errors throughout the world raising up wars and persecutions against the Church, the good will be martyred, the Holy Father will have much to suffer, various nations will be annihilated."

18. These prophecies are also derived from the predictions of St. John Damascene, particularly, the following: "Thus the Devil does not himself become man after the Incarnation of the Lord – God forbid! – but a man is born of fornication and receives into himself the whole operation of Satan, for God permits the Devil to inhabit him, because He (God) foresees the future perversity of his will. So, he is born of fornication, as we said, and is brought up unnoticed; but of a sudden he rises up, revolts, and rules … [H]e shall come in signs and lying wonders … and he will seduce those whose intention rests on a rotten and unstable foundation and make them abandon the living God …" (St. John Damascene, "Orthodox Faith, Book four," Fathers of the Church, Inc., pp 398-400) Also of interest is what the oldest extant Christian catechism states, "[T]he whole time of your faith will not profit you unless you are made complete in the last time. For in the last days false prophets and corrupters shall be multiplied, and sheep shall be turned into wolves … and then shall the deceiver of the world appear, pretending to be the Son of God, and [he] shall do signs and wonders, and the earth shall be delivered into his hands" ("Didache" 16:3-4, ca. 70 AD).

CHAPTER 3:

1. This story only slightly resembles the facts underlying the case of Roe vs. Wade, the landmark 1973 U.S. Supreme Court decision that declared a Constitutional right to abortion. The young plaintiff in the real case, Norma McCorvey, claimed she had been raped and challenged a Texas law prohibiting abortion. It took three years to litigate, so her baby was born and put up for adoption. But, since that time, McCorvey has insisted that she actually had not been raped and that she had been a "pawn" of two ambitious, young lawyers, Sarah Weddington and Linda Coffee. For years McCorvey had lived a promiscuous lifestyle and worked in an abortion clinic. However, in 1995, she experienced a Spiritual conversion, was baptized a Christian, and repudiated her lifestyle and work. Now, she is an anti-abortion activist and a member of the Catholic Church. In 2005, she petitioned the Supreme Court to overturn the earlier decision armed with voluminous testimony of the harm abortion has caused women since the Constitutional change. The petition was denied. By the end of the 20th century, induced abortions had accounted for over fifty million American deaths, more than all American wars combined.

In addition to the tragedy of human death, the loss of so many younger members of the American workforce undermined the actuarial tables for the entitlements that America's retiring baby boomers hope to receive someday.

2. Source: U.S. Fish and Wildlife Service

3. This paragraph is an exact quote from a May 6, 2010 report from AFP News, "World Needs 'Bailout Plan' for Species Loss: IUCN."

4. All of these are on the Endangered Species List of the U.S. Fish and Wildlife Service.

CHAPTER 5:

1. http://www.gendercide.org/case_infanticide.html. Also, in the Mail Online expose', "Gendercide: China's Shameful Massacre of Unborn Girls," posted 4/10/10, Peter Hitchens reports the following: "By the year 2020, there will be 30 million more men than women of marriageable age in this giant empire… Nothing like this has ever happened to any civilization before."

2. http://www.reformedblacksofamerica.org/downloads/Abortion_by_race_Bradley.pdf - based on US Centers for Disease Control data through 2001.

3. www.toomanyaborted.com, "Black Children Are an Endangered Species, The Truth in Black and White."

4. http://www.johnstonsarchive.net/policy/abortion/wrjp339.html

5. http://www.un.org/esa/population/publications/sixbillion/sixbilpart1.pdf

CHAPTER 6:

1. Dana Priest, "Fort Hood Suspect Warned of Threats Within the Ranks," Washington Post, 11/10/09.

CHAPTER 7:

1. See: http://www.washingtonpost.com/wp-dyn/content/article/2010/08/13/AR2010081305098_pf.html

CHAPTER 8:

1. See Eusebius, "The History of the Church." Penguin Classics.

2. Except for John witnessing the execution, this is generally described by ancient historians Tertullian, Origen and Eusebius.

3. This paragraph summarizes much of the first book of Tertullian's "Ad Nationes" which is a refutation of the calumnies against the early Christians.

4. Fr. John J. Pasquini, "*Ecce Fides:* Pillar of Truth" Shepherds of Christ Publications, Foreword.

CHAPTER 9:

1. This television critique is quoted from a National Public Radio's Morning Edition segment by Susan Jane Gilman that aired on October 19, 2009. The excerpted transcript follows:

> ***"When I first heard that R. Crumb had illustrated the Book of Genesis, I thought: "Oh. This oughta be good." Crumb, after all, is the godfather of the cartoon counterculture ... [H]is most recent project was a book titled "Robert Crumb's Sex Obsessions."***
>
> ***"His depiction of the Bible, I assumed, would therefore be the funniest, most subversive, most profane ever. But, to my surprise, "The Book of Genesis Illustrated" is straight-faced ... It's a cartoonist's equivalent of the Sistine Chapel, and it's awesome ... [T]his God is a somber, craggy, commanding presence ... And, we all know there's sex in the Bible — and Crumb reproduces this, too... Reading it, you wonder: Is this blasphemy? Is it art? Does it make a mockery of the Bible simply by illustrating it?***
>
> ***"All I can answer is this: You expect it to be sardonic, but it is not. You may expect it to be psychedelically spiritual — it's not that, either. Rather, it's humanizing. Crumb takes the sacred and makes it more accessible, more down-to-earth, less idealized. And this may be a blessing, or it may be subversion itself."***

2. This radio report is quoted from a National Public Radio's Morning Edition segment by Barbara Bradley Hagerty and reported by Dianna Douglass on October 19, 2009. The excerpted transcript follows:

> *"Last month, atheists marked Blasphemy Day at gatherings around the world, and celebrated the freedom to denigrate and insult religion. Some offered to trade pornography for Bibles. Others de-baptized people with hair dryers. And in Washington, D.C., an art exhibit opened that shows, among other paintings, one entitled 'Divine Wine,' where Jesus, on the cross, has blood flowing from his wound into a wine bottle. Another, 'Jesus Paints His Nails,' shows an effeminate Jesus after the crucifixion, applying polish to the nails that attach his hands to the cross ... It's about the future of the atheist movement — and whether to adopt the 'new atheist' approach — a more*

aggressive, often belittling posture toward religious believers.

"New atheists like Oxford biologist Richard Dawkins and journalist Christopher Hitchens are selling millions of books and drawing people by the thousands to their call for an uncompromising atheism. For example, Hitchens, a columnist for 'Vanity Fair' and author of the book 'god Is Not Great,' told a capacity crowd at the University of Toronto, 'I think religion should be treated with ridicule, hatred and contempt, and I claim that right.' His words were greeted with hoots of approval. Religion is 'sinister, dangerous and ridiculous,' Hitchens tells NPR, because it can prompt people to fly airplanes into buildings, and it promotes ignorance. Hitchens sees no reason to sugarcoat his position. 'If I said to a Protestant or Quaker or Muslim, 'Hey, at least I respect your belief,' I would be telling a lie,' Hitchens says. Asked why he feels compelled to be so blunt, he responds: 'I believe it's more honest, more brave, more courageous simply to state your own position.'

"'The more outrageous the message the better,' says PZ Myers, who writes an influential blog that calls, among other things, for the end of religion. On Blasphemy Day, Myers drove a rusty nail through a consecrated Communion wafer and posted a photo on his Web site ... 'Edgy is what young people like," Myers says. "They want to cut through the nonsense right away and want to get to the point. They want to hear the story fast, they want it to be exciting, and they want it to be fun. And I'm sorry, the old school of atheism is really, really boring.'"

"... The new atheists counter that they believe in reason, science and freedom from religious myth. And, as Lindsay, who replaced Kurtz, puts it: 'We take the high road, the low road, country roads, interstates, highways, byways, — whatever it takes to reach people...'"

3. Mr. Myers misses the point that atheism, in fact, ***is*** a religion. It is faith in the impossibility of God's existence. In fact, some argue that atheism requires greater faith than belief in God. After all, the atheist's knowledge is necessarily limited – just as any single individual's knowledge must be – yet, he dismisses the many millions of witnesses, through the centuries, who not only say they have faith but that they have had personal experiences that support that faith.

4. Source: National Child Abuse and Neglect Data System, for federal fiscal year 2007, http://www.childwelfare.gov/pubs/factsheets/fatality.cfm#children.

5. In 1634, Mother Anne of Jesus Torres heard the Virgin Mary predict, "At the end of the nineteenth century and for a large part of the twentieth century, various heresies will flourish on this earth, which will have become a free republic. The precious light of the faith will go out in souls because of the almost total moral corruption… there will be great physical and moral calamities… My [religious] communities will be abandoned; they will be swamped in a fathomless sea of bitterness and will seem drowned in tribulations… The spirit of impurity, like a deluge, will flood the streets, squares and public places. The licentiousness will be such that there will be no more virgin souls in the world… Gaining control of all social classes, sects will… penetrate… into the hearts of families and destroy even the children. The devil will take glory in feeding perfidiously on the hearts of children. The innocence of childhood will almost disappear… Priests will abandon their sacred duties and will depart from the path marked for them by God."

6. The Fatima prayer is, "O my Jesus, forgive us our sins, save us from the fires of hell, lead all souls to Heaven, especially those in most need of Thy mercy."

CHAPTER 11:

1. This story is found in Randall Sullivan's excellent book, "The Miracle Detective."

2. These prophecies can be found in Yves DuPont's "Catholic Prophecy, The Coming Chastisement."

3. This prophecy is from Emmerich's "The Life of Jesus Christ" Vol. 4, p. 356.

4. Revelation 22:18

5. Source: Wikipedia, "List of Cities Claimed to be Built on Seven Hills": Amman, Jordan; Asunción, Paraguay; Bamberg, Germany; Barcelona, Spain; Bath, England; Brussels, Belgium; Budapest, Hungary; Cagliari, Sardinia; Ceuta, Spain; Cincinnati, Ohio; Dunedin, New Zealand; Edinburgh, Scotland; Gorzow, Poland; Guaranda, Ecuador; Iaşi, Romania; Istanbul, Turkey; Jerusalem, Israel; Kampala, Uganda; Kiev, Ukraine; Lisbon, Portugal; Los Angeles, California; Lynchburg, Virginia; Lviv, Ukraine; Macau, China; Mecca, Saudi Arabia; Melbourne, Australia; Moscow, Russia; Nevada City, California; Plovdiv, Bulgaria; Prague, Czech Republic; Providence, Rhode Island; Pula, Croatia; Richmond, Virginia; Rome, Georgia; Rome, Italy; Saint-Etienne, France; Saint Paul, Minnesota; San Diego, California; San Francisco, California; Seattle, Washington; Sheffield, England; Somerville, Massachusetts; Tallahassee, Florida; Tehran, Iran; Thiruvananthapuram, India; Tirumala, India; Torquay, England; Turku, Finland; Worcester, Massachusetts; Zevenbergen, Netherlands.

6. The following are from Birch's, "Trial, Tribulation and Triumph," p. 65.

7. From Josh McDowell's "Evidence for Christianity," Chapter Six.

8. The following prophecies quoted by Fr. Alonzo are from the books cited in the Sources section that are preceded by an asterisk.

9. See "The Stigmata and Modern Science" by Rev. Charles M. Carty.

10. Matthew 7:15-16.

11. 1 John 4:2.

12. Source: BBC News, http://news.bbc.co.uk/2/hi/americas/4034787.stm

13. For greater detail on this subject, see "Scripture Alone?" by Joel Peters.

14. 2 Thessalonians 2:15.

15. John 21:25.

16. Joel 2:28, Acts 2:17.

17. 1 Corinthians 12:3.

18. This quote is from "I Am Sending You Prophets" by Edward D. O'Connor, C.S.C.

CHAPTER 12:

1. From http://www.guardian.co.uk/environment/2010/may/21/un-biodiversity-economic-report.

2. In Michael Chrichton's "Next," [pp. 422-423] the author notes a few important conclusions from his research on the novel. A corrupting unfluence of the scientific process in America is one of his complaints: "As a result of this legislation [the Bayh-Dole Act of 1980], most science professors now have corporate ties — either to companies they have started or to other biotech companies. Thirty years ago, there was a distinct difference in approach between university research and that of private industry. Today the distinction is blurred, or absent... Now, scientists have personal interests that influence their judgment." Likewise, government has expanded its roll significantly inuniversity funding. Consequently, the author of this work recommends a healthy dose of skepticism regarding the increasingly alarming "scientific" predictions of global catastrophes that allegedly can be averted with large quantities of other peoples' money.

3. Among others, see http://www.epa.gov/cfl/cflcleanup.html

4. The story of the Chinese government official was relayed to the author by an American who had travelled to China seeking industrial opportunities.

CHAPTER 13:

1. Desmond A. Birch, "Trial, Tribulation & Triumph," p. 389.

2. Venerable Mary of Agreda, "The Mystical City of God, Volume II," p. 228.

3. Birch, p. 393

4. This and the following prophecies from Sr. Marianne are found in "Trial, Tribulation and Triumph," p. 327.

5. The complete text of the "Didache" can be found at: http://www.scrollpublishing.com/store/Didache-text.html

CHAPTER 15:

1. See Exodus 32:13: "... I will give your descendants all this land I promised them, and it will be their inheritance forever." Also, for those who believe the Bible is the Word of God yet doubt Israel's claim on the Promised Land, the author recommends studying the following verses: Hebrews 11:9, Deuteronomy 19:8, Deuteronomy 34:4, Exodus 12:25, Exodus 3:17, Joshua 22:4, Numbers 14:16, Numbers 14:23, Acts 7:5, Ezekiel 30:5, Joshua 23:5, Genesis 28:15, Genesis 50:24, Nehemiah 9:23, Nehemiah 9:8, Ezekiel 20:42, Psalm 47:4, Leviticus 20:24, Jeremiah 32:22, Jeremiah 2:7, Isaiah 58:14, 1 Chronicles 11:10.

CHAPTER 16:

1. In Malachi Martin's "Hostage to the Devil," some signs of demonic possession include: whitened, taut facial skin; cold body temperature; and a cacophony of unnatural voices referring to the exorcee in the third person.

2. Many of these details are taken from "Hostage to the Devil," Appendix One, "The Roman Ritual of Exorcism."

3. This is quoted from the Roman Ritual of Exorcism.

4. Luke 11:24-26.

CHAPTER 19:

1. Many of these facts are from Nino Lo Bello's "The Incredible Book of Vatican Facts and Papal Curiosities."

2. R.A. Scotti, "Basilica," p. 27.

3. Scotti, p. 14.

4. Maria Luisa Ambrosini with Mary Willis, "The Secret Archives of the Vatican," chapter II.

CHAPTER 23:

1. Excerpted from words of Chris Matthews, MSNBC Hardball, 12/24/09. Full quote is as follows: "Well, to reach back to one of our heroes from the past, from the '60s, Saul Alinsky once said that even though both sides have flaws in their arguments and you can always find something nuanced about your own side you don't like – and it's never perfect – you have to act in the end like there's simple black and white clarity between your side and the other side or you don't get anything done. I always try to remind myself of Saul Alinsky when I get confused." Alinsky's most famous book, "Rules for Radicals" was dedicated to "…the first radical known to man who rebelled against the establishment and did it so effectively that he at least won his own kingdom -- Lucifer."

CHAPTER 25:

1. See Paul Johnson's "A History of Christianity," p. 278.

2. These quotes are from Will Durant's "The Story of Civilization, Volume 6, The Reformation," pp. 351-357.

3. E.R. Chamberlin, "The Bad Popes," p. 255.

4. Chamberlin, pp. 259-260.

5. Some of these details come from R.A. Scotti's "Basilica," chapter 19.

6. Scotti, p. 160.

7. Exodus 10:3.

8. Luke 18:14.

9. James 4:10.

10. To this day, Swiss Guards are sworn in on May 6th.

11. Details in the above three paragraphs are found in R.A. Scotti's, "Basilica," Chapter 19, and Maria Luisa Ambrosini's "The Secret Archives of the Vatican," pp. 179-181, as well as Will Durant's "Heroes of History," Chapter 16.

12. Scotti, p. 163.

13. LW 49:169.

14. See Will Durant, "The Story of Civilization – The Reformation, Volume 6," pp. 447-449.

15. Durant, p. 450.

16. Durant, pp. 449-451.

17. Scotti, p. 168.

CHAPTER 27:

1. John 15:12-17

2. For an excellent review of Messianic prophecy, see Josh McDowell's "Evidence for Christianity," Chapter 6. The following prophecies and fulfillments are from that book.

3. Prophecy: Psalm 41:9; Fulfillment: Matthew 10:4.

4. Prophecy: Zechariah 11:12; Fulfillment: Matthew 26:15.

5. Prophecy: Zechariah 11:13; Fulfillment: Matthew 27:5.

6. Prophecy: Zechariah 11:13; Fulfillment: Matthew 27:7.

7. Prophecy: Zechariah 13:7; Fulfillment: Mark 14:50.

8. Prophecy: Psalm 35:11; Fulfillment: Matthew 26:59-60.

9. Prophecy: Isaiah 53:7; Fulfillment: Matthew 27:12.

10. Prophecy: Isaiah 53:5 and Zechariah 13:6; Fulfillment: Matthew 27:26 and John 19:11.

11. Prophecy: Isaiah 50:6 and Micah 5:1; Fulfillment: Matthew 26:67 and Luke 22:63.

12. Prophecy: Psalm 22:7-8; Fulfillment: Matthew 27:29 and 27:41-43.

13. Prophecy: Psalm 109:24-25; Fulfillment: Luke 23:26.

14. Prophecy: Psalm 22:16 and Zechariah 12:10; Fulfillment: Luke 23:33 and John 20:25.

15. Prophecy: Isaiah 53:12; Fulfillment: Matthew 27:38 and Mark 15:27-28.

16. Prophecy: Isaiah 53:12; Fulfillment: Luke 23:34.

18. Prophecy: Isaiah 53:3 and Psalm 69:8 and 118:22; Fulfillment: John 7:5&48 and Matthew 21:42-43 and John 1:11.

19. Prophecy: Psalm 69:4; Fulfillment: John 15:25.

20. Prophecy: Psalm 38:11; Fulfillment Luke 23:49 and Matthew 27:55-56 and Mark 15:40.

21. Prophecy: Psalm 109:25 and 22:7; Fulfillment: Matthew 27:39.

22. Prophecy: Psalm 22:17; Fulfillment: Luke 23:35.

23. Prophecy: Psalm 22:18; Fulfillment: John 19:23-24.

24. Prophecy: Psalm 69:21; Fulfillment: John 19:28.

25. Prophecy: Psalm 69:21; Fulfillment: Matthew 27:34 and John 19:28-29.

26. Prophecy: Psalm 22:1; Fulfillment: Matthew 27:46.

27. Prophecy: Psalm 31:5; Fulfillment: Luke 23:46.

28. Prophecy: Exodus 12:46; Numbers 9:12; Psalm 34:20; Fulfillment: John 19:33.

29. Prophecy: Psalm 22:14; Fulfillment: John 19:34.

30. Prophecy: Zechariah 12:10; Fulfillment: John 19:34.

31. Prophecy: Amos 8:9; Fulfillment: Matthew 27:45.

32. Prophecy: Isaiah 53:9; Fulfillment: Matthew 27:57-60.

33. John 14:6

34. John 14:9

35. Most of these descriptions of the deaths of the apostles come from Fr. John J. Pasquini's "The Existence of God," University Press of America, Inc., pp. 52-53.

36. Fr. John J. Pasquini, "*Ecce Fides,* Pillar of Truth," Shepherds of Christ Publications, p. vii.

37. Luke 6:37-38.

38. Luke 6:35.

39. Luke 6:27-28.

CHAPTER 29:

1. For more detailed descriptions of the Medjugorje prophecies contained in this chapter, please refer to the books that are cited in the Sources section and preceded by a plus symbol.

2. Particularly for Medjugorje skeptics, the author highly recommends “The Miracle Detective” by former Rolling Stone journalist, Randall Sullivan.

3. This summary of prophecies of saints is more broadly found in “Trial, Tribulation & Triumph” p. xlii, as well as other books on Catholic-approved prophecies listed in the Sources section.

4. These details are in all of the author’s listed Sources that cover the apparitions of Medjugorje. Approximately 40 million religious pilgrims have visited Medjugorje since 1981.

5. See “The Thunder of Justice,” p. 245. A century earlier, Pope Leo XIII was given the same divine message. Ibid, pp. 4, 5 and 237.

CHAPTER 30:

1. “Ritual Sacrifice of Children on Rise in Uganda,” Jason Straziuso, Associated Press, 4/5/10.

CHAPTER 32:

1. Ingrid Newkirk, Washingtonian Magazine, August 1, 1986.

2. Source: http://www.donatelife.net/UnderstandingDonation/Statistics.php.

CHAPTER 34:

1. This paragraph is loosely based on the early life story of John Corapi. As a young man he lived without regard for the faith in which he had been raised. After a surprising conversion, Corapi became a priest and, eventually, an effective media advocate for the Catholic Church. Unfortunately, in 2011, he left his order under a cloud of accusations. Perhaps, he became one more priest who fell victim to the very purposeful demons that were prophesied.

2. John 3:5.

3. Matthew 26:41.

4. Although Mark 14:50-52 only describes a “young man,” the visionary Blessed Anne Catherine Emmerich identified that person as the Apostle John. (“The Life of Jesus Christ and Biblical Revelations” vol. 4, pp. 27-28.)

5. This description is based on reports from former abortionists, such as Dr. Bernard Nathanson. Dr. Nathanson once directed New York’s largest abortion clinic and has claimed responsibility for over 75,000 abortions. He also co-founded NARAL (the National Abortion and Reproductive Rights Action

League). In the late 1970s, however, Dr. Nathanson had a change of heart and became a staunch opponent of abortion. He is creator of the pro-life video "The Silent Scream" and author of the book "The Hand of God: A Journey from Death to Life by the Abortion Doctor Who Changed His Mind." Also, the article, "Innocent blood: How lying marketers sold Roe v. Wade to America" by David Kupelian, describes many of the unethical, immoral and illegal practices of many abortionists. It can be found at http://www.wnd.com/index.php?fa=PAGE.view&pageId =28544.

6. Statistics from peer reviewed studies conducted by the Elliott Institute and found at http://www.theunchoice.com/resources.htm

7. Based on Luke 13:6-9

8. 1 Corinthians 2:9.

9. John 14:6.

10. Luke 12:48.

11. Luke 6:37.

12. Proverbs 23:7.

13. Philippians 4:8

CHAPTER 36:

1. Sun Tsu, "The Art of War."

2. The following teachings are from Niccolo Machiavelli's "The Prince."

CHAPTER 37:

1. "You will hear of wars and rumors of wars, but see to it that you are not alarmed. Such things must happen, but the end is still to come. Nation will rise against nation, [which is also translated 'ethnic group against ethnic group'] and kingdom against kingdom. There will be famines and earthquakes in various places. All these are the beginning of birth pains." Matthew 24:6-8.

2. Forbes.com, "Report: Union Pensions Funds Lag," Asher Hawkins, 9/4/09.

3. The Saudi details, descriptions and quotes in this chapter, including Petro SE, are from Gerald Posner's "Secrets of the Kingdom."

CHAPTER 39:

1. The Iranian details, descriptions and quotes in this chapter are from Mark Hitchcock's "The Apocalypse of Ahmadinejad."

2. Gerald Posner's "Secrets of the Kingdom," p. 34.

3. Posner, pp. 173-174.

4. Posner pp. 183-184.

5. Posner, pp. 26-27.

CHAPTER: 46:

1. The "Sedition Act of 1918" was signed into law by President Woodrow Wilson on May 16, 1918. It forbade the use of "disloyal, profane, scurrilous, or abusive language" about the United States government, its flag, or its armed forces or that caused others to view the American government or its institutions with contempt. Under this negation of Constitutionally-protected free speech, an estimated 1,500 Americans were prosecuted. The unpopular Act was repealed in 1920.

2. This last sentence is from journalist Walter Lippmann, the Pulitzer Prize winner who is revered by today's journalists. He offered the advice to Franklin Roosevelt, in 1933. "Journal of Libertarian Studies, Volume 15, no. 4" (Fall 2001), pp. 107–16, 2001 Ludwig von Mises Institute.

CHAPTER 52:

1. Philippians 4:4-7

CHAPTER 53:

1. The character B. Abu Ladin is loosely based on the life of international terrorist Abu Nidal, or "father of the struggle." Some of his information is from internet sources including http://en.wikipedia.org/wiki/Abu_Nidal.

CHAPTER 54:

1. St. Zenobius (d. 417) prophesied, "Antichrist, the son of perdition will be born in Corozain, will be brought up in Bethsaida and shall begin to reign in Capharnaum, according to what Our Lord Jesus said in the Gospel: 'Woe to thee Corozain ... woe to thee Bethsaida ... and thou Capharnaum that art exalted up to heaven, thou shalt be thrust down to hell.'" (Luke, 10:13)

CHAPTER 55:

1. See 2 Corinthians 11:14.
2. From John 1:23.
3. Luke 4:18-20.
4. Luke 4:21.

CHAPTER 56:

1. It has been said that a variation of the comforting command "Be not afraid" is expressed in the Bible 365 times. One for every day of the year.

2. The author does not wish to minimize the tragedy of suicide. Clearly, when one believes that "voices" are prompting it, mental illness is the likely cause. For more information on the Catholic Church's pronouncements on suicide, please see "The Catechism of the Catholic Church" 2325 which states, "Suicide is seriously contrary to justice, hope, and charity. It is forbidden by the fifth commandment." Further, 2280 - 2282 stress that God must remain the master of life and that it is our responsibility to preserve it. However, 2283 advises that we should not despair of the eternal salvation of persons who have taken their own lives. Only God knows and judges the human heart. Still, as 1010 points out, "Because of Christ, Christiian death has a positive meaning: 'For to me to live is Christ, and to die is gain.'" (Phil. 1:21) Of course, this story is symbolic. God does not ask us to "commit suicide for Him" but, instead, to "commit everything to Him." So, under the extraordinary circumstances of this fictional tale, we now better understand why the site was named Holy Sacrifice Monastery.

CHAPTER 57:

1. St. Hippolytus (d. 235) wrote "Treatise on Christ and the Antichrist," discussing the number 666 that is associated with the Antichrist in the Book of Revelation. Using the relevant correlation of letters and numbers, St. Hippolytus specified just two names that equate with the number 666: **Evanthas** and **Titan.** Earlier, St. Irenaeus (130-200) mentioned the same two names. However, Dr. Huntington Cyst - aka "The Prophet of Technology" - represents the False Prophet written about in various chapters of the Book of Revelation.

SOURCES

ADELS, JILL HAAK, "The Wisdom of the Saints," Barnes & Noble Books, 2004.

AGREDA, MARY OF, " The Mystical City of God," Vols. 1-4, Tan Books and Publishers, Rockford, IL, 2006.

ALLEGRI, RENZO AND ROBERTO ALLEGRI, "Fatima – The Story Behind the Miracles," Servant Books, Cincinnati, OH, 2001.

AMBROSINI, MARIA LUISA AND MARY WILLIS, "The Secret Archives of the Vatican," Barnes & Noble Books, 1996.

AMORTH, REV. GABRIELE, "An Exorcist Tells His Story," Ignatius Press, San Francisco, 1999.

BANDER, PETER, "The Prophecies of St. Malachy," Tan Books and Publishers, Rockford, IL, 1973.

*BIRCH, DESMOND A., "Trial, Tribulation & Triumph – Before, During and After Antichrist," Queenship Publishing, Goleta, CA 1996.

BONDANELLA, PETER AND MARK MUSA, Editors, "The Portable Machiavelli," Viking Penguin, New York, 1988.

BOYER, REV. O. A., "She Wears a Crown of Thorns," Rev. O. A. Boyer, Mendham, NJ, 1958.

BROWN, HAROLD O.J., "Heresies," Hendrickson Publishers, Peabody, MA, 1998.

BROWN, RAPHAEL, "The Life of Mary as seen by the Mystics," Tan Books and Publishers, Rockford, IL, 1991.

CARTY, REV. CHARLES M., "The Stigmata and Modern Science," Tan Books and Publishers, Rockford, IL, 1974.

CATHOLIC ANSWERS: EDITORS, "The Essential Catholic Survival Guide," Catholic Answers, San Diego, CA, 2005.

CATHOLIC CHURCH, "Catechism of the Catholic Church," Doubleday, New York, 1995.

CHAMBERLIN, E. R., "The Bad Popes," Barnes & Noble Books, New York, 1993.

CLAVELL, JAMES, "The Art of War by Sun Tzu," Delacorte Press, New York, 1983.

+CONNELL, JANICE T., "The Visions of the Children," St. Martin's Griffin, New York, 1997

+CONNELL, JANICE T., "Meetings with Mary – Visions of the Blessed Mother," Random House, New York, 1995.

*CONNOR, EDWARD, "Prophecy for Today," Tan Books and Publishers, Rockford, IL, 1984.
CRICHTON, MICHAEL, "Next," Harper Collins, New York, 2006.
CRISTIANI, LEON, "Evidence of Satan in the Modern World," Tan Books and Publishers, Rockford, IL, 1974.
CRUZ, JOAN CARROLL, "Eucharistic Miracles – And Eucharistic Phenomena in the Lives of the Saints," Tan Books & Publishers, Rockford IL, 1987.
CRUZ, JOAN CARROLL, "Miraculous Images of Our Lady," Tan Books and Publishers, Rockford, IL, 1993.
*CULLETON, REV. R. GERALD, "The Prophets and Our Times," Tan Books and Publishers, Rockford, IL, 1974.
*CULLETON, REV. R. GERALD, "The Reign of Antichrist," Tan Books and Publishers, Rockford, IL, 1974.
DELANEY, JOHN J., "A Woman Clothed with the Sun – Eight Great Apparitions of Our Lady," Image, New York, 2001.
*DUPONT, YVES, "Catholic Prophecy – The Coming Chastisement," Tan Books and Publishers, Rockford, IL, 1973.
DURANT, WILL, "Heroes of History," Simon & Schuster, New York, 2001.
DURANT, WILL, "The Story of Civilization – The Reformation," Simon & Schuster, New York, 1957.
EMMERICH, ANNE CATHERINE, "The Life of Jesus Christ and Biblical Revelations," Vol. 1-4, Tan Books and Publishers, Rockford, IL, 1979.
ENGLAND, RANDY, "The Unicorn in the Sanctuary – The Impact of the New Age on the Catholic Church," Tan Books and Publishers, 1991.
EUSEBIUS, "The History of the Church," Penguin Classics, London, 1989.
FALEY, ROLAND J., "Apocalypse Then & Now," Paulist Press, New York, 1999.
FICOCELLI, ELIZABETH, "Bleeding Hands, Weeping Stone – True Stories of Divine Wonders, Miracles, and Messages," Saint Benedict Press, Charlotte, NC, 2009.
*FLYNN, TED AND MAUREEN, "The Thunder of Justice," MaxKol Communications, 1993.
FORTEA, REV. JOSE ANTONIO, "Interview with an Exorcist," Ascension Press, West Chester, PA, 2006.
GERSTER, GEORG, "The Past from Above," Getty Publications, Los Angeles, 2005.
GHEZZI, BERT, "Mystics & Miracles," LoyolaPress, Chicago, IL, 2002.
GROESCHEL, REV. BENEDICT J., "A Still, Small Voice," Ignatius Press, San Francisco, 1993.

GUITTON, JEAN, "Great Heresies & Church Councils," Harper & Row, New York, 1965.
HAHN, SCOTT, "Reasons to Believe," Doubleday, New York, 2007.
HITCHCOCK, MARK, "The Apocalypse of Ahmadinejad," Multnomah Books, Colorado Springs, CO, 2007.
*HUCHEDE, REV. P., "History of Antichrist," Tan Books and Publishers, Rockford, IL, 1976.
JANSEN, G.H., "Militant Islam," Harper & Row, New York, 1979.
JOHNSON, PAUL, "A History of Christianity," Touchstone, New York, 1995.
JOHNSON, PAUL, "Modern Times," Harper & Row, New York, 1983.
JOHNSON, PAUL, "The Papacy," Barnes & Noble Books, New York, 2005.
JOHNSTON, FRANCIS, "Fatima – The Great Sign," Tan Books and Publishers, Rockford, IL, 1980.
JOHNSTON, FRANCIS, "The Wonders of Guadalupe," Tan Books and Publishers, Rockford, IL, 1981.
+JONES, MICHAEL KENNETH, "Medjugorje Investigated," Devotions, Medjugorje, Bosnia & Herzegovina, 2006.
KEATING, KARL, "Catholicism and Fundamentalism," Ignatius Press, San Francisco, 1988.
KONDOR, REV. LOUIS, "Fatima in Lucia's Own Words," The Ravengate Press, Still River, MA, 2004.
LARSON, BOB, "In the Name of Satan," Thomas Nelson Publishers, Nashville, TN, 1996.
LAURENCE, RAY, "Traveller's Guide to the Ancient World Rome," David and Charles, Cincinnati, OH, 2008.
LAURENTIN, RENE, "A Short Treatise on The Virgin Mary," AMI Press, Washington, 1991.
LINDSEY, HAL, "Planet Earth – 2000 A.D." Western Front, Ltd, Palos Verdes, CA, 1994.
LOZANO, NEAL, "Unbound," Chosen Books, Grand Rapids, MI, 2003.
MARTIN, REV. MALACHI, "The Keys of This Blood," Touchstone, New York, 1990.
MARTIN, REV. MALACHI, " Hostage to the Devil," HarperSanFrancisco, 1992.
MARTIN, RALPH, "The Fulfillment of All Desire," Emmaus Road Publishing, Steubenville, OH, 2006.
MCCALL, THOMAS S. AND ZOLA LEVITT, "Satan in the Sanctuary," Thomas S. McCall and Zola Levitt, 1983.

MCDOWELL, JOSH, "Evidence of Christianity," Thomas Nelson Publishers, Nashville, TN, 2006.
MCDOWELL, JOSH AND DON STEWART, "Understanding Secular Religions," Here's Life Publishers, San Bernardino, CA, 1982.
MIRAVALLE, MARK, "Meet Mary," Sophia Institute Press, Manchester, NH, 2007.
MURK, JIM, "Islam Rising," 21st Century Press, Springfield, MO, 2006.
NELSON, THOMAS, "Nelson's Complete Book of Bible Maps and Charts," Thomas Nelson, Inc., 1993.
+ODELL, CATHERINE M., "Those Who Saw Her," Our Sunday Visitor, Huntington, IN, 1986.
PALMER, ALAN, "The Decline & Fall of the Ottoman Empire," Barnes & Noble Books, New York, 1992.
PASQUINI, REV. JOHN J., "The Existence of God," University Press of America, Lanham, MD, 2010.
PASQUINI, REV. JOHN J., "*Ecce Fides* – Pillar of Truth," Shepherds of Christ Publications, China, Indiana, 2007.
PECK, DR. M. SCOTT, "Glimpses of the Devil," Free Press, New York, 2005.
Peters, Joel, "Scripture Alone?" Tan Books and Publishers, Rockford, IL, 1999.
PETROSILLO, ORAZIO, "Vatican City," Musei Vaticani, Vatican City, 2000.
POSNER, GERALD, "Secrets of the Kingdom," Random House, New York, 2005.
ROSENBERG, JOEL C., "Epicenter," Tyndale House Publishers, Carol Stream, IL, 2006.
RUGGLES, ROBIN, "Apparition Shrines," Pauline Books & Media, Boston, MA, 2000.
SCOTTI, R. A., "Basilica – The Splendor and the Scandal: Building St. Peter's," Plume, New York, 2007.
+*SULLIVAN, RANDALL, "The Miracle Detective," Grove Press, New York, 2004.
TRIFKOVIC, SERGE, "The Sword of the Prophet," Regina Orthodox Press, Boston, MA, 2002.
VAN DEN AARDWEG, GERARD J. M., "Hungry Souls," Tan Books and Publishers, Rockford, IL, 2009.
VAN IMPE, JACK, "Final Mysteries Unsealed," Jack Van Impe, 1998.
VAN IMPE, JACK, "Millenium: Beginning or End?" Word Publishing, Nashville, TN, 1999.

VAN IMPE, JACK, "Revelation Revealed," Jack Van Impe Ministries, 1982.
VON CLAUSEWITZ, CARL, "On War," Princeton University Press, Princeton, NJ, 1989.
WALSH, WILLIAM THOMAS, "Our Lady of Fatima," Image, New York, 1990.
+WEIBLE, WAYNE, "Medjugorje – The Message," Paraclete Press, Brewster, MA, 1989.
WILKINSON, TRACY, "The Vatican's Exorcists – Driving Out the Devil in the 21st Century," Warner Books, New York, 2007.
WOLLENWEBER, BR. LEO, "Meet Solanus Casey," St. Anthony Messenger Press, Cincinnati, OH, 2002.

CPSIA information can be obtained at www.ICGtesting.com
Printed in the USA
LVOW091419051211

257903LV00001B/39/P